SHALLOW
END

Other Stonechild and Rouleau mysteries:
Cold Mourning
Butterfly Kills
Tumbled Graves

A STONECHILD AND ROULEAU MYSTERY

SHALLOW END

BRENDA CHAPMAN

DUNDURN
TORONTO

Cover image: © Ian Lim/123RF
Printer: Webcom

Library and Archives Canada Cataloguing in Publication

Chapman, Brenda, 1955-, author
    Shallow end / Brenda Chapman.

(A Stonechild and Rouleau mystery)
Issued in print and electronic formats.
ISBN 978-1-4597-3510-1 (paperback).--ISBN 978-1-4597-3511-8 (pdf).--
ISBN 978-1-4597-3512-5 (epub)

    I. Title. II. Series: Chapman, Brenda, 1955- . Stonechild and Rouleau mystery.

PS8605.H36S53 2017   C813'.6   C2016-905282-6
                                        C2016-905283-4

1 2 3 4 5   21 20 19 18 17

Conseil des Arts du Canada   Canada Council for the Arts   ONTARIO ARTS COUNCIL CONSEIL DES ARTS DE L'ONTARIO an Ontario government agency un organisme du gouvernement de l'Ontario

We acknowledge the support of the Canada Council for the Arts and the Ontario Arts Council for our publishing program. We also acknowledge the financial support of the Government of Ontario, through the Ontario Book Publishing Tax Credit and the Ontario Media Development Corporation, and the Government of Canada.

Care has been taken to trace the ownership of copyright material used in this book. The author and the publisher welcome any information enabling them to rectify any references or credits in subsequent editions.

— *J. Kirk Howard, President*

The publisher is not responsible for websites or their content unless they are owned by the publisher.

Printed and bound in Canada.

VISIT US AT

dundurn.com | @dundurnpress | dundurnpress | dundurnpress

Dundurn
3 Church Street, Suite 500
Toronto, Ontario, Canada
M5E 1M2

To my niece Laura Russell

*The shallow consider liberty a release from all
law, from every constraint.*
— Walt Whitman

*Evil is unspectacular and always human
And shares our bed and eats at our own table.*
— W.H. Auden, *Herman Melville*

CHAPTER ONE

Sunday, September 4

Jane Thompson lifted a hand to the window and widened two slats of the metal blind so that she could see the street below. The sun struck her full in the eyes, and for one disorienting moment, blinded her. She tilted her head and squinted through the dazzling light toward the sidewalk across the street. The homeless man who'd taken up residence was gone. The media camped outside for the past week also appeared to have given up their daily vigil. By the angle of the sun, darkness would have completely descended in another hour. The reporter and photographer would be off having supper, likely complaining about their thankless assignment. Hopefully, they'd tire of waiting for her by morning.

She wasn't counting on it.

She let the slats fall back into place and turned to look around her new living quarters on Regent Street. She'd deliberately picked this cramped second floor apartment in a three-unit rental outside of the downtown. The building was a converted house with two units on the main floor and hers taking up the second. One of the downstairs units was empty, the young couple with a baby slipping off in the night the week before, owing two months' rent. The landlord was having trouble renting it again since most of the university students already had places for the upcoming school term. Not helping his cause were the three university boys who shared the larger unit below her. They played their music loud through most of the day and enjoyed entertaining their buddies at odd hours. Jane couldn't afford much but she had enough to make the first and last month's rent and felt lucky to have found this one-bedroom apartment even with the annoyances. Where she lived hadn't mattered so long as she remained in Kingston.

The confined space made her feel safe.

The bedroom and living room came furnished with somebody's castoffs. The bed, visible from where she stood, consisted of a saggy mattress on a frame — not even a headboard to make up for the discomfort. An old dresser with a mirror filled one wall, the mirror warped with age so that her reflection came back slightly distorted. The closet was small with room for a few pairs of shoes. A crooked pole at eye level was empty except for the green fall jacket she'd been given.

She made the three steps to the couch and slowly lowered herself onto the cushions. The slanted roofline had meant pulling the couch out from the wall so that she didn't bang her head. The window that she'd been looking out toward the street was behind the couch, wide and nar-row, halfway up the wall. The couch faced an old, cumbersome television sitting on a wood veneer stand — and that was it for furniture. Not even a carpet to soften the space. The first evening, she'd gotten down on her hands and knees and crawled across the hardwood floor, counting twenty-three cigarette burns on its pitted face in the living room alone. A scarred space. Like her.

Jane stared at the blank television screen. She hadn't turned it on yet, not wanting to let the out-side world into her private space. *Not yet.*

Should she chance a walk to the grocery store for milk and bread? It was several blocks from her apartment in a high traffic part of the city. The idea of going there scared the hell out of her in daylight when she could be recognized. Her trips outside had all been done under the cover of darkness up until now. But she needed an early night. Maybe, if she settled in earlier, she'd be able to sleep. She closed her eyes. Tomorrow morning, she had to go out, regardless. Eight thirty she was to be at the Sally Ann on Division Street to begin her job sorting clothes. The store was open from ten to five thirty, six days a week, but she'd be in the back and had to get there before opening time. She'd leave the apartment extra early to avoid the reporter in case he was sent another day.

The higher you go, the harder the fall. Her God-fearing mother had been right about that. Wrong about a whole lot of other stuff, but bang on with the dire predictions.

Jane stood and crossed the narrow space to the bedroom. She opened the closet door and for a moment stood staring into the empty space. Adam had promised to come by with her clothes but hadn't returned her calls. She knew that he was away. She'd walked the back streets to her old home on Silver Street her first night out and three evenings after that, each outing filled with disappointment.

She took her jacket off the hanger and slipped it on, pulling the hood over her head. Adam knew her release date was Monday. He'd deliberately taken Olivia and Ben out of town to send her a message. He wanted her out of their lives. He'd let her see them when he was ready, on his terms. She felt resolve course through her. She had nothing left to lose except her relationship with her children. Adam may have divorced her a year in, but she was still their mother. Adam couldn't make that go away, much as he'd threatened to sever their ties with her.

She paused for a moment in front of the mirror. A diet of prison food had made her lose weight. So much so that she barely recognized the jutting cheeks and narrow jaw of the woman before her, even considering the wavy effect of the glass. Her last haircut, two days before her release, had shorn the length into a cap — long bangs and cropped short above her ears. A pixie cut, the girl had called it, before Jane's locks of blond hair fell to the floor.

Jane had called it a fresh start.

She grabbed her keys from the top of the dresser and headed for the door. She'd sneak out the back way just in case someone was lingering out front.

The fence behind the detached garage had a gap that she could easily slip through. It led into an alley with the brick wall of a house lining the other side of the path. The opening allowed her to come and go unobserved — an escape route already coming in handy as she began her new life in the shadows.

Flashes of light pierced the night as the car sped through the darkness on Highway 401 toward Kingston. The interior of the car was warm — too warm — and Naomi could feel her eyes getting heavier. She blinked and repositioned herself in the passenger seat, stealing a glance at Adam's rigid profile behind the wheel. He'd stopped talking after their pit stop in Bowmanville. The kids had bought burgers and drinks at McDonald's but she and Adam decided to wait until they got home. "I'll whip up some omelettes," she'd said. Her promise had seemed easier two hours earlier when she wasn't so tired.

She looked into the back seat. Olivia's blond head was bouncing in time to the music flowing into her ears from her iPod. Ben was reading a book while also listening to music on his device. They both had their mother's direct blue eyes and fair colouring. She wondered if Adam found these constant reminders of Jane painful, but she wouldn't ask. He'd made it clear early on that the topic of his ex was off-limits.

"We're almost home." He turned his head from the road for a moment and looked at her. His eyes caressed her face from a distance. Warmth spread up her belly and into her throat. The longing she felt for him was growing in strength, not abating with time.

"It'll be good to sleep in our own bed." She smiled and let the statement hang suggestively between them.

He smiled back. "No kids in the next room to stifle creativity."

"Or enthusiastic noises."

"Or that." He grinned and she saw a glimpse of the boy he'd once been. He winked before looking back at the road.

She turned to stare out the side window. They were nearing the first off-ramp into Kingston. She knew that if Adam could have prolonged their time away, he would have. He'd been more and more on edge as their two weeks at the rental cottage outside Sudbury drew to a close. No matter how Naomi tried to make him relax, he'd fall back into a gloomy space that had no room for her. Long walks or fishing trips in the boat with his kids kept him away from the cottage while she lay around reading or concocting intricate meals to feed them upon return. She may as well have fed them hamburgers and Kraft Dinner for all the appreciation she'd received.

"Do they know Jane's getting out of prison next week?" she'd asked Adam while washing dishes from a fettuccine alfredo meal that the kids had barely touched. The recipe was one of her best and she'd been hurt by their rejection.

"They know."

He'd closed off the opening she'd offered to talk about Jane's return. It was as if he was shouldering some horrible burden alone as penance for his ex-wife's sins.

Naomi had met Jane once, a few months before the sky caved in on her. Before her arrest and trial. Naomi had kept the encounter from Adam, knowing instinctively that he would not have been pleased. He'd kissed her by then, full on the mouth as he passed by her on his way to his desk, but nothing more than that. He'd admitted later that it had been spur of the moment and he'd immediately felt guilt for the impropriety of his impulse. No promise of anything further no matter all the erotic fantasies floating around her imagination.

It had been a grey November Saturday morning when Naomi had followed Jane's car from her house to the grocery store. She'd caught up with Jane in the fruit aisle. Bent over, reaching for McIntosh apples, Jane had been inspecting each one before dropping it into a plastic bag. She'd been wearing a red wool coat and high black boots, her white-blond hair gathered into a messy bun at the nape of her neck. She'd turned when Naomi bumped her cart with her own. The look in her startling blue eyes had gone from somewhere far away to focus in on Naomi.

"So sorry," Jane had said. "Was I in the way?" When she smiled, her face had glowed as if a lamp was backlighting her skin and Naomi had felt the bottom fall out of her dreams. Adam would never leave this woman for her. She knew that even her youth couldn't compete with Jane's smile that wrapped around a person like warm honey and the warmth in her dreamy blue eyes that was as intriguing as sex, for Naomi was experienced in this department, having lost her virginity when she was fourteen to her sixteen-year-old cousin. She'd been the one doing the pursuing, although she knew that all the bleeding hearts would twist her into a victim if they'd known. Never mind that she found sex enjoyable from the get-go. It didn't hurt that getting a guy to drop his pants gave her a sense of power over him that she'd become an expert at exploiting.

Naomi studied the distracted way Jane tucked a piece of loose hair behind her ear with long, graceful fingers. Her fingertips then slid down her cheek and across her full lips before landing on the silk scarf tied around her neck. The movement was sensual as hell and Naomi found herself staring. If Jane was aware of the vibe she gave off, she gave no sign. "No, I was the one who bumped into you." Naomi started backing up, eager to get away.

"Say, aren't you one of the students from teacher's college doing a work term in my husband's class at Rideau Public? Adam Thompson?"

"Yes, that would be me." There was nothing for it. She held out a hand. "Naomi Van Kemp. Nice to meet you."

Delight radiated from Jane's face like a child suddenly handed a wonderful surprise. She reached out and clasped on to Naomi's hand. "Jane Thompson. So nice to meet you. I saw your photo on Facebook, you see. Adam was talking about what a natural you are in the classroom and he showed me your profile. Are you planning to work in elementary when you graduate?" At last she released Naomi's hand.

"I'm hoping to get a grade four class."

"Like Adam." Jane laughed, a husky playfulness in her voice. "He tried the grade seven and eight level but likes teaching the younger ones. I, on the other hand, love working with the intermediates. I'm at Winston Churchill Public."

Believe me, I know that. "Are you baking a pie?"

"Pie?" Jane looked down at the bag filled with apples. "Goodness, I got carried away thinking about something else. No, I'm afraid these are for lunch bags. I'm really not much of a cook."

At least Naomi had something on her. Her parents had owned a bakery, and she'd cut her teeth on recipes and putting concoctions into the oven. Still, her skill in the kitchen felt like an inferior triumph. "Sorry again to have bumped into your cart. I have to get a move on."

"Lovely to have met you. Keep up your good work."

Again, her beatific smile, and Naomi had slunk away, certain then that Adam was as far out of her reach as the moon. She'd finished her student teaching placement without further incident. It was serendipity that she received a call to supply teach in the classroom next to his the week after his wife was arrested.

And as Jane's fortunes had plummeted, Naomi's had grown to fill the gap.

She looked across at Adam again and thought about the night ahead when they would be alone in his king-size bed. Cooking wasn't the only talent she had to make Adam happy to leave his life with Jane behind. She'd put on the silk teddy and thong that she had picked up before they went away and remind him of all the benefits of living with a twenty-six-year-old.

Just in case he needed reminding.

CHAPTER TWO

Tuesday, October 4

Jacques Rouleau paid for his coffee and slipped between tables until he reached his team at the far end of the cafeteria. Gundersund moved into the chair on the other side of Woodhouse and Rouleau took his vacated seat at the head of the table. Kala Stonechild sat alone on Rouleau's right. She looked up at him from her plate of scrambled eggs and bacon.

"Anything exciting to report, sir?"

"No. Still quiet on the major crimes front. That turned out to be the quietest September on record."

Gundersund nodded. "Following up on a quiet summer." He speared a sausage on his plate. "I can't say that I've minded though."

Rouleau caught the look that Woodhouse gave Stonechild. Something was going on between the two of them. Woodhouse hadn't wanted her on the team — it wasn't difficult to figure that out — but so far, the team was holding together. He could count on Gundersund to let him know if anything was getting out of hand. In any case, Stonechild would not appreciate his interference, of this he was certain.

"Look, Bennett's back." Gundersund pointed toward the entrance and Rouleau turned in his chair. Gundersund raised a hand to wave Bennett over. "He's looking fit."

"The young heal fast," said Rouleau. Hard to believe Bennett had been in intensive care for two weeks from a gunshot wound five months earlier. He'd come as close to death as a person could without actually checking out.

Bennett sat in the empty seat next to Stonechild after he grabbed a cup of coffee. He took a drink and said, "Coffee hasn't gotten any better since I was off, but it's good to be back otherwise. What've I missed?"

"Nothing much." Woodhouse bit into a cinnamon bun. "Your absence was barely noticed." He smiled, a glob of icing hanging from his top lip.

"Well, I missed you." Kala tilted her head sideways and smiled at Bennett.

Bennett's dimples appeared. "Then it was worth taking a bullet."

Woodhouse tapped his temple. "Getting shot has turned you into a soppy wuss. Good thing you've returned to work so I can toughen you up before it becomes permanent."

Gundersund cleared his throat. "Welcome back, Bennett. You look completely recovered."

Bennett swung his eyes over to Gundersund. "I am. My mother's relentless cooking helped. I never thought I'd say it, but I'm actually glad to be away from all the homemade pasta and casseroles. By the way, thanks for all the phone calls and text messages, everyone. Especially you, Woodhouse, but no need to keep sending me those dirty jokes and videos." He paused a few beats. "Really, no need."

Woodhouse swiped at his mouth with a napkin. "Kept your spirits up, did I?"

"Sure, if you say so."

Woodhouse tossed the last of the bun into his mouth and wiped his hands on the front of his shirt. "Laughter is the best medicine. Especially if it includes a dwarf, a goat, and a bar."

"Right," Rouleau cut in, looking up from his cellphone. His glance landed on Woodhouse for a moment. "Our quiet fall has officially ended. A body's been found at Murney Point. Cause of death does not appear to have been natural. Gundersund and Stonechild, you take this one. Woodhouse and Bennett can tag along and will be at your disposal. Officers are on site and Fiona and the forensics team are on their way."

"Any indication of who was killed?" Gundersund was already on his feet, scooping napkins and tossing cutlery onto a tray.

"No idea," Rouleau said. "A homeless guy found the body. Check in when you have something to tell me."

Without a major crime to solve, the team had been lethargic and adrift for months. Already Rouleau could sense an excitement in their faces as they organized to leave. They were hungry to get going, never a bad quality in a detective. Too bad it took someone else's misfortune to give focus to their days, but this was the reality of their work. When it came right down to it, murder was the jam on their bread and butter.

Kala tried to breathe deeply and centre herself before getting out of the car. Gundersund turned left off King Street and showed his ID to the officer guarding the entrance to Murney Point. He was waved through and drove slowly around the bend into the parking lot facing Lake Ontario. A number of squad cars filled one end of the lot and Kala could see police scouring the shoreline. She glanced back at Murney Tower, a round, grey limestone fortress with a red band of windows rimming the border under a conical roof. She'd been meaning to take a tour of one of the two Martello towers open for summer visitors that guarded the Kingston shoreline since she arrived in Kingston the year before, but never got around to it. She was too late again this year as both museums closed their doors for the season in August.

Gundersund pulled into a spot some distance from the ambulance and turned off the engine. Wind off the lake buffeted the car and waves rolled in gusty swells against the shore. The day had the depressing feel of late fall as nature hunkered down for the first snowfall. Kala took a deep breath before stepping outside. The air had turned cool overnight and a wispy fog coated the landscape. She inhaled the dampness and cold and zipped her leather jacket as she joined Gundersund. A triangle of geese honked their way south overhead and she looked up. She could barely make them out against the grey sky.

Gundersund squinted and pointed toward the shoreline. "I see the top of someone's head. The body must be just over there. It's not a very steep drop to the water."

They started toward the lake and passed a man with a scraggly grey beard and crochet cap sitting on a park bench with a small dog on his lap. An officer was standing in front of him with her notepad out.

A cop named Bedouin walked from the top of the cliff toward them. "Hell of a day for a murder."

"Not one I would have picked." Gundersund tipped his head toward the lake. "What've we got?"

Bedouin pointed toward the grassy section of land that sloped toward the rocky shoreline. "A kid, maybe sixteen, seventeen years old. Male. The homeless guy's dog made a bit of a mess running around the body, which blended into the break wall at the base of the hill and was tucked into some bushes. I guess we're lucky the mutt led his owner there in the first place. Might have taken a while to find the body otherwise. His name's Bert by the way."

"The dog?"

"No. The homeless guy. He's a regular in the liquor store parking lot on Princess. I didn't catch the dog's name." Bedouin smiled, revealing over-sized front teeth that had earned him the nick-name Gopher.

Kala asked, "How long's the body been there?"

"Overnight. Probably not much longer." He looked back at Gundersund. "Your wife should be able to tell us more. She's been down inspecting him for a good fifteen minutes."

Gundersund stared out across the lake. He said without looking at Kala, "Why don't you head over and have a chat with Fiona while I double back and talk to Bert?"

"Don't you want to see the body before he gets moved?"

"I won't be long."

She watched Gundersund head over to the park bench and sit down next to the homeless man. Her six-foot-three partner made an imposing figure next to Bert, who obviously hadn't been surviving on a healthy diet. Bert laughed at something Gundersund said and Kala turned toward the hill.

She walked to the crest of the cliff and looked down into the gully, which was thick with white mist. A bell was clanging somewhere off to her left and the rushing sound of the wind was steady in her ears. Her home was further along this same shoreline on the western outskirts of the city. She stepped carefully toward Fiona on the slippery rocks and stopped a short distance away. Fiona's long blond hair was tucked under a plastic cap and she was wearing the white suit and boots of the forensics team. A young man dressed in the same white suit stood next to her, typing notes into an electronic device. Every so often, he fought to stay upright as a blast of wind attempted to push him onto the rocks. His eyes travelled across the space toward Kala and he bent to tell Fiona. She looked up and stared for a second in Kala's direction before lowering her head and resuming inspection of the body.

Kala surveyed the bobbing line of flotsam along the shoreline and the rolling grey waves with the white haze blotting out the horizon. The whistling wind and crashing waves muffled all other sound so that her ears felt stuffed with cotton batting. She planted her feet and scanned the band of rocks and bushes at the base of the break wall, finally coming to rest on the dead boy whom Fiona was crouched over. He was on his stomach, legs splayed and face turned away from her. She could make out short black hair and broad shoulders but not much else because of the angle of her view and the mist. While she waited for Fiona to finish up, she replayed her last encounter with her partner's wife. Fiona had walked into their office looking for Gundersund but he'd left for a dental appointment. They were alone and Fiona walked over to stand in front of Kala's desk.

"I suppose Paul's told you that he's asked for a divorce."

"No, we don't discuss …"

Fiona spoke over her. "We've been to see a mediator and she wants us to see a marriage counsellor. Paul doesn't want to, but I'd like it if you could encourage him. He … he respects your opinion."

Kala experienced dismay at being drawn into her partner's marriage and, for the first time, pity for Fiona. From what little Kala had gleaned from water cooler chatter, Fiona had brought this upon herself by leaving Gundersund for a year to move in with a doctor. The affair had already ended when Kala arrived in Kingston the year before, and Fiona had taken every opportunity since then to wrangle her way back into her husband's life. He appeared reluctant, but Fiona was attractive and persistent. The office pool gave convincing odds for his capitulation by Christmas. The desperate look in Fiona's eyes had been a first and Kala had had to force herself not to react to it. "Your husband and I don't discuss our private lives," she'd said, "and I'm not getting involved. Sorry."

Fiona had stared at her with a half-smile on her lips, the desperate look hardening into something tough and calculating. Her voice dropped. "If you think I'm leaving my husband for you to trap like a sneaky bitch, you can think again. You might fool the men with your big doe eyes and quiet suffering, but I've got your number. You're as conniving as they come but you have no idea who you're messing with. Consider yourself warned."

She'd stormed off before Kala could respond to the stunning attack, disturbed not only by the threat but also the twisted version of her friendship with her partner. Kala had promised herself that she'd steer clear of Fiona and keep Gundersund at arm's length outside of work hours. So far, she'd managed both. She hadn't been surprised when Gundersund had started leaving work on his lunch hours twice a week to go for counselling because she'd known that Fiona wasn't going to let him go easily. After each session, he'd returned to the office stone-faced and uncommunicative and Kala hadn't encouraged him to talk about it.

Fiona straightened from a crouched position and said something to her assistant. Then she climbed the rocks until she stood a few feet from Kala. Even from the short distance away, she had to speak loudly above the noise of the wind and waves battering the shore.

"No ID on his body. He was dragged down the hill but he was already dead."

"How did he die?"

"Blunt force trauma. The back of his head is a mess. Whoever hit him wasn't holding back. He took a couple of good blows. I'd say somebody was extremely angry." Fiona glanced at her before looking away and the words hung an unspoken challenge between them. Kala was tiring of this silent game but felt helpless to end it.

Fiona started climbing and passed as close to Kala as she could without brushing against her. "I'm cold and want to get out the wind. I'll have my report later this afternoon."

Kala waited a few moments before turning to follow her. She looked up and saw two paramedics who were carrying a stretcher appear at the top of the incline with Gundersund following behind. He met Fiona and stopped to speak with her before continuing on down the hill toward Kala. His mouth was set in a grim line.

"The station received a call that a seventeen-year-old boy named Devon Eton is missing. He didn't come home last night but his parents thought he was at his friend's place. They often played video games late and Devon would sleep over. This morning his mother found out he wasn't there and hasn't been able to find him any of the other places she thinks he might have gone."

"Do you have a description?"

"From what Fiona just told me, he matches the kid down on the rocks." Gundersund looked toward the body. His blond hair was beaten straight back by the wind. He raised his voice to be heard above the breaking waves. "The mother was upset about something but didn't want to get into it on the phone. She's going to be even more upset when she finds out her kid is dead. Ready for a closer look?"

Kala pushed back a strand of hair from her eyes and nodded. "After you," she said.

They'd have a few minutes with the boy before he was carted up the hill into the waiting ambulance. She tried to hang on to the inner calm she'd found in the car as she followed her partner across the slippery rocks.

CHAPTER THREE

Rouleau met them in the hallway of the station at one o'clock. "Hilary Eton identified her son. She says that she knows who killed him."

They were quiet for a moment. Kala knew that convicting someone was never as simple as this. Knowing and proving were different animals entirely. She looked at Gundersund when he said, deadpan, "Well, that makes our job way easier." He gave her a crooked smile before asking Rouleau, "Is she alone?"

"Yes, her husband left this morning for business in Calgary. She's reached him at the Calgary airport and he's on his way back."

"Where's Mrs. Eton now?" Kala asked. She looked from Gundersund to Rouleau and thought he looked tired. She'd been worried about him since his ex-wife, Frances, died in the summer. He'd stopped gathering the team unless he had to and never went with them for a drink after work as he had before Frances's death.

"I brought her into my office and am giving her a bit of space to make some phone calls. She should be about done."

"Then I guess we'll find out who it is that she suspects."

She and Gundersund followed Rouleau into the main office. Woodhouse was on the phone and Bennett was pouring a cup of coffee by the window. Kala smiled at Bennett on her way by. She'd been hoping for some time to sit with him and catch up, but there'd be no break while this case got underway. She'd been surprised by how much she'd missed Bennett while he was in Ottawa recuperating at his parents'. One quick trip to Ottawa at the beginning of his convalescence had been more to reassure herself that he was going to recover than anything else, a way to ease some of the guilt she felt at getting him shot. She hadn't been oblivious to his interest in her and knew he placed more importance in her visit than she'd intended, but he'd get over his crush, for that was how she saw it. She was thirty to his twenty-five and the age difference felt like a lot.

Mrs. Eton was framed in the window when they entered, arms folded across her stomach and looking out. Her hair from behind was golden-brown cut into a short bob. Wealth and style were evidenced by her well-cut wool coat and high leather boots. When she finally turned and acknowledged their presence, her grey-blue eyes swept over them without focusing. Watery black mascara had tracked down her cheeks, which were as pale as ivory. The lack of colour in her face was disconcerting, and Kala feared that she might pass out.

Rouleau must have had the same thought because he immediately crossed the room and guided her by the elbow to a chair directly behind her. "Can I get you some tea?" he asked, bending so that he was in her line of vision.

Her shoulders rose and her back straightened, and Kala blinked at the transformation on her face. Mask firmly in place, this woman would not be letting them see inside. Though still pale, her eyes were resolute. "No, thank you." She looked at Gundersund and Kala as they took seats on the couch. Her chin lifted. "Will this take long?"

To Kala, the woman's upper-crust British accent spoke of a moneyed upbringing and private schools, much like the upper class characters in PBS crime dramas. Mrs. Eton could have been a faded version of the actress who played the lead detective in *Prime Suspect*. Kala wracked her brain to remember the actress's name. She came up empty.

Rouleau took the seat next to Hilary Eton and she turned slightly to face him. "Just a few questions. We know how difficult this is for you but we want to find whoever killed your son as soon as we can."

"Of course. I'm not sure where she's living now, but you should be able to track her down without difficulty. She'll be answering to somebody, I imagine."

Rouleau's face remained sympathetic, no sign of impatience to be found. "I'm sorry, Mrs. Eton, but I don't know what woman you're speaking about. Perhaps you could tell us her name and why you suspect her."

Kala watched Mrs. Eton carefully to see if the shock of her son's death had affected her mind. She was aware of Rouleau and Gundersund silently waiting with her to see where this would lead. Shock and grief could make even the most rational person lose their grasp on reality for a time. Mrs. Eton's back arched higher into the chair. "You don't remember my son's case? It was a few years back, but still …"

Kala could see the gears turning in Rouleau's head. He glanced over at Gundersund, who looked perplexed before comprehension dawned in his eyes. "Your son was one of the schoolboys assaulted by the teacher, what was it, five years ago?"

"Four. Four years ago. Sexually assaulted. We were notified that Jane Thompson was out on parole five weeks ago, a day I'd been dreading since she was sentenced. I've been jumping at shadows since I heard, but then …" She shrugged her shoulders. "One has to carry on, doesn't one? I didn't want to live in fear and my hope was that she'd leave Kingston to go somewhere that nobody knew her. From what I've heard, her husband divorced her and wants nothing to do with her. Could anyone blame him? Besides, Devon is that much older. He was only twelve years old when it happened." For the first time, her voice broke. "I thought … I thought he could handle what she'd done to him."

Rouleau leaned closer to her and spoke quietly. "I'm sorry to have to ask you questions at this terrible time."

Her voice got louder, her British accent more pronounced. "No, I want to help. I need to help. Devon deserves retribution. We, that is, Mitchell and I, have felt that she ruined our son's life when she corrupted him. She was convicted of that, you know.

Corruption of a minor, gross indecency, and sexual assault. She was in a position of trust and the judge said that was the greatest evil of all when he sentenced her." She got to her feet in one abrupt motion. "I have to go, Sergeant. I need some time. Could we resume this when my husband is back this evening?"

Rouleau nodded. "I'll have an officer drive you home. Do you have other children, Mrs. Eton?"

"We have a daughter, Sophie. She's thirteen, in grade eight. I don't know how I'm going to tell her about Devon. She adored him." She stopped and looked panic-stricken around the room. "My purse? I don't remember where I dropped my purse. Did I leave it in the taxi? Oh my God."

Kala spotted a black bag on Rouleau's desk. "There it is," she said and motioned that she was on her way to get it. The purse was Italian leather with a designer label and heavier than expected when she picked it up. The zipper was partly open and Kala caught sight of an iPad and two pill bottles before she crossed the distance to hand the purse to Hilary Eaton. Was she taking medication for an illness? The unnatural pallor to her skin could be from a medical condition.

Mrs. Eton accepted the bag with a large sigh and clutched it to her chest as she walked toward Rouleau standing by the office door. "What time is your husband's flight?" he asked as he opened the door and stepped aside to let her pass in front of him.

"Eight o'clock. He's got a car in overnight parking at the airport and will be driving straight home. I'm certain he'll want to speak with you as soon as possible."

"We'll come by tonight. We'll be keeping you both apprised every step of our investigation."

"Thank you." She stopped two steps into the hall and turned to look at Rouleau. "I thought abusing my son was the greatest evil, but now, I know it wasn't even close. Letting that woman out of prison to seek revenge on my family was far, far worse."

Rouleau walked with her to the outer office, telling Kala and Gundersund that he'd be back after he saw that she was delivered safely home. Gundersund trailed behind Kala to the coffee machine sitting on a filing cabinet at the far corner of the open concept office. He stood behind her while she poured two cups. She added cream and sugar to both and handed him one. Gundersund looked as if he was trying to get a read on her mood.

"Seems to be more cases of female teachers having affairs with underage students," she said. "Makes you wonder what's going on when a married woman finds a boy sexually attractive and risks everything — her marriage, her relationship with her children, her job."

"I don't get the attraction either, but we may as well get started on the leg work. Why don't you read up on Jane Thompson while I track down her parole officer and find out where she's living? We'll be going over to pick Jane up once Rouleau gets back." He took a sip from the mug.

"Works." Kala started back to her desk. "I've got a burning question for you," she said to Bennett on her way by. "Who was the British actress who played the lead on the TV series *Prime Suspect*?"

Bennett cocked his head and thought for a second. "Got me. Must have been before my time."

"Helen Mirren," Woodhouse said without taking his eyes from his computer screen, "played DCI Jane Tennison in the *Prime Suspect* series."

"I knew Hilary Eton reminded me of someone. She could be Mirren's well-heeled sister," Gundersund said. "Well done figuring it out, Stonechild."

Woodhouse added, "The series is a classic. You don't know what you're missing, Bennett."

Kala dropped into her desk chair and adjusted the computer screen. She did a quick search and brought up an image of the actress. "They do look alike. It's uncanny, really." She closed the window and clicked back on the Google search.

Time to get down to business.

CHAPTER FOUR

Later that afternoon, Rouleau gathered the team in the area they'd set up behind a couple of dividers. They'd cordoned off this space to post photos of the crime scene and work out scenarios on a whiteboard. It had the feel of a secret clubhouse, not visible to anyone entering the office. Already he'd had photos mounted from the crime scene with Devon Eton's body lying next to the beach wall. Devon's black hair was matted with blood, and dirt covered one side of his face. He had been a healthy, athletic kid; muscular build but still not as filled out as a grown man. Much too young to die. Kala Stonechild had tracked down the whereabouts of Jane Thompson and Rouleau had sent officers to bring her in for questioning. They'd come to get him when she arrived.

"What have you found out about Devon Eton?" he threw out to nobody in particular.

Woodhouse looked up from his laptop. "Ed Chalmers was lead detective on the Eton sex case and I was off on training most of that summer so wasn't involved. Officer Cathy Bryden replaced me before she transferred into the canine unit. Gundersund was working drugs, if I recall."

"That's right," said Gundersund. "I followed what was going on but mainly because the arrest and trial created a lot of press. People were fascinated that a married female school teacher would seduce a boy in her class. The press loved her. She was attractive and as the trial went on, they painted her as one cool customer without remorse. Her nickname was the Seductress. Devon Eton was a good-looking kid and made a sympathetic victim. The entire case was disturbing but impossible not to watch unfold."

Woodhouse clicked a few keys. "I made some notes. Devon Shawn Eton turned seventeen years old in January and was living with his parents, Mitchell and Hilary Eton, and thirteen-year-old sister, Sophie, at 5342 Beverley Street. I had a look on Google Earth. It's at the north end and one of the bigger homes on the street. Fenced in, white pillars, black shutters, big front porch, and a two-car garage."

"So further north and west from where his body was found but within walking distance."

"Yup." Woodhouse scrolled further down the page. "Mitchell Eton owns a computer company employing thirty staff that designs accounting software for small- to medium-size businesses. Hilary Eton lives off his avails."

"I believe she's called a stay-at-home mom," Gundersund said.

Woodhouse looked up. "Give it whatever tarted-up name you want. She was freeloading. Never worked a day after they got married."

"Anything else?" Rouleau asked. He wasn't about to chase Woodhouse down this particular rat hole.

"Devon played defence on the high school football team and this was his graduation year. I thought about heading over to the school with Bennett to interview teachers and classmates tomorrow."

Rouleau nodded. "Good plan but I'd like Stonechild and Gundersund to handle those interviews. You and Bennett can go door to door to speak with the neighbours. Can you refresh us on the Jane Thompson case, Gundersund?"

Gundersund's eyes met his with silent approval. He'd long been encouraging Rouleau to do something about Woodhouse's negative influence on the team. *If only it was that easy,* Rouleau thought. Woodhouse knew what lines not to cross and had the police union behind him. Rouleau had had a union rep in once for a hypothetical chat and come away dismayed with the little leeway he had to act. Woodhouse hadn't done anything to warrant reprimand. At the moment, Woodhouse was glaring daggers at him but wisely keeping his thoughts to himself. He knew exactly how much he could get away with.

Gundersund pulled his notebook from his breast pocket. "Jane Thompson was a grade seven and eight English and history teacher at Winston Churchill Public School. Devon Eton and another boy named Charlie Hanson were in one of her grade seven classes. Devon had skipped a grade and was mature for his age, but then, he was a January baby. From all accounts, before it came out that Jane was having an affair with him, she was popular and considered one of the school's all-star teachers, not uncommon for this kind of thing, apparently. I found a few articles on past cases where a female teacher was convicted of having sex with one of her students. Anyhow, Devon's mother, Hilary Eton, discovered a pair of women's lace underwear when cleaning out his gym bag. Remember he was only twelve years old at the time and hadn't even had a girlfriend yet as far as his parents knew. After the school psychologist was brought in, Devon spilled that he'd been having sex with Mrs. Thompson. She'd been tutoring him after school to help him maintain his high English grade and that was when a physical relationship developed. She had opportunity and never denied that. Forensics found various text messages between the two, setting up meetings that she swore later were all innocent. Some naked photos of Devon were found on her home computer along with some other child porn, supporting what he told his mother. Charlie Hanson also had seen them together in a couple of compromising positions a few months earlier and said that Devon had confided in him that Mrs. Thompson had started coming on to him and they'd been having sex."

"So did she ever admit to it?"

"Not before or during the trial. Her defence was that she'd been set up. However, the clincher was her DNA all over the lace undies in Devon's gym bag. So after initially saying the boys were lying, about a year into her sentence, she confessed."

"So she was convicted."

"Yeah. The circumstantial evidence combined with the two boys' testimony convinced a jury. Plus, one of her co-workers said he'd seen them alone together one Saturday afternoon in her classroom, so that was damning combined with everything else. The judge sentenced her to three years but she got out last month after serving two-thirds of her sentence." Gundersund checked his notes. "Her husband Adam Thompson divorced her the beginning of the second year of her sentence and got sole custody of their two kids."

Rouleau was surprised. "Three years. Isn't that unusually harsh for this kind of crime?"

Gundersund nodded. "Usually women get off lighter than men. Two years is about the longest sentence for a woman teacher in Canada. The States gives slightly longer sentences, but not by much. The judge said in this case that because Jane Thompson wouldn't admit to what she'd done, he was upping her time. No remorse and possible she'd reoffend without treatment."

"How did she refute the prosecution's evidence?" Kala was leaning forward, elbows on her knees. She'd been listening intently to everything Gundersund said. He looked across the room at her.

"She said that she was meeting with Devon to tutor him in English because he'd missed out on the grammar rules when he skipped grade six and his writing was suffering. Nothing major and the prosecution argued that the tutoring was a smoke-screen for their affair. According to Mrs. Thompson, Devon told her that he was worried his father would make him quit football if his average dropped at all. She said they met at different times when they could both fit it in, but that was all. No touching. No sex."

"What about the photos on her computer?"

"She said she had no idea how they got there."

Rouleau asked, "Anything else?"

"She'd confided in her sister that she was thinking of leaving her husband before this blew up. The sister" — he looked at his notes — "named Sandra Salvo said that Jane suspected he'd been unfaithful but had no proof. Under cross-examination, Adam Thompson admitted they'd had a bit of trouble but said it was because he'd been working long hours and had nothing to do with having an affair. He lost his temper on the stand and said that Jane was grasping at reasons for her unforgiveable behaviour."

"That was a nail in her coffin," Bennett said. "Pretty damning when you add it all up."

Gundersund nodded. "That's how the jury saw it, too."

Rouleau looked between the dividers. Jim Nichols was standing by the entrance to the office. "We're over here," Rouleau called, and Nichols crossed the floor to join them. He looked around the space, then back at Rouleau.

"Quite the clubhouse you've got here, Mouseketeers. They've brought in Jane Thompson and she's waiting in the meeting room downstairs."

Rouleau stood. "Stonechild can you take the interview with me? I'd like a female present. Gundersund, you can stand inside the door. We go carefully on this one."

"What are you worried about?" Gundersund asked.

Rouleau tried to put his reservations about the path this case was taking into words. "I don't want to rush to any conclusions. Jane Thompson was guilty of sexual misconduct but that's not in the same ballpark as murder. We have to make absolutely certain of the facts before we arrest her because a lot of people would like to see her hang for this whether or not she's guilty."

The woman sitting across from Rouleau was not the person he'd been expecting. Dressed in a charcoal grey hoodie and black sweatpants, her spiky blond hair made her look more like a teenager than ex-teacher and mother. Her head had been lowered when they walked in, as if she'd fallen asleep, and she only looked up after Rouleau sat down across from her and called her by name. Her face, bare of makeup, was milky white with purplish bruising under her eyes. He had trouble picturing her as the seductress that media had labelled her until her eyes met his. The startling blue of her gaze sent a physical jolt through him. She transformed from average to mesmerizing with one wide-eyed stare. He could well understand the effect her eyes would have had on her young male students. Rouleau was aware of Stonechild slipping into the seat next to him, and he glanced back at Gundersund leaning on the wall next to the door. Both had settled into stillness but he knew they were watching Jane Thompson's every move, undoubtedly as transfixed by her eyes as he was.

"Thank you for coming to speak with us this afternoon, Mrs. Thompson. I know it's late in the day. My name is Staff Sergeant Jacques Rouleau."

"My pleasure." Her voice was low and pleasant, husky and sensual at the same time. The slight lift to her mouth let him know that she meant the opposite.

"For the record, we're recording this interview, Tuesday, October 4. Time is now 4:35 p.m. Detectives Kala Stonechild and Paul Gundersund are with me. You know why you're here, Mrs. Thompson?"

"Not really. I haven't broken parole so hope this isn't about me."

She smiled again, but Rouleau saw a guarded expression in her eyes this time. She'd be foolish not to be wary, he thought, and she looked far from a stupid woman. "You were released from prison not that long ago."

"Just over a month."

"Have you had any contact with your ex-husband and children since your release?"

"I've spoken with Adam on the phone. They were out of town when I first got out and we've had trouble arranging a date for me to see the kids. I'm hoping it'll be within the next few days."

"Have you been back to your old neighbourhood?"

Her eyes travelled across his face to Stonechild sitting next to him and back again. "Why did you bring me here, Sergeant? Surely not to talk about my relationship with my family. Unless ..." She straightened and lifted a hand to cover her heart. "Something has happened to one of them. Has something...?"

Rouleau raised a hand. "No, no, your family is fine." He looked down at his notebook, open on the desk in front of him, to give her a chance to regroup. He hadn't meant to scare her and was not convinced that he had, because if she'd killed Devon, she'd know full well that they'd be interviewing her and would have prepared her reactions. He looked up. "You admitted to having had a sexual relationship with Devon Eton a year into your sentence and undertook counselling and rehabilitation courses in prison."

"I did." Her face had relaxed and she was leaning back in the chair, her hands folded on the table. "I learned many important things about myself. The reasons that my strict upbringing led me to become the monster I am, my sexual need to be with children arising from being raised by a cold mother, techniques for holding myself in check. I undertook rehabilitation with an open mind and am now fully aware of my predilections and how to restrain myself, but on guard. Always on guard, like a recovering alcoholic."

Her direct gaze hadn't wavered and he wondered at the self-mocking lilt to her words. The smile was back, as if she'd shared a dark, intimate secret with him. He paused and forced himself not to look away from the trap set in her incredibly blue eyes. "Devon Eton's body was found this morning by a homeless man walking his dog along the waterfront."

He tried to see a reaction but could not. Her face remained a polite mask, no sign of disturbance on the smooth, clear surface. He might have given her a weather report for all the impact his words generated. Her silence stretched into uncomfortable seconds but he remained still and observant. At last a flicker of something crossed her face that looked like regret but could have been anger.

"Are you telling me he's dead?" Her voice was huskier, lower than before.

"Yes. He was murdered last night and left on the shore of Lake Ontario at Murney Point."

She shook her head before dropping her chin to her chest and closing her eyes. The room was silent, the seconds ticking by. This time, Rouleau didn't try to outwait her.

"I'm sorry if I've upset you with this news."

"I have mixed emotions." She opened her eyes and he couldn't begin to guess what was going on inside. "He was a student in my class once upon a time. I felt responsible for his well-being."

The irony filled the space between them. She looked down at her hands still resting on the table.

"Where were you yesterday evening?"

"Nowhere near Lake Ontario."

"Can anyone confirm your whereabouts?"

"I doubt it. I worked my shift and then went back to my apartment around six. I don't speak to anyone as a rule, except when my sister Sandy and I talk on the phone. We might have last night."

"You don't remember?"

"All of our conversations are the same. She usually calls when I'm half-asleep so I can never remember which night we spoke."

Rouleau knew his team would be checking and didn't press the issue. "Did you go out after you got home, say, to the grocery store?"

Jane appeared to think deeply before shaking her head. "You're going to have to take my word for it that I wasn't at Murney Point last evening." The Mona Lisa smile came and went. Her eyes were iridescent pools that a man … a twelve-year-old boy could drown in.

Rouleau shut his notebook. "We'll leave it there for now. We'll need to ask you more questions as the investigation unfolds."

"Of course. If there's one thing I know how to do, it's answer questions from the police. I could give lessons if ever called upon to teach again. Can I go now?"

"Yes, you're free to go."

She pulled the hood of her sweatshirt over her head and stood. When she reached Gundersund, he opened the door and escorted her into the hall.

"What do you think?" Rouleau turned to look at Stonechild. She'd started to rise from her chair but lowered herself back into the seat. Her dark eyes were thoughtful.

"There's a lot going on in her head but not on her face. I got the sense that she's holding in anger, but I'm not sure if it's directed at the system or the people who've deserted her." Kala paused. "You couldn't help but notice her eyes. They're mesmerizing, and that voice … I got the sense she was downplaying her looks, but she couldn't hide the fact she's a magnet for men."

"I thought much the same. She's going to be hard to figure out." Rouleau checked his watch. "You're going to have a busy day interviewing people tomorrow. Head home and get some supper and some sleep. Everything going okay?"

"No complaints, sir. Thanks."

They stood at the same time. Rouleau was aware that she'd withdrawn from him and the rest of the team over the summer. He'd been half expecting her to announce her departure for some time, but had felt helpless to change the situation.

They walked side by side down the hallway and he left her at the door to their office, continuing on toward Heath's office for a command debrief so that Heath could face the media for the nine o'clock news. *At this rate*, Rouleau thought, *I'll be lucky to make it home for supper before Dad has himself tucked in for the night*. As usual, the first hours of a murder investigation would fill every waking hour, but this was the time Rouleau liked best. The thrill of the hunt was fresh, the trail still warm, and the slow-going slog of following up on leads that led nowhere hadn't started to grind the team down yet.

CHAPTER FIVE

Gundersund looked across at Stonechild as he pulled on his seat belt. "Thanks for the lift. My car will be ready tomorrow afternoon."

"I can pick you up again in the morning. What time?"

"Seven thirty works. We can head directly to the school to start interviews and I'll grab a cab to get my car at some point before the shop closes."

"Okay."

She drove along the waterfront heading out of town, past the spot where Devon Eton's body had been found. Shafts of sunlight blinded them as the sun had descended to a point just above the tree-tops. The morning wind had stilled and the waves rolled gently onto the beach.

Gundersund wondered whether to tell Stonechild that he'd seen her niece the day before when he'd driven past Frontenac Secondary School. Kala hadn't wanted to talk about Dawn after Child Services had taken her away, but he knew she was hurting. He decided to give it a shot. "I drove by Dawn's school yesterday and saw her in the yard.

She seemed well." He looked out his side window so Stonechild wouldn't think he was watching for her reaction.

"Was she alone?"

"She was with a couple of girls, probably from her class."

"That's good."

They were silent for a moment. Gundersund asked as casually as he could, "Are you planning to see her?" This time, he turned his head to look at her. He could see the muscle working in her cheek. She lifted one hand from the steering wheel to push her sunglasses further up her nose.

"I think she's better off if I don't interfere in her life. A clean break always works best."

"Do you honestly believe that?"

"Yeah, I do. As a kid who moved homes at least every year, I know it's easier if you don't look back."

She'd never spoken about her childhood before. Gundersund knew it had been bad. He'd read the Marci Stokes article in the *Whig* about her years homeless and drunk on the Sudbury streets. "Perhaps it would have helped if someone had made an effort to keep in touch with you."

"But they didn't."

"And that was a shame."

"Maybe … and maybe they did me a favour."

They passed the Kingston Penitentiary, closed for some time, the inmates moved to other locations where they were crammed in like sardines, if media could be believed. The road wound northwest past large older homes with glimpses of the river down

the hill. Shadows filled the spaces as the sun continued its descent. Ten minutes later, they reached the
turnoff to their side road.

"I've got more experience with this kind of separation thing," she said as if fifteen minutes hadn't
elapsed since his last comment. "And I turned out
just fine."

"You did." He hesitated. "But you are not without issues."

She laughed. "No, I've got my share, but then
again, so do you and you had a normal two-parent
upbringing." She glanced over at him.

He could see her point and smiled back. "Touché."

They reached his driveway and she pulled in,
stopping halfway. He opened his door and set one
foot on the ground, his elbow resting on his knee.
"Thanks for the lift, Stonechild. See you tomorrow."

"Yeah. Bright and early."

Gundersund walked slowly toward his front
door, turning before the steps to watch her truck's
tail lights disappear from view. He would have liked
to suggest they take their dogs for a walk down by
the water, but Fiona had taken to dropping by unan-
nounced. Until he finished the sessions with the
marriage counsellor and continued with the divorce,
he had to be careful not to give Fiona reason to get
worked up. He was biding his time until she came
around to accepting that the divorce was the only
way to get on with their lives, as he had. A clean
break would be better than this dragged-out ending that Fiona had insisted upon. No regret and no
looking back. Stonechild's cynical view of severing

relationships would have been a fitting end to his marriage, even if he found the childhood that had led to her world view overwhelmingly sad. The difference was that he was an adult trying to get on with his life, while she'd been a kid with no life experience to know that not everyone let you down. Her words spoke of an absence of hope; he was only beginning to get some of his back.

Kala still missed coming home and finding Dawn sitting at the kitchen table waiting for her. She'd only had custody of her niece part of a year but it had been enough time to get used to having her around. Now it was only Taiku who met her at the back door.

"Hey, boy." She bent and gave the dog's back and head a good rub before opening the door wide to let him outside. "I'll be out to join you in a minute." She flicked on the wall switch and the kitchen sprang into light. She took a quick look around before crossing to the fridge and taking out a pot of stew she'd had the night before. Leftovers always tasted better the day after. She tucked the pot into the oven, turned on the heat, and grabbed her warmer jacket from the hook behind the back door.

Taiku was sniffing around the back steps when she stepped outside. He waited for her to walk down the steps and bounded in front of her across the lawn toward the lake. Kala knew the way even in the darkness, but tonight the sky was clear and the moon and stars gave the night air a silvery sheen. They walked along the shoreline, the damp breeze blowing back Kala's hair and cooling her face. The beach was filled with rounded stones of different sizes and she stepped carefully until she reached a flat rock that made a comfortable seat. She sat cross-legged and let herself relax into the rhythm of the waves striking the shore. The night was scented with autumn richness and she breathed deeply, letting the calm of the night air fill her soul. Taiku lay next to her, his warm body pressing against her thigh as if sensing that she needed him nearby.

Gundersund's words had hit closer to home than she had admitted to him. She hadn't told him how many times she'd driven to Dawn's school to see her, only to drive past without stopping. Once, a month after Dawn had been taken from her, she'd phoned the number that the child care worker had given her. A woman named Colette finally had answered, but after Kala told her who she was, the woman's voice had lost its welcome. "Dawn is just beginning to settle in," she'd said. "This might not be a good time to re-enter her life. Perhaps in a few weeks I could get back in touch with you. We need to go carefully, as you know. She's had so much upheaval."

Colette had never called back. Kala had backed away except for her weekly trips past Dawn's school that felt like a pathetic inability to let go.

Kala thought about Jane Thompson and the sad mess she'd made of her life. Had she been biding her time in prison to kill the boy who'd put her there? Was she a woman bent on revenge? Kala knew Jane Thompson was the logical choice for Devon's murder given her recent release from prison. Had her release set somebody else into motion? Tomorrow, she and Gundersund would start to fill in the blank spaces. She was going to need to be rested and clear-headed to figure out relationships and motives. She'd keep Jane as a possible suspect but not the only suspect.

"Time to head back." She reached down and ruffled Taiku's silky head. "No answers for us out here tonight." The stew would be warm and she was suddenly hungry. Supper and a hot shower would hit the spot, and hopefully a dreamless sleep would find her soon afterward.

CHAPTER SIX

Gundersund slid into the front seat and handed Kala a travel mug, keeping a second one for himself. "My way of saying thanks for picking me up," he said. "Did you get Rouleau's email?"

She inhaled the smell of roasted coffee and took a sip before saying, "He's going to speak with the Etons while Woodhouse and Bennett go door to door. You and I start with Jane Thompson's sister, Sandra Salvo, before we carry out interviews at the school."

"I take that as a yes."

"Sorry. I meant yes." She smiled and set the mug in the cup holder and began backing out of the driveway. She stopped the truck before backing onto the main road and looked over at him. He appeared to have had a rough night, the scar on his cheek redder than usual against his pale skin. He'd tried to tame his blond curls but not quite succeeded. Gundersund would have been a Viking back in the day — a giant man with unruly locks and scarred face. She forced herself back from an image of him on the prow of a dragon boat. "Did you get Sandra's address?"

"She's in a new subdivision in the east end on Rose Abbey Drive."

"I wonder why Jane didn't move in with her sister when she was released."

"Good question. We'll have to ask her."

Sandra's house was a taupe and brown two-storey with double garage on a street tightly lined with similar homes. A plump woman with grey-blond hair to her waist opened the door before they had a chance to knock. She looked past them as if searching for somebody before hustling them into the hallway. A black cat with frostbitten ears nearly made it through their legs and outside to freedom, but Sandra slammed the door shut in time.

"Popcorn tries to get out every chance he gets. You'd think he hates living here." She laughed and held out her hand. "I'm Sandra. Thanks for coming by. Going into the station would have been problematic for me." She led them into the kitchen, which fed into a family room. Kala blinked. Two babies were crawling around a penned-in area and three more pint-size children were eating cereal at the kitchen table.

Sandra jumped when the doorbell rang and a relieved smile crossed her face. "My helper just arrived. We can meet in the den once I let her in."

Gundersund looked at Kala and mouthed, "Why Jane chose to live elsewhere."

The den was a cramped room with a desk and office chair taking up half of the space, and two leather chairs in front of a window that looked into the neighbour's kitchen, where Kala saw a man in a housecoat pouring a cup of coffee. Two walls of Sandra's den were lined with bookcases overflowing with paperbacks. Kala and Gundersund squeezed past the desk and sat in the leather chairs to wait for Sandra.

"Doesn't look much like her sister," Gundersund said. "She appears to be a lot more wholesome. Do you want to take the lead on this one?"

"If you like."

A baby's crying filled the house but didn't last long. Sandra appeared a moment later and shut the door. She took the desk chair and rolled it a few feet toward them. "Sorry about that. Luckily, two of the kids are home sick today and I get three more four-year-olds at lunch hour, and even though my second helper shows up at eleven thirty, as I explained to your sergeant, this really is the best time for us to meet. Now, I believe you have questions about my sister, Jane?"

Kala glanced at Gundersund and back at Sandra. "Are you aware that Devon Eton was murdered two nights ago?"

"Of course. I read the paper but I haven't spoken to Jane about it, as you requested. I can assure you though that she didn't do it."

"How can you be so certain?"

"Jane didn't hate him, although I must say that I would have in her shoes. I mean he was responsible for ruining her life."

"You don't agree that Devon was the victim?"

"Jane is not a child rapist nor is she a killer."

"Did you speak with Jane by phone on Monday night?"

"Yes. I called at seven as I usually do. We, or I should say I, talked for half an hour. Jane never says very much. She's been depressed since she got out because that prick Adam has been keeping the kids from her. Olivia is eight and Ben is twelve so they need their mother now more than ever especially since that tramp he's dating isn't much older than Ben. I imagine Adam will be using this kid's death as another reason to keep them apart. I'm angry as hell about all this. The so called friends who just turned their backs. After all that Jane did for ..."

Kala was beginning to understand why Jane let her sister do all of the talking on the phone. Sandra was like a nonstop wind-up toy without an apparent need for air. Kala cut in. "What kind of childhood did the two of you have?"

"What, me and Jane? Not great, but thanks for asking. Our mother was old school. She believed in beatings and God — not the usual combination, but we always got an earful of scripture after our punishment. Jane took the brunt of it being the oldest and the one who daydreamed when she should have been doing chores. Drove my mother half around the bend. You wouldn't believe how wild my mother got when Jane discovered boys, or maybe it was the other way around. I mean, have you seen my sister? She had them lining up in grade school." Sandra clamped a hand over her mouth. "I didn't mean that like it sounded," she said through her fingers.

"Did you visit your sister in prison?"

"I tried to get there once a month. It's hard with this daycare business I'm running. I take in kids most weekends too and a few of the parents work shifts." Her head snapped toward the door. A child was screeching and shortly afterward a second child started screaming uncontrollably.

Kala raised her voice. "Just a few more questions. Have you seen Jane since she got out of prison?"

"I invited her for dinner a few times but she never came. As I said, she was depressed, hanging around her apartment after work, waiting for Adam to let her see her kids. Tragic how far she fell in life. Everything my mother said about Jane came true."

"What would that be?"

"That she was living in a dream world. Getting above herself and heading for a fall. I'm just glad my mother's in a home now with Alzheimer's so she can't yell 'I told you so' at Jane anymore. It was bad enough when Jane was found guilty of having sex with that kid."

The screaming had grown louder and moved just outside the door. Gundersund spoke for the first time, raising his voice above the child's. "For the record, where were you Monday night, Sandra?"

She thought for a second. "Why, right here. I didn't have any kids staying over so I had a bath after I spoke with Jane and called it an early night."

"Can anyone vouch for you?"

"No. I live alone. I only have a helper come to work when I have more than four kids so neither was here that day because most of the kids were off with the flu."

"How close are you to Jane?"

"Are you asking if I'm close enough to kill on her behalf?" Sandra smiled and suddenly Kala saw her resemblance to Jane in their identical expressions that could have been taken as mischievous but came across as secretive. "My sister and I had to learn to band together when we were kids to survive in my mother's house of spare the rod. I'd take a bullet for Jane but that doesn't mean I'd commit murder for her."

Gundersund was writing down details of their visit in his notepad while Kala drove toward the school. The sky had brightened since their morning drive to Sandra's house and Kala felt her spirit lift. At this time of year, a warm, sunny day was to be savoured. The warmth had to carry them into the winter months that were just around the corner.

Gundersund clicked the pen with his thumb a couple of times and set the notepad on his knees. "What's your take on Jane and Sandra?"

"Their childhood would make an interesting study. They both chose to work with kids even with a lousy role model. I find that interesting."

"I hadn't made that connection. You'd have to wonder how much impact their mother's discipline and preaching had on them and on the way they interact with kids. Did the mother's parenting come up at the trial, do you know?"

"Not sure."

"Yeah. I'll make a note to check. From what I've been reading in the file, Cathy Bryden kept meticulous notes. Sandra doesn't have an alibi but she doesn't seem high on the suspect list. For one, she could have killed Devon at any point over the past three years if she'd wanted to and wouldn't have implicated Jane since she was in prison."

Kala pumped the breaks as she eased up to a stop sign. She looked over at Gundersund. "Unless she *wanted* Jane to be implicated. Who knows what's really going on between the two of them? The fact Jane hasn't been to see her a month after her release and appears to barely tolerate her phone calls makes me wonder how close they really are."

"Layers inside of layers." Gundersund picked up the notepad. "Never trust anyone."

"That's right. Jane Thompson may very well have killed this kid, but it's also possible that somebody was waiting for her to get out of prison so they could pin this on her. That leaves the field wide open."

"But why? The only ones I can see who would want revenge would be family and friends of Devon. They'd hardly kill him to get back at Jane Thompson. Makes no sense."

"Well, there's Jane's sister Sandra as we just discussed and an ex-husband, for starters. Sounds like Adam Thompson is keeping Jane from their kids. Maybe he wants her back inside so he never has to deal with her again. He kills the boy she was having an affair with and vents some pent-up anger from their affair that must have made him look less than manly. What was the name of the street the school's on?"

"Kingston Collegiate. Make a left here on Frontenac. It's that three-storey red brick building at the end of the block."

CHAPTER SEVEN

The Eton home was furnished with an eclectic mix of modern and antique — darkly stained oak and walnut tables with elaborately carved designs contrasted with the sleek lines of minimalist sofas and chairs upholstered in expensive silk fabrics. The art on the walls ran to hunting scenes and landscapes in the Turner tradition, a reflection of Hilary's British heritage. She'd led Rouleau into the spacious living room when he arrived at 9:00 a.m. and invited him to sit on a plaid-covered couch in front of a bay window that looked out over the backyard. Oak trees lined the back of the property, their leaves a slash of scarlet against the blue backdrop of sky. The room smelled of smoke from a recent fire in the brick-lined hearth. Charred logs still rested in the grate.

"Mitchell will be right down. He's with our daughter, Sophie. As you can imagine, she's having great difficulty accepting Devon's death." Hilary positioned herself in the wingback chair across from them. The sombreness of her long black skirt and black sweater was softened by the glint of a wide sterling silver bracelet wrapped around one wrist and a heavy silver chain with a heart locket resting between her breasts. Dark eyeliner rimmed the redness in her eyes that came from crying or lack of sleep. *Probably both*, Rouleau thought.

He sat forward, trying to bridge the distance between them. "I know how difficult this is for you and your family and I'll try to intrude as little as possible, but we want to find whoever harmed your son and hold them responsible. The sooner we learn all we can about Devon's movements last week, the more quickly we can make an arrest."

"I've already told you who murdered Devon. I can't understand why that bloody Thompson woman isn't already in custody." Hilary crossed her arms across her chest and sat rigidly in the seat. Her eyes looked over Rouleau's head and out the window.

He didn't contradict her. Nothing would be gained by challenging the accusation. He said, "My team has been collecting evidence and is even now interviewing everyone who knew Devon. Once we have proof for a conviction, we'll arrest whoever is responsible."

"It shouldn't take long." Mitchell Eton's voice boomed across the space as he strode toward them. He didn't notice that his loud entrance had made Hilary jump and grab on to her chest. "Have you taken the harlot in for questioning yet?"

Rouleau stood and extended his hand. "I'm very sorry for your loss, Mr. Eton. We're doing everything we can to bring your son's killer to justice. That includes interviewing Jane Thompson."

Mitchell Eton was not a handsome man, but he commanded the room with his deep voice and piercing brown eyes. Unlike his wife, he had no trace of a British accent and exuded an aggressiveness that would serve him well in the business world. He gripped Rouleau's hand before sitting next to him on the couch, legs spread wider than considered polite. Like Devon, he had broad shoulders, although his body was thicker without Devon's height. He had the same shock of black hair, too, but silver threads glinted at the temples. Rouleau could see an angle to his nose where it had been broken and not set properly, giving him a thuggish air reinforced by the bullish way he held himself. Rouleau wouldn't have placed him with aristocratic-looking Hilary, yet they'd married, raised a family, and lasted as a couple longer than most. Mitchell hadn't made eye contact with his wife since he entered. Rouleau could see the strain they both were under. He hated having to add to it, but he had no choice. "Can you tell me anything about the day your son was killed, Mr. Eton?" he asked.

Mitchell took his time answering and spoke in a measured voice when he did. "It was a regular day. I saw him at breakfast early. I was heading to the office and he had a football practice before school started. Neither of us is a morning person so we didn't have any prolonged conversation, something you can imagine I regret now. Devon turned down my offer of a ride and was heading to the washroom last I saw him. Sophie and Hilary were both moving around upstairs when I left. I had a dinner meeting after work and got home around eleven. I thought Devon was already in bed. Hilary mentioned the next morning that he hadn't come home but was likely at Charlie's and hadn't called. She said she was going to track him down when I left for the airport."

Hilary added, "I called around as soon as Mitchell left and nobody had seen him. That's when I phoned the station to say he was missing. I didn't know what else to do."

"I still don't know how you could lose track of the kids." Mitchell finally looked over at her. "It's not like you had anything else pressing to take up your attention."

"Fuck you, Mitchell." Her voice was low and controlled, her words shocking in the silence of this tranquil room. They seemed out of character with her proper English bearing. "You have no idea what I do or don't do in a day since you're never here." Her eyes swung over to Rouleau. "I apologize, Sergeant. My husband can be an ass when he feels people have not lived up to his expectations."

"Hilary." Mitchell's voice was conciliatory but seemed to hold a warning. "Let's not let the stress of this situation make us say things we'll regret. We have to keep our eye on the ball and that's helping put that woman back behind bars."

"Mom?"

They all looked across the room to a girl standing in the doorway. She was tall and slender with long, white-blond hair hanging loose to her waist, and on the edge of the teen years. Her blue-grey eyes were identical to her mother's. Hilary started to stand but Mitchell beat her to it. He rose and began walking toward his daughter, arms spread wide. "I'm here, Sophie."

"I want to talk to Mom." Tears began streaming from her eyes. She looked ready to keel over and Rouleau got to his feet.

"Coming darling." Hilary rushed across the room and Mitchell stopped to let her by. He watched without making any effort to intervene. She put her arms around Sophie and looked over her head at him. "I'm going to take Sophie to her room. I'll stay with her."

"As you wish." Mitchell turned and strode back to sit in the chair that Hilary had vacated. He looked at Rouleau. "This is a bloody nightmare. My family is falling apart around me and it's all because of that Thompson woman."

Rouleau had seen murder bring families together and he'd seen it rip them apart. The Eton family had been through more grief than most, and whatever fissures had been under the surface of this marriage looked to be splitting open. "I'm all done for now," he said. "If you have any questions or remember anything you think might be important, please don't hesitate to call me. Here's my card with my email address and cellphone number. I'd like to talk to Sophie but will wait a few days until she's up to it."

Mitchell looked toward the door. "We just need a bit of time. Sophie is a strong kid, but this is going to take time to get over. That's our focus now. I know it looks like Hilary and I aren't getting along, but we have a solid marriage. We're both reeling from Devon's death."

Rouleau asked, "Can you tell me if Devon had a girlfriend and the names of his friends?"

"Girlfriend?" Mitchell appeared to pull himself back from the dark place his mind had taken him. "Hilary would know better than I do but they never last long. His best friend is Charlie Hanson. They go back to grade school and have remained tight through ... well, through everything. Devon hung out with some of the guys on his football team. His coach will know their names."

Rouleau started toward the door. "We'll be in touch. Again, I'm very sorry for your loss. We'll do everything we can to find out what happened to your son."

"We already told you who murdered Devon." Mitchell's voice had returned to its booming self-assuredness. "Now all you have to do is prove it."

Woodhouse thanked the woman in the yellow bathrobe and she closed her front door. He could hear a chain being scraped into place as he started down the front steps. He was directly across the street from the Eton home on Beverley Street. The drapes were closed on all the Eton windows as if they stupidly believed they could keep the dirty world away. He'd give his left nut to interview that family. Get them to talk about what made their kid Devon tick. If he knew Rouleau, he'd have pussyfooted around them like he always did and gotten nothing to help move the case along. The man had gotten soft since his wife kicked the bucket.

Woodhouse loosened the collar on his coat as he walked toward Bennett waiting for him on the sidewalk. Damn cold weather had disappeared overnight and now he was overdressed. Kingston weather was as changeable as a woman's mind. He reached Bennett and pointed to the house he'd just left. "Lady was as helpful as that tree stump over there. Did the next-door neighbour have anything enlightening to say?"

Bennett closed his iPad. "Cheryl Gladstone saw Devon leave for school the day he was killed when she was putting out the garbage. He said hello to her as he always did when they crossed paths. She didn't see him return home but she was at work at the hospital on the evening shift. Says they're a quiet family who keep to themselves for the most part."

"Did she make any mention of seeing Jane Thompson hanging around since her release?"

"No. Said she hadn't noticed anyone unusual on the street."

Woodhouse let out a loud sigh. As if it wasn't enough of a pisser that they had to go door to door and carry out interviews that any monkey could do, they hadn't gotten one bit of useful information. Not to mention he was stuck again with a pretty boy partner who had the IQ of a lemming. And then there was Stonechild. The idea of her getting the plum lead assignment on this case instead of him made him want to hit somebody. His BlackBerry rang and he took it out. When he finished the call, he put his phone away and said to Bennett, "Rouleau is leaving the Etons' and returning to the station. We're to finish up here and go back to Murney Point where the kid's body was found and interview the people in the apartment building across the street."

"That could take a while."

"You think ... genius?" Woodhouse muttered the last word under his breath. He started toward their car, parked at the end of the block. Bennett appeared to be in no hurry to follow him but Woodhouse would let it ride. As long as it didn't turn into insubordination. A few steps from the car and his BlackBerry rang a second time. He checked the number. *Well, well, well.*

"Yeah?" He was a little surprised to be hearing from Marci Stokes from the *Whig-Standard*. The last time they'd spoken, she'd torn a strip off him for going over her head on the Stonechild article. He still believed the public had a right to know one of their protectors had spent a chunk of time as a homeless drunk on the Sudbury streets. Stonechild had no right to be on the force when she'd demonstrated such weakness of character. No matter how much people said they'd changed, they never really did. He believed that with every atom of his being.

Her voice was sharp, all business. "Have you got anything for me on the Eton murder?"

He waited a few beats, letting her hang. He kept his voice nonchalant. "Maybe. That is, if you have something for me."

"I'm quite sure the ledger is in your favour at the moment."

Woodhouse smiled. "I'm assuming you're asking me to help you for a reason."

"Your HQ isn't saying much." A pause. "Is this related to Jane Thompson and her release?"

"You seem overly eager to get a jump on this story. What's the rush?" He saw Bennett approaching out of the corner of his eye. He dropped his voice. "Listen, why don't we meet, say, seven tonight at the usual spot?"

She exhaled in his ear and Woodhouse could picture the battle going on inside her head. Get the story even if it meant dealing with him or let it slip away. He wasn't surprised to hear her say, "Fine. I'll be there."

The phone went dead and Woodhouse looked at Bennett, trying to figure out if he'd overheard anything. He couldn't be sure by the sulky look on Bennett's face. He tucked the phone into his breast pocket and patted his crotch. "Setting up a date for tonight. Nice to have a hot lady in my life."

Bennett opened his car door and leaned on it. He glared across at Woodhouse. "I'm happy for you Woodhouse, but I really don't need to know about your personal life. Really don't need to know." He got inside the car and slammed the door.

Woodhouse ducked his head and smiled. Baiting the kid was too easy. It didn't compensate for their demotion to a supporting role in this case, but would keep the job from getting dull. Maybe if he pushed Bennett hard enough, he'd pack up and take Stonechild back to Ottawa. Rouleau might even come to his senses and start giving the murder cases to the best investigator on the force, which was none other than himself. All he needed was the chance to prove it.

Kala and Gundersund were shown into an empty classroom at Frontenac Secondary. They rearranged two desks, putting them side by side. Gundersund set a chair directly in front while Kala put two chairs behind the desks. She invited their first interviewee, Rhonda Peters, to sit in the single chair facing them. Rhonda was a portly woman, her belly jutting out further than her breasts under a shapeless blue dress. She'd been Devon Eton's homeroom and math teacher.

"Yes, Devon was in class Monday and no, he didn't act as if he had anything weighing on him. I handed back a calculus test, which he'd aced as usual. He planned to go into the sciences next year. He'd applied to Queen's and U of T, but I believe Queen's was his first choice."

"So he was a good student?" Gundersund asked.

"Devon was brilliant at math and science. Not as gifted in the arts, but that's to be expected. It's unusual for someone to be equally as adept in all fields of study."

"And what was he like as a person?" Kala still had no real feel for him.

Rhonda's crisp replies faltered as she appeared to be searching for words. Kala and Gundersund waited her out. "Well," she began, "he was polite. I suppose you're aware that he was involved with his grade seven teacher at his elementary school. We were all wary of getting too close to him, as you can imagine."

Kala forced a smile from reaching her lips. Rhonda Peters likely didn't need to fear the attentions of the teenage boy population. "Did Devon have a girlfriend?"

"Well, he was friends with Charlie Hanson. I never heard that Devon was dating anyone in particular but I chaperoned a few dances and he was always out there with one girl or another. He was a good-looking boy and part of the football team, the reason he came to this high school, I believe. The fact he'd been involved with his teacher gave him a certain status with the girls. As you know, this generation has received nothing but sexual marketing from the time they could click on a computer key."

Gundersund leaned forward. "Did you meet Devon's parents?"

"Of course. Devon was in my math class for the past two years so his parents came to the parent-teacher interviews. I had the sense that they expected a lot from him. The father is very successful through his own hard work. He's also philanthropic and made quite the name for himself in the community. Do you know that an entire wing in Kingston General is named after him?"

Kala glanced at Gundersund. Mrs. Peters was acting a little star-struck. Time to get the interview back on track. "Have you any stories about Devon that might give us insight into his personality?" she asked.

"Let me see." They waited while Rhonda again dug into her memory bank. "He got a B+ on a math test when I taught him in grade nine and he stayed after the other students had gone. He was upset and tried to get me to change the mark. He was practically crying when I said no. After that, he stopped answering questions in class, but he was back to getting A and A+ on his work. That's really all that stands out." She stood. "I need to get to my next class." She hesitated. "I didn't mean to imply that Devon was a crybaby because it was only the one time. In fact, I'd say he was the opposite."

"How so?" Kala asked.

"Oh, he seemed tough skinned to me. Not a bully, but you'd never call him a victim." She laughed. "I don't know what I mean. Just disregard all that. I really am late." She hurried from the room, banging her hip on the door as she swung it open.

Kala turned to Gundersund when they were alone. "So what we have on Devon is that he was brilliant and driven to succeed, maybe more than was good for him. Girls liked him but he didn't have a girlfriend. He was polite and quiet for the most part and toughened up after his first semester in high school. Have I left anything out?"

"Not that I can tell. So far, there's no reason for anybody to have killed him."

"Except Jane Thompson if we believe his parents. Let's see if his classmates prove more enlightening than his teachers."

For the rest of the morning and late into the afternoon, each one of Devon's classmates and football teammates took turns funnelling into the classroom to give their version of his life and last day at school. One after the other, they provided the same critique: Devon had been brilliant, standoffish, best friends with Charlie Hanson. Asked to describe Charlie, they'd fallen silent before revealing they hadn't liked him much, not certain why.

One girl in their biology class said that Charlie was Devon's shadow. "Devon was the one we all tried to date. I guess that teacher he had the affair with put him off long-term relationships. We all wanted to give him true love and save him." She giggled. "None of us could figure out what Devon saw in Charlie, but they were always together."

When the last of the football teammates picked up his knapsack and hiked out of the room without looking back, Kala flung her pen onto the table and pushed back her chair so that its front legs were up in the air.

"We learned practically nothing about why Devon got himself murdered, but if anyone knows, it'll be this fellow Charlie."

Gundersund stood. "I'll go see where he is. He should have been here by now."

Gundersund was gone ten minutes and on his return stood at the entrance to the classroom. "Charlie Hanson left after first period. We need to get over to the Hansons' now. I got his address from the office secretary."

Kala gathered up her notebook, pen, and cellphone and shoved them into her bag. "Great. The one person we really need to speak with and he's quit the premises." She'd have preferred to speak with Charlie at the school on neutral turf and wasn't happy to have to track him down. She could tell by the expression on Gundersund's face that he felt the same way.

"All set," she said. "Let's go find out what it is about this Charlie Hanson that made Devon Eton become his buddy and makes the other kids dislike him."

CHAPTER EIGHT

Kala drove to Macdonnell Street where Charlie resided with his mother, Roslyn Hanson, and two sisters. They lived a few streets west of the Etons and further north, facing the back side of Winston Churchill Public School. The Hanson house was modest in comparison to the Etons' — a two-storey with white siding and windows that could have used an update. An overgrown cedar hedge took up most of the front yard.

Kala parked her truck on the street and wondered why she had a bad feeling. She forced herself to shake it off. An untended yard and rundown home didn't equal an evil spirit. Gundersund sat silently while she scanned the other side of the street. She finally turned to face him, smiling to keep the uneasy thoughts from showing in her eyes. "That last talkative girl we interviewed said Charlie's father, Wally Hanson, died a few years ago. Guess he was the handyman around this place because it looks like the yard could use some work."

Gundersund was watching her. "What is it?" he asked, ignoring her attempt at levity. His blue eyes questioned hers. "You seem put off by something."

"I don't know. Sometimes I get a feeling … probably nothing. Let's go check this kid out. I think he might respond better to you than me." She opened her door and stepped out quickly. She didn't know which was more unsettling: the feeling that had risen up her spine or the fact that Gundersund was starting to read her.

Charlie's mother answered the door. She was older than Kala expected, with kinky grey hair to her shoulders and a lined face. "I don't have money for charity this month," she said, and started to close the door.

"Roslyn Hanson? We're from the Kingston police, Homicide Division." Gundersund raised his badge to eye level through the gap. She stopped and pulled the door wider, moving a step closer to read their names.

"Who is it, Mom?" A girl in her early twenties entered the hallway. She was wearing a pink nursing uniform and shrugging into a jacket while holding her purse in one hand. She looked at Gundersund and Kala and stopped. "You're here to question Charlie."

"You carry on to work and we'll be fine." Roslyn stepped back and helped her with the sleeve of her jacket. She looked at Gundersund. "This is Ashley, my oldest. She lives in student housing on campus and is a fourth-year nursing student. My pride and joy."

"Oh, Mom." Ashley gave her a peck on the cheek. "I'll see you at breakfast because you'll be in bed when I get home. I'll be staying over one more night and then back to my dorm." She gave Gundersund a chest-high wave as she walked past him. "Go easy on my brother. He's taking Devon's death hard."

"Well, come in then." Roslyn started down the hallway. "Don't mind the mess."

They followed her into a small living room filled with furniture — a blue couch too big for the room was pushed against the window, blocking half of the view. Two recliners angled in from each wall facing a giant-screen television set on a stand. A rectangular oak veneer coffee table, home to a stack of fashion magazines, empty coffee cups, and an overflowing ashtray, took up most of the remaining space. Overpowering air freshener competed with stale cigarette smoke, making Kala's eyes water. She felt a cough tickle the back of her throat. Gundersund made a clearing noise in his as they took spots next to each other on the couch.

Roslyn stood in the doorway. "I'll just go get him, shall I?" She was gone before they could respond and they listened to her heavily climb the stairs while calling Charlie's name.

Gundersund swiped at his eyes. "Something in this room is giving me a full-on allergy attack. What is that smell anyway? Gardenia?"

"Chemical flowers in a spray can." Kala spotted a family photo on the wall above one of the recliners. "My guess is roses."

The picture had to be a few years old. Charlie's dad stood next to him, both with the same prominent nose and wavy brown hair, although the father's was peppered with grey. In the photo, Roslyn had less grey in her hair than now but the same pinched look on her face. Ashley had pulled her wavy hair into a ponytail at the top of her head and wore a tight T-shirt that showed off her fleshy arms and healthy chest. She was the only one smiling. The younger girl looked to be eleven or twelve. Someone had cut off her hair in an unattractive style. Her looks weren't helped by round glasses and a sour expression on her face that spelled a whole lot of woe for somebody.

"Is that the dad?" Gundersund got to his feet and squeezed between the couch and the La-Z-Boy. "Charlie must be fifteen in this photo, so two or three years ago. Family's not exactly best in show, are they?" He plunked back down on the couch and Kala bounced as he landed.

"I wonder if he had a heart attack." Kala looked toward the door to make sure Charlie hadn't entered unnoticed.

"I think his classmate said that Charlie's dad died unexpectedly. Might have been his heart or one of those quick-moving cancers. Although an aneurysm can get you pretty quick, or a stroke. Man, I'm starting to scare myself."

They stopped talking as shoes clunked down the stairs and toward them along the hallway.

"You're up, tough guy," Kala said.

A slightly older version of the boy in the photo entered the room with his mother close behind him. They crossed the short space and each swung a recliner around to face Stonechild and Gundersund.

"He's eighteen," Roslyn said as she sat down. "But guess it won't do no harm for me to listen in."

"You're welcome to be here for our interview." Gundersund smiled at her and then repositioned himself on the couch.

Kala could feel every movement her partner made as the cushions shifted under his weight. She glanced over. Gundersund was a bear of a man and he angled himself to fill Charlie's sightline. She looked back at the kid. He was watching Gundersund with alert eyes framed by black-rimmed glasses but had a relaxed expression on his face, arms folded across his black T-shirt, which was emblazoned with a large Google logo. His face had filled in, but his hair was the same unruly mess of waves as in the photo on the wall.

"First let me say how sorry I am that you lost your friend. I understand you were close."

Charlie nodded. He looked down at his hands. "Thanks."

"When was the last time you saw him?"

"Monday at school."

"Not after school?"

Charlie looked at his mother and back at Gundersund. "Usually we got together but he said that he had something to do."

"Any idea what?"

"Nope. He was secretive about it. In fact, he'd been secretive a lot the past month or so. I thought he might be seeing someone and didn't want to tell me yet."

"A girl?"

"I guess."

"You were his friend when Jane Thompson was accused of sexual interference and you saw them together, is this correct?"

"You seem to already know what happened."

Kala lifted her head from taking notes. For the first time, she heard an edge to his voice verging on insolent.

"I'd like to hear it from you." Gundersund's voice was firm and Kala knew he'd also caught Charlie's attitude.

Charlie slumped deeper into the chair. "Yeah. Devon told me that he and Mrs. Thompson were having sex. I saw them together a few times after he told me. Once, she kissed him. I never saw them getting it on though." His mouth twisted sideways. Kala couldn't tell if it was a smirk or a grimace of distaste.

Roslyn moved in her chair but didn't say anything.

"How did Devon feel about her getting out of prison last month?"

"He never said."

"I imagine the trial must have been difficult for him."

Charlie shrugged. "I guess. We all liked Mrs. Thompson but she shouldn't have come on to Devon. We were just kids."

Kala heard a whine in his voice that kids used when feeling hard done by. He wasn't that far from being a child even though he looked like a grown-up young man.

"Was Devon worried about anything? Anybody bothering him?" Gundersund asked.

Charlie's glasses reflected the light and Kala didn't see his eyes before his head dropped. "Not that he told me." He wiped the back of his hand across his nose. "I still can't believe he's dead. Seems like he'll walk through that door any minute. We were best friends since grade five." He dropped his head further and covered his eyes with one hand.

"I think that's enough for now." A flurry of activity and Roslyn was on her feet, looking down at them on the couch. She put her hands on her hips. "Charlie needs time to grieve."

Gundersund took a long look at Charlie. "If you remember anything that could help us, Charlie, no matter how trivial it might seem, call us and we'll follow up. Officer Stonechild and I will leave our contact information with your mom."

Charlie nodded but he didn't make any move to get out of the chair. Kala followed Gundersund and his mom out of the living room. She stopped in the doorway and glanced back over her shoulder. Charlie was lying with his head against the headrest reading something on his cellphone.

She reached Gundersund in time to hear him say, "You have another daughter."

Roslyn was pulling the front door open. "Tiffany. That's her coming up the walk."

Tiffany's wavy brown hair was now down to her shoulders but the scowl from the photograph was still on her face.

"How old is she?" Kala asked.

Roslyn turned to look at her. "Fifteen going on thirty. She started grade ten but doesn't like school much. Hard to believe my three kids all have the same genes, they're that different."

Kala smiled. "I've heard so many parents say the same thing. Where do you work, Mrs. Hanson?"

"I'm a cashier at the Loblaws behind Princess. Doesn't pay much but luckily Ashley got scholarships for nursing school and works part-time. The universities are fighting over Charlie. The one coming up the walk is my biggest trial."

"Well, sounds like you're doing a great job."

Mrs. Hanson smiled at Kala for the first time. "It hasn't been easy." She caught Tiffany by the shoulders as she was trying to skirt by them. "Tiffany, this is Officer Stonechild and Officer Gundersund. They're here about Devon. Did you see him on Monday?"

"Why would I see him on Monday? He was Charlie's friend, not mine. Ask Charlie."

Kala moved to cut Tiffany's escape into the house. "Did you or did you not see Devon on Monday?"

Tiffany stared at her with defiant eyes, a peculiar grey-green shade that reminded Kala of lichen. Her gaze was laser straight and unnerving.

Roslyn stepped in. "Don't be cheeky, and answer the officer."

"No," Tiffany mumbled, her mouth holding the "oh" sound long enough to be rude. She turned her head to look at her mother. "I didn't see him on Monday. Can I go now?"

"Mind you do your homework before supper. I don't want another note home from your teacher."

"I just have some math questions. What's for supper? Not that rotten hamburger casserole again."

"Hot dogs, just so you'll stop complaining."

Tiffany scrunched up her face and stuck out her tongue before slipping past her mother and up the stairs.

Roslyn shook her head. "God keep me from striking that child. Ever since Wally passed … I don't know how to handle her most days. I keep waiting for her to outgrow this phase."

"Thanks for your time, Mrs. Hanson," Gundersund said as he walked down the steps, leaving Kala to offer words of encouragement and their business card. Kala followed her partner into her truck.

"That family depresses the hell out of me," he said. "Makes me never want to have kids. I'll check in with Rouleau, and hopefully, we can call it a day."

Kala sat with her hands on the wheel, staring straight ahead. Did she want kids? Did she want Dawn back?

Gundersund looked across at her and hit his hand against his forehead. "How insensitive of me. I'm sorry, Stonechild."

"It's okay. Those kids depress me too."

"I should clarify that I'd gladly be a dad if I could guarantee that all my kids would turn out as great as Dawn."

She started the truck and glanced at him as she turned to make a shoulder check. "But there are no guarantees. There isn't even a guarantee that Dawn will turn out okay with all she's had to deal with. That's my biggest fear in all this, that she turns into another kid like Tiffany in there with nothing but anger to get her through the night."

CHAPTER NINE

Kala dropped Gundersund off at the car lot just after six and was home by six thirty. Not quite a twelve-hour day. They'd gotten off lucky.

As they were leaving the Hansons', she'd received a message from Rouleau to be at the station for a seven o'clock meeting the next morning, so another long day ahead on Thursday. She knew Forensics was also working late hours going through the physical evidence, including Devon's cellphone and computer and all the notebooks they'd taken from his locker. When she called earlier, they had nothing to report. Three days after the murder and they had no motive and no suspects, aside from the obvious one. Jane Thompson could have sought revenge, or maybe Devon had rebuffed her attempts to start up again. Love and obsession could warp a person. Kala had seen the carnage wreaked by more than one rejected lover. In every case, temporary madness had consumed their being like a poison in the blood.

She pulled into her driveway, stepped outside her truck, and inspected the property. Creeping darkness had cast long shadows across the lawn. The air had a crispness to it in the mornings and early evenings that hadn't been present a week earlier. She'd think about taking Taiku for a week in Algonquin Park if this case ended quickly. Put the canoe in the water and paddle to a wilderness campsite. The leaves would have turned and the colours would be at their peak. Time away might help cure the fatigue that had overtaken her waking hours.

She walked around the side of the house to the back deck. Taiku would have heard her arrival and be at the back door, waiting to be let outside. Her phone buzzed in her pocket as she reached the steps. She didn't recognize the number but clicked on RECEIVE as she climbed.

"Kala Stonechild?" the caller asked.

A woman. Kala tried to place her voice but couldn't. "How can I help you?" She opened the back door but Taiku wasn't waiting in his usual spot. *Strange*.

"I'm Dawn's new child care worker, Caroline Russell. I've had a call from her foster family that she's been skipping school. I understand you're the closest she has to a relative with her parents in prison. I've been going over her file and would like to meet with you, if you have the time in the next week or so."

Had the universe been reading her mind? Kala took a second to get her head around the implications. "What happened to her other social worker? Tamara Jones?"

"Tamara's taken a leave of absence. The court has put Dawn in my charge."

Another one bites the dust. Tamara had been young and unbending — thought she knew it all because she graduated from a university course. Self-preservation told Kala not to get involved. The system had the power to destroy her hope. She hesitated but the persistent longing to see Dawn won out.

"Tell me when and where," she said.

Woodhouse checked the bar to the right of the Delta lobby to make sure none of his colleagues was lurking before he joined Marci Stokes. She'd chosen a high table near the window overlooking the harbour. Her back was to the room and he saw that she already had a drink in front of her with slices of lemon and lime bobbing in the clear liquid. He'd lay money that it was her usual gin and tonic. He strode to the bar and ordered a beer before he hoisted himself into the seat across from her. She was typing on her iPad and didn't look up.

"Don't mind me," he said. "I'll sit here nice and quiet while you finish whatever important document you're working on. Your time is much more valuable than mine." He took a long drink of beer. Man, she was ragged around the edges, older than last time he'd seen her in the summer. Getting less attractive the older she got. He could see grey in the roots of her hair, which looked like it needed a brushing. Her black trench coat was open, showing a wrinkled blue blouse. She could have been a good-looking woman if she'd put a bit of effort into her grooming.

She glanced up. "Thanks. Just sending off an email to my editor." She finished typing and tucked her iPad into the open handbag at her feet. She took a drink from her glass and stared at him. "It's been a while."

"I figured you'd be back when we got an interesting case. How've you been?"

She shrugged. "Not much to tell. I spent the past few months in New York but like the air better here. So did the teacher whom Devon Eton put in prison kill him?"

"That's my guess. Rouleau has us checking out every other possibility, but I'd bet money she's back inside by the end of next week."

"What've you got on her?"

"Kid's parents say she did it. Plus, what are the odds he gets murdered the month after she gets out?"

"Maybe someone took the opportunity so she'd get blamed."

"Yeah, maybe, but not very likely."

"Could you let me know when you're about to make the arrest?"

She made the question sound offhand, but Woodhouse heard something in her voice that sounded like desperation. He had to wonder why. Instead of answering her, he said, "As I recall, you weren't all that happy with the information I gave you last time. In fact, you were less than appreciative. Why should I help you now?"

"Because you owe me. The information that you gave me, and that my boss published without my permission, made Kala Stonechild lose custody of her niece. I'm sure Rouleau wouldn't be too pleased to know the hand you played in all of that."

"If he even believed you. You wrote the story after all. Plus, aren't you bound by the reporter oath to never give up a source?"

"I am. I also regret writing that story every day. I'm not sure which is the stronger pull on my loyalty." She raised her empty glass until she caught the eye of a passing waitress. She motioned for another and then looked over at him. "Do we have a deal?"

"So you keep quiet about who gave you the information that Stonechild was a homeless drunk, and I feed you information about this case? Why did you really come crawling back here?"

She grimaced. "I wouldn't exactly call it crawling." She put her elbows on the table and leaned toward him. "All right, Woodhouse, here it is. I quit my job at the *Whig* and went back to work for my ex on the *New York Times* only to discover I hated working for the self-serving prick. The *Whig* wasn't pleased as you can imagine, but they let me come back to work on probation. I have to bring them something big or they're going to hire the person they had lined up as my replacement. My ex at the *Times* is doing his best to spread the word through all the media outlets that I'm washed up, vindictive asshole that he is. I want to prove him wrong."

"I thought you were tight with Rouleau."

"Not since the Stonechild story broke with my name on it."

Woodhouse smiled. He wasn't sure yet how he'd use her misery to his advantage, but he knew that he would in time. For now, he'd play along. "Well, maybe I owe you. Sure, I can help you out."

The waitress set her drink down. "Would you like another, sir?" She picked up his empty beer glass and set it on her tray.

"No, I'm heading out. Just put my drink on the lady's tab. She's in a buying mood tonight." The waitress left and he stood. "I'll be seeing you around then, Stokes. Good to have you back in town." He rapped his knuckles twice on the table top.

She stared at him with a look on her face like she'd swallowed something distasteful. She reached down and pulled her iPad from her bag. "You have my number. Use it when you have something useful to tell me."

He gave a mock salute and headed out of the bar toward the front entrance. Still nobody he recognized in the lobby, which didn't surprise him. This hotel wasn't one of the police force haunts. He felt no guilt about stringing Marci Stokes along or giving her information from time to time. His retired partner, Ed Chalmers, had always said that milking sources was part of the job. He'd called it a chess game where you always had to stay a few moves ahead of your opponent to win. "No matter what it takes, Woodhouse, you have to come out on top. Otherwise, the bad guys win."

Woodhouse waited for a geriatric couple pulling their luggage to clear the door before he stepped outside and went in search of his car. Time to head home and cook the steak waiting for him in the fridge. It would go nicely with a few pints of beer and the sports channel.

CHAPTER TEN

Thursday, October 6

Jane Thompson sat on the vinyl-covered kitchen chair sipping an instant coffee and smoking a cigarette, watching the sky lighten above the trees and buildings across the street. Even though Thursday was her day off, she still rose at five and went for a morning jog while the world was in darkness. The cigarette was her reward. She was working on quitting and had gotten herself down to two a day. She'd have the second after supper. Soon, she'd have to cut them out altogether, but not just yet. She'd started smoking in her early twenties and quit when she found out she was pregnant with Ben. She started up again in prison because her life had felt so hopeless. The idea of getting lung cancer had seemed like a fitting end. In the depths of her despair, she'd forgotten how much her kids needed her.

She reached inside her pocket and pulled out the letter from Ben that she kept with her as a reminder that she had to hold on. He'd sent it the month before she got out, without Adam's knowledge, she knew. The words were ingrained into her memory but she still liked to see his handwriting and imagine him forming every word carefully so that she'd be able to read his writing. He was infamous for his poor penmanship.

Olivia and I can't wait to see you. We know you worry that we don't love you anymore, but we do. Dad is still angry but we know that you did what you did for a reason. We want to live with you when you get out. I know it'll take a while to happen, but that's what we both want. This is so messed up. Come home Mom.

Ben and Olivia. Her reasons for everything she'd done and was about to do.

Adam had cancelled two visits but had agreed she could see them today after school. She'd thought about going behind his back but her parole officer had warned her that this wasn't a good idea if she wanted to keep regular visits a possibility. Adam was angry and letting her know that he held all the power. If she crossed him, she knew that he'd keep the kids from her. She'd been right to be patient and outwait him. Only a few more hours.

She took a long drag of the cigarette and held the smoke in her lungs. The burning felt good before she let the smoke out in a long, slow stream through her nose. She stubbed the end out in the ashtray and got up to make a second cup of coffee. The phone rang in the bedroom as she was filling the kettle from the tap. For a split second, she considered not answering, and then thought better of it. Her parole officer said to always be available, and for now, she had to play by the rules. She leaped across the small space into the bedroom and grabbed the receiver.

"Hello?"

"I can't believe they think you killed that kid. How could they ... my God. How are you doing?"

"I'm fine, Sandra. How did you find out?" She shifted the phone from one ear to the other and lowered herself onto the edge of the bed.

"The *Whig-Standard*. You made the front page. Photos from your trial and even a wedding picture of you and Adam. The reporter is named ..." A pause and rustling of paper that Jane could hear over the phone. "Yeah, here it is. Marci Stokes wrote that you were taken into the station. I'm so relieved to find you at home."

Jane closed her eyes. *Not again*. "The police asked me some questions yesterday but let me go. I assure you that they have nothing on me."

Sandra was quiet for a moment. "Of course they don't. You aren't a killer." Jane heard less certainty in her sister's voice. "Will this affect your visit with Ben and Olivia?"

"Why should it? I haven't been charged."

"It's just Adam can be a real jerk."

"Well, he knows how much this visit means to me and how long I've waited. Besides, he doesn't read the *Whig*." She ignored the buzz of worry starting in her belly. Today was her day to finally hold her kids and nothing would get in the way.

"I guess you're right. Not even Adam could be that cruel."

"Sandra … I have to go. I have a busy day ahead and need to get in the shower."

"Are you still coming for supper on Saturday?"

"Yes. Are you sure I can't bring anything?"

"Just yourself. And Jane?"

"Yeah?"

"Nothing. Just keep your head down. Don't give them any reason to arrest you again."

"I'm trying. Thanks for the call."

She hung up, annoyed at Sandra for the worry behind her words. The big blond detective had spoken in the same disbelieving tone when he asked where she'd been the evening Devon went missing. She stood and shrugged out of her sweatshirt, unhooking her bra as she crossed the bedroom to the bathroom, letting the clothes fall in a scattered trail behind her. Well, soon none of their opinions would be worth a damn. She had plans that didn't include sitting in the women's pen for the rest of her life, letting others call the shots. If she'd learned anything in the past four years, it was to stay a step ahead. She wouldn't let the same mistakes she'd made four years ago trip her up now, because she wasn't the same woman she'd been when the police first came knocking at her door.

Rouleau poured a cup of muddy-looking coffee from the pot and checked for cream. When none was to be found, he added a scoop of sugar to cut the bitterness. He picked up the file he'd been reading and crossed to the meeting area and noticed that everyone but Woodhouse was holding a Tim Hortons cup. Rouleau had forgotten that Woodhouse made the coffee on Thursday mornings.

"You didn't send me a text reminder," he said as he passed by Gundersund.

Gundersund smiled and raised his cup. "We're trying to encourage him to be more domesticated, remember?"

"It seemed like a good idea at the time."

Rouleau noticed Kala Stonechild sitting separate from the others, head down, reading her phone. Bennett had followed him into the space and was dragging a chair closer to her, but she didn't look up. Woodhouse was on the other side of Gundersund with a few cops sitting between them. Rouleau had asked Heath for some dedicated uniforms and was happy to see Bedouin, first one on the murder scene, and Tanya Morrison, a smart cop with twenty years' experience. He'd heard from Vera that she'd put in a request to join his team. Heath was considering expanding the unit the next fiscal if some funding came through. Rouleau took a second to welcome them before checking the chart of people involved in Devon Eton's life that they'd started on the whiteboard. The connections were growing as the detectives added names from their door-to-door and interviews.

"Right," he began. "I have the report from Forensics and it shows cause of death was from a couple of violent blows to the back of his head. They aren't able to determine what was used, but it was a large solid object and not somebody's fist. Time of death estimated between midnight and

2:00 a.m. October 4, although it could have gone an hour either side. He'd eaten a hamburger and fries sometime around six based on the stage of digestion. He'd also drunk a good quantity of beer, possibly explaining why he was easily overpowered. He was fit with no chronic medical issues. He'd had a broken collarbone that had healed and some faded bruising that was consistent with football injuries."

"Could he have gotten into a drunken brawl with somebody?" Woodhouse asked. He looked over at Stonechild as if to imply that she was experienced with drunken brawls.

Gundersund responded quickly. "There were no other injuries, which would be probable if he'd been involved in a fight, especially on his hands. He was likely ambushed. If he was half inebriated, he'd be easy to overpower."

"No drugs in his system?" Bennett asked.

"Not on preliminary analysis but more tests are pending." Rouleau turned and wrote the details in a column on the whiteboard. When he finished, he asked, "Anything come from the door-to-door?"

Woodhouse shook his head. "Neighbour saw Devon leave for school at the normal time. She said he was polite as always and didn't notice anything off. She worked night shift at the hospital and didn't see him come home. Nobody else saw anything. We also checked out the apartment building across from the park. Nobody saw anything."

Rouleau looked back at the whiteboard. "Gundersund, I see that you and Stonechild interviewed his best friend, Charlie Hanson, is it?"

Gundersund looked at Stonechild but she was busy typing on her phone. He looked back at Rouleau. "Yeah, they were thick as thieves by all accounts. Charlie said that Devon had something to do after school, that he was keeping a secret, and that he never saw him after class got out. Classmates said Charlie wasn't popular like Devon, and I have to say, the kid was a bit creepy."

Woodhouse said, "Creepy is the norm for most teenage boys."

Gundersund stared across at him. "Since when did you become an expert on teenage boys?"

"If Woodhouse is an expert on teenage boys, we're all in trouble … and maybe in for a lawsuit." Bedouin waited for the laughs to die down before asking, "What do you want Tanya and me to do today?"

Rouleau shook his head at Gundersund and said, "Woodhouse and Bennett will work through Devon's computer, iPad, and phone. Heath is holding a media briefing today and the parents will be speaking. We'll be announcing a call-in number for anyone who might have seen anything or who might have information. The family is offering a reward for information that leads to a conviction. Bedouin and Morrison, I'll need you both to answer the phones and sift through the calls. We've got others on standby to check out the bars on the off chance Devon was in one drinking after school."

"Kala and I will continue interviewing people." Gundersund stood and stretched. "Devon's football coach was home sick yesterday but he's at the school today. We have a teacher from Jane's last school to track down and we also plan to speak with Adam Thompson about his ex-wife."

Rouleau nodded. "Keep Jane Thompson in your sights. We'll need to bring her in again for questioning before long, but not before we have a better idea of her involvement with Devon and his family."

Kala caught up with Gundersund at his desk after making a visit to the washroom. He was reading something on his computer screen that he minimized when he realized she was behind him. He hadn't been quick enough though. She'd seen the website for a law office on King Street that specialized in family law. She sat down in the guest chair and he swivelled his seat to face her.

"Devon's football coach at Frontenac has a spare at ten and will meet us in his office in the gym." Gundersund glanced at his notebook. "Name is Laurence Lee. I'm still waiting to hear from Jane's previous colleague ..." He trailed a finger down the page. "Nicholas Wagner. He had the classroom next to Jane at Winston Churchill and was one of the few to take the stand in her defence during her trial. He's changed schools but is still in the district."

"Good. Gundersund, I hate to do this but I have an appointment that I can't get out of at four o'clock. Are you okay if I bow out for a bit?" For some reason, she didn't want to tell him that it was with Dawn's new social worker. She hadn't decided if she was going to get involved again.

"No problem. I can take the Adam Thompson interview alone."

"I might be able to join you partway through."

"And if not, I'll fill you in."

The office to the right of the gym doors was cramped and smelled of stale body odour and warm tuna sandwiches. Kala stepped around a basketball and squeezed into one of the two visitor chairs wedged up against the filing cabinet that was capped with trophies and packages of new tennis balls. Laurence Lee was standing and talking into his cellphone. He was attempting to calm down what appeared to be an irate parent and rolled his eyes at Kala as he listened to their end of the conversation. Gundersund remained standing near the door, a hulking presence in Lee's cramped, messy kingdom.

Kala waited impatiently for Lee to end the call. He was short, maybe five eight, but muscular under a white T-shirt. The buzz cut gave his black hair a military look and his stare was penetrating — not a man you'd want to meet in a dark alley. His head bobbed up and down a few times before he cut off the caller with a curt, "Take it up with the principal." He shoved the phone onto his desk and dropped into the chair, keeping his eyes on Kala. "Sorry about that. One of my football players has an overprotective mother who's making his life a misery. But you're here to talk about Devon Eton, not my ongoing parent problems. What would you like to know?" He grabbed a volleyball from the floor and leaned back in the chair, juggling the ball from one hand to the other while he waited for her question. The muscles in his arms bulged with every toss. Green Chinese lettering was tattooed on the underside of both forearms.

Kala held his unblinking gaze. She felt like she was twelve again in a staring contest with a boy in her class. "We're gathering as much information about Devon as we can at this stage. Did you see him on Monday?"

"He was at practice in the morning. Seemed okay and nothing stands out. I saw him by his locker talking to Charlie Hanson after last class. They appeared to be arguing about something."

"Any idea what?"

"No, but Devon was telling him off from what I could see. I could never figure out their relationship. Charlie was quiet and not brilliant by any stretch, although not stupid either. Who really knew what was going on in his head?"

"Did you see them leave together or separately?"

"Honestly, I couldn't tell you. It's a busy time of day and I was on hall patrol."

"We're asking everyone their impression of Devon and if he was upset about anything."

Laurence Lee hesitated. "I imagine you've been told that he was polite, good student, popular and intelligent."

Kala read a subtle change in his body language. "I hear a 'but.'"

Lee let the volleyball drop, then watched as it bounced across the floor and landed on his gym bag.

"Devon appeared to have all these stellar qualities and I can't put my finger on any one thing that made me doubt the authenticity of the kid, but I don't know, there was something about the way he looked at you when he thought you weren't paying attention. I wouldn't call it malicious exactly, but it was definitely cold." Lee met her eyes again. "Not much to go on, is it? A gut feeling about the expression in someone's eyes won't hold up in court I'm guessing, but then again, Devon won't be on trial for his own murder."

"Did he do anything that backs up your gut feeling?"

"Well, he was involved in that case against his grade seven teacher and I don't know how something like that warps a kid. He was quiet and a hard worker on the team, but almost too intent on winning. I try to teach my boys that winning isn't everything. Devon looked at me whenever I said that like I'd grown another head. I know he came here because of our reputation as a football school and he hoped to keep playing in university. We played Gananoque High School in a regional final two years ago and their coach took me aside after the game. One of their players said Devon had hurt him intentionally after the play. Nobody saw it so I had to let it go after speaking with Devon. He denied it of course. Quite convincingly, I might add."

Kala kept her voice non-judgmental. "I imagine the Jane Thompson affair sent a ripple through the teaching community in Kingston."

"You got that right. I'd met her a couple of times at teacher conferences. She reminded me of one of those ice goddesses who breathe the glorified air reserved for the insanely beautiful. Could have knocked me over when I found out she was getting it on with a student. I mean she's hot, but with a kid in her grade seven class? Come on."

Kala thought about how small Kingston was. Like a large town in some ways when the majority of university kids went home for the summer. "Do you know Adam Thompson, Jane's ex-husband?"

Lee made a non-committal noise in his throat. "I'm more familiar with his girlfriend."

"And who would that be?"

"Naomi Van Kemp. We dated for a while when she was supply teaching at Rideau Public, my previous school. She dumped me when she got a full-time job in the classroom next to Adam. It was a while later that I found out they were seeing each other outside of school. And before you ask, Jane was already under arrest when they went public so I have no idea when their relationship started. I would have thought he was too old for her, but what do I know? The Thompsons appear to have a thing for the younger set."

"You must have been upset to lose her like that."

"I wasn't too pleased but not for the reason you think. I was getting serious about Naomi but in hindsight, I can see that she was using me to help her get a permanent job. The woman would do anything to get herself ahead. Just about anything."

Lee jumped up from the chair and grabbed the volleyball from where it perched on his gym bag.

He bounced it on the floor before tossing it at Gundersund, who caught it easily with one hand. Kala could hear the gym filling up with male voices and stomping feet.

Laurence Lee motioned for Gundersund to throw the ball back and he did. Lee tucked it under one arm and reached for the whistle lying on his desk. "Sorry to cut this short but duty calls, Officers. I wish I could be more help to you. Whoever killed Devon deserves to be caught and thrown in jail just like they did to Jane Thompson when she molested him, only this time they should throw away the key."

Gundersund waited until Lee was in the gym calling to the boys to get dressed without any horsing around. He said, "Laurence Lee is the only one who's painted Devon Eton in a bad light."

"Lee might have his own agenda. He was also casting suspicion on Naomi Van Kemp, likely wanting a bit of revenge for her ditching him." She'd found the entire exchange peculiar. "It'll be interesting to find out more about Naomi and Adam and when they started up."

"Which brings us to our next interview — Jane Thompson's former colleague Nicholas Wagner, although I see he's also moved schools. They taught together at Winston Churchill Public but Wagner's now teaching intermediate at Kingston Collegiate & Vocational Institute. Everyone has been consistent in believing she got what she deserved so it will be interesting to speak with her one supporter on staff. He must have felt betrayed when Jane later pled guilty to having sex with Devon. I hope we're not going down the wrong path checking on Jane Thompson's past transgressions."

"Maybe we are, but we'd be negligent not to pursue such a glaringly big piece of the puzzle. At the very least, we should find out what made Devon Eton tick and that could lead to whatever behaviour led to his death."

Kala stepped closer to Gundersund, who stood leaning against the wall by the door. She'd been avoiding being alone with him since Fiona let her know that they were working on their marriage. She wondered if catching him checking out a family law website meant he was exploring options. Even so, Fiona wouldn't be easy to deter. From all the talk around the precinct, Fiona had always been able to lure him back, no matter how outrageous her own behaviour.

Gundersund's brilliant blue eyes met hers. For one confusing moment, she imagined him bending down to kiss her and the thought made her face burn hot. Gundersund stood still, watching her face. His eyes held a question and she saw a tenderness in them that made desire rise up from her belly. She fought the urge to reach out a hand and run her fingertips along the scar on his cheek, instead scowling while she fumbled to find the phone in her pocket. Her hand grasped it and she pretended to read a message. "I need to answer this," she said, head down.

When she dared to look back up, Gundersund's face was closed off and he was looking past her. "I'll meet you by the front door." His voice was normal, as if she'd imagined the charged moment between them. He smiled at her and pushed himself off from the wall, leaving her alone with the feeling that she'd dodged making a complete fool of herself.

She took a second to still her heart and tucked her phone back into her jacket before slowly following in his footsteps out of the office. Laurence Lee was tightening the volleyball net to a post in the centre of the gym and the boys were emerging from the change room in twos and threes dressed in shorts and T-shirts. She searched near the entranceway but Gundersund had already disappeared out the gym doors.

CHAPTER ELEVEN

Gundersund was in the truck when Kala finally joined him. He'd been typing on his phone and glanced over at her when she started the engine. "We have an hour to kill. I just got a message from Nicholas Wagner. He isn't available until two o'clock because he was asked last minute to give up his spare to fill in for a teacher who got sick."

"Good. Gives us time to grab something to eat." She avoided looking directly at him and put the truck in gear. The last thing she needed was for it to get awkward between them, or more awkward than it was already. A few minutes later, they were heading into the downtown. They decided on take-out sandwiches and coffee from the Pilot House on King Street and crossed over Clarence and followed it to the pathway bordering the lake. They started walking east into the wind.

"Getting chilly," Gundersund said. "This should do." He lowered himself onto a park bench and Kala took the other end. "Is that a man windsurfing out there?"

She squinted across the water, ruffled with white-caps. "Looks like it. He probably jogs in thirty-five-below weather too, and bikes to work in blizzards."

"Yeah, I don't get that either." Gundersund set his coffee cup on the bench while he unwrapped his club sandwich. "Exercise doesn't have to be torture. You can work out in a gym with other sane people when the weather is crap."

Kala took a bite of her roast beef on a kaiser and thought about Jane Thompson and what her affair with Devon Eton had cost her. Her family, her job, her reputation. The wind tossed Kala's hair around her face and she pulled a strand out of her eyes. Jane hadn't struck her as a stupid woman. Would she really have killed Devon so soon after getting out of prison? Surely, she would have known that she'd be the main suspect. Then again, she had nothing else to lose and revenge could be a strong motivator. After all, she'd had more than two years in prison for her losses to crystallize into hatred. Kala ate quickly as she pondered the mystery that was Jahe Thompson.

Gundersund crumpled his sandwich wrapper into a ball. "I'm going to hike a bit further," he said. "Coming?" He was looking straight ahead toward the lake. The wind had tangled his blond hair more than usual and he had a few days' growth of beard.

She took the last bite of her sandwich and stood, wiping her hands on her jeans. "Sure, why not."

They walked the length of the pathway with the wind from the lake tossing the tree branches to and fro, making leaves fall in handfuls to the ground.

Kala zipped up her coat and wished she'd brought a hat. Her hair was whipping around her face and getting into her eyes. Gundersund was a strong, silent presence beside her. The comfortable feeling that she got when she was around him had been strained since Fiona had warned her off, and it was nice to feel the ease return. She was sad knowing that their friendship would not be surviving Fiona's return into his life. He might be conflicted about his marriage now, but history showed that he couldn't bring himself to leave it.

"I'm going to meet with Dawn's new social worker this afternoon," she said with no forethought. She knew Gundersund had wanted her to become proactive in Dawn's life but she hadn't been able to explain to him why she couldn't. She couldn't even explain it to herself.

He nodded and shot her a sideways glance. "I think that could be a good idea."

"Maybe." They kept walking and she was glad that he didn't press her to talk about her change of heart. As they neared the park bench where they'd had lunch, she checked her watch. "Guess we should get to the school. Wagner's class will be wrapping up soon."

Gundersund lifted a hand to shield his eyes from the sun and pointed with his other. "Look, that windsurfer has gone farther out. The man must be mad."

They stopped to watch for a moment. He didn't seem to be in any difficulty even though from shore his situation looked precarious.

"I guess some people don't mind taking big chances," she said. "That will change once he gets into trouble a few times."

They left the path and started cutting across the grass toward Clarence Street and the truck. "I'm glad we had this break," Gundersund said. "I'll try to drop by your place after supper to fill you in on my last interview and to find out how your meeting goes."

"If you like." She wouldn't hold her breath. It was no coincidence that Gundersund had stopped coming over after the article about her drunken past hit the paper and they'd taken Dawn away.

Nicholas Wagner met them in the front lobby of Kingston Collegiate & Vocational Institute, or KCVI as the school was known, and escorted them to a small office at the end of a long green hallway lined in grey lockers. "The guidance counsellor is letting us meet in her office," he explained. "We won't be interrupted." He ran a hand through his floppy blond hair and studied them with sad cow eyes. He was a tall, slightly stooped man with an earnest, friendly smile. Kala thought that kids would take to him. "We've had some famous graduates at KCVI," he said as they settled in. "Sir John A. Macdonald and former MP Peter Milliken were two of them."

"What subject do you teach, Mr. Wagner?" she asked.

"Music, with a dash of history and geography for my sins." He gave her a self-depreciating smile.

"I had planned a career performing on stage, but that fell apart. Please call me Nick."

"I'm sorry to hear that. What instrument do you play, Nick?"

"Guitar and piano, occasionally vocals. I thought I'd be the next Arlo Guthrie, but the music industry didn't see my talents the same way. How about you? Play any instrument? Ever wanted to be in a band?"

Before she could respond, Gundersund interrupted, "So how well did you know Jane Thompson?" They were sitting in blue plastic chairs curved to fit their backs, and he looked as uncomfortable as Kala had ever seen him. The chair was too small for his weight and wobbled as he tried to settle into it. Kala could see the irritation on his face, and she should have felt some sympathy for him, but had to hold back a smile.

Nicholas also noticed Gundersund's discomfort and his lips twitched before he took his eyes off Kala to focus on the question. "We taught across the hall from each other for three years when I worked at Winston Churchill Public. She was friendly with the rest of the staff but spent all of her time focused on the kids when she was at school. I probably interacted with her as much as anyone."

"Did you see any signs that she was having an affair with Devon Eton?" Gundersund asked.

The sad expression returned to his eyes. "At first, I was her strongest defender so I was gobsmacked when she confessed. I mean, sure, the boys all thought they were in love with her. She has this certain sultry sexuality of which I'm convinced she is unaware. Her eyes alone could have launched a thousand ships." A blush crept up his neck. "You'd think I was smitten as well, the way I'm talking."

"And were you?"

"I'd be lying if I said that I wasn't intrigued, but she was married at the time. I thought happily."

Kala said, "She didn't confide in you about her marriage."

Nick's eyes swung back to her. "No, and her husband taught at another elementary school. Winston Churchill, if I recall correctly. Jane's a private person, which worked against her in the end. Nobody knew what she was up to in her classroom or after hours. Speaking of which, the teacher who saw Devon go into her classroom one Saturday had no reason to lie. The school was empty but Bob came to get some tests that he'd forgotten to take home. He agonized about telling the police but did in the end."

"We'd like to speak with him. Is Bob still at Rideau Public?" she asked.

"I wish you could, but Bob suffered a heart attack and died a year after Jane was arrested. A few parents have said that the school is cursed. The principal was forced into retirement after the trial, and last I heard, she suffered a stroke. We were all painted in a negative light as suspicions swirled. There was even talk of a sex ring originating out of the teachers' lounge, although this was later acknowledged to be nonsense. We were uneasy for a long time, even about being alone with our classes. Some got threatening phone calls. It got ugly."

Kala hadn't considered the full impact of the trial on the rest of the staff until now. Jane Thompson's lapse in judgment hadn't only hurt Devon and their families. "When did you leave?"

"I liked the school, the kids. I didn't want to turn tail and run as if we'd done anything wrong, but I wanted a fresh start and took the job here the year after she was convicted. I don't regret it."

Kala nodded. "Did you visit Jane after she went to prison ... or since her release?"

"No to both. I kept my distance from her if only to protect myself. I'm not sure if I should be ashamed of that."

"How so?"

"Jane seemed very alone and struggling. I could have reached out — we'd been friends after all — but I chose my reputation over her."

Gundersund shifted and the chair made a cracking noise. He grimaced but didn't comment on his precarious situation.

"One last line of questions, Mr. Wagner. We'd be interested in knowing if you can shed any light on Devon Eton and Charlie Hanson. Were they in any of your classes at Winston Churchill?"

"Yes, I taught them both. Devon was outstanding in math and science but closer to average in English and the arts. Skipping grade six meant he didn't get some grammar basics, so it made sense to me that Jane would help him out. She was dedicated to the kids." Nick paused. "Charlie and Devon were typical teenage boys to me. Gawky, growing into their bodies, not particularly popular, although

Devon was into football and was good-looking enough. He was more popular after the trial than before it. In the teenage world, he became a folk hero of sorts. I can't say that either boy stood out for me while I was teaching them. They were quiet and polite in class. Likely bored. Gifted kids latch onto ideas without effort and are often putting in time while their classmates figure out concepts. I naturally put most of my efforts into teaching the average students and gave the gifted kids projects to do on their own. Not a perfect system but mainstreaming, few resources, and large classes dictate the agenda."

"Would you say that Charlie was brilliant or gifted too?"

"Hard to say. He didn't talk in class and I had the feeling he wasn't interested in school. I never figured him out."

"Were Devon and Charlie outsiders in your opinion?"

"Devon was popular after a fashion. Charlie was definitely not. I'm not sure either would see themselves as part of the in crowd. As you know, the teenage population is narcissistic in nature, particularly during this age of social media, but I find that when you probe beneath the bravado, most of the kids are struggling with self-worth and finding their place. These are years that most of us would not want to repeat."

Kala met Gundersund's eyes before looking at Nick and smiling. "I think that's all our questions for now. Thank you again for taking this time out of your schedule."

She and Nick stood at the same time while Gundersund tried to push himself out of the chair. It appeared attached to his back and he took a few attempts to break free. It fell to the ground and tipped over onto its side. He straightened, leaving the chair as it lay, and walked ahead of Kala out of the room without saying a word.

"Nice," he said when she caught up with him. "That guy was enjoying my discomfort. The sadistic, affected bastard."

Kala tried and failed to hide her laughter. "I thought the whole thing was going to collapse and you sat there saying nothing. My God, when it cracked …" She threw back her head and laughed louder.

"And give him the satisfaction?" Gundersund shook his head, but amusement crinkled the corners of his eyes. "I have my pride."

"Well, you know what they say." She waited a beat. "About that going before a fall."

Gundersund laughed. "Shit, I thought the chair legs were going to give out. Took me right back to every hateful class I ever sat through." He tilted his head and grinned at her. "But I'd happily sit on a bed of nails if it meant hearing you laugh again."

Jane arrived at the Coffee & Company café on Princess Street half an hour before Adam was to meet her with Ben and Olivia. Her stomach was too excited to eat but she ordered a pot of Earl Grey tea and a banana muffin so that she could sit for a while without feeling that she was loitering. The boy behind the counter had looked at her with puzzled eyes as if trying to place her, but another customer had taken his attention and Jane made her way across the room to the table by the window.

The day had turned cooler and windy as happened often in this seaport town. She'd lost track of the unpredictable Kingston weather when she was inside. She'd always liked the changing seasons but after a year locked away, depression had coloured every waking moment as one day melted into the next, without beginning or end. A steady stream of traffic passed by outside the window where she sat, Princess being a one-way street heading south toward Lake Ontario. Pedestrian traffic was lighter — too early for school kids to be released from their classrooms or for the dinner and bar crowd to start filling their favourite haunts.

Jane sipped her tea and left the muffin uneaten on its plate. The table next to her changed customers twice while she waited. Quarter to four came and went and Jane's unease grew into full-fledged anxiety. By four o'clock, when Adam and the kids were fifteen minutes late, she had to talk herself down from total despair. They might have gotten held up at school or needed to run an errand on their way to meet her. She broke off a piece of muffin and nibbled on it while she looked out the window. Adam had been a lot of things during their marriage but he'd never been deliberately cruel. Even after all that had gone on between them, she couldn't believe that he would agree to meet her and not show.

At ten after four, she scanned the street one last time before wrapping the muffin in a napkin and slipping it into her purse. She turned to lift her coat from the back of the chair and had her head down, putting one arm into a sleeve, when she heard the door to the café open. She looked up. Adam filled the entrance, his dark brown hair longer than she remembered, his blue eyes sweeping the room until they found her. She eagerly looked past him for Olivia and Ben, but they weren't with him and her spirits sank like rocks in her stomach. Adam strode toward her and dropped into the seat across from her while she struggled to control her feelings.

"You cut your hair," he said. "I always liked it long."

She kept her hands from self-consciously touching her hair. He'd been obsessed with her looks when they were together. She'd often wondered what would happen when she got older and they started to go. She didn't have to care about that any longer. "You promised to bring Olivia and Ben." She watched his face tighten but he kept his voice even, devoid of any emotion that would betray the depths of his anger.

"That was before your boyfriend was found dead and your face and our family were plastered on the front page of the *Whig*. I can't expose them to any more of this, Jane. You've hurt them … us enough."

"I had nothing to do with what happened to Devon. Nothing. I deserve to see my kids. I need to see them. The court said that I could."

The look on his face spoke volumes. He didn't buy her pronouncement of innocence and was struggling to keep control. He prided himself on his reasonableness. He wore it like a sanctimonious cloak every day of their marriage. "You can't honestly think meeting you now is a good idea. I only came to tell you that we have to wait for this investigation to play itself out." He'd used his patient, explaining voice that made her want to scream. He checked his watch. "The police called before I left the school to meet you and they'll be at the house in twenty minutes to interview me. I only came so you wouldn't be here waiting and wondering what happened to us."

"When will I see them?"

He stood. "When the police arrest Devon's killer." He smiled. "I'm assuming it won't be you, although you've been known to surprise me."

"You're aware that you're being cruel." She said the words to the back of his head as he walked away from her toward the entrance. He didn't look back.

She sat staring at the yellow and red leaves rolling down the sidewalk, tossed into the air by gusts of wind. She was lost in thought, her hands wrapped around her cold cup of tea, while university students ordered coffee and noisily filled the tables all around her. It was only when the boy from behind the counter began wiping down the table next to her that she came back to herself and pulled her eyes away from the street. The boy's face was tilted in her direction with a look of recognition in his curious eyes. Jane turned away from him and grabbed her purse from the back of her chair. She jumped up and hurried toward the front door with her head down, narrowly avoiding colliding with an elderly couple on their way inside.

CHAPTER TWELVE

Gundersund watched a white Mazda wheel into the driveway from where he stood on the front steps of the Thompson house. A young woman in a brown suede coat and boots leaped out of the driver's seat and started toward him. Her two fair-haired young passengers exited from the back seat more slowly and appeared to be in no hurry to follow her. He first thought she was the child caregiver but realized his mistake when she introduced herself as Naomi Van Kemp, the name he recognized as belonging to Adam Thompson's live-in girlfriend. She looked closer in age to the two kids than to Jane Thompson.

"Sorry to keep you waiting." She said the words over her shoulder, half out of breath, as she unlocked the front door. She pushed it open and motioned Gundersund to follow her inside. "I've just sent Adam a text since it's him you've come to see. He had an errand to run but expects to be home shortly."

"No problem. Perhaps you and I can chat first."

The look on her face said she'd rather not, but she recovered quickly. "Of course. Let me get Ben and Olivia a snack and settled and then I'm all yours. Would you like a coffee or tea?"

He waited in the family room for her and she sat across from him ten minutes later after serving cups of coffee brewed in one of the fancy one-cup contraptions. He noticed that she'd taken the time to brush her long straight hair and apply fresh makeup. Her perfume lingered on the air — a light, youthful scent that he didn't recognize.

"I'm not sure I know anything that will help you with the murder investigation." She was leaning on the arm of the couch with her stocking feet tucked under her, sipping on her coffee and watching him as he set his small tape recorder on the coffee table. The look in her eyes reminded him of Fiona and the way she'd study him as she searched for a way to get him to do what she wanted. He'd heard Naomi with the kids in the kitchen while he waited. She'd been on the bossy side and done most of the talking.

The girl, Olivia, had gone upstairs to do her homework, but Ben was sitting at the counter eating an apple with a book open in front of him. Gundersund had a feeling that the boy was listening to their conversation while pretending not to be. He was the older of the two kids, likely twelve years old by the look of him. That would have put him at eight when his mother's trial was underway and plenty old enough to feel the impact. He'd know something new and terrible was hovering around his family again. Perhaps, he'd become the silent listener. How could a kid not become anxious with all that had gone on in this house? Gundersund looked back at Naomi, who'd pulled her iPhone out of her pocket and was checking messages.

"I understand you supply taught at Winston Churchill when Devon Eton was there. How well did you know him?"

Naomi dropped the phone onto the couch next to her and looked at him. Her eyes were guarded. "I knew who he was, of course," she said. "Kingston is a small town and the teaching community is tight, so we all know the Jane Thompson fall-from-grace story. Devon was in one of the grade eight classes that I supplied in for a few weeks."

"How did he seem to you?"

"Seem?"

"Was he friendly, closed off, happy? What was your impression of him?"

"Devon was quiet but everyone was aware when he was around. I thought he might be milking the damaged, angst-filled victim role, but the girls were all in. Justin Bieber, loner bad boy … every girl at that age wants to save the rebel."

"He had a best friend named Charlie Hanson."

"Charlie Hanson. I never understood why Devon was hanging with him, but they'd been friends since grade five or something. Charlie's kind of creepy." Naomi's phone pinged and she grabbed it from the couch. "Adam just pulled into the driveway." She leaped off the couch and disappeared down the hallway.

Gundersund heard her greet Adam before their voices lowered to a murmur. He looked over at Ben. The boy had his head tilted so that he could hear

Naomi and his father, but he was still pretending to read the book resting on the counter in front of him. He straightened up as his father walked into view. Adam nodded to his son but kept walking confidently toward where Gundersund was sitting. Gundersund had the impression of a man used to taking charge.

"Officer, sorry to keep you waiting. I see Naomi has given you coffee. Would you like a refill?"

"No thanks. If you have time for a few questions, I won't keep you long."

"Of course." Adam sat down in the spot vacated by Naomi. He ran a hand across the stubble on his cheeks and let his fingers rest on his neck. "I imagine you're here about Jane." He turned toward the kitchen. "Ben, I'd like you to go upstairs and get started on your homework."

"I don't have any."

Naomi shook her head from where she stood behind Ben. "I told him to go to his room after his snack but he's been stalling."

Adam said, "Benjamin." He started to rise from the couch.

"All right, Dad. All right. I'm going." Ben's voice held a touch of panic. He slid off the stool but took his time crossing the kitchen floor once he realized his father wasn't coming after him. He disappeared from view and Gundersund heard his footsteps on the stairs.

Adam sank back into the couch. "Sorry about that. Ben is entering the defiant stage of adolescence made doubly bad by his mother's maddening behaviour."

Gundersund asked, "Have you seen Jane since she got out of prison?"

Adam laughed, a short, sharp bark. "Actually, that's why I'm late. I met Jane downtown to tell her that she won't be seeing the kids until this murder is resolved. I won't have her popping into their lives only to ... well, find out she's embroiled in something."

"Do you think Jane killed Devon Eton?"

Adam stared into Gundersund's eyes. Gundersund was struck by the anger he glimpsed before Adam laughed again. "Of course I don't think she killed that kid."

His words rang hollow to Gundersund and he couldn't decide whether this was what Adam had intended. Protest while meaning the opposite. He realized that he didn't like Adam Thompson much, but whether or not the man was a decent human being wasn't germane to the case at hand. His actions were, however. "Where were you and Naomi Monday evening?"

Adam glanced back to where Naomi was wiping down the counter. She stopped when he said, "What were we up to Monday night? Do you remember, babe?"

Her forehead creased. "You went to the gym after supper and I went shopping at the Cat Centre. Remember I bought the new bedding at the Bay?" She looked at Gundersund. "The Cataraqui Centre, if you want me to be explicit." She smiled.

"That's right. I was already home when you showed up back here around nine thirty."

"Were you with anyone?" Gundersund directed his question at both of them.

"I was by myself," said Naomi. "I had planned on meeting up with a girlfriend, but she texted that she couldn't make it."

"And I worked out alone. There were guys around but nobody from my usual crowd. It was later than I normally hit the gym."

"Any reason you went later than normal?"

"Naomi had a parent interview and we ate late. Ben is old enough to babysit so we got them settled and headed out for a few hours."

Gundersund had the uneasy feeling that their stories had been rehearsed. They'd had lots of time to get their routine down. He said, "One last question. Naomi met Devon when she was supply teaching. Did you have contact with him after the trial, Mr. Thompson?"

"Are you kidding me?" Real emotion at last. "He's the last person I wanted to see from that time. I didn't hate the kid because I think Jane manipulated him, but my way to heal was to forget he existed."

Gundersund thought, *And now he doesn't.*

He stood to leave. "Well, thanks for your time." He looked up the stairs on his way to the front door and thought he spotted the top of Ben's head on the landing. He would have loved to talk to the kid, but without his father or Naomi present. He bet that Beh knew more secrets than CSIS. Too bad he wasn't a few years older so that he could be interviewed without an adult present.

"Come in and have a seat. Caroline will be right with you."

Kala nodded at the woman's back and looked around. A torn red leather couch took up one wall. It looked more comfortable than the plastic chairs on either end, so she picked a corner and settled in with a *Glamour* magazine that had been lying on the end table. The pages were dog-eared and somebody had taken a purple pen to the models, giving them moustaches, beards, and Harry Potter glasses. After flipping through the pages, Kala closed her eyes and leaned her head against the wall. She let her mind relax and pictured a northern river under a prairie blue sky. She imagined herself in her canoe with Taiku in the front. She was trailing the paddle behind her and enjoying the sound of a loon calling up ahead. Gentle waves were lapping against the boat.

"Officer Stonechild?"

Kala's eyes fluttered open.

"I'm Caroline Russell. Thank you for coming." A short, middle-aged woman with purple hair and multiple piercings in each ear reached out her hand. Kala lifted herself to her feet and shook the offered hand, still groggy from her short nap.

"Let's meet in my office, shall we?" Caroline's voice was warm and friendly, the opposite of Tamara Jones's, the young court worker she was replacing. Caroline's eyes were creased in laugh lines.

The office was small and cramped. The fluorescent overhead lights were off and a desk lamp left shadows in the corners of the room. Kala eased into the visitor chair and wedged her knees against the desk. The room smelled of Earl Grey tea and oranges. She spotted a large teapot and flowered mug on the window ledge. Caroline had a file open in front of her. Her eyes scanned a page and then she lifted her head and smiled at Kala.

"So Dawn lived with you for a few months earlier this year. How did that go in your view?"

"Does it matter? Tamara placed her with a family. She was clear that they're better suited to raising a teenager than a single, Aboriginal cop."

"Hmm." Caroline squinted at something written in the folder. "Yes, they've had some success with a couple of kids but Dawn doesn't appear to be one of them, at least that's my initial assessment."

"I'm not surprised. Her life hasn't been stable or happy the last while." Kala remembered the vibrant twelve-year-old kid she'd first met in Ottawa and sadness filled her. You didn't need a crystal ball to know where Dawn's life was heading. This case worker might be having second thoughts, but she would be helpless to stop the plans already set in motion.

"There's a note in the file that you called the foster mom to set up a meeting with Dawn. Did this take place?"

"No." She could mention the roadblocks set up by the foster parents, but chose to remain silent. Her experience was that those working in the foster care system stuck together. Long hours, inhuman workloads, sad, sad stories, and burnout — mistakes were inevitable, given the system and lack of resources. Kala figured that each of the case workers had clients they'd felt helpless to save. They only had so much time to give to each foster kid before they had to move on to the next.

Caroline's eyes searched Kala's face. "Would you be willing to take Dawn for an afternoon?"

"I'm not sure I understand where this is coming from. Would her foster parents be in agreement?"

"I can convince them." Caroline leaned back in her chair. "Let me be frank, Officer Stonechild. I visited Dawn at her foster home last week because her teacher had reported her skipping school on two occasions. I didn't see any rapport between Dawn and the couple. In fact, Dawn appeared to be largely invisible in the home as they have two young kids of their own and two other foster kids, one of whom is physically disabled and takes a lot of care. They're good people but stretched thin. I spoke with Dr. Lyman, who's counselling Dawn, as you know. She's also concerned and was opposed to having Dawn moved from your home. It seems her advice was factored out of the decision made by my predecessor."

Kala felt the old anger course through her. Dawn had been removed from her and placed with a family that didn't have the time for another kid. The insane waste. She thought about how a meeting with Dawn would open the girl up for more pain when the system decided to move her somewhere else. Seeing Dawn again would be the same as slowly tearing off a Band-Aid. These people had no idea what it did to a kid to start a relationship with someone only to have them disappear from their life.

She planted her feet and worked her way into a standing position. "Can't you simply move her back with me?"

"It's not that easy, I'm afraid, but I'm going to see what I can do. A visit would be a good first step."

Kala didn't know whether to trust this woman, who was making no promises. She could be replaced by someone new or Tamara Jones could return. "Let me think about it," she said. "I'll give you my answer in a few days once my work settles down again. I want to make certain that I do what's best for Dawn, and I'm not sure if what you're proposing is the answer. I'll be in touch."

Caroline sighed and got to her feet on the other side of the desk. "I suppose that's the most I could ask for given what has gone on. I'll wait for your call. Thanks for coming by."

Kala stopped at the door, her hand on the knob. She looked back at the social worker. She'd closed Dawn's file and had turned to work on her computer positioned on a side table. The photo of a boy who looked to be three years old filled the screen, with a file number under his picture. Kala bowed her head and kept walking, the lost expression in the little boy's wide blue eyes staying with her as she stepped outside into the gathering dusk.

CHAPTER THIRTEEN

A wave of nausea made Jane double over and grab her stomach. The surge of fear that gripped her chest like a vice had her feverish and light-headed. Sweat ran into her eyes, blurring her vision. She tried to slow her breathing, to ignore the panic coursing through her in a monster wave. Her throat was closing in and she struggled to breathe. One minute, two minutes crawled by. She needed to get out of this apartment because she was surely going to die or go crazy if she didn't escape the stifling room. She staggered toward the door.

The night air was cool on her skin and chilled the sweat beaded on her face and arms. She'd grabbed a sweatshirt on her way out, knowing that she'd be shivering when the sweating stopped, and she yanked it over her head and pulled the hood up as she ran the length of the block, trying to outpace the demons clawing to get out. She inhaled deeply, several full, slow breaths, and gradually the fear lessened and she felt back inside her body. She slowed her pace to a brisk walk and kept going in the direction of the lake, relief replacing the panic. The headlights from passing cars slid by, but she kept to the shadows.

At the corner of Victoria and Princess, she hesitated as the light turned green and looked behind her. Somebody was hurrying toward her, their long coat flapping around their legs as they ran. She felt her chest begin to constrict again but the figure appeared too small to be a man, and as the woman got closer, Jane forced herself to relax. She turned and crossed as the light blinked to yellow. She had been so certain that she'd left the panic attacks behind her in prison that this one had come as a shock. It had rattled her to her core. She picked up speed as she walked, trying to swallow the anguish that threatened to make her break down and weep.

Head down, at first she didn't hear her name being called. She turned her head sideways. The woman in the open trench coat was almost next to her, breathing hard and trying to get her attention. She was an older woman with messy auburn hair and concerned brown eyes. Jane slowed her steps.

The woman's voice was apologetic. "I'm sorry to bother you, but you looked so upset running out of the door of that apartment building. Are you okay?"

"I'm fine. You knew my name. Do I know you?"

"No. My name is Marci Stokes and I'm a reporter with the *Whig-Standard*. I don't mean to intrude and this is totally off the record. Can I buy you a cup of coffee or a drink or something? You look ready to pass out."

Jane was not a stupid woman. She knew that Marci Stokes had been waiting outside her apartment hoping for an opportunity to question her, but the panic attack had left her shaken and in need of distraction. At least this reporter had been up front about her profession. She looked intelligent and warm, like someone Jane would have befriended back when she had a life. She spotted a coffee shop up ahead.

"I could sit for a minute."

They walked without speaking and Marci held the door open, saying, "Why don't you find a table and I'll get two coffees. Do you take cream and sugar?"

Jane nodded even though she didn't take sugar. She felt drained and sugar might give her some energy. She took a table near the window and looked listlessly out at the street. She thought about Ben and Olivia and imagined herself back in her house before all the ugliness. Their faces from four years ago floated on the glass in front of her. Her sweet children, the only good thing in her life. She was so deep into the memory that she forgot all about Marci until she set a coffee cup in front of her and sat down with a groan. "This has been one long day. I'm beat. Thanks for keeping me company."

Jane wrapped her hands around the coffee cup, finding pleasure in its warmth. Now that they were sitting close together, she regretted having agreed to share the table with a reporter who would no doubt be looking for a sensational angle, not that there weren't lots of them already out there.

Marci lifted her cup and grimaced after the first swallow. "I always think I'm going to enjoy this beverage more than I do. Must have something to do with the smell of coffee being so seductive. I read up on your story, by the way. I don't pretend to walk in your shoes, but I understand making a fool of yourself over love. I keep doing it over and over myself."

"At least you never went to prison for it."

"At least not that."

They smiled at each other and Jane finally raised the cup to her lips. The coffee was sugary sweet and hot. Marci appeared content to sit without speaking and Jane felt herself relaxing. She looked at their reflections in the window. Marci was younger than she'd first thought. Probably in her forties, but she didn't appear to care much about her appearance. This gave Jane the confidence to say, "My husband Adam was in love with how I looked. At first, I liked all the attention and compliments but toward the end, his obsession with my physical self became … unbearable."

"Is that why you started up with Devon Eton?" Marci tilted her head to one side.

Jane looked down at her hands. They were dry and chafed. She'd meant to buy some hand cream but kept forgetting. She spoke quietly. "I wanted out. I couldn't do it anymore. And for all I gave up, he won't let me see my children." She lifted her head.

Marci nodded as if she understood. Jane knew that she didn't. How could she?

"Surely, he can't keep you from seeing them. You are their mother."

"He has sole custody. Devon's death gives him another reason to keep them from me."

Marci hunkered forward, her brow furrowed in rows of concentration. "Does Adam believe you killed him?"

Jane laughed. "Is this your way of asking me if I did it?"

"I guess it is. Sorry to have come at it that way." She grinned an apology.

"You'll forgive me if I give this a pass. I've been misquoted almost every time I spoke to a reporter before you." Jane took a last drink from the cup and got to her feet. She left the cup on the table. "Thank you for the coffee. I'll finish my walk now and hope you understand when I say that I'd like to be alone."

"Of course. You look like you're feeling better. Maybe, we can talk on the record sometime. I could tell your side of the story. Here, take my card."

Jane hesitated, but she accepted the card and tucked it inside the pocket of her jeans. "Thanks," she said, "but I wouldn't hold my breath waiting for me to call."

"There's no time limit." Marci lifted her coffee cup in Jane's direction. "Consider my offer open-ended. It's never a bad idea to get your side of the story out there. I could be your voice."

Marci finished her coffee and returned to the counter for a refill and a honey cruller. She ate the doughnut at the same table where she'd sat with Jane Thompson and thought over their conversation. Jane had looked so ill and frightened when she'd spotted her coming out of the apartment building — as if she was being pursued by an axe murderer. It took a second for her to recognize Jane, having only seen photos and video news footage from around the time of her trial. The short hair was a surprise and she was thinner but still undeniably attractive. When Jane had careened out of the front door, Marci had watched for a few moments to see if anyone was following her. When it became obvious that Jane was alone, she set out in pursuit. What or who had spooked her? That never became clear.

Marci licked sticky honey from her fingers as she pondered what it was about Jane Thompson that didn't ring true. She pulled out her cellphone and checked for messages. Nothing yet from Woodhouse. Maybe, she should stop barking up that tree. The guy was something of a snake.

She tucked her phone back into her pocket and took out her mini tape recorder. She'd turned it to record before she brought the coffees to the table but had kept it in her pocket. Not exactly ethical, but she wasn't planning to use anything Jane said, not that Jane had said much.

On her way back to her car, she clicked play on the tape recorder and plugged in an ear bud. Jane's voice was low and pleasing to the ear. She was stunning up close. Marci had never seen eyes so blue. Hypnotic and hard to look away from. Had Devon Eton been seduced the first time that he looked into those eyes?

Marci stopped walking. She hit rewind on the tape recorder and listened a second time to Jane explain how she couldn't take it anymore. Marci had thought that Jane was speaking about her wanting out of her claustrophobic marriage. Yet, the last sentence didn't fit. Marci realized that Jane could have meant something entirely different.

I wanted out. I couldn't do it anymore. And for all I gave up, he won't let me see my children.

What had she given up that made her think she'd get to see her children? Marci popped out the ear bud and took her car keys from her pocket, so deep in thought that she walked past her car the first time. She checked her watch. Going on ten o'clock and she was tired, but her reporter nose was twitching. She'd head home, pour a Scotch and spend an hour on the internet. Something told her Jane Thompson had more story to tell but needed to be coaxed along. Time to get out the rake and start rooting through the dirt to see if she could get a new angle on this sordid tale.

CHAPTER FOURTEEN

"Sorry I didn't get over to your place last night. Something came up and it got too late." Gundersund wasn't about to tell her he'd had an exhausting standoff with Fiona. He'd finally gone to sleep in the spare room when she refused to leave. He'd tried again to tell her that their marriage was over while she kept saying it was time for her to move in. Part of him thought it might be easier to concede and give it another shot. The idea of letting her back into his life didn't make him feel good. In fact, it made him feel trapped.

"No problem. I got your email update." Kala dropped into her desk chair and swivelled around to look at him. "You look like hell."

"Only because I feel like hell." He stretched one aching shoulder. The mattress on the spare bed had seen better days. By the look of her, Stonechild hadn't gotten a good sleep either. Her eyes were exhausted. "How'd it go with the court worker? What did she want?"

"For me to get involved with Dawn again."

"Are you going to?"

"I'm thinking about it." She paused. "Believe me, I want to see Dawn, but I'm worried that if I keep popping in and out of her life, I could do irreversible damage. The next court worker might decide I'm a bad influence or they might move her to another town."

"Sometimes, you have to make a leap of faith, Stonechild. Dawn needs you." He could have added, "and you need her," but he thought it wiser to let the thought go unspoken. If he'd learned anything about his partner, it was that she didn't like anyone interfering in her personal business. "So what's on our plate today?"

She was looking at her computer screen, seemingly relieved with the change of subject. "Rouleau is meeting with Heath now and said to hang around until he gets back. He wants a quick powwow."

Woodhouse spoke from behind Gundersund. "Your relatives would know all about that, aye Stonechild?"

Gundersund turned. "And yours would know all about eavesdropping. Why didn't I know you were sitting at your desk?"

"Because I crept in while the two of you had your heads together." Woodhouse rolled his chair past Gundersund and stopped inches from Stonechild. He leaned in and pushed his face close to hers. "Like a thief in the night, I hear all and see all and steal your secrets." He wriggled his fingers in the air as if conjuring up some voodoo before he pushed his chair slowly back toward his desk with his feet, all the while keeping his eyes glued to her face.

She held his gaze. "Are you naturally creepy or do you have to work at it?"

Woodhouse laughed. "The lady has teeth," he said looking up at Gundersund as he rolled past. "You'd better watch out or she might take a bite out of you."

The irrational part of Gundersund wanted to punch Woodhouse in the jaw, but the rational part knew Woodhouse would enjoy the fallout too much. The best way to get to Woodhouse was to ignore him. Gundersund turned and looked at Stonechild. "Hey partner, do you want to go for breakfast while we wait for Rouleau?"

"No, that's okay. I've got stuff to do." She glanced at him before lowering her head to look at something on the computer screen. Her mouth was set in a tight line.

"Good thing one of you has a work ethic." Woodhouse was leaning back in his chair, hands folded across his rounded belly.

Gundersund walked over to his desk without commenting. If he'd said anything it would have been to ask Woodhouse if he'd always been such a prick. He sat and turned his back on Woodhouse, grabbing the mouse for his computer and scrolling through emails. He reached the end of the unopened list when Bennett sauntered in, looking lean and fit in a black leather jacket and jeans. He was young, fresh-faced, and happy, everything Gundersund had lost along the way.

"Sorry I'm late. Doctor's checkup." Bennett stopped at Stonechild's desk and Gundersund wasn't sure he liked how her face lit up. They chatted for a bit and he heard her laugh. Gundersund noticed Woodhouse watching them with an intensity he found disconcerting. For a second, he felt hatred radiating out of the man. Was it directed at Stonechild or Bennett or both? Rouleau walked in at that moment and Woodhouse's focus shifted.

"Anything to report, boss?" Woodhouse asked. His expression had relaxed into its usual surly state.

"Let's gather in our meeting area," Rouleau said. "This won't take long." He called across the room for Bedouin and Morrison to join them.

Gundersund stood and followed Stonechild and Bennett into the meeting area. He wondered if he'd read too much into Woodhouse's face the moment before. Woodhouse was a jerk, a male chauvinist pig, but harmless enough. Even helpful when necessary, with a cunning kind of intelligence.

They found places to sit or lean while Rouleau had his back to them writing on the whiteboard with a black marker. He was copying times and names from a paper that he held in his hand. When he finished, he turned to face them.

"Good morning everyone. Thanks for entering all your reports into the system." He waved the paper. "I got word from Forensics about Devon's cellphone records. He made a few calls and texts the day he died. At 3:30, his mother called him. He received a phone call from a pay phone at 3:42 and called Charlie Hanson at 4:05. He texted his sister Sophie's phone a few minutes later and again five minutes after that. Forensics is still tracking down information on the pay phone, but we probably won't be able to identify the caller. The calls and messages stopped after that."

"What were in the text messages to his sister?" Stonechild asked.

Rouleau looked at her. "The first was 'Need to talk' and the second was 'See you in a few.'"

"Did she respond to either?"

"No. However, she might know something about what he was up to that afternoon and we're going to have to talk to her. I'd like to get her away from her parents if possible, although we're going to need their permission. Try the mother first."

Stonechild nodded. "We'll pay them a visit this morning."

"Have another chat with Charlie as well and find out what Devon called him about. I couldn't find any reference to the call in your notes."

Gundersund said, "He never mentioned a call. Just said that he didn't see Devon after he left school. They might have been having an argument at their lockers so we'll be checking that out too."

Rouleau looked at the whiteboard. "The call lasted thirty-five seconds so Charlie must have picked up or there was a voice mail message."

Woodhouse grunted. "Shouldn't we be bringing in Jane Thompson for more questioning? Seems to me she's the one we should be investigating. Has anyone checked *her* phone calls? We're spinning our wheels if we focus on these kids."

"Heath is on the same page as you." Rouleau stopped as if recalling the conversation. "He wants her movements accounted for and you and Bennett can get on that. Get as much detail as you can on her interactions from the moment she left prison last month. We need to know if she was in contact with Devon. It's reasonable to assume that they could have bided their time to start something up again. According to past cases where a female teacher and a student had an affair, they often reconnect after the teacher serves her time." He turned to Bedouin. "Anything interesting from the call line?"

"We're checking out a couple of leads but I'd say nothing too promising at this point."

"Okay, well, let's keep digging everyone. Heath wants something for his next news conference scheduled for end of day."

Rouleau left, and Stonechild and Bedouin followed him out.

"If it was a male teacher and a female student, they'd lock the teacher away and pitch the key into Lake Ontario," said Woodhouse as he stood up. "Appears to be a double standard for pedophiles based on your particular gender."

"You're actually right about that," said Gundersund. "Male teachers are dealt with much more harshly in the courts, both in Canada and the U.S."

"And in public opinion," said Bennett.

"Wasn't there a woman teacher in the U.S. who kept getting caught with her student every time she got out of the pen? I think she had his baby in prison. Whatever happened to her and the student?" Woodhouse asked.

Gundersund took out his cellphone. "They got married. She got seven years after she was caught with him after serving her first six-month sentence.

When he turned eighteen, they got married. He was twelve years old and she was married with four kids when they hooked up the first time."

Woodhouse shook his head as he got to his feet. "Man, I just don't get it. Saddling yourself with a sad old lady when you're still a kid. He missed out on all the firm young flesh at his randy disposal."

Gundersund tried to signal Bennett with his eyes to let it rest but he was too late to stop Bennett from taking the bait. "Christ, Woodhouse. You really are a disgusting excuse of a man." Bennett pushed past his partner, who dropped back into his seat clutching his stomach. Woodhouse's laughter followed Gundersund and Bennett like a cackling crow all the way back to their desks.

Kala hung up the desk phone and reached for her jacket slung across the back of her chair. "I spoke with the secretary at Sophie's school. Sophie didn't make it in today and hasn't been in class all week. We can take a run to the Etons' and hopefully get a chance to speak with her."

"I'll be right with you," Gundersund said, covering his cellphone with his hand. He switched the phone to his other ear and said, "I've got to go. Yeah, I'll meet you for supper at The Keg. I'll be there but I don't have time to talk right now."

Kala could have sworn Gundersund's eyes were sheepish when he looked her way. "Fiona?" she asked.

"Yeah." His jaw tightened. He stood and motioned with his hand for her to lead the way. "Let's get going."

And that'll be the end of searching for a family lawyer, Kala thought. *Fiona wins another round.*

Gundersund drove. He didn't say anything as they headed down Division to Union, turning west and winding through the university campus until they reached Beverley Street. Kala used the time to run the facts of the case through her mind. She was comfortable with Gundersund's silence, yet something about the closed-off look on his face made her think he had worries beyond the case. She took quick peeks at him as he drove, trying to guess what was eating at him. It couldn't be his marriage, which appeared to be improving if he was having supper with Fiona. She was glad now that she hadn't asked him over for dinner as she'd planned that morning when she pulled a couple of steaks from the freezer.

He pulled into a parking spot across the street from the Eton house. The day was an autumn jewel with clear blue sky and vibrant red, orange, and yellow foliage. Kala stepped out of the car and crunched leaves with her boots as she followed Gundersund across the street. An ancient oak had shed its leaves like rain overnight and stood dark and barren amongst its counterparts. The tree was dying and would have to be cut down before long.

"You should take the lead with Sophie," Gundersund said, waiting for her to catch up.

"If you like. I don't see any cars in the driveway."

The house had an empty feel to it and she wasn't surprised when their knocks on the front door went unanswered.

"Let's swing by Mitchell Eton's workplace and see if he knows where they are," Gundersund said as he clumped down the steps behind her. "If we have to come back later, Charlie Hanson might be home from school and we can kill two birds with one stone. You okay working a bit of overtime?"

"Sure. We could pay a visit to Jane Thompson. She should be at work. What about your dinner with Fiona?"

"She'll understand if I'm running late. Woodhouse and Bennett are doing more background work on Jane. Maybe we should wait until they've finished before we approach her again."

Kala sighed. She wanted to get something going on this case but every lead had been a dead end and now they were playing hurry up and wait. "Fine," she said, "although it sure would be nice if we could stop chasing our tails and figure out what Devon Eton was doing Monday night after school that got him killed."

"I'm with you on that," said Gundersund. "We're almost a week into this case and no closer to solving it."

Kala looked both ways before starting across the street. She glanced back at him and smiled as she stepped off the sidewalk. "Well, we might be frustrated with the pace, but nobody on the team can say that they're bored anymore."

"I'll give you that," he said. "This beats the long summer of twiddling our thumbs. Too bad it's at the expense of a dead seventeen-year-old boy."

CHAPTER FIFTEEN

Friday morning, Naomi woke with stomach cramps. Rolling spasms in her lower belly that were uncomfortable but manageable on the pain scale. The cramps were a monthly occurrence that she tolerated stoically since she could do little about them. She reached a hand across the bed to feel for Adam before remembering that he'd gone in early to help with preparations for a track meet. He'd been running with the students every morning before school started, beginning in late September. Naomi lay for a moment collecting her thoughts. She'd promised him the night before that she'd get the kids off to school and already could hear them stirring in their bedrooms. Adam would be displeased if he found out she hadn't followed through.

Slowly, she rolled onto her side and swung her legs over the bed frame. A phone call to the school dispatcher and then she was in the shower, which helped to relieve the ache but not enough to change her decision to take a day off. She wasn't well enough to face a classroom full of boisterous fourth graders.

It wasn't as if she ever used up her quota of sick leave. She'd earned a day to herself.

She chanced Adam's cold anger and told Ben and Olivia that she wasn't feeling well, and they'd have to get their own breakfast and see themselves off to school. God knows, it wouldn't kill them to fend for themselves for once. Their father coddled them outrageously and expected her to do the same when he wasn't around. His strict devotion to them was beginning to wear on her patience.

She could hear them clumping around in the kitchen, talking and laughing like they did when they didn't know that she was in the house. Her stomach had stopped hurting since her period started but she felt lethargic and snuggled under the covers. Yes, a day off was what she needed. Life had been stressful since Jane got out of prison. Adam had always been hard to read — one of the things she liked about him, truth be told — but since Devon's murder, he'd been downright un-approachable. More brooding than Heathcliff.

Some running up and down stairs and finally the front door slammed as the kids raced out to catch their school bus that would take them to Calvin Park Public. Silence filled the house like a thick blanket. Naomi turned and looked over at the clock. *Quarter to nine.* She sat up and stretched. An entire day ahead with no obligations and nobody to bother her. She threw off the covers and wriggled out of her silk night-gown. No matter that she'd had a shower. A soak in a bubble bath would make her feel better and then …
well, then she'd do whatever she damn well pleased.

By eleven o'clock, she'd read a magazine in the tub for half an hour, drunk a pot of tea, read the paper, and watched Mike Holmes fix someone's disaster of a house on the Home and Garden channel. Four trips to the kitchen for something to eat, and twenty minutes into watching Whoopi on *The View*, and she was officially out-of-her-mind bored. How did people stay home all day and not go crazy?

She looked around the living room from where she sat slouched on the couch. Jane had decorated the house and Adam hadn't wanted to change anything. "The kids don't need to go through any more trauma" was how he'd put it when she'd brought out a furniture brochure from Urban Barn. Jane's taste had run to clunky traditional pieces — browns and beiges with splashes of garish red. Naomi would have chosen a grey palette for this space with modern, sleek lines. Maybe some nice sapphire blue cushions and modern prints for the walls. Update this Silver Street seventies infill.

She knew that she should have warmed to Ben and Olivia more than she had. Their features and colouring, so like Jane's, put her off every time she looked at them. They watched her with defiant, untrusting eyes and never hesitated to undermine her with Adam whenever they saw an opening. The problem wasn't whether or not she liked kids — which she did. It was that in particular she didn't like these two kids. They took up too much of Adam's focus and were always underfoot. They were ungrateful, trailing their messes all over the house for her to clean up after them.

The door to Adam's den on the other side of the kitchen was shut as usual. Adam locked it whenever he was finished working on his computer, which he liked to do some evenings and on the weekends. He said that he needed a private space that he knew wasn't being invaded by the kids. She had an uneasy feeling that he sometimes put her into the same category, but then she'd remember his touch when they were alone in his big bed. He didn't treat her like a child when her tongue flicked across his chest, that was for sure. Adam kept student files in his den and said that he had to ensure student privacy was not breached. Naomi stared at the door, willing it to open. The idea of breaching student privacy was a bit of a stretch. Who was going to make off with the information? Her? Ben and Olivia?

She crossed the kitchen floor and paused in front of the office door, nervous enough to check behind her to make certain that nobody had entered the house unnoticed. If one of the kids saw her, they'd report her to Adam in a heartbeat. The tap was dripping in the kitchen sink, but other than that, the house was silent. She raised her hand to try the doorknob. A mix of surprise, delight, and finally, uneasiness coursed through her when the handle turned and the door opened. She checked over her shoulder again and stepped inside.

This was the only space in the house where Jane's old-fashioned taste wasn't staring you in the face because Adam had decorated this room himself. A toffee-coloured leather chair with a footstool sat in front of the window with an antique walnut desk taking up the other half of the room. Framed photographs of Ben and Olivia were on the walls as well as two taken with Jane when they were one big happy family. In the blown-up photo, Jane's smile was wide and open, her arms wrapped around Olivia with Ben next to her, his skinny arms twined around her neck. Their three blond heads and clone-blue eyes must have been focused on Adam, who would have been behind the camera urging them to smile. Naomi would have preferred if he'd taken that picture down. She felt jealous at the possible reason why he hadn't.

Adam had positioned the desk so that he looked out the window into the back garden when he sat typing on his computer. Her eyes jumped to the screen saver. Balloons in primary colours were drifting skyward at regular intervals. *Had Adam forgotten to log off?* He must have been called away quickly to leave the door unlocked, and he'd forgotten to return and shut things down. She stood still for a moment, thinking about the wisdom of what she was about to do.

"Well, if he has nothing to hide ..." she said aloud before crossing to his desk. She didn't dare move anything in case Adam noticed such things about his space. She clicked the keyboard and the screen saver disappeared, replaced by a lesson plan he'd been working on. She leaned closer. He'd been making notes on a history game he was going to use later in the week. She hit the icon on the top of the page to minimize it and the main page appeared in its place. She clicked on the photo icon, curious to see what he kept on file after seeing Jane's face still hanging on the wall.

The photos were arranged in subfolders by date. The most recent was two days before. She opened the yellow file folder and tried to comprehend what she was seeing. A string of snapshots taken with a telephoto lens of ... she enlarged one and squinted ... a woman with short blond hair. Her face turned toward the camera in the next photo and Naomi held a hand to her mouth. *Jane*. He'd been taking pictures secretly of his ex-wife as she waited for a bus. Naomi checked the date and time stamps. He'd taken them after work when he said he'd had a meeting. She moved the arrow and clicked on each photo in sequence. Jane was skinny as a rail in a grey T-shirt and black track pants, her eyes hidden behind oversized black sunglasses. Her hair was short and messy, making her almost unrecognizable ... but still gorgeous in her ethereal, waif-like way. Naomi thought she might very well hate her. A second folder dated two weeks earlier contained a series of photos of Jane walking downtown. He must have been positioned in his car on the side of the street by the angle of the photos. She moved the arrow over to the file marked Monday and hesitated. Monday was the day that boy was killed. Adam said he'd been at the gym all evening. Had he lied about that too?

She closed her eyes and clicked. Before she could look at the screen, the sound of the deadbolt shooting open in the next room made her jump like a scared rabbit. Her thigh banged hard against the desk. She stifled a scream with her hand and searched the room for somewhere to hide. The only place was under the desk, but that would be crazy. If Adam came into the house and found her there, she'd look guilty as hell. Her next thought was to start running. Run out of the room, out of the kitchen, and out of this house. Leave lying Adam and his coddled kids and never come back. She looked toward the open office door while her fingers hit the keys to shut down the photo album. She even remembered to enlarge the lesson plan that Adam had been working on before she skittered across the floor and slipped out of the room.

A heavy-set woman was standing in the doorway with her back to the kitchen. She was bent over, placing her shoes on the mat. She straightened, lifting a pail as she did so and turning. Her eyes swept the kitchen and found Naomi standing frozen against the wall. The woman let out a yelp. She grabbed her chest and dropped the bucket of cleaning supplies that she was holding in front of her. The bucket rolled and its contents scattered. "You gave me a fright," she said in Naomi's direction as the fear left her face. She knelt to start picking up bottles. "Nobody's ever here when I come."

Naomi rushed over and picked up a container of Vim that had reached the dishwasher. "I'm so sorry. You must be Myrna. I forgot that you came on Fridays to clean." She handed over the bottle. "I have a day off." She was angry that her voice was so apologetic.

"Mr. Thompson told me about you," Myrna said. Her rheumy eyes settled on a point over Naomi's right shoulder. "I wasn't sure you were still holding

Jane's place now that she's out of jail." She dropped Mr. Clean into the pail with a thud and motioned toward the door. "Well, I have my system. I'll be starting in the kitchen and I'll do your bedroom last so you might want to make yourself scarce."

"Thanks," Naomi heard herself say. "I'll be in my room until you tell me to move."

Kala and Gundersund returned to the station after they tracked down Mitchell at his office and he told them that Hilary had taken Sophie to visit her grandparents in Coburg until Sunday morning.

"Not a great move when we have a murder investigation going on," Gundersund said to him.

"Neither of them is coping so I wanted them to have a break before Devon's funeral," Mitchell said. "I could answer your questions if you like."

"We'll come by on Sunday." Kala signalled to Gundersund to let it rest and they'd left without further comment.

They spent the afternoon working on a court case at which they had to appear the following week, and got into their separate vehicles at four thirty to rendezvous at the Hansons'. They'd need both vehicles so that Gundersund could make his dinner date with Fiona while Kala would head directly home to let Taiku outside.

She followed him through the downtown and along the side streets until he slowed and turned onto Macdonnell. He found a space halfway down the street and she parked her truck a few vehicle lengths in front of him, between a van and a motor-cycle. They got out at the same time and met in the middle of the road. She looked at the Hanson house and waited for the bad feeling to return, but it didn't.

"The hedge looks like it's grown half a foot since we were here last," Gundersund said. They crossed to the sidewalk. "I saw a curtain move in the living room."

"So much for our sneak attack."

"Mom's working," said Tiffany when she opened the door. She was wearing tight ripped jeans and a crop top that showed off a pierced belly button. Her curiously coloured eyes were surrounded in thick liner and dark shadows that gave her a raccoon-like stare. She started to close the door before Gundersund's foot intervened.

"We're here to speak with your brother, Charlie. Is he home from school?"

"Yeah, I guess. My mother might not like you talking to him without her here, but she'll get over it. He is eighteen after all."

Kala asked, "Mind if we step inside? We can talk to him in the hallway. We only have a few follow-up questions."

Tiffany shrugged. "Sure, why not?" She left them in the narrow corridor and walked to the bottom of the stairs. "Charlie!" she called. "Cops here to see you." She turned and smiled at them, and for the eeriest of moments, Kala felt like she was looking at one of the girls she'd known in foster care. "Go up if he doesn't come down," she said before she disappeared into the back of the house.

"Do you think her mother approves of that makeup?" Gundersund asked. "I'd take a face cloth to her if I were her dad."

"They're all coating on the pancake makeup. It's called fashion."

"Well, in my day, girls tried to look pretty, not like wild animals you'd be scared to meet in a back alley, much less take out to the movies."

"Dating yourself, Gundersund, not to mention showing your sexist side."

"So I'm a chauvinistic prude. Shoot me. How old is she again?"

"Her mother said she'll be fourteen next month."

Gundersund frowned but stopped what he was about to say as footsteps thudded across the landing. They both looked up and watched Charlie descending the stairs. He was wearing a black Grateful Dead T-shirt, faded almost to grey and a few sizes too large. A red bandana crossed his forehead and flattened his messy curls. The sweet smell of weed travelled with him down the stairwell.

"You wanted to see me?" he asked. He stood with his back against the banister.

"Are you okay with answering a few follow-up questions without your mom here?" Kala asked.

Charlie lifted one shoulder in a shrug. "Sure, why not."

Gundersund moved a few steps closer to him. "Going through phone records, we became aware that Devon called you Monday afternoon after school. Can you tell us about that phone call?"

"I can't say that I remember any call."

"It happened at 4:05 and lasted twenty-five seconds."

Charlie looked to be thinking it over. Finally, he said, "Yeah, maybe he called but we talk all the time."

"This was the day he died, so whatever you talked about could be important. Do you remember the conversation?"

"Nothing stands out. I think he told me that he was sorry to cut out so soon but we could hang out Tuesday after school. Nothing of import."

"Did he give any indication of where he was going?"

Charlie glanced over at Kala. He looked uncomfortable for the briefest of moments before he looked back at Gundersund. "Not really."

Gundersund's voice hardened. "Is that a yes or a no?"

"That's a no."

"Someone saw you and Devon arguing at your lockers before he left school on Monday. Can you tell us what that was about?"

Charlie rubbed his nose with the back of his hand and took his time lowering it. "I don't think we were fighting about anything.... Oh, yeah. I owed him five bucks and he was mad that I couldn't pay him back yet. It was nothing."

Kala stepped forward and Gundersund moved sideways to let her stand next to him. "Were you and Devon dealing drugs, Charlie?" she asked. "Or could Devon have been buying drugs the night he was murdered?"

She knew she'd missed the mark by the sudden relaxing of Charlie's shoulders. The cockiness returned to his face. He laughed. "No, nothing like that." He glanced upstairs and back at them. "We might smoke some pot but that's about it. It's pretty much legal anyhow."

"But not quite." Gundersund looked at Kala. "Anything else?"

She nodded. "Charlie, you said that Devon wasn't worried about Jane Thompson being out of prison. Do you know if he was looking forward to seeing her again ... or if they'd made contact?"

Charlie pulled his phone out of his pocket and looked at the screen. He clicked on keys with his thumb. He was either buying time or trying to annoy them. Kala repeated her question and he looked up at her. She could tell that he had no intention of sharing anything more.

"He never said."

"Let's go, Gundersund." She shut her notepad. "Charlie needs a bit of time to think over his answers because I'm sure he wants to do everything he can to find his best friend's killer."

Charlie's lowered head jumped slightly at her words but he continued to move his thumb quickly on his phone's keypad. "I'll tell Mom you were by when she was working," he said before he began backing up the stairs.

"You figure he was warning us about talking to him without his mother around?" Gundersund asked as they crossed the street to their vehicles.

"Probably." She unlocked her truck. "I'll see you tomorrow. Have fun at dinner."

"Yeah, see you tomorrow."

His face was lined with worry before he turned away and Kala hesitated with her fingers on the door handle. Should she ask him if something was bothering him or wait until morning? Before she could decide, he was in his car and reversing to angle out of his parking spot, arm slung over the seat and head turned. Kala pulled her truck door open and swung a leg inside. *Maybe it's nothing,* she told herself. *He was only thinking about the case and all the disturbing people we're interviewing along the way. Once he has a night off, he'll bounce back to his old self.*

CHAPTER SIXTEEN

Rouleau set the last of the reports onto his desk and removed his reading glasses. He was rubbing the bridge of his nose with his thumb and finger when Vera poked her head through his office door.

"Heath would like to see you," she said. She was slightly out of breath. "I was afraid you'd already left."

Rouleau checked his watch. "I'm running a bit late. Let me make a call and I'll be right there."

"Okay." Vera beamed at him before pulling the door closed behind her.

He called his father to make sure all was well and to let him know to go ahead with supper. His father's health issues were a constant worry at the back of Rouleau's mind. He knew his father wouldn't be around forever, but losing him now would be a second cruel blow after Frances's death a few months earlier. Rouleau sometimes felt as if everyone he loved was slipping through his fingers and he was powerless to hold on.

He was surprised to find Vera in the main office waiting for him. She normally wore her white ash–blond hair in a bun, but today it was loose around her shoulders. She was dressed in a tight cashmere sweater and pencil skirt with her usual high heels. He'd heard her called the fashion plate by more than one cop. Her other nickname was Marilyn after the famous blond bombshell. She looked slightly uncomfortable and he wondered why. They fell into step and he waited for her to say whatever was on her mind.

"I was wondering," she started and paused.

"What is it, Vera?"

"I'm involved with a hospital fundraiser and we're having a musical evening on Tuesday to raise money for new neonatal incubators. I have an extra ticket."

"That I'd be happy to purchase."

"Are you sure? I know it's bad form to sell stuff at work, even if the money goes to charity. You can say no and I won't be offended."

"Let me know how much and I'll write a cheque."

"That's so great. Thanks, Jacques." Vera smiled again and walked behind her desk to get her coat. "I'm off then. I'll leave the ticket on your desk tomorrow with a note on how much you owe me."

"Perfect." Rouleau didn't like musicals, but his dad did and might be free. He kept walking toward Heath's open door where he found Heath on the phone. Heath raised his pointer finger as he cut off whomever he was talking to and told them he'd have to call them back.

"So." Heath folded his hands across his stomach and leaned back in the chair. "What's the news on the Eton murder?"

"I wish I had some. The team is out beating the bushes but nobody is coming forward with solid information. We have no idea what he was doing at the seawall or why he was killed."

"Which circles us back to the Thompson woman."

"I know. I agree that we need to refocus our efforts to find out more about her and what she's been up to since her release. I didn't want to over-look any other suspects in a rush to judgment, but it's looking like we can't ignore the obvious anymore."

Heath gave the thumbs up. "Glad you've been thorough, but it's time to put the pressure on her and get a confession."

"Of course we'll follow up on all leads if new information becomes available."

"I'd expect nothing less. I'll time the next press conference right after you've brought her in for questioning. At least we'll look like we aren't sitting around twiddling our thumbs. By the way, have you anything going on this Thursday evening?"

"Not at the moment. Do you need me to sit in on a board meeting?"

"Actually, I was hoping you might come to a cocktail party Ingrid is throwing. This is an import-ant evening for her and I promised that you'd be on the guest list. She thinks a lot of you, by the way."

Rouleau had only met Heath's wife once before and was surprised to hear that she had an opinion of him one way or the other. "I'll certainly do my utmost to be there. Thank Ingrid for the invitation."

Heath's head bobbed up and down. "Great. I'll tell her you'll be there. She'll be pleased." He picked up his cellphone from the desk. His eyes travelled across Rouleau's face as he added, "Well, here's the tricky part. Since you're coming, I'd like you to bring Vera's cousin. You remember Laney Masterson? She was helping you to find a house last year." Heath looked down and tapped some keys. He kept his eyes focused on the screen.

Rouleau was momentarily at a loss for words. He stared at Heath and wondered how much Ingrid knew about his ongoing affair with Laney. Ingrid had to be suspicious if Heath was asking Rouleau to be Laney's date. He took a second to formulate a response that would extricate him from the evening without angering Heath, a man who'd so far been a supportive, hands-off boss, a relationship that Rouleau needed to maintain. Yet, he wanted to avoid deceiving Ingrid even more than he wanted to be on Heath's good side. Rouleau had another reason for turning down the evening. He'd found Laney attractive on their few interactions the summer before and believed that the interest had gone both ways, but he had no intention of being alone with her. He started into his refusal but Heath cut him off, his cherub face awash in feigned delight.

"All set then. I've sent Laney a text that you'll pick her up around eight. I'll forward her address and coordinates to you later this evening. Thank you again, Jacques. You have no idea the trouble you're saving me from on the home front." Heath laughed a jolly, forced belly laugh as if sealing their good old boys' fraternity. "Now if you'll excuse me, I have to return that call. See you tomorrow, shall I?" Heath was already holding the cellphone to his ear and he nodded goodbye to Rouleau, saying hello into the receiver at the same time.

Rouleau shook his head and started his refusal again but Heath swivelled his chair to face the far wall and pretended not to see or hear. Rouleau left when it became obvious Heath would outwait him. An email with his regrets in the morning would have to do. No way in hell would he let Heath get him involved in his marriage mess. As Rouleau's father once advised him some years earlier when Rouleau's replacement in charge of a volatile unit kept calling with his problems, "That isn't your circus, son. Those aren't your monkeys."

The trick would be convincing Heath that his monkeys weren't Rouleau's problem to solve either.

He returned to his office for his coat. He was glad to see that everybody had gone home. A murder investigation could wear down the team if they didn't take breaks when they could. He headed for the main entrance and said good night to the desk officer, who motioned to Rouleau that he had a visitor. Rouleau turned to look toward the lobby. Marci Stokes was waiting sprawled in one of the visitor chairs, her tan trench coat open over a hunter green turtleneck and jeans. Bright red running shoes competed with her messy shock of copper hair. Her rumpled appearance suited what little Rouleau knew of her: brash, unapologetic, and immune to social niceties. Rouleau groaned inwardly at the sight of her. The day had been a long one and he had no desire to fend off her requests for inside information on the Eton case.

He walked past her without comment and pushed the front door open, stepping outside into the cool of the evening. The sun was almost down and shadows were thickening. A north wind had come up, promising changeable weather overnight. He took a cleansing breath and waited for Marci to work her way in front of him, which she wasted no time in doing.

"Hey Rouleau. Long time, no see."

"I heard you'd left Kingston for greener pastures."

"I took a trip down memory lane and spent a few months in New York. Now I'm back."

Her voice was matter of fact, but her coffee-coloured eyes showed a vulnerability and more than she'd meant him to see. He'd found their previous interactions enjoyable but knew he couldn't trust her. When she wrote a piece that threw Stonechild under the bus, he'd broken off their connection. He'd learned the hard way that Marci had no loyalties except to the story and would do whatever it took to get it.

"Let me guess," he said. "You're on the Devon Eton case, looking for inside information. Sorry, I can't be of any help this time around." He stepped past her and began walking toward the parking lot. The wind pushed against him, cooling his bald head and making him think about getting home for a Scotch in front of the gas fireplace.

Marci spoke from behind him. "I figured as much, but I wanted to give you something this time. An insight into Jane Thompson."

He kept walking and tossed over his shoulder, "Why?"

Marci caught up to him and matched his strides. The face she turned toward him in the circle of light from the street lamp looked pensive. Her eyes were luminous dark pools. "There's something about Jane that's so, I don't know, unbelievable. How can she find the strength to keep going after all she's been through? Don't you want to study her like a bug under a microscope? I know I do. It got me thinking ..."

"Jane Thompson brought about her own downfall by having sex with her student. She may very well have killed him, too."

"Yeah, I get it. She deserves to wear the scarlet letter A, right? Corrupting a twelve-year-old. Betraying her husband and children. Killing the kid in a fit of anger ... maybe. What's to defend? I've been going through the court transcripts all day and am struck by how Jane pleaded innocent throughout the trial until almost a year after she was found guilty. She refused to apologize to the Etons when given the opportunity before sentencing, even though her lack of remorse impacted negatively on her sentence. Why would she do that, Detective?"

"She was in denial. I don't pretend to know the psychology behind these women who fancy themselves in love with young boys, but I would imagine they lie to themselves about their behaviour and the responsibility they bear." They'd reached his car and Rouleau took out his keys. He turned and leaned against the door. "Just what are you driving at, Marci? Why were you waiting for me tonight, since you don't appear to have anything pressing to share?"

Her face reflected the confusion going on inside her. "I'm not a sentimental woman, Rouleau. I couldn't be and work in this male-dominated business and expect to be a success. But I can smell a story, and I believe Jane Thompson hasn't told hers yet. She confessed to the affair with Devon Eton, and her husband left her two weeks later. There has to be something in the timing."

"He divorced her when he had proof positive she'd been lying about her guilt."

"Maybe, but I think there was more to it."

Rouleau pushed himself off the car door, turned, and opened it. He stopped with one foot inside and his hand on top of the door frame. "We'll be bringing her in for questioning in the next few days, so maybe she'll tell us. I'll pass along your questions to the team."

"And I'll keep digging. Have to win that Pulitzer somehow to complete my bucket list." She smiled and left him shivering inside his car with the heater up full even though it was blowing cold air. He looked toward the last place he'd seen her before her bright hair bobbed out of sight. Her belief in her hunches reminded him of Stonechild and her uncanny intuition. Could both women have the same unsettling ability to sense the invisible? Kala Stonechild and Marci Stokes were as different as two women could be, or so he'd believed. Maybe, it was time to rethink the two of them.

He put the car into drive and pulled out of the parking lot and headed for the downtown and his father's condo on the waterfront. It was late and he was tired and he wanted nothing more than some supper and that Scotch neat. Time to put aside Heath, Laney Masterson, and Marci Stokes — and all the nonsense of the day — for a few hours so that he could face it all over again in the morning. "Not my monkeys," he muttered under his breath as he cranked up Fleetwood Mac on the radio and turned left onto Princess.

Fiona was sitting at the bar in the King Street Keg when Gundersund arrived twenty minutes late. She was halfway through a Keg-size cranberry mojito and smiled when she saw him approach. She turned a cheek for him to kiss, and he remained standing in front of her since the place was packed, every bar stool taken.

"You smell good, like a spicy Irishman," she said, adding, "Our table's ready."

"I made it home in time for a quick shower." *And to let the dog out for a pee.* His hair was still damp and his shirt collar felt wet on his neck. He ordered a Mill Street beer and they followed the waitress as she threaded through groups standing around the bar to lead them to their table in the back dining room. The noise level was slightly lower, conversations rising and falling around them. Fiona had always loved the energy of a crowded room after spending all day in the lab. Tonight, her face was flushed and her eyes were sparkling. Gundersund thought she was one of the most beautiful women he'd ever seen. He'd thought that from the first moment he'd laid eyes on her and age was making her more, not less, attractive. She was wearing a scooped silk top, a royal blue colour that accentuated the creaminess of her skin. She'd pulled her blond hair back in a loose braid and the silver hoop earrings he'd given her on their third wedding anniversary glinted in the light as she moved her head to study the room.

They ordered their usual meals: the scallops and bacon appetizer to share, prime rib with a twice baked potato and Caesar salad for her, and the New York sirloin with mushrooms and garlic mashed potatoes for him. Each selected a large glass of Californian Belle Glos Pinot Noir to accompany the meal. This Keg had been a haunt when they were together.

"We are creatures of habit, aren't we, darling?" Fiona asked him after the waitress had gone.

"Fiona ..." he started, but she interrupted.

"Let's not get into anything tonight. We can pretend for one meal, can't we?"

He studied her more closely. Redness rimmed the edges of her eyes as it only did when she'd been crying. He felt guilt at the thought that he might be the cause.

"We can," he said.

He wished he still loved her. He could try again to let her into his heart and the feelings might return. He knew he could fall back into the marriage with her. They'd learn to be a couple again, but he knew that it would cost him in the end. She might be faithful for a year, maybe two, but it wasn't in her to be faithful forever. He didn't want to go through the pain when she left him again — and she would.

She held his gaze and her expression changed as she seemed to sense his mood. She said softly, her voice small, defeated, "This isn't going to work, is it, Paul? You've decided that I'm not worth giving a second chance."

Gundersund reached over to take her hand. She rarely gave up fighting for what she wanted or showed weakness. This moved him more than anything else she could have said or done.

"I'm not sure that marriage is for us. I'm a safe place for you to land, but I don't think it's enough. You have to be honest with yourself, Fiona. You owe this to yourself … and to me."

Her shoulders straightened and she picked up her glass. Her voice started out wobbly but grew in strength. "Well, since we agreed to keep this light tonight, I'm going to keep my end of the deal and tell you about my day. Only one body this morning and it was a natural death. Too much fast food, smoking, and a sedentary lifestyle killed him at forty-nine. I taught a class at the university after lunch and then made it back to the morgue to start preparing for another autopsy. A suicide this time. I always find those the saddest." She took a drink, swallowed, and said, "You think I'd be used to young men offing themselves by now, but I never am."

"Some things we aren't meant to get used to."

He met her eyes and neither looked away until the waitress arrived with the appetizer. They took their time unwrapping their napkins and simultaneously reached for the same scallop with their forks.

Fiona laughed, ducking her fork under his and spearing the scallop. She popped it into her mouth. "Any progress on the Eton case?" she asked as she chewed. "Mmmm, this had to be the best scallop on the plate."

He shook his head and smiled. "We're eliminating suspects before zeroing in on the likely culprit."

"The teacher — what was her name? — Jane …"

"Thompson. Heath has her in his sights and we're to question her more forcefully to get her to confess."

"I know that tone. You aren't convinced."

"She's one cool customer. I can't see her handing us her own head on a platter. Stonechild thinks we have to come at Jane more subtly to get her to talk. Stonechild has a terrific way of drawing people out." He noticed Fiona's smile waver and silently cursed himself for bringing up his partner. He knew they didn't like each other much.

The waitress picked that moment to deliver their main courses, and Fiona left his comments about Stonechild alone. They busied themselves eating and Gundersund steered the conversation to safer subjects. The table next to them changed customers, and Fiona knew the woman from yoga class. Introductions were made and Fiona kept the conversation going between the two tables. Over coffee and liqueurs, she told Gunderson her news.

"I wasn't certain until tonight, but I've been offered a four-month teaching position at the University of Calgary and I'm going to take it. I've already discussed the idea of taking a short sabbatical with my boss so now I just have to accept and get all the details ironed out."

He didn't know how to feel. This was what he wanted, wasn't it? "It sounds like a good opportunity."

"It'll be a change. It'll give us both a chance to step back and think about what we want. Really, to figure out what you want, because I already know. You and I belong together. Will you give me the four months before reaching a final decision about our marriage?"

Another delay. Four months wasn't really a long time in the scheme of things. He owed Fiona nothing but he'd compromise this one last time. Perhaps, she'd decide to release him of her own accord once she got away. She'd meet someone else and forget about rekindling their marriage.

"Four months," he said, "and then we do what's best for us both. Agreed?"

Her smile was wide and self-assured and her eyes had regained their sparkle. She raised her glass to clink his. "Agreed."

A stop on the way home for groceries with a detour to Sima Sushi at the bottom of Princess Street for a takeout order of spicy salmon roll with crab, cream cheese, and cucumber, and Kala was turning onto Old Front Road as the sun was beginning to set over the treetops. She opened the window all the way and breathed in the fresh fall air, slowing as she passed Gundersund's property. A quick glance toward his house and she noticed that his car wasn't in the driveway, but she hadn't expected it to be. She remembered that he was having dinner with Fiona as they worked on patching up their marriage.

It looked as if Woodhouse was going to win the office pool. She hadn't wagered any money on whether or not Fiona would reel Gundersund back in. She hoped for his sake that he knew what he was doing. She could understand how Fiona's chameleon-like ability to transform herself into whatever men wanted would fool somebody like Gundersund. He was a kind man, surprisingly unsure of himself when it came to women. A beautiful, self-absorbed feline like Fiona would keep him off balance and thankful for any crumbs. Kala was happy that she'd nixed the feelings she'd started to have for him. *Very happy.* Not only did he have a wife, but he was also her partner. Two big reasons to run the other way.

The question was why she craned her neck to look for him every time she drove past his house.

Lining the entrance to her driveway was a tangle of bushes and trees that had grown thicker the past year that she'd been living in the house, looking after it while Marjory was living up north researching a land claims case. Marjory called periodically and had been back for a few weekends. During her last phone conversation two weeks before, she'd told Kala that she was thinking of selling the house and moving to Vancouver. "I've been asked to take on a new land claims case when this one wraps up in a few months. I always wanted to live on the West Coast."

Kala drove slowly up the drive. She parked half-way to the house and stepped outside. She could hear the waves rolling onto the beach at the end of the property, and already the first stars were poking through the deepening blue sky. An owl hooted from the woods on her left and a small animal rustled in the leaves not far from where she stood, likely a field mouse. The thought that she'd soon have to leave this place and look for a new home made her sadder than she would have expected. She couldn't pinpoint when she'd begun to feel at home here, but this was the first time she'd had the sense of belonging anywhere since she left Birdtail Creek to live with a foster family in Ontario just before her eleventh birthday. Taiku loved the freedom of the beach and woods. She liked knowing that Gundersund was down the road.

Once again, Taiku was not waiting for her at the back door. She could hear him bound across the landing and down the stairs after she called his name and jangled her keys. He galloped down the hall toward her, his tail wagging, and he jumped against her legs and waited for her welcome. But while she set her bag down and put her supper into the fridge, he flopped down near the kitchen table instead of heading to the back door to go outside. *Strange.* Worried, Kala crossed the kitchen and knelt down beside him. "Are you sick, boy?" She touched his nose, but it felt wet and cool as it should. She was relieved that he stood when she did, and she let her fingers run through the soft ruff of fur around his neck. "Let's go outside for a run."

On the back deck, they stopped at the head of the stairs and Kala watched the sun going down to the west over the lake. Taiku ran down the steps and disappeared into the bushes. She could hear him rummaging around, but he was right next to her as she crossed the lawn to climb down the short cliff to the stone stretch of beach. He seemed content to stay next to her, and again she wondered at his lack of energy. Usually, he was all over the property after a day shut up indoors. When the sun was completely down, they returned to the house and she poured his supper from the bag of dog food and refilled his water bowl. His tail wagged, but he only ate a few bites before going to lie down in his spot by the table.

Now, this is getting really odd, she thought while retrieving her sushi from the fridge and pouring a glass of milk. She squeezed in next to Taiku — he always stretched out in the same spot by her feet — and ate while watching to see if he was exhibiting signs of sickness. He slept, snoring softly and twitching while he dreamed. He seemed to be breathing without problem and his eyes had been clear when he'd looked up at her, but Kalą promised herself that she'd take him for a checkup first thing after the weekend. He probably could use a visit to the vet, anyhow, since his sixth birthday was coming up in a few weeks.

CHAPTER SEVENTEEN

Kala woke from a deep sleep disoriented with her heart pounding. Eyes wide open, staring into the darkness, she forced herself to lie still and listen. The wind had come up since she'd come to bed and the curtains were billowing sails snapping into the room. Taiku paced restlessly in the hallway and Kala thought this combination of sounds must have been what awakened her. The rest of the house appeared quiet.

She jumped across the room to pull the window shut and called to Taiku to come as she leaped back into bed. The temperature outside had dropped at least ten degrees, and she shivered under the blankets. Taiku's paws padded across the hardwood floor, and he settled with a loud sigh on the rug next to the bed.

Kala tossed and turned, trying to get comfortable. An hour later and she was still wide awake. Her eyes inspected the shadows past the open doorway. Her senses had been on high alert all week and she wasn't certain why. Was it the murder investigation making her jumpy, or was it

Taiku being out of sorts? Whatever was creating her uneasiness had entered her home like an invisible ghost. All week she'd felt another presence. She'd walked through the rooms each evening carefully looking for signs that somebody had been in the house but had found nothing out of order. Nothing that she could put her finger on. Yet, still she couldn't relax.

At twenty after three, she got up, slipped into her bathrobe and walked downstairs in the dark, Taiku silently following behind her. She gave him a biscuit while she heated up some milk on the stove. She didn't bother to turn on any lights except the dim one over the stove. Her eyes had adjusted to the gloom, and she hoped the natural light would help her body become sleepy. They settled on the couch, Taiku's head resting against her thigh while she sipped the milk and thought about how to approach Jane Thompson because they'd be bringing her in for questioning late morning. Rouleau was going to take the lead, which suited her. He had the most experience and Jane wasn't going to give anything away easily, but perhaps, Kala could suggest some questions ahead of time. Rouleau always appreciated input.

A crash against the window made Kala jump off the couch and slop milk onto her housecoat. Taiku was instantly beside her on the floor, growling low in his throat, the fur on the back of his neck standing straight up. Kala put down her mug on the coffee table and crossed to the window, craning her neck to see into the darkness. "Wait here, Taiku."

She walked silently into the front hallway and found the switch to turn on the outside light. When she opened the door, a gust of wind pushed her back, the cold cutting through her thin housecoat. She pulled the fabric tighter around her neck and stepped outside in bare feet. Her eyes took a few minutes to adjust to the shadows outside the shallow pool of light, but she made out a large branch lying under the picture window. The wind had ripped it from the oak tree and tossed it against the house. Leaves were swirling across the lawn and the trees were black and swaying. Clouds filled the night sky, blocking out the moon and stars. She took another look around the yard before slamming the door and throwing the deadbolt.

"Nothing to worry about," she said to Taiku as she returned to the couch. She stooped to rub his neck until he stopped growling and his body relaxed under her hand. She picked up the mug from where she'd set it on the coffee table. "Let's head upstairs and see if we can fall asleep again."

Taiku appeared on the same wavelength and led her to the hallway, checking that she was following as he started up the stairs. Kala stopped at the bedroom where Dawn had stayed the few short months she lived in the house. The window was open and the room was cold. Kala entered and closed the window before returning to her own bedroom and climbing back under the covers. She finished her milk in the darkness and gradually stopped shivering under the blankets. Fatigue made her limbs heavy and she let her mind wander until all her thoughts were a kaleidoscope of colours and shooting images behind her closed eyelids.

She and Taiku were both sound asleep when the thunder and driving rain rolled in at 5:00 a.m.

Woodhouse was the only one in the office the next morning when Kala arrived a half hour late. Even though it was Saturday, Rouleau had asked them to show by nine so that they could prepare for Jane Thompson's interview later in the morning. The effects of the terrible night's sleep had made her sluggish and she'd taken longer than normal to get herself out the door.

Woodhouse raised his arm and made a show of looking at his watch. "Up late partying, were you?"

She dropped her bag on the floor and sat down at her desk, ignoring his question. She turned on her computer screen and brought up her email before looking across at him. "Where is everyone?"

"Rouleau and Gundersund went for breakfast in the café. They said for you to join them if you like when you get in. I expect they're almost done by now."

"That's okay. Where's Bennett?"

"Washroom. I expect he's almost done, too." Woodhouse grinned, leaned back in his chair, and pretended to grab his crotch.

Kala stared at him without reacting. He was always ruder with her when nobody was around to witness. She could still make complaints against his behaviour but preferred to bide her time. She knew he was making Bennett's life a misery. That bothered her more than his harassment of her. She could handle whatever he had to throw at her, but Bennett wasn't as hardened by bullies the likes of Woodhouse. Bennett took things personally.

She looked past him to the door as Bennett entered like a ray of sunshine. He smiled when he saw her and walked over to sit in Gundersund's chair. "Rouleau and Gundersund are on their way. Woodhouse and I are heading over to pick up Jane Thompson while you three go over the case to make sure Rouleau has all the information before Jane's interview." He rolled the chair closer as if trying to block out Woodhouse. He dropped his voice. "Say, has Vera sold you a ticket to her fundraiser yet?"

"No. What is it?"

"A musical put on for the hospital. I have two tickets and wonder if you'd like to come with me? It's Tuesday evening and we should have this case about wrapped up by then."

"You might be a tad optimistic, but sure, I'll come with you if we don't have to work overtime. How much do I owe for the ticket?"

"This is on me."

They both looked up at the same time as Gundersund and Rouleau walked in together. Gundersund's eyes went from her to Bennett and she felt guilt flood through her, as if she and Bennett were up to no good. Bennett must have felt it, too, because he immediately got out of Gundersund's chair with an apology and headed to his own across from Woodhouse.

"Brought you a coffee," Gundersund said as he set the cup on her desk. He was frowning as he shrugged out of his leather jacket. "Hell of a storm going on out there. Did you get wet coming in?"

She picked up the coffee cup. "Thanks. No, I managed to stay dry. How was your dinner last night?"

"All right. Can't go wrong with a Keg steak." He sat down and stretched out his legs, crossing them at the ankles. He yawned. "Fiona's taking a four-month teaching position in Calgary beginning next month."

Which explains the lack of sleep. He can't stand the idea of her being away. Kala wasn't a fan of Fiona but felt the need to make him feel better. "The time will go fast. She'll be back before you know it."

"I'm counting on it." He started to say something else but Rouleau appeared in the doorway to his office and called them both over. Gundersund looked across at Woodhouse and Bennett and said, "Time to go pick up Jane Thompson. She'll be working at the store in the back today. She knows you're coming."

Rouleau and Kala let Jane sit alone for twenty minutes in one of the smaller rooms before they entered. Kala could see immediately that Jane was on edge, more so than the last time they'd questioned her. Her blond hair looked freshly washed, and her clothes were simple but clean — a sweatshirt and faded jeans — but they were loose on her slender frame, and Kala thought she'd lost weight in the week since they'd first questioned her. Her face was pale as ivory and she had the look of suffering around her eyes, still mesmerizing in the fluorescent lighting. Kala hoped that she'd be up to their questioning. Rouleau was looking Jane over, too, and appeared to reach a similar conclusion.

"Can we get you a drink, Jane? Coffee or a soft drink? Water?" His voice was kind, the one he used when speaking to people in distress. He'd said in his office that when people were violent and mentally ill, he was torn between the need to bring them to justice and compassion. He'd feared that Jane Thompson's hold on reality might be tenuous, but her conversations with her psychologist in prison were protected for the most part.

"No. I'm fine. How long will this take?"

"Do you have to be anywhere?"

"Not really."

Rouleau looked at his notes. "We shouldn't keep you too long if you tell us what you know."

"Then ask away." Jane settled back in the chair, arms wrapped around her waist. Her eyes darted between him and Kala.

Kala turned her chair slightly so that she was angled toward Rouleau, trying to make Jane focus on him. He'd be asking the questions, gaining her trust and drawing her out. She pictured Gundersund, Woodhouse, and Bennett behind the two-way glass observing.

Rouleau walked her through her earlier whereabouts the week that Devon was murdered. Her responses were short, never elaborating or offering more than asked. Kala didn't hear any inconsistencies. Jane once again denied being in contact with Devon while she was in prison or after she got out. Rouleau looked down at his notes and then back up. He was wearing a green sweater that made his eyes a deeper green than usual, and Jane seemed unable to look away.

"Jane, what happened for you to change your mind about confessing to having sexual relations with Devon? You denied all of the allegations and refused to apologize when you had the chance in court. Why did you suddenly admit to everything?"

"What does it matter?"

"Everything about this case so far appears to hinge on your relationship with Devon Eton, so I'd like to know what you were thinking when you decided to change your plea."

"Nobody believed me when I said that I hadn't slept with him, but everyone believed me when I said I had." She shrugged. "So, it must be true, right, Detective?"

"Tell me why you admitted to everything when you did."

Jane dropped her eyes and was silent. She began to say something but her voice caught and she raised a hand to cover her mouth, fighting to gain control. When she lowered her hand to her lap and looked at Rouleau, her composure was back in place. She said, "It seemed like the right time to tell the truth."

"Your husband announced your divorce two weeks after you confessed, a year into your sentence."

"He did, but it had nothing to do with my decision to confess to my sins."

"When did you start to have feelings for Devon?"

She blinked and bit her bottom lip. She took her time responding. "Let's say that my feelings for Devon blossomed after he decided."

"Decided … what?"

"Decided to have the affair."

"You're saying that he instigated what went on between you?"

"Most certainly. He set everything into motion."

Rouleau checked his notes. "You've never said this before. In fact, Devon and Charlie Hanson both claimed that you made the first moves."

"I know what they claimed."

"You must have been upset when Devon admitted to everything that had gone on. He'd have known what it would do to your career and marriage."

"I was upset, yes."

"Were you upset with him when you got out of prison?"

"No. I'd accepted what happened. I only wanted to see my kids again."

"What would you say if I told you we have a witness who put you in the neighbourhood the night that Devon was murdered?"

She closed her eyes. "They'd be lying."

Kala glanced at Rouleau. They had no such witness and he was walking a fine legal line with the wording of his question. He was watching Jane with a curious look on his face. As far as Kala could see, he hadn't gotten any closer to getting her to confess to killing Devon. In fact, she was slipping further away from them the more he probed. Kala was struck by the waste this woman had made of her life and the loss. What she'd done had harmed Devon, his family, the school, and her own family, but her actions had destroyed her most of all.

Rouleau looked at Kala. "Anything else you'd like to ask Jane?"

Was he admitting defeat or was he trying to throw Jane off? Kala thought for a moment. "What are your plans going forward, Jane, you know, after all of this is settled?"

Jane's head swivelled in Kala's direction. Her initial startled expression quickly disappeared. "No plans. I'm hoping to see my kids on a regular basis once Adam has time to set up a schedule. I might start taking classes at the college. I'm going to need to make a career change."

"Will you continue living where you are now?"

"For a while. I'm thinking of moving out of Kingston but will see how everything goes. For now, I'm staying for my children."

Rouleau checked his watch and Kala did as well. Six hours had gone by without learning anything new. Kala thought it might have been too early to bring Jane in this second time without all the forensics completed. They didn't have any evidence to leverage a confession. On the other hand, it never hurt to get the main suspect giving statements on record that could be later disproven. Somewhere in all of Jane's six hours of testimony, she might have made a slip.

Rouleau asked, "When you were in prison, could you see yourself starting back up with Devon when you got out? Did you see a future with him?"

"God, no."

"How do you feel about his death?"

"Shocked but not devastated, if that's what you're after."

Rouleau closed his notebook and studied her with his penetrating green eyes. After a few moments of silence, he got to his feet and looked down at her. "We're done for now, Mrs. Thompson. Please be ready to come in again and keep to your routine. The officers who brought you will take you wherever you like."

Once alone in the hall, Rouleau said to Kala, "Got time to meet at the Merchant? It's been a long afternoon and I could use a beer."

She was sorry to turn him down. "I have to get home and take Taiku out. He's been acting strangely and I want to keep an eye on him."

"Another time then."

Kala returned to the office and grabbed her leather jacket. The rain was still coming down when she stepped outside but lighter than it had been. She zigzagged around puddles as she ran to her truck, her hair soaked by the time she made it inside the cab. She pulled out her phone to check for messages before turning on the engine. Caroline Russell had left two voice mails. Kala accessed the messages and listened as the rain pattered on the roof.

Caroline's voice was loud in her ear. *Had she made a decision about a visit with Dawn? Please call back as soon as she got the chance.* Kala erased both messages without listening to the second and turned the key in the ignition. After all the system had done to her and to Dawn, now they were pressuring her to fix things after Tamara Jones made it clear that her involvement was no longer wanted. The foster mother Colette had brushed her away like a bothersome fly.

Kala turned on the windshield wipers and put the truck into gear. She glanced in the rear-view mirror and stared into her own reflected eyes. The anger and pain gave her pause. *This isn't about you. Stop taking this personally — Dawn's welfare trumps your wounded feelings.*

She pulled out of the parking spot and bounced through the puddles toward the exit onto Division Street. As soon as she got home, she'd call Caroline Russell and agree to a meeting. She'd want Caroline to promise that this would be a long-term arrangement and that Dawn wouldn't be used like a yo-yo that they'd pull back when it suited them. The social worker's word wouldn't be worth much if her own history was anything to go by, but she'd tuck away her misgivings and give the system another chance for Dawn's sake.

Decision made, Kala felt lighter at the thought of seeing Dawn again.

Jane refused the offer of a lift home from the blond police officer who looked like a Viking and caught the bus instead. Luckily, she reached the bus stop as one was pulling in and she was on schedule to make her four-thirty meeting at the Iron Duke on Wellington Street. The bus would take her close enough that it would be a short walk in the rain.

As she paid her money, she scanned across the street. A plain blue sedan was idling half a block away and was pulling into traffic as she took a seat at the back of the bus. Through the back window, she watched the car follow the bus toward the downtown. Two men sat in the front seat, neither of whom she recognized, but she knew they were undercover cops. She took careful note of their faces.

The car was a block back when she got off the bus. She kept her head lowered and stepped around puddles as she cut across to Wellington Street. The wind was brisk and wet and she pulled the hood up on her coat. A quick glance back at the street and no sign of the blue sedan, but she had no doubt it was somewhere close by.

She looked around the restaurant's interior and chose the empty table wedged into the corner near the brick archway that separated the main rooms. She'd be able to keep an eye on the door without looking obvious and was away from the windows. As instructed, she would wait for her contact to find her. She hoped the cops would stay outside but wasn't counting on it.

She studied the menu. She was way past hungry after her day in the police station and decided to splurge on the meatloaf with cheddar mashed potatoes and gravy. She ordered a glass of red wine when the waitress came by for her order. She'd earned a drink, the first since her release.

While she waited for her meal, a young Asian man carrying a beer slid into the booth across from her. He had spiked, straight black hair dyed red at the tips and was wearing a green duffle coat. He smiled when she looked up. "Kimmy said you were a looker. She wasn't kidding."

"Hieu?"

"Yes."

"Thanks for coming. How's your sister?" Jane glanced toward the door. One of the cops was coming into the restaurant and looking around. He spotted her and walked into the other side.

"Good. She's good. Said to say hi. She's signed up for that college nurse helper course now that she has her grade twelve. She says you turned it around for her."

"Kim did it for herself. Tell her how happy I am that she's going back to school."

"Our mom wants you to come for supper so we can all thank you."

"That would be nice, but maybe not for a while."

The smile reached Hieu's eyes. "Of course. I'll let her know you're on vacation, having some family time."

"Hopefully, you'll be right. Don't look now but a cop just came in and we have to act like you're trying to pick me up."

"Not a problem."

The waitress arrived with Jane's meal. Hieu said to Jane, "So, are you from around here?"

"I don't mean to be rude, but I'd rather eat my supper alone if you don't mind."

The waitress eyed Hieu. "Everything okay, ma'am?"

"Yes, no problem. I can handle it."

The waitress took a last hard look at Hieu before she walked away.

Hieu said from behind his raised glass. "How do you want to do this?"

"I left my jacket on your side. The packet is underneath. You can take it and exchange it with yours whenever the moment seems right."

"Cool." He reached into his jacket pocket and dropped something onto the floor. "Damn," he said and hunched over to pick it up, twisting his body sideways in the booth. When he straightened, he lifted his beer and stood. "Maybe I'll see you around."

"Yeah, thanks for understanding I'm not up for company tonight."

Hieu's face expressed fake disappointment. "We could have gotten to know each other better."

"Another time."

"Yeah, another time."

Jane watched him saunter over to the bar on the other side of the arch and take a chair near the front of the room. He immediately pulled out his cellphone and began scrolling. She ate her meal slowly and avoided looking at Hieu. When she finished eating and pushed her plate away, he'd left the bar. She signalled for the waitress to bring her bill.

"The gentleman who just left paid for your dinner. I guess he was sorry for bothering you." The waitress smiled. "This is your lucky day."

"Thanks. He was cute but I wasn't in the mood. A long day, you know?" She smiled. *And I really hope you're right about my luck changing.*

"Yeah, I know what you mean. Some nights you don't need the hassle."

Once outside, Jane pulled her hood up over her head and went in search of a bus stop. She didn't feel like making the forty-minute walk home in the cold rain. She wondered what the cops would think if she crossed the street and knocked on their window and asked for a ride home. The thought made her smile. She'd seen the one talking with her waitress, likely finding out what had been going on between her and Hieu. She was counting on their role-playing to be enough to put the cops off the scent.

When she got home, she took the packet from Hieu out of her jacket pocket. He'd wrapped the three passports in brown paper and put them into a zip-lock bag. She pulled them out and carefully looked through each. She touched Ben's and Olivia's faces with her fingertips. The passports looked real to her. Kim had promised that Hieu would come through. Jane hoped she'd be able to thank them properly sometime but wasn't counting on it. Once she and the kids got out of Canada, all ties would have to be broken.

Before taking a hot shower, she hid the passports under a floorboard that she'd worked up under the carpet in the living room. Sitting on the bed afterward in her housecoat with her hair in a towel, she called Sandra.

"Good thing we cancelled tonight's dinner. My interview went late. Does tomorrow still work? I can take the bus. No, it's no trouble. I know how much you hate driving. Are you sure I can't bring anything? Yeah, I'm looking forward to seeing you, too."

CHAPTER EIGHTEEN

Rouleau was having trouble sleeping. Ever since Frances's death, he'd been unable to put his grief away and let his mind relax. It was okay during the day when he was busy, but nighttime was another story. This morning, he woke at three thirty, but lay in bed until five so as not to waken his father in the next bedroom. Then he got up and had a quick shower before going to the kitchen to make breakfast. He got the coffee brewing, then turned his attention to scrambled eggs, sausage, and hash browns with toasted English muffins. Rouleau liked to give his father a good meal to start the day since he never knew how long he'd be at work with a murder case underway.

Rouleau sat at the table with a cup of coffee and his laptop reading the news while his dad shuffled around in the next room, getting set for the day. Henri had aged over the past year. A broken leg followed by a heart attack had left him physically weaker. Frances's death had devastated him. Even though Rouleau and Frances had been divorced, she'd always kept in touch with Henri and they spoke often on the phone. Rouleau only found out after she died how often she'd made the trip from Ottawa to Kingston to visit his father the years before Rouleau moved back.

Henri told Rouleau at her funeral, "I feel like I've lost my child."

His dad was dressed in grey slacks and his favourite frayed pullover. His white hair was combed back and damp from the shower. He sat in front of the place setting that Rouleau had arranged for him and lifted the napkin from the placemat and shook it out. "You're turning into quite the gourmet breakfast cook." His sharp blue eyes surveyed the kitchen and landed on Rouleau. "Rough night again, son?"

Rouleau got up and poured his dad a cup of coffee before refilling his own. "I was awake early but got a few good hours in."

"You need to be sharp to solve this murder case. How old was the boy again?"

"Seventeen. In grade twelve."

Henri shook his head. "Such a waste of a life. I understand he had a sad history, as well. I followed that trial with the Thompson teacher. For the longest time, I thought she was telling the truth."

Rouleau turned from the stove where he was spooning eggs onto their plates. "What made you think that?"

"Something in her eyes and the set of her shoulders when the media filmed her going to and from the courthouse. Call it an old man's intuition. Obviously, I was wrong. Does it look like she killed him? I ask this knowing you can't say much."

Rouleau scooped hash browns and sausages onto their plates and brought them to the table. He buttered the toasted muffins and set the plate on the table next to his dad before sitting down. "We've no evidence linking anybody yet."

Henri took a mouthful of eggs. "Excellent eggs. Just how I like them." He chewed slowly before taking a sip of coffee. "What else is on your mind besides the case?"

"An HR problem. One of the members of the team is disruptive but hasn't given me enough grounds to get rid of him."

"That cop Woodhouse, is it?"

"The very one. I thought a new partner would help straighten him around, but he's become something of a bully to the new young recruit. He's also barely civil to Kala Stonechild." Rouleau spread jam on his muffin. "I had a beer with Gundersund last night and he's worried. Thinks Woodhouse's attitude will drive both Bennett and Stonechild to take jobs elsewhere."

"What are you going to do about it?"

"My first step will be to speak with the two of them to see how big the problem is. Then I'll have to figure out a way to bring Woodhouse into line."

"What about moving him sideways into another division?"

"All options are on the table."

They finished eating and Rouleau stood to pour one last cup of coffee. "What are your plans today, Dad?"

"I'm going to watch the afternoon World Series game, and if the weather clears, I'll take a walk down to the water. Might get in a nap."

"I'm driving into work but will check in to see how the game's going. Pork chops okay for supper?"

"I'll cook up some applesauce between innings."

"I'll try to be home by six."

The team gathered in the meeting area when Rouleau arrived in the office at nine o'clock. They appeared listless, but it was the end of the first week with no real leads, the time when spirits tended to flag. Rouleau gave some inspirational words before launching into what they had so far and making the day's assignments.

"The bar-to-bar inquiries turned up nothing. If Devon Eton was drinking beer in a pub or restaurant, nobody remembers him. The door-to-door in the apartment building and houses across from Murney Point turned up nothing either."

"See no evil, hear no evil," commented Bedouin. He looked at Tanya Morrison and back at Rouleau. "We've checked out a few of the calls from the hotline but nothing panned out."

Morrison nodded agreement. "And the calls are drying up. Will you be making another plea for information in the media?"

Rouleau said, "Yes. Heath is waiting for us to give him something new to talk about but he'll call a press conference by mid-week regardless. Anybody else?"

When they remained silent, Rouleau continued, "I had a couple of officers tailing Jane Thompson last night after we interviewed her. She took the bus to the Iron Duke and had supper. An Asian fellow joined her for a bit, but the waitress confirmed that he was trying to pick Jane up and she rejected his advances. The waitress said that the guy was not a regular and didn't know his name. He paid in cash."

"Any follow-up needed?" Gundersund asked.

"We don't have the resources to track him down based on the little information we have. The officers tailing Jane said he was unknown to her, so no red flags."

"Are they following her again today?"

"Heath isn't keen on using resources to keep tabs on her but said we could follow her during regular hours. No overtime."

Stonechild spoke for the first time. "So she's on her own between four in the evening and seven in the morning."

Rouleau nodded. "Not ideal, but nothing links her to the murder yet. From what the officers are reporting, she doesn't do much except go to work and then home and periodically out for groceries or a walk. She jogs in the morning. Nothing exciting so far."

"Should we start re-interviewing witnesses?" Stonechild asked.

Rouleau nodded. "We have to figure out where Devon went after school and who he was with. Re-cover old ground and see if anyone has remembered anything. Maybe some of his classmates were away or held something back. It's worth another attempt."

Gundersund stood. "Woodhouse and Bennett, we'd like you to go to Devon's school tomorrow and re-interview his football team, classmates, and teachers. Read through the files and see if you can work out anything we missed. Cross-check the class lists because we didn't interview some of the students who were away the day we were there. Bedouin and Morrison will be back at the neighbourhood next to Murney Point on a second canvass. Stonechild and I will be visiting the Etons, Hansons, and Jane Thompson's family."

Rouleau said, "Remember to share anything new that you find out. Forensics should have its full report in tomorrow, so hopefully, they'll have something concrete for us to work with, specifically the exact cause of death and the tox screen results. We should also be getting a report on the contents of Devon's computer and iPad early this week. Thanks again for working another weekend. We'll take a day off soon, especially those of you who were in yesterday as well as today."

The team broke up to spend the rest of the morning on the phone and combing through documents. Rouleau retired to his office and sifted through the pile of paperwork that Vera had left for him. The bureaucratic end of his job was what would drive him into retirement, although that was still a few years off.

Stonechild knocked on his door at two o'clock, waving a tray with sandwiches and coffee from a nearby deli. "Lunch is served," she said, and accepted his offer to sit and keep him company while they ate.

"Where are the others?" he asked, taking a bite of ham and cheese.

"Knocking on doors. Woodhouse and Bennett offered to help Bedouin and Morrison canvass near Murney Point. Gundersund is running a few errands and plans to be back in half an hour."

"Good. I've been wondering what your take is on Jane Thompson."

"She's hard to read. I'm not sure if she was always so closed off or if her years in prison made her that way. She strikes me as smart but extremely guarded ... no pun intended." She smiled. "What do you think?"

"Much the same. The *Whig* reporter Marci Stokes waylaid me the other evening after work, and she's questioning why Jane confessed after holding fast to her innocence throughout the trial and one year into her sentence."

"That struck me as odd, too. Jane's answer to your question about why she suddenly confessed seemed evasive."

"Sometimes people who perpetrate sexual crimes on kids don't believe they've done anything wrong. We've all heard about the underground network of pedophiles giving one another validation and mutual approbation. Often, they feel superior and above the rules."

"I could try to get close to Jane and get her to talk."

"Except that you sat in on her interview and she's unlikely to let her guard down." Rouleau thought for a moment. "I know she's not our favourite reporter, but Marci Stokes managed to make a connection with Jane and even bought her a coffee."

Stonechild met his gaze. "I'm not holding a grudge against Marci for writing a story about me, even if I wish she hadn't. Everything she wrote was true." She shrugged. "If you like, I can track her down and see if she'll try again with Jane."

"At this point, it couldn't hurt. Meet with Marci and see if she'll give us a hand."

"I'll call her when I get back to my desk."

Marci Stokes agreed to meet Kala at five o'clock at a café at the corner of Ontario Street and William, a stone's throw from Lake Ontario. Kala drove toward the waterfront and parked her truck on a side street a few blocks away. The short walk was invigorating. It felt good to be in the fresh air after sitting at her desk all day. The rain had stopped early afternoon, and while the air felt damp, the breeze was lighter than when Kala had stepped outside her house in the morning and surprisingly warm.

The Common Market sign, bolted into the limestone wall above red awnings, was a painting of shipbuilders and sailboats with gold lettering inside a navy border. Kala had driven by on occasion but never entered the building and was charmed by the brick fireplace, limestone walls, and warm woodwork. The tables and chairs were mismatched but the decor worked, especially when she smelled the rich scent of coffee and fresh baking — breads and croissants, chocolate and cinnamon. Kala searched the tables of customers but

Marci hadn't yet arrived, so she walked to the counter and ordered a caffè latte and lemon square. The girls at the table next to the fireplace got up to leave and Kala grabbed their spot. She settled in and took a moment to savour the lemon pastry and milky coffee.

The front door opened as Kala took the last bite of the tart and Marci rushed into the café. She spotted Kala and signalled a greeting before heading straight to the counter. She arrived at the table with a scone and coffee and shrugged out of her trench coat as she sat down. "Sorry I'm late. I had to finish a story before I left the office."

"Thanks for meeting me on short notice."

"Yeah, well, I was glad you called because I've been wanting to apologize for that article about your homeless stint. If it means anything, I had second thoughts after I wrote it, but my editor printed the story without my knowledge. The worst part was that he edited out the paragraph where I expressed my admiration for the way you turned your life around. I hope the story didn't cause any problems. Rouleau reprimanded me with a rather terse email."

"Forget it. I have. I actually wanted to meet with you about Jane Thompson. I understand you had coffee with her."

Marci looked at Kala while biting into her scone, her eyes searching Kala's face. "So no make-up sex," she said, smiling. "I guess I can't blame you or Rouleau if you were pissed at me." She slumped back in the chair. "Yeah, I had coffee with Jane. Understandably, she's not doing well. Her former colleagues and neighbours painted a picture of this dreamy, smart woman. Good with kids, family-focused. Principled and seemingly above the tawdry. I'd say she lost all that mattered to her when she slept with her student. Now, she's alone, suspicious, and haunted."

"Did you make a connection with her?"

"Hard to know." Marci reached into her bag and pulled out her tape recorder. "I recorded our conversation without her knowing. And before you think I'm a total miscreant, I had no plans to use it." She clicked play and Kala leaned closer to listen.

The tape finished and Kala straightened. "A bit muffled but clear enough. She doesn't give anything away, does she?"

"No. She wouldn't even deny killing Devon when I gave her the chance. I thought she might have. The part I find interesting is when she says that after all she did, her husband is keeping the kids from her. That doesn't fit in anywhere unless she killed Devon as a way to show her husband she was atoning?"

Kala replayed Jane's words in her mind. "You're right. Something is off. Would you be willing to make contact with her again and try to gain her confidence?"

"I'm guessing off the record."

"We can discuss releasing the information after you meet with her and we see what she reveals."

Marci tore off a piece of scone and popped it into her mouth. Her eyes again studied Kala's face while she decided whether to play along. "You and I are a lot alike, you know. We both work in male-dominated professions and have to toil twice as hard to get half as far. Where do you plan to take your career, Kala Stonechild? Where do you see yourself in five, ten years?"

Kala had no idea how to respond. Where did she even see herself next week? "I haven't given it much thought."

"Let me give you an important bit of advice. Have a plan and stick to it. Don't let anyone or anything distract you along the way. I knew where I wanted to go — editor-in-chief of a major newspaper — and I let myself get sidetracked by a man, who now wants nothing more than to destroy me. I've been reduced to compromising my integrity to stay in the game."

"You're a good reporter. I started following your work after you wrote that piece about me."

"I'm a damn good reporter, and I would have made a damn good editor-in-chief. Now, I'm reduced to making deals with the police to get a story ahead of the CBC. Yeah, I'll have another go at Jane Thompson, but only because I smell a story and I owe you one."

"You could record her again, and I'll stay in the background."

"We aren't forgetting that this is a woman who stuck by her claims of innocence for a year after she went to prison. She's not going to get tripped up at this point for murder."

"No, but she might give us something to follow up on. If she gets comfortable with you, she might make a slip."

"I wouldn't bet the farm on it."

Jane sat in her sister's kitchen and tried to imagine herself somewhere else, a trick she'd mastered in the prison cell. Sandra had been bustling around since her arrival, putting a roast chicken into the oven, peeling potatoes, and whipping up a dessert of cream puffs and chocolate sauce. She'd refused Jane's offer of help and sat her at the dining room table with the bottle of Merlot that Jane had brought and was now steadily making her way through. At last, no more work was to be done and Sandra couldn't avoid sitting with her any longer. Jane pulled herself out of a daydream and offered to share her wine.

"I'll get a glass." Sandra was up and flitting around the kitchen again, her long, braided hair swishing back and forth as she moved. Jane watched her and tried to decide if this activity was more frenetic than usual. She concluded that it was.

"What's got you upset?" Jane asked when Sandra had settled back across from her. Jane filled her glass almost to the brim and topped up her own. The bottle was empty and she hoped her sister had another on hand for their meal.

Sandra stared at her. "You mean besides the fact that my sister just served three years for having sex with a student who happened to get himself murdered a month after she gets out of prison?"

"I've got it under control."

"That's the same thing you said after they arrested you."

"I won't make the same mistakes."

Sandra's lip lifted in a half-smile. "You've changed then, because you never planned ahead. Up until you were charged, you drifted through life and always stepped over the bad stuff without getting your shoes dirty. Speaking of which, have you been to see our mother since your release?"

"No. From what you said, she won't recognize me, anyway."

"Some days are more lucid than others. She might pull herself together enough to give you one final raking over." Sandra laughed and her large chest lifted and fell under her flowered smock top.

"I wouldn't put it past her. She must have been in pig heaven knowing that every bad thing she envisioned for me came true."

"Man, the harder she came down on you, the harder you were to pin down. You drove her absolutely crazy, you know. She couldn't figure out how to make you hurt enough to repent."

But she had, over and over again. Jane was good at pretending, but only because she couldn't face the reality. She became a dreamer and compliant to survive. Even now, she cringed at the thought of seeing her mother's face again. At the end of her life together with Adam, her mother had been like an ugly black cloud following her around. Jane had believed that Adam and the kids and a teaching job would make her mother happy, but they'd only revved up her religious zeal. "Your perfect husband married you for sex and how long will that last? He's bound to find out how wicked and vain you are. I fear for your children if he doesn't. God sees all and knows all and if you don't repent your sins …" (Her mother always moaned at this point as if in unspeakable agony.) "Well, all I can say is that there'll be a day of reckoning for you, my girl. My only hope is that I'm around to see you brought down off your high horse. Why I didn't stop at one daughter, I'll never know."

Adam had used his charm to win her mother over — as far as her mother could be won over — but he avoided her as years went on, passing pleasantries with her on the phone before handing it over to Jane. "I don't know why you don't make a break from her," he'd say afterward, and she couldn't explain why she kept on taking the calls. Perhaps it came down to the belief that her mother was right. She didn't deserve her life. She was shallow and evil inside where nobody could see and her mother was her penance.

Sandra raised her wine glass and clinked Jane's. "To never letting our mother's fire and brimstone justice bring us down again."

Jane met her sister's eyes. "I'll drink to that."

They swallowed gulps of wine.

Sandra got up to take the chicken out of the oven to let it rest before cutting. She put potatoes and stuffing into bowls and set them back into the oven to keep warm. "I used to be so jealous of you," she said, returning with a salad and plates. "You were such a beautiful little kid, like a blond angel with eyes that could charm the devil. I think Mother was jealous too, if it comes down to it. Dad tried to get custody of you after he took off with Judy, did you know that?"

"No."

"Well, he did. Just you, though. He was quite willing to leave me with her."

The bitterness in Sandra's voice was raw pain and Jane reached out her hand to cover her sister's larger one. She felt the familiar anxiety fluttering in her chest trying to escape. "I'm sorry, Sandra," she said. "I wouldn't have left without you." Why hadn't she known her father had wanted her with him? Her mother had told her so many times that she and Sandra were the reason he ran away that this version of the truth was part of her DNA. "He didn't want to be saddled with you kids." This realignment of the truth shook her to her core, but now was not the time to say so.

Sandra took the foil off the chicken and cut off pieces with a long, sharp knife. She filled the platter and brought it to the table, returning for the potatoes and stuffing. Mercifully, she made one more trip to the wine rack for a bottle of pinot noir.

"You'll stay tonight," Sandra invited. "I don't like to think of you alone on the bus half corked."

"I'd like to stay, thanks." The surprise was that Jane meant it. She looked at her sister's bowed head as she cut into a piece of chicken and thought about all the misunderstanding over the years. They'd competed for crumbs of affection and become competitors until Jane moved out and married Adam, her saviour, or so she'd believed. She'd shut Sandra and her mother out of her married life except for the odd phone call, wanting to be free of them both. Now, the only one to stand by her was her sister. "Thanks for all your visits while I was inside. I never had a chance to thank you. They meant a lot."

Sandra looked up and the bit of happiness in her face made Jane's breath catch. "You're welcome, sis," Sandra said before standing with effort and picking up their plates. "How about I get us some of that dessert to go with the rest of the wine?"

"Perfect. You're spoiling me though. It'll be hard going back to my own cooking."

"You never could master putting a meal together." Sandra rolled her eyes and laughed. "I never could figure out how you got by in life…." Her voice trailed away and she turned her back to scrape their plates into the recycling bag.

I couldn't figure it out either, obviously, or I wouldn't be living in a student apartment, working in the Sally Ann, and wondering if I'm ever going to see my kids again.

"Well, I'm still standing."

Jane reached for the bottle and refilled their glasses.

CHAPTER NINETEEN

Monday, exactly one week after Devon Eton's body was found at Murney Point, the homicide team got down to business with renewed purpose. Bedouin and Morrison took a few officers to complete the door-to-door canvass that had been started the day before. They remained hopeful of finding a witness they'd missed on the first go around even though the odds were getting slimmer with every passing hour. Woodhouse and Bennett returned to Devon Eton's school to re-interview classmates and teachers while Kala and Gundersund started their morning by driving together to the Etons' to finally interview Devon's younger sister, Sophie. Hilary Eton had confirmed by phone that they were back from their trip and waiting at home for the officers to arrive at eight thirty.

"Sophie needs the kid glove treatment so you have the lead on this one," said Gundersund. "I'll try to get the parents to give you some space."

"I have a feeling that won't be easy."

"Maybe they'll be less intense since it's been a week for them to absorb what happened to their son."

"Or their rage will have grown because we haven't arrested Jane Thompson. I can understand their hatred for the woman."

Mitchell Eton yanked open the front door before they had a chance to ring the bell. He filled the doorway dressed in a navy suit, the tailoring expensive enough to hide his square bulk. His black hair was glistening with gel and combed back from his broad forehead. Kala could see by the set of his mouth and the fire in his dark eyes that a week hadn't been long enough to mellow his anger.

A car pulled up and idled at the curb. Kala and Gundersund turned and looked at the same time as Mitchell said, "I was hoping to see you before my cab arrived. I have to catch a shuttle to Toronto, so Hilary will take the interview with Sophie." He stooped and picked up a satchel on the floor next to him. "Sophie is still fragile so please go easy on her. Hilary isn't doing much better. If I didn't need to be in Toronto today for an emergency board meeting, I'd be here to help them through this. I suppose it's no use asking, but I'll be returning late afternoon if you could postpone until then? I phoned the station but you'd already left."

"We wanted to speak with you as well, but we can come back another day for that. We'd prefer to speak with Sophie and your wife now."

Mitchell looked inside the house, appearing undecided. He took a deep breath and let it out in a sigh. "Go easy on them," he said again, and stepped aside to let them into the hall. "Hilary had a heart attack two years ago and stress is the last thing she needs. If this meeting wasn't about a takeover of my company, I would not be going. I'll be doing my damnedest to be home by five."

Gundersund and Kala walked unescorted into the living room, where they found Hilary and Sophie sitting on the couch. Sophie's long white-blond hair was loose and she reminded Kala of a gangly colt, all leg and knobby knees under a pleated skirt. Hilary was again dressed in black and looked marginally less distraught than on their last visit, but not by much. Kala pulled a chair closer so that she sat directly in Sophie's sightline. She asked, "How are you both doing?"

Sophie looked at her mother. "We're okay."

Hilary squeezed Sophie's hand. "We'll be having a celebration of Devon's life on Friday afternoon. Just family and closest friends. Mitchell and I decided against a funeral."

"That will bring some comfort." Kala crossed her legs and folded her hands on her thigh. "Sophie, can you tell me about last Monday?"

"I went to school."

"Did you see Devon in the morning?"

"No, he had football practice and left before I got up."

"Were you in contact in the afternoon?"

Sophie looked at her mother. Hilary took over responding. "He tried to reach her but they never met up."

"Is that correct, Sophie?"

"Yes. He wanted … he wanted to meet me but I had to stay at school to speak to my teacher and she kept me late. I never saw him."

Kala had interviewed a lot of witnesses over her career and knew the tells when someone was lying. Sophie's breathing had changed and her voice was higher and shallower than before, the physical responses to a change in her heart rate and blood flow. She'd raised a hand to her throat, an automatic response that people did when trying to protect themselves. The repeated words and sudden movement of her head toward her mother were further tells. Kala asked, "Why did Devon want to meet you?"

"We ... we were ... we were going to go shopping. Mom's birthday is coming up and he said that we could pick out a gift together."

"Where were you supposed to meet?"

"At the park."

"But he didn't show up?"

Sophie nodded.

"Did he let you know he wouldn't be coming?"

This time, Sophie shook her head and looked down at the floor. Kala glanced at Hilary, who was sitting motionless with lips pursed and eyes staring straight ahead. *She knows that Sophie is lying.* Kala asked Sophie, "Were you worried when he wasn't home when you got there?"

"I thought he might be with Charlie." Her words were barely above a whisper.

"Did you tell your mother that he hadn't come home when he texted you that he would see you in a few minutes?"

Sophie shook her head again. Hilary could have been made of stone, her body so rigid and still.

"How did you get along with your brother?"

"Fine. He was … out a lot."

"Anywhere in particular?"

"I don't know. With Charlie, I guess."

"Do you like Charlie?"

"Yeah, he's okay."

Kala was running out of ideas and patience. She looked over at Gundersund. He flipped a page in his notepad before asking, "Sophie, do you hang around with Charlie, or Tiffany, perhaps?"

Sophie turned her head and met his eyes. Kala saw panic in her expression. "Tiffany is a year older than me. We have *nothing* in common."

Hilary stirred from her catatonic state and put an arm around Sophie's shoulders. "Devon and Charlie were friends, but we didn't have anything more to do with the family."

Gundersund nodded as if this was what he'd known all along. "Your husband said that you've been ill, Mrs. Eton," he said. "How is your health now?"

"Mitchell worries too much. I'm still on medication but that will probably be for the rest of my life. My doctor says I'm to resume all normal activity."

"I'm glad to hear that. Well, we won't take up any more of your day, but we'll be keeping you up to date on the investigation. We have counselling services if you'd like us to arrange a visit. I know that we offered this before, but maybe you're ready to consider speaking with someone now." He looked at Sophie and back to Hilary.

"No, I don't think that will be necessary."

Kala said, "Sophie might benefit …"

"I said we're fine." Hilary's voice hardened, much like the tone of voice she'd used when she snapped at Mitchell.

Kala studied her for a moment and said, "We understand, but know that we have help on hand if ever you should need it."

Caroline Russell phoned at lunchtime and set up a place for Kala to meet Dawn after school on Wednesday. The foster parents were fine with the meeting, but nothing could be arranged before mid-week. Kala added the time and place to her electronic calendar. Wednesday was two days off and she would try to put the visit out of her mind until then; otherwise, she'd be climbing the walls at the thought of Dawn floundering in foster care for even one more hour.

Gundersund stopped by her desk. "Rouleau wants to see us in his office."

Rouleau was speaking on the desk phone but he waved them in. He made his apology to the person on the other end and hung up. "The forensics report is in. Devon Eton was hit in the back of the head with a blunt object three times and died from massive hemorrhaging at the base of his skull. Time of death was between ten and midnight Sunday evening, although closer to eleven is the most likely time."

Kala looked up from her notepad. "No blows to other parts of his body?"

"No. The other marks on his body came from being in the elements overnight. Forensics says that identifying the object is difficult but it was broad and rounded."

"Any drugs in his system?" Gundersund asked.

"Traces of marijuana and about the legal limit in alcohol."

"So not impaired."

"Not legally. He was healthy and fit. Nothing else of note except maybe that he'd eaten chips and peanuts but nothing else since lunch."

"It sounds like he was in a bar," said Kala.

"The officers had no luck finding the one he was in if so, but I agree that he does appear to have been in a bar by his stomach contents." Rouleau handed them printouts of the report. "I'm joining Heath shortly to ask the public if anyone remembers seeing him that night, particularly in a pub. Bedouin and Morrison will be back on the phone lines tomorrow. I've got other officers on the lines for the rest of the day."

"He was supposed to meet his sister in the park but never showed up, according to Sophie. She went home and thought nothing more of it," said Gundersund.

"I don't think she was telling us the entire truth," said Kala.

"It's too bad you couldn't interview her without a parent present. She might have done something after school that her parents didn't know about, like meeting up with a boy. Kids of that age don't like to share with their parents," said Rouleau.

"I know, but the mother wasn't pressing Sophie to tell us everything. They both seemed to be hiding something, in fact."

"What's your next move?"

Kala looked at Gundersund. "We need a strategy meeting."

Gundersund checked his watch. "I have an appointment with the computer techie in a few minutes to go over what they found on Devon's machines. Do you want to sit in? We could start strategizing afterward."

"That's okay. The computer debrief won't take two of us. We can connect later."

She waited until Gundersund left for his meeting before grabbing her jacket and going to get her truck from the parking lot. She had an idea that this witness might speak to her alone without Gundersund present. If nothing came of it, he'd never have to know.

From her vantage point across the street from the school, Kala spotted Tiffany Hanson clumping down the front steps a few metres behind a group of boys. She was wearing a black hoodie over tight black leggings and high-top runners, slouching away from the school property and lighting up a cigarette halfway down the street. She let the cigarette dangle from a corner of her mouth while she checked her cellphone as she walked with head down. Kala looked back toward the school entrance and debated waiting for Charlie to appear or chasing after Tiffany. The opportunity was too good to pass up. She got out of her truck and raced after Tiffany's retreating figure.

"What the hell?" Tiffany clutched her chest. "You scared the crap out of me." She glared at Kala through eyes smudged in kohl, once again sporting the startled-raccoon look.

"Sorry about that. Can I walk with you for a bit?" Kala put her hands into her jacket pockets and fell into stride with Tiffany.

"What're you doing here?" Tiffany glanced sideways at her and then back at her cellphone. She flicked her lit cigarette onto the street.

"I was at the school checking on a few things when I saw you leaving. How are you doing?"

"Fine."

"I imagine you must feel bad about Devon."

"What do you mean?"

"He was best friends with your brother and always hanging out at your house. He might even have felt like another brother."

"Are you *kidding me*? Devon was *not* like my brother." She smiled for the first time. "There's only one Charlie Hanson, if you haven't noticed."

Kala smiled back. A small connection that lessened the tension. They kept walking. Kala said, "I've been trying to understand Devon and Charlie's friendship. Who would you say was the leader between the two?"

"I don't want to talk about my brother behind his back. Especially not with the fuzz."

"Do you know what they were fighting about before Devon left the school?"

Tiffany stopped walking and turned to look at her. "Are you trying to pin this on Charlie, because

I can tell you that he didn't kill Devon. He didn't have the guts no matter how he acts."

"I'm not trying to blame this on Charlie. I'm trying to figure out what was going on with Devon that day. He was supposed to meet his sister, Sophie, and never showed up."

An odd look crossed Tiffany's face before she turned and resumed walking. She started picking up speed and Kala quickened her pace.

"What is it, Tiffany? Any detail or bit of insight could help us to find Devon's killer. Are you friends with Sophie?"

"No, we aren't friends. I wasn't friends with Devon either and I don't care that he's dead. Maybe you should arrest me. Mom tells me often enough I'm going to end up locked away if I don't shape up and get better grades. I'm riding the rails to hell."

"It's normal to try things out at your age. You strike me as a smart kid."

Tiffany turned her head and stared at Kala. "Yeah, I read that you were homeless in your teens. A drunk. What was that like?" Her face was impossible to read behind the black eye makeup and thick foundation. Her lips were tight together in a shimmery white line.

"Not something I'd recommend." Kala might have resented the question from someone else but could see that Tiffany wasn't trying to be rude. Real curiosity lay behind her question.

"Did you turn tricks or what?"

"No, I just drank. Cheap whiskey was my beverage of choice."

"But where did you get the money to buy booze?"

"Panhandling. People are amazingly generous if it means they don't have to think about you for the rest of their day. Running away from home is a tough go, Tiffany. It's better if you can make things work with your mom."

"I guess."

They were nearing an intersection and Kala thought about turning back to get her truck. She'd likely missed Charlie and had somewhere else to be. Tiffany started talking before she had a chance to say goodbye.

"My dad drank, too, but he didn't know when to quit. The diabetes and alcohol gave him a heart attack and put him into a coma." Tiffany shoved her middle finger skyward. "And then he died."

"I'm sorry."

"Yeah, me too. He was a good guy in spite of being hammered half the time."

Kala touched her on the arm. "I'm heading back to my truck. If I give you my personal cellphone number, will you promise to call me if you're thinking about a residence change or need to talk something over? I'm a good listener ... even if I am the fuzz."

Tiffany stopped walking and clicked a few keys on her phone. She looked up. "Okay, give it to me."

Kala dictated the number while Tiffany typed it into her address book. "Here's my business card, too, with my work number. Leave a message on either voice mail and I'll call you back as soon as I can."

Tiffany shoved the card into her jacket pocket. "You might regret giving these to me. I could sell them to a telemarketer."

"I hope not. I'd have to come and find you."

"Good luck getting me to confess."

Kala jogged back the way she'd come. She passed several groups of students but saw no sign of Charlie.

Evening darkness was settling in earlier with every passing day, and while Kala liked the changing of the seasons, she wasn't looking forward to another long, wet winter in Kingston. In the North, once November arrived and snow covered the forest, the frozen temperatures lasted until spring. In Kingston, a week of minus thirty could be followed by a week of rain. She would never get used to the vagaries.

The sun was hovering above the buildings and the wind had died to a ripple when she found a parking spot on one of the side streets a short distance from Jane Thompson's apartment. She got out of her truck and cut across the streets until she was behind Jane's building. Jane was still at work and would be there until seven, according to the officer who was following her. He said that he was off duty at five but was confident she wasn't free to go anywhere in those two hours. He'd checked with her supervisor who'd confirmed her hours.

Kala had driven home before arriving at Jane's and picked up Taiku. She'd stopped to buy a burger on her way back into town and ate it in the truck, giving half to Taiku before she left him stretched out on the front seat of the locked truck. She approached Jane's apartment building from the rear. The property had a small yard surrounded by a high wooden fence that didn't have a gate. The only way in was through the back door of the apartment building. She backtracked along the properties, checking for something to help scale the fence. Three houses down, someone was building a fence and she spotted a stack of boards off to the side near the garage, easy enough to reach unseen. She borrowed a sturdy-looking plank and carried it back to the yard, leaning it at an angle against the fence and carefully climbing until she reached the top. She pulled herself over and dropped into the yard, landing on all fours. She stayed crouched and checked to see if anyone had seen her. Music blared from the bottom apartment but nobody appeared in the windows. The second floor apartment, which she knew to be Jane's, was in darkness.

Kala got to her feet and brushed off the dirt from her jeans. She made a search along the outside perimeter and found a gap in the fence on the far side that she might have missed if she hadn't noticed the absent nails and the odd angle of the board. She lifted the board and squeezed through to the other side. She found herself in an alley that led onto a street and an unobserved exit. Jane was being watched from the front of the building. Had she found this way to escape the media and police watch?

Kala walked back down the alley and climbed through the gap until she was again in Jane's backyard.

She placed the board back as it had been and crossed to the other side of the yard, squatting in the shadows next to overgrown raspberry bushes that could have used some loving care. They matched the patchy grass and tall weeds. The downstairs tenants were into country music and a series of deep-voiced male singers with varying degree of twang kept her entertained during the next hour while she waited.

A light came on in Jane's apartment at close to eight o'clock. While she watched, Jane entered and left the room facing the yard. Some fifteen minutes later, she re-entered the room, her naked body visible in the light from the overhead bulb, her hair wrapped in a towel. She stood in the window looking out at the night, rubbing her hair with the towel and stretching her arms over her head. Kala looked away and back again as the blind was pulled down. She could still see the outline of Jane's slender shape backlit from within. Jane hadn't seen her in the shadowy end of the yard, and Kala stood for a moment to get the circulation flowing again in her legs. She stayed in place another two hours until Jane's bedroom light went out. Then she slipped back through the gap in the fence and went in search of her truck after replacing the piece of wood she'd borrowed. Taiku would be sleeping in the front seat and ready for a walk. She'd take him along the beach at the end of her property as a reward for his patience after she called Marci Stokes and set a plan in motion for the next night.

CHAPTER TWENTY

Naomi sometimes felt as if she was an actress on one of those reality television shows, living out a drama of sex, love, and betrayal. Ever since she'd found the photos of Adam's ex on his computer, she'd been on edge, but not completely in a bad way. Her sex with Adam was hotter than it had ever been. They'd met after work Monday in a bar downtown and done the deed in one of the toilet stalls in the ladies' bathroom. Adam had performed in record time and only just gotten out the door before a group of university girls came in, talking about some guy who'd been trying to pick one of them up. Naomi had adjusted her skirt and walked past them with wobbly legs and a sore back from where Adam had pressed her up against the stall door. She still felt a bit tender this Tuesday morning.

She stood up and clapped her hands. Her grade four students got back into their seats and the chatter stopped. The student teacher from Queen's took over the math lesson and Naomi gratefully found a chair and empty desk at the back of the room where she marked notebooks while half-listening to the teacher-in-training giving her lesson on decimals. The kids were paying attention and all was going well. Nobody noticed when Naomi slipped out to get a coffee in the staff room.

"You, too?" Liam Brody was leaning against the counter holding a cup of coffee and smiling at her. They were alone in the sun-drenched kitchenette, which contained the coffee machine, kettle, and microwave for communal use. Liam had arrived at the school in the fall to take over retiring Mrs. Humphries's grade five class and had used every opportunity to flirt with Naomi even though he knew she was living with Adam. She didn't mind. In fact, the idea of having sex with Liam had begun to dominate her daydreams. He was early twenties and a soccer player with the lean body type and long sandy hair that she liked.

"Thank God for student teaching weeks." She smiled and brushed against him as she reached for her coffee mug.

"You smell good today." He leaned in and inhaled the scent from her hair. "Like roses after a spring rain."

"Have you been teaching love poetry again?" She gave him a playful shove in the arm. His biceps felt rock hard and a spasm of longing made her bite her bottom lip so as not to moan.

He turned sideways and reached across her to lift the coffee pot from the machine. "Allow me."

"Ever the gentleman."

As he poured, he looked at her and said, "I wonder if you might like to help me work on a lesson plan Thursday after school, that is, if you aren't busy."

She tilted her head, knowing this made her look cute while showing off the large diamond stud earrings Adam had given her on their six-month dating anniversary. "Why, Adam has a track meet on Thursday in Ottawa with his team and won't be home until after supper. I think I have some time to help you out." She was supposed to be home to watch Ben and Olivia, but they could fend for themselves for an hour. She'd make up some excuse that Adam would buy later if they ratted her out.

"I'd heard Adam was taking the track team to Ottawa. How coincidental is it that I need help on the exact same day?"

This time, Liam's arm pressed against her breasts as he returned the coffee pot to the machine. Naomi slopped some of the coffee onto the floor and used both hands to lower her mug to the counter. "Shall I come in ... or I should say, *to* your office when the kids leave?" she asked.

Liam's breathing quickened. "Why don't we meet off-site, say the Holiday Inn? We can spread out and relax."

"Why, that sounds delightful. I look forward to sharing some of my best teaching tricks."

She glanced back when she reached the door to the staff room. Liam was watching her walk away, and she was happy she'd put on a tight grey skirt and high heels. She knew that she should feel some guilt at setting up this rendezvous with Liam, but ever since she found the photos of Jane on Adam's computer, she felt that the fidelity rule was off the table. Lusting after his ex was way worse than her having a meaningless physical encounter with another man. Not to mention, it would be nice to be with someone closer to her own age. She wouldn't have to sneak looks at her iPhone after sex like she did with Adam, who said that he couldn't understand her need to be constantly online.

At seven thirty that evening, Marci Stokes was waiting in her car for Officer Stonechild to arrive on the side street where Stonechild had told her to park, a few blocks from Jane Thompson's apartment. She wasn't convinced that Jane would open up to her, but didn't mind giving the plan a try. At the very least, this would get her back into the good graces of Stonechild, and hopefully Rouleau. A truck pulled up behind her and she recognized Stonechild at the wheel. She got out of her car and met Stonechild in the road.

"Jane Thompson got home twenty minutes ago," Stonechild said. "Here's a recorder. Turn it on and leave it in your pocket. It's sufficiently powerful to record the conversation so that it can be used in court if necessary."

Marci accepted the device and made sure she knew which button to push before slipping it into the pocket of her coat. "Any words of wisdom?"

"Tell Jane that you want to help her get her story out. Don't overplay your hand or she'll get suspicious." Stonechild gave a sideways smile. "I have my doubts about this, as you must, too. Jane doesn't strike me as a woman who's going to spill her guts, but she might let her guard down enough to give us a lead. Rouleau asked that we make an attempt."

"I'll give it the old college try. Where will you be?"

"Not far. I've got a spot to watch in the backyard. If you run into any trouble or feel threatened, walk over to one of the back windows and wave. I'll get to you within a minute or two."

"Great. I feel much safer, although if she wants to off me, a few minutes might be too much leeway."

"If she sees me, you won't get anything out of her." Stonechild appeared to reconsider. "I could follow you up the stairs and hide in the hallway."

"No, your first plan is better. I can handle myself."

Marci left Stonechild and walked two blocks over to Regent Street to stand in front of Jane's apartment building. The main door was locked, and she rang the buzzer to Jane's apartment. She had to buzz a second time before Jane came on the intercom. Marci spoke quickly before Jane could tell her to go away.

"It's Marci Stokes. I bought you a coffee the other night and wanted to make sure you're okay." *No response*. She thought of Stonechild's lack of faith in her ability to draw Jane out and searched for something to make a connection. "I've been worried about you." A few more seconds passed and she made one last attempt. "I'm here as a concerned friend only. Strictly off the record."

Silence for almost half a minute, and then the buzzer sounded to let her in. Marci jumped across the space and grabbed the door. She pushed and walked into the narrow entranceway at the bottom of the stairwell. She could hear male voices in a first floor apartment that faded as she climbed the stairs. Jane's apartment took up the entire second floor of the house. The carpet on the landing was stained and nearly worn through in front of the door. She tapped lightly and waited. Streaky light filtered in through the dirty window high up on the end wall, casting the landing in gloomy greyness.

It took a while for Jane to open the door, but as soon as she did, she stepped into the hallway and shut it behind her. She was dressed to go out in jeans, running shoes, and a jacket. Her hair was damp from a recent shower. She stepped past Marci and said, "Let's go for a walk."

Jane was halfway down the stairs before Marci could respond. She hurried after her, hoping that Stonechild would realize what was going on, but not counting on it. Hadn't Stonechild said that she'd be watching from the back of the house? Still, Marci rationalized that she should be safe outside if Jane decided to turn on her, although she strongly doubted this would happen. Her reporter instinct told her that Jane would rather have her company than kill her.

"Can I buy you a drink?" Marci called as she ran to catch up. "Or a cup of coffee?" She tried not to breathe hard and let Jane know how dreadfully out of shape she was. God, she needed to get on an exercise regimen. She hoped Stonechild heard the front door slam or her yelling to Jane.

Jane looked back over her shoulder. "Sure, why not? I know the perfect place for a glass of wine."

Jane appeared in a buoyant mood and Marci wondered what had changed since their last encounter. She was intrigued, but remembered Stonechild's warning and didn't press for information until they were settled in high-back chairs at a table next to the large brick fireplace in an establishment named Tom's Place, a restaurant and bar that had been around for ages, or so Jane told her. "Adam and I used to come here for supper when we first started dating. I imagine that it's too staid for Naomi, given the lack of trendy decor that her generation prefers."

Marci marvelled at the way Jane put her ex-husband in his place with one dry observation about his much-too-young girlfriend. As she lifted her gin and tonic and eased her aching feet out of her shoes, she spotted Stonechild slipping into a chair on the other side of the dividing curtain of fabric that separated the tables. Marci forced her eyes to rest on Jane's face so as not to have her turn to see who had caught her attention. Jane lifted her glass of Cabernet Sauvignon to her lips. The satisfied smile on her face as she swallowed the expensive wine — Marci had ordered the very best — reminded her that before Jane's trial and incarceration, this woman had had standing in the community and a solid middle-class lifestyle. "Do you miss it?" she asked.

"Miss it?"

"Your life ... before all this."

Jane ran her tongue along her bottom lip to remove a drop of wine as she pondered the question.

"Some of it. My kids and my house, but not my marriage. Money is nice to have because it buys freedom, but I'm not as enamored with possessions after my time inside. Living in prison has a way of putting what's important into perspective." She laughed. "Maybe, everyone should have to spend a year locked up."

"Not something I'd like to see put into law, but I can understand what you're saying. Have you had the chance to visit your kids?"

"No, but I hope to soon. Adam wants to make sure I'm not charged with Devon's murder before he invites me. I lost custody when I was inside."

"He doesn't trust in your innocence?"

Jane's laugh was harsher this time. "I've done nothing but confuse him since even before I was accused of the affair."

Marci hunched forward so that she was closer to Jane. Now was the moment. "If I was to write about you, what would you want me to tell readers? What don't they know about you that will help get your side of the story out?" She lifted her drink to her lips and tried to appear relaxed while she waited.

Jane's eyes turned from pensive to anguished. "People only want the sensational, and take what is presented on the surface as fact. The more titillating the better. I was painted a seductress who preyed on her twelve-year-old student. People believed the worst because they had no interest in looking any deeper."

"And what would they have found if they had looked below the surface?"

"It's too late, Ms. Stokes. I could have used you four years ago. Now, I have nobody to rely on but myself, and you know what?"

"What?"

"I think I prefer it this way." Jane looked around the room and as if imprinting it in her memory. She turned to glance behind her and Marci held her breath, relieved when Jane turned back around without appearing to have seen Stonechild. "How long have you been a reporter?" Jane asked before taking a long drink from her glass.

"Going on twenty-five years. I think about changing careers every so often but can't seem to make the leap. Reporters aren't as relevant as they once were with all the new social media, but I believe we still need objective, informed reporting, maybe now more than ever."

"There was a day I couldn't ever see myself being anything but a teacher. I might become one again someday if I get a chance. I miss it." Jane drank the last of her wine. "I should be going."

"Can I get you another glass?"

Jane stood and smiled down at her. "To loosen my tongue? I'm sorry, but I'm heading out now. Thank you for the drink and the chat, even if you're doing this to write a story. I appreciated the diversion from my solitary existence. It was particularly nice to drink a good glass of wine again." She took a few steps away.

Marci called to her. "You haven't told me the entire story, have you, Jane?"

Jane squared her shoulders before turning back around. "No, but maybe someday I will. I have your card if I ever feel the need." She smiled and continued walking toward the entrance. A moment later and she was gone.

Stonechild rounded the corner and took her vacated chair. She reached out a hand and said, "I'll take the recorder. Not a confession but interesting all the same. Stay here and finish your drink. I'm going to follow her once she's had a few seconds head start. Sorry you'll have to hike all the way back to your car, but thanks for this."

Marci reached for the tape recorder in her pocket and passed it across the table. "No problem. What do you make of what she said?"

Stonechild looked toward the door and back at her before taking the recorder and slipping it into her jacket pocket. "Hard to tell, but I'd better be going. See you around?"

"Yeah, see you around."

After Stonechild had followed Jane into the night, Marci called over the waitress and ordered another gin and tonic. She took out her iPad and typed as much as she remembered of their conversation into a Word document before it faded. Somewhere in their cryptic, jumbled exchange was the making of a story. While she'd promised not to write one now, who knew what the future would hold?

The waitress set down her fresh drink on the table and Marci thought, *What the hell? I've got all night and nowhere to be.* She opened a new page and started typing an opening paragraph. She'd start a profile piece and flesh it out with facts from Jane's life and trial. If Jane was to be charged with murder sometime down the road, she'd be just that much farther ahead.

Kala followed Jane back to her apartment, cutting through the alleyway and pushing through the opening in the fence. She saw the light go on and off in the kitchen and then on in the room that Kala had decided was the bedroom. A moment later and Jane was framed in the window dressed in her nightgown as she reached up to pull the blind closed. She stood looking out for several seconds with her hand raised to draw the blind, face tilted back to stare into the sky.

What are you thinking about? Kala stayed crouched near the raspberry bushes letting her mind replay the conversation she'd overheard between Jane and Marci. Jane played her cards close to her chest, but Kala had the feeling that Jane was killing time, waiting for something to unfold. She tried to put herself in Jane's place. What would she do if placed in the same situation? The certainty of what that would be struck her full force. She had to remind herself that Jane was not her and might have a different reaction, but the idea was enough for Kala to change her plans and return to the station.

The office was empty and she left the overhead lights off, crossing to her desk and turning on her desk lamp. She took a while to retrieve the videos they'd made of Jane's interviews but was able to find them filed in the common drive. She turned up the volume to listen for every inflection in Jane's voice while she studied her facial expressions. The camera in the interview room was mounted high on the wall and had captured Jane's every move like a bug under a microscope. When she'd viewed them a second time, she took out the recording that Marci had made that evening and listened to it several times. Once satisfied that she'd gotten all she could out of the tapes, she slumped back in her chair and closed her eyes to think.

We've been looking at this all wrong. The knowledge made her weary. If she was right, Jane Thompson would look even guiltier of Devon's murder. Kala had found herself drawn to the silent strength of the woman and a part of her had been hoping that she hadn't resorted to revenge and killed Devon Eton with no regard to the consequences. She was going to have to face the likely possibility.

Kala opened her eyes and checked her watch. It was nearly midnight and much too late to come up with a plan. She got out of her chair and grabbed her jacket from the desk where she'd tossed it. Long past time to head home to Taiku and get him outside for his nighttime run.

Her cell rang as she was pulling into the driveway. Kala threw the truck into park and felt around for her phone, which she'd tossed on the seat next to her. She checked the number and thought it looked familiar. "Stonechild here."

"Kala, it's Fiona."

"Fiona? I can hardly hear you."

"'S … me, all right. I thought you should know I'm leaving. Four months in Calgary."

Her speech was slurred and Kala was having trouble making sense of what she was saying. "Why are you calling me now?"

"I want you to stop chasing my husband. We're getting back together...." Her voice trailed away.

"There's nothing going on between us. How many times do I have to tell you?" Kala wondered if she had something written on her forehead that only Fiona could see, or perhaps it was her highly tuned radar for female competition, because Kala had never knowingly given her cause to be jealous. "Have you been drinking, Fiona? Where are you?"

"I love him," Fiona said and broke into noisy, sloppy sobs. "I need him," she wailed between hiccups.

"Go to bed and sleep it off," Kala said. "Things will look brighter in the morning." *Or not, if you have a hangover.* "I'm signing off."

Kala disconnected, the words, "Need you to stay away," playing in her ear. Just what she wanted to hear at the end of a long day.

She stepped out of the cab of the truck and onto the ground. The wind had come up and she could hear waves crashing onto the shoreline even from this distance. The clouds were scudding across the sky overhead but not yet thick enough to block the stars completely. A crescent moon cast light onto the lake. She shivered inside her jacket and thought about skipping the walk with Taiku, but knew she couldn't after he'd been stuck inside all day. She'd take her penance for neglecting him and take him for a long walk the length of Old Front Road. Perhaps, the exercise would clear her head and help her to fall asleep when she finally crawled into bed.

CHAPTER TWENTY-ONE

Rouleau felt as if the energy had been sucked from the room as he surveyed the troops at the daily morning meeting. It was already October 12, nine days into the investigation with no breakthroughs. Heath was getting anxious and calling nightly for updates. Everyone was in their accustomed place, faces tired while their hands were busy fiddling with cellphones and iPads. He needed to provide some motivation, but his energy level was lower than theirs. He'd been having trouble concentrating and difficulty caring about work. He wondered if he needed a holiday, or perhaps retirement, to let someone with more drive lead the team.

"Right," he began, tucking his thoughts away for the moment, "I have a meeting with Heath shortly but wanted to hear developments. Who wants to go first?"

Woodhouse volunteered but had little new to impart. Bedouin recounted the calls from the information line that they'd followed up on but had led nowhere. Gundersund reported that Forensics hadn't come up with anything enlightening on Devon's computer.

Rouleau looked over at Stonechild. She was as tired-looking as the rest of them, but her eyes were alert and watchful. He followed the direction of her gaze as she tracked around the room. Woodhouse was reading something on his phone, Bedouin and Morrison had their heads together looking at a sheet of paper, and Bennett had gotten up to refill his coffee cup. Gundersund was looking down at his iPad and reading silently with his lips moving. "Anything?" Rouleau asked Stonechild, trying to forget for the moment that he was late for his meeting with Heath.

She shook her head. "I'm working on a few things but nothing worth reporting yet."

Gundersund raised his head. "Is this something I should know about, *partner*?" He emphasized the last word and a look passed between them.

"I can fill you in, but I wouldn't say that I've uncovered anything you need to know."

Rouleau watched the two of them locking eyes for a moment before he said, "I'll leave you to it then. Keep plugging away everyone. Something is bound to break before much longer." He said the words with false certainty because he knew the longer this dry spell went without a decent lead, the tougher the case would become. He had no desire to face Heath now with so little progress.

On his way past Vera's desk, he found her by the filing cabinet with a handful of documents. She smiled at him and walked over to join him. Her eyes were sparkling and her face glowed more than usual. "Have you some good news?" he asked.

"Just that I'm looking forward to the performance tonight." Her eyes dimmed as she looked him over. "You've forgotten, haven't you?"

He reached back in his memory and landed on the benefit ticket she'd given him the week before. "Of course not." He wondered if his father would go on such short notice. He couldn't think who else to give it to. He added, "I won't let it go to waste."

"Perfect." She seemed uncertain but the smile was back. "Heath said to show you right in. He's scheduled another media scrum after lunch."

"He's not going to be pleased to find that we haven't any new information for the public."

"Oh, I wouldn't think that would worry him too much. He always shows well, regardless of how little substance there is in his briefings." She flashed a Mona Lisa smile before returning to her filing and left him to make his own way into Heath's inner sanctum.

Heath was standing by the window when Rouleau entered. "Well?" he asked, turning. "Anything worth going to the media?"

Rouleau remained standing. "I'd say not yet, although we could make another appeal for people to come forward with information. It might be time."

Heath ran a hand through his curls. "I suppose I could have Vera arrange to get the parents in again for another public plea. You're off the hook, by the way. Ingrid cancelled tomorrow night's party."

Rouleau took a second to remember what Heath was speaking about. Another invitation that had slipped his mind. "That's too bad," he said. "I was looking forward to it. I imagine you'll let Laney know?"

"Of course. Ingrid isn't feeling up to entertaining." He turned back to the window and Rouleau took this as his cue to leave.

Gundersund was waiting for an opening to speak with Stonechild about what she was working on. Since the morning meeting, she'd been on the phone and unavailable. He knew too well that her preference was to work alone. He'd thought she was finally coming around to the idea of being his partner, but obviously not entirely. She'd left the office an hour earlier to pick up sandwiches, and he planned to prod her into a conversation over lunch at their desks.

"Hey, Gundersund."

He looked over to see Tanya Morrison walking toward him, a smile on her face and a paper waving in her hand. She dropped into the chair next to his desk. "I think we've caught a break." She handed him the paper. "Narendra Ahujra, desk clerk at the Limestone Spa Hotel, remembers seeing Devon Eton the afternoon that he went missing."

"At last." Gundersund grinned back at her. "I could kiss you right now."

"I know, aye? I can't tell you how pleased I am to know that a week answering nutter calls has led to this gem."

"Is Narendra Ahujra working today?"

"His shift starts at three. I told him that a couple of detectives would be by then. I hope that's okay."

"That gives us an hour to finish up here and get to the hotel."

Stonechild sauntered into the office carrying a couple of sandwiches and a tray with two coffees. "What's going on?" she asked as she set everything on her desk.

"A lead." He handed her the paper. "Narendra Ahujra saw Devon at the Limestone Spa Hotel after school the day he went missing. We'll head over to speak with him at three."

"Hurray." Stonechild returned their smiles with one of her own. "We needed a break." She waved goodbye to Morrison before sitting down at her desk and saying to Gundersund, "Vera caught me in the hall and Rouleau needs some information from you before a media briefing. Can you give him a call? Here's your sandwich and coffee."

He accepted both and pulled out his phone. "He'll be happy to hear about this tip. We should head over to the hotel around twenty to three. I don't mind driving."

"I plan to take my truck so I'll meet you there."

Exasperation made him say, "For God's sake, Stonechild, it won't kill you to share a ride."

She went still. "I have to be somewhere right after the interview." She met his stare and looked away.

He knew something was bothering her but had no idea what. The evasiveness in her eyes made him cautious and bite back what he was about to say. Instead he asked, "How about meeting up at the Merchant after you get finished with your appointment?"

Her eyes met his again. "I really can't today. Rain check?"

"Sure." He lifted the phone to his ear while she opened a file on her computer and began reading at the same time as she bit into her sandwich. *What is going on with you?* He tried to set aside his unease while giving Rouleau his full attention. When he finished the call, Stonechild was gone from her desk and hadn't returned when it was time to leave for the hotel. He sent a text to confirm that she would meet him in the Limestone Spa parking lot and set out. By the time he reached his car, she'd texted that she was on her way as well.

Narendra Ahujra was working behind the front desk when Gundersund arrived at the hotel at quarter past three. Stonechild was already waiting for him by the front entrance. Ahujra was checking in a woman and they waited for him in the lobby while he completed the transaction. The lobby walls were tropical terracotta, the floor pale brown tile. Two turquoise-coloured couches were arranged in front of a white plaster and stone fireplace, and they took positions kitty corner to each other.

A compact man with a fringe of greying hair and a humourless face, Narendra arrived ten minutes later and sat next to Gundersund facing Stonechild. He took the photo of Devon that Gundersund handed him and confirmed that this was the young man he'd seen the Monday before.

"He was here close to seven o'clock that night."

"Was he with anyone?"

"He was alone but he took the elevator to one of the rooms."

Stonechild asked, "Do you know who he was visiting?"

"We had an IT conference going on that week with the rooms booked on the third floor and he went to one of their rooms. I know because I was on the elevator with him on the ride up. I had a customer phone down because his room card was not working so I ran a new one up to him. This young man got off on the same floor but he went one way and I went to the other end of the hall."

"IT?"

"Sorry, information technology. Computers. People were here from all over Canada. They used one of the larger conference rooms Monday and Tuesday until late afternoon."

Gundersund asked, "Could you give us a list of names and addresses for the guests staying in those rooms?"

Narendra nodded. "I can do better than that. I saw which room this young man entered and I checked the name of the occupant. My manager said that it would be fine if I co-operated with your inquiry." He returned to the desk and retrieved a print out that he handed to Gundersund. "I cannot tell you why this boy made me curious except that he would not meet my eyes and then I had a memory of seeing him in the hotel one other time, I think it was in late May or early June."

"What was he doing here then?"

"He was in the lobby, sitting for some time in that striped chair over there near the fireplace. After half an hour had passed, I asked if I could help him but he told me that he was waiting for someone who was late. I cannot tell you what made me think he was out of place, but after all these years working in the hotel industry, one gets a sense. We run a clean, family hotel and are always on the lookout for … the unsavoury. I didn't see him leave that time because I got busy."

Stonechild looked unconvinced. She said, "Surely Devon wouldn't have stood out so clearly after such brief encounters. You must see thousands of people come and go in this hotel."

Narendra shifted from one foot to the other, appearing to be struggling with how much to reveal. "The day he was so long in the lobby, one of the other clerks pointed him out to me as the boy who had the affair with his teacher. She was in his class at school. Naturally, I checked him out. When he sat in that chair for such a long time, I wondered what he was up to and so I approached him. We run a clean establishment, Officer."

"So you said already." Stonechild didn't look impressed with what Narendra was implying about Devon.

Narendra forged on, perhaps emboldened by her skepticism and feeling a need to convince her otherwise. "Well, he was known to like older women, wasn't he? At the risk of being indelicate, some women will pay for an experience with a young man. He was good-looking and carried himself with a certain arrogance. He was already corrupted, Officer."

"Do you think that's what he was up to in your hotel? Soliciting older women for sex?"

Narendra pursed his lips. "That's not for me to say."

"So no proof or complaints."

"No."

"Well thanks for your time," Gundersund said, shooting Stonechild a "let's wrap this up" look.

They didn't speak until they were outside the hotel standing under the protection of the covered entrance. A wind was whipping the flags atop the buttress so that they snapped like sheets on a clothesline. Gundersund thought it might be time to pull out a warmer jacket.

"Already *corrupted*?" Stonechild said as if she couldn't believe that Narendra had had the audacity to say the words. "The man made himself judge and jury."

"He certainly held Devon's past against him."

"To be fair, Narendra has a job to do." She did up her jacket. "Keeping the hotel clean and all. Do you think he might be right about Devon being here for unsavoury business?" She used her fingers to make quotation marks around the last two words.

"It's a possibility, but not high on my list. He was visiting a man in the IT field, which could be related to his father's business. Maybe, he was meeting up with his father in one of the rooms. The more I think about it, the more plausible it is that Mitchell Eton was at the conference."

"Then why didn't Mitchell tell us about meeting Devon here the two times we questioned him?"

Gundersund was silent. He checked the paper that Narendra had handed him. "The room that

Devon entered that day was occupied by one Ivan Bruster and his address is in Ajax. I'd like to question him face to face. What's your gut tell you?"

"The same. I think we should hold off talking to Mitchell until we've had a chance to grill Bruster. We don't want Bruster tipped off that we're coming. It's just after four o'clock and I have an appointment. Want to clear it with Rouleau and take a drive to Ajax tomorrow morning?"

"Yeah, I'm heading back to the station so I'll talk to Rouleau. I'll text the time that I'll pick you up tomorrow. My turn to drive." Gundersund waited for her to give him grief and was relieved when she accepted his plan without comment.

CHAPTER TWENTY-TWO

Caroline Russell arranged to drop off Dawn at the Starbucks at the bottom of Princess Street. Kala arrived a few minutes early and scouted inside the coffee shop for Dawn before going back outside to wait on the sidewalk. She was nervous and apprehensive about how the visit would go, oblivious to the wind and cold swirling around her. The last time they'd been together was when social worker Tamara Jones had taken Dawn away from the house on Old Front Road. Kala had pretended that she was in agreement with Dawn's move to a foster home because she'd had no choice. Tamara held all the cards and she wasn't bending. Kala would never forget the betrayed look in Dawn's eyes when Kala told her to leave.

She spotted Dawn before Dawn saw her. She'd grown taller and leaner over the almost five months of separation. Nearly fourteen and so like her mother, Rose, at the same age; so much so that for one brief moment Kala almost believed it was Rose. Dawn's hair was plaited in two long braids and she wore a red jacket and jeans. When she lifted her gaze from the sidewalk and saw Kala, a series of conflicting emotions crossed her face in the space of a few seconds. The last was wary and closed off as she slowed her steps. Kala waited for Dawn to reach her.

"It's so good to see you," Kala said, needing to reach past the animosity to the child she'd once known. "I've missed you."

"Caroline said to tell you she'd be back to get me in an hour." Dawn looked past Kala and waited motionless, her mouth in a straight line, her eyes defiant.

I deserve your anger. "Would you like to get a drink and then we could walk down by the water?" Kala didn't dare touch her even though she wanted to take her in her arms. There was a time not so long ago that she would have.

A shrug and head nod, and Kala went inside for iced drinks while Dawn waited outside. They walked toward the lake at the bottom of Princess Street without talking. Kala was willing to wait for Dawn to find her way, but after the silence stretched into minutes, Kala reminded herself that Dawn had never been one to talk much. She was going to have to initiate conversation or there wouldn't be any.

"How are they treating you in the foster home?" she asked when they were standing at the railing looking out over the whitecaps beating against the seawall and sipping iced coffee through straws. A fine spray dampened their hair and faces. She had to speak loudly to be heard above the sound of the wind.

"Fine. They don't bother me."

"Are you still playing baseball?"

"No."

"That's too bad, but I guess school takes up a lot of time."

"I don't care about school."

Kala wasn't sure she'd heard right at first. She didn't want to ask her to repeat the words in case she had. It was too early to probe. "Let's go sit out of the wind."

They fought their way back against the wind until they rounded a bend in the path, but there was no relief from the cold dampness gusting off the lake. They crossed the lawn and started up a side street where the limestone buildings gave some protection. Traffic was heavy with people heading home after a day's work but few were on foot. The weather was bad enough to curtail all but the hardiest.

They waited at the stoplight at Clarence and King, and Kala could see that Dawn wasn't holding herself as rigidly as she had been. She reached over and touched Dawn's shoulder without speaking. It felt too soon, too precarious to share more than this. Dawn didn't pull away and Kala was grateful for the small concession.

Dawn kept her eyes on the opposite side of the road. The light turned green, but she stayed rooted in spot. Kala took a step forward but then stepped back to wait beside her.

"Why are you doing this?" Dawn asked, glaring at Kala. "You said that you didn't want me with you anymore."

Kala understood this anger. She'd lived it most of her teenage years. She leaned closer so that her mouth was close to Dawn's ear. "I always wanted to see you. I only said that I didn't want you living with me because I thought it would be easier for you to leave. I had no choice but to let you go."

The light turned red and a group of boys jostled up next to them, their voices boisterous above the wind. Kala and Dawn waited until the light turned green a second time and the boys had passed them by. They trailed across the street behind them.

"I have new friends," Dawn said when they reached the curb. "They don't ask where my parents are or why I'm living in foster care. They think I'm okay." She'd huddled deep into her jacket so that her chin was buried under the collar.

"Of course you're okay. You don't need to explain yourself to anyone." Kala had never felt so helpless. She'd failed this girl and she didn't have any idea how to make it better. "I was wrong to let you go so easily. I promised to fight for you and I didn't." Her words were taken by the wind and she wasn't certain that Dawn had heard them.

Dawn began walking a few steps ahead of her and Kala let her have her space, keeping a short distance behind without letting it get any wider. They continued up Clarence and kept going on Brock as far as Barrie when Kala checked her watch. An hour had sped by as if pushed forward by the pummeling wind and Kala didn't dare keep Caroline Russell waiting. This visit had been a test and she was determined to pass it. "We have to head back," she said to Dawn pointing toward the lake. Dawn nodded and they turned right, starting down the hill, this time walking together. They reached the Starbucks parking lot a few minutes late, but ahead of Caroline.

"Taiku misses your walks," Kala said. The window to make headway was quickly disappearing. "Maybe, I could bring him next time."

Dawn opened her mouth to say something but stopped when Caroline wheeled her car into the parking lot. She parked next to them and leaped out of the driver's seat, leaving the engine running. The wind swooped under her coat and blew it over her head before she trapped the cloth with her hands. "My goodness, this weather." She tried to smooth her hair but it would not be tamed, tossing about her face and whipping into her eyes. "Sorry I'm late. How did your visit go?" she asked, smiling at Dawn and questioning Kala with her eyes.

"We had a walk by the lake." Kala wasn't sure what more was expected.

Caroline put an arm around Dawn's shoulders as the silence lengthened. "We'll be on our way, then. Thank you for coming by, Officer Stonechild. Perhaps, we can do this another time. Maybe when the wind dies down."

Dawn stared at Kala but didn't say anything. Caroline searched Dawn's face before directing her toward the passenger door. She said to Kala, "I'll be in touch."

Kala nodded and turned to walk up the street to where she'd parked her truck. This visit had been a terrible failure, but had she truly expected it to be anything else? Would she have acted any differently than Dawn in her situation?

She picked up speed until she broke into a jog, trying to escape the force of the wind and the knowledge that Dawn was lost to her. All that was left was the gaping emptiness in her heart and the glaring fact that she hadn't fought hard enough to keep this from happening.

Gundersund pulled into Stonechild's driveway at seven thirty the next morning. He hoped he didn't look as rough as he felt. He'd driven Fiona into Ottawa to catch a flight to Calgary after work the day before when she called him last minute. She'd be gone for five days and then back to finish out one last week of work before beginning her four-month teaching stint. He hadn't gotten to bed until close to two a.m. By then, the steady wind had lessened to a cool breeze and the stars had been visible. The moon had grown slightly larger than a sliver and shone a pale light that he gazed up at while waiting for Minnie to do her dog business before bed.

Stonechild came out of the house thrusting one arm into her leather jacket while talking into her cellphone, tucked between an ear and shoulder. Her long black hair hung wet and loose about her face. She slammed into the passenger side and cursed.

"I left Bennett waiting for me at the charity event last night. I totally forgot all about it."

For one guilty moment, Gundersund was pleased that she'd stood up Bennett. He tried to sound sorry. "That's too bad. Did he say how it went?"

"Yeah, good. Vera was expecting Rouleau, and Bennett said she looked disappointed when he didn't show either. At least they had each other for company." She buckled herself in. "I need coffee."

"My first destination." He backed onto Old Front Road. "There's a truck stop restaurant on Sydenham Road that has good coffee and it's not far out of our way. We should be in Ajax in just over two hours if traffic is good."

"Have you got Ivan Bruster's home and work addresses?"

"I do, and the Ajax police received a courtesy call to let them know we're coming. A buddy on the force checked and Bruster spent the night at home."

"Good to know we aren't on a fool's mission then. It crossed my mind this morning that he could be away on business."

She stopped talking and Gundersund knew better than to engage in conversation before she'd had caffeine. They decided to eat in the diner before getting on the road since they were both hungry and muffins weren't going to do it. Kala ordered fried eggs, sausage, home fries, and a double order of toast, and Gundersund said to make his the same. Two coffee refills and a cup each for the road and they were on the 401 to Ajax by eight thirty. Stonechild appeared relaxed and the dull ache behind Gundersund's eyes had almost disappeared.

When they'd passed the exit to Napanee, Gundersund broached the case. "Have you uncovered something that we should discuss?"

Stonechild kept staring through the front windshield. She took a sip of coffee. "No. I've been going over Jane Thompson's interview tapes but haven't anything more than a feeling."

"What's your feeling?"

She appeared to ponder the question before saying, "I don't want to lead us on the wrong track and prefer to wait until I have something more than a gut reaction to share."

"Fair enough." He'd learned that this was how she worked best and he needed to step back and give her space, but not too far back. "Let me know when you need my help."

"I will."

He had one more bit of probing to do, and this would likely not be well received either. "How did your meeting with Dawn go yesterday?"

She turned to look at him. "How did you know?"

"I'd say a gut feeling, but I overheard your last call with the court worker."

Stonechild looked back at the road and sighed. "Not good. She's angry like I was at her age. A teenager with all the shit that goes along with that and then believing she's been abandoned. Not a good combination."

"Will you see her again soon?"

"It will be up to Dawn. I made overtures but she wasn't all that receptive. She tells me that she has new friends who accept her as she is. I intend to find out who these friends are and make sure they aren't into anything they shouldn't be."

"I'd be happy to help with that."

"I might take you up on the offer. I'll do whatever it takes to make sure she's safe."

Gundersund had Stonechild place a call to his police friend as they pulled off the highway into Ajax at close to ten o'clock. The cop answered right away and reported that Bruster was working from home, it appeared, and his BMW was still in the driveway. Stonechild confirmed directions, and ten minutes later they pulled up in front of a two-storey, faux grey brick building with a three car garage in a new subdivision. The houses were large and closely spaced with saplings planted in the postage-stamp size front yards. Very little differentiated one house from another. He could tell by the look on Stonechild's face that living here would be her idea of hell.

"Well, let's go find out what Devon Eton was doing in this man's hotel room the afternoon that he went missing," Stonechild said, opening her door.

"Sounds rather ominous when you put it like that."

A pretty blond woman in her thirties opened the door. She had a two-year-old with playdough on his hands riding on one hip and another baby growing in her belly. Gundersund wasn't an expert, but he guessed she was due any day. "Can I help you?" she asked.

"We're here to speak with Ivan Bruster about a police matter." Kala held up her badge. "Would he be home?"

The woman's face crinkled in puzzlement. "Are you sure you're wanting *my* Ivan Bruster? He's not done anything wrong."

"We only have a few questions about a person he came across in Kingston two Mondays ago while he was there on business."

She opened the door wider. "Oh, yes, at the conference. He's in his study at the back of the house. Down this hall to the end. If you don't mind finding your way, I have somebody's hands that need cleaning up. My name's Katie, by the way."

"Nice to meet you, Katie."

If Ivan Bruster was surprised to see them, he didn't let on. He stood and shook their hands and invited them to sit in two leather chairs in a space that looked out over the small backyard. A young maple stood starkly empty of leaves in the centre of the space. The room smelled of cigarettes and air freshener. He pulled over his desk chair and sat facing them. "Can I get you coffee? Tea?"

"No, thank you. Do you know why we're here?" Stonechild was taking the lead as they'd agreed in the car. Gundersund tried to make himself blend into the furniture so that Bruster wouldn't feel intimidated. A tough feat, given Gundersund's size.

For a moment, Bruster looked confused. "I thought you were my new clients."

Kala took out her badge. "I'm Officer Stonechild and that is Officer Gundersund. We're with the Kingston police investigating a homicide. We're hoping you can help us to track the final movements of Devon Eton last Monday, October third."

The confusion turned to shock. Bruster stared at her as if she'd grown another head. "You've got to be kidding me. Devon Eton is dead?"

"I'm afraid he died that Monday night. He was seen entering your room at around seven o'clock on the evening he went missing. Can you tell us about that?"

Bruster ran a trembling hand through his hair until it stood on end. "Good God," he said. "Dead?"

He shook his head. "Who saw him entering my room? I don't understand."

"Someone who works in the hotel."

"Okay." Bruster took a deep breath and seemed to get his bearings. Some of the colour returned to his face. "His father is a friend of mine. I met Devon the day before by chance and invited him to come by to talk about a possible summer job."

"Summer is quite a ways off."

"Yeah, but it never hurts to line someone up. The computer market is competitive and good interns aren't that easy to find, believe me. His dad asked me as a favour to consider Devon and I was following up since I happened to be in town."

"Did Mitchell know that his son met with you last Monday?"

"No, unless Devon told him, but I think Devon wanted to keep our meeting under wraps for the time being. He didn't want to raise his father's hopes … you know, about getting a job." His voice was stronger now, more confident. Gundersund could imagine him running a business of like-minded geeks. Round rimless glasses and floppy brown hair made him look bookish but this impression was countered by a strong jaw and direct grey eyes.

Stonechild asked, "Do you own an IT company, Mr. Bruster?"

"I do. I have a staff of sixteen and am looking to bring the number up to twenty next year. Business is booming."

"What was Devon like?"

"Seemed fine. Type one personality, I'd say, which is linked with intelligence. Why, what have you heard?"

Gundersund found Ivan's response oddly worded, and so did Stonechild, by the sharp way she focused on him. "I believe that I asked you the question."

Bruster laughed as if caught in a joke. "Yeah, so you did, but I didn't know him that well. He was a football player and bright, verging on genius when it came to math — not the stereotypical jock by any means. I'm sure you've heard that he had a bit of trouble with his teacher in middle school, but that didn't impact my decision to hire him. Everyone deserves a do-over."

"Now that you've had a few minutes to take in his death, do you have any idea why somebody would want to murder him?"

"None. None whatsoever."

Gundersund asked, "Did you speak on the phone with Devon that afternoon?"

"No, we ran into each other at the mall on the Sunday.... Wait, he did call now that you mention it. He wanted to make sure our meeting was still on. I was working on a project and told him just to come up to the room for his interview."

"The interview was at seven? Wasn't that late?"

Bruster looked confused. "He came to my room at four thirty."

"Are you certain about the time?"

"Yes. Whoever said they saw him must have been mistaken."

"How long was he in your room?"

"Maybe half an hour. Forty minutes tops. I told him that he could start after term ended in the spring and he was happy about that. I'm glad his last day was a good one." Bruster paused and frowned. "How did he die?"

"He was found near the lake. Did anybody see him leave your room?"

Bruster shook his head. "I wouldn't know. He might have run into somebody in the elevator or outside the hotel. I just don't know."

Stonechild shifted the direction of her questions. "When's the first time you met Devon?"

"His father came to Ajax on business a year or so ago and brought Devon only because they were on their way to Toronto to a Jays game and some guy time. Devon spent most of the day at my offices and worked with one of the other programmers."

"What was your impression of him when you met?"

"Seemed like a nice kid. As I said, highly intelligent."

Stonechild looked at Gundersund. "Anything else before we leave?"

"I think that covers it. We'll be back if anything else comes up." He liked that Ivan Bruster looked uncomfortable. He added, "Don't bother seeing us out. We know the way."

"What do you think of his story?" he asked Stonechild once they were back in his car.

"Sounded plausible." She kept talking almost as if working through her train of thought out loud. "But hard to believe he didn't know Devon was dead since he's friends with Mitchell. I imagine the community isn't so large that the death of another business owner's kid wouldn't spread quickly. He sounded rehearsed. Did you have that sense, too?"

"No. He put on quite an act, if so. I'm wondering if it was Narendra Ahujra or Bruster who got the time wrong?"

"We can go back and speak with Narendra."

"Somebody should check. The time has a bearing, although we don't know what Devon did before or after his interview with Bruster."

"He could have met someone in the bar or run into someone else he knew in the hotel. A fake ID giving his age as nineteen was found in his wallet. He drank beer and smoked some pot somewhere."

"I think we should pay Mitchell a visit to find out if he asked Bruster to hire his son."

"We can be at his office around two if traffic is good."

"Let's do it." She leaned against the headrest and closed her eyes. "I've been having trouble sleeping," she said. She opened her eyes and turned her face to look at him. "I hear Fiona is going on a teaching gig for four months."

"Yeah, I took her to the Ottawa airport last night. She'll be back for a week and then gone for the duration."

"How do you feel about that?"

He was surprised that she was asking since they'd both steered away from discussing his marriage. *How do I feel about Fiona leaving?* "She thinks that given enough time and counselling, we'll become a couple again. She's having trouble accepting the truth."

He glanced over. Stonechild's dark, unfathomable eyes were watching him. "And what is the truth?" she asked in a voice as soft as a cotton sheet falling onto the floor.

"The truth is that our marriage is over."

CHAPTER TWENTY-THREE

Adam was working late getting his track team ready for the next day and Naomi was supposed to watch his kids after school. She phoned to let Ben know that she'd be on her way as soon as she finished supervising detention. After she disconnected her phone, she looked up at Liam, who was standing next to her desk.

"Okay, I have twenty minutes. I can meet you for a coffee, but we can't be seen together."

Liam agreed and she watched him leave. She imagined his muscles flexing and relaxing under his loose black slacks. His butt was as tight as the soccer balls he kicked around the field and she was weak at the knees thinking about his muscular thighs on top of her. She stood and got her spinning hormones under control before following him at a discreet distance to the parking lot.

As she crossed the parking lot, she caught sight of Adam standing near the field talking to kids in running gear. He was wearing his Jays ball cap and blue Columbia jacket over jeans, always perfectly turned out for any occasion. She hesitated before getting into her car, knowing full well that she was about to cross a line by meeting Liam off school property. Then she reminded herself of the photos Adam had on his computer that he'd taken of Jane. The shock of finding them was as sharp now as it had been when she'd seen the first photo of Jane standing at the bus stop.

Two nights earlier, she'd asked Adam if he'd seen Jane since her release from prison, other than the time he'd met to tell her that she wouldn't be seeing the kids until Devon's murder was solved. He'd gone a bit ballistic, asking if she trusted him, wanting to know what even made her ask … going on and on. After he'd left for his nightly workout at the gym, Naomi realized he'd never answered her question.

She unlocked her car and got in. Since that awful day when she'd almost been caught spying in Adam's den, she'd begun watching him more closely. He was going to the gym more often — or so he said — and the part of him that she'd found to be mysterious and so attractive initially was becoming increasingly suspicious. He also seemed to be tracking her own whereabouts more closely and she was beginning to feel on edge.

Liam was waiting for her at a corner table in Sipps coffee shop on Brock Street, out of the way enough that they shouldn't run into anyone from the school. To be honest, the idea of getting caught together was part of the excitement. Maybe not wise, but definitely a turn-on. Two cups of coffee and a slice of tin roof cheesecake were already on the table. Liam handed her a fork and they both dug into the luscious chocolate cheesecake, loaded with chocolate-covered peanuts and capped with tiny marshmallows.

"I love this place," said Naomi. "Limestone and brick walls, good coffee, and desserts to die for." She watched Liam as she ran the tip of her tongue back and forth across her chocolate-covered fork. She smiled when his pupils enlarged as he followed the last flick of her tongue with his eyes.

"Still set for tomorrow after school?" he asked.

"Are you sure you're up for it?" she teased. "Your voice sounded a little hoarse just now. Perhaps you're coming down with a terrible disease."

"And maybe you've got the cure for what ails me."

"There you go again with the love poetry." She smiled, scooped up another forkful of cake and waved it in the space between them. "I'll set it up with Adam's kids tonight." *Believe me, just as soon as I get home.* Ben was aching for more independence and she'd play on that, telling him and Olivia that this would be a test and one that they should keep to themselves since Adam worried more than was good for him.

On the drive home, Naomi pondered her options. She was disenchanted with her current living arrangements and could see the day when sex with Adam wouldn't be enough to keep her there. The problem was that they worked in the same school and he had this possessive streak that might be tough to get out from under. He'd gotten jealous a few times and the memory of his anger followed by a round of intense lovemaking sent a shiver up her back, whether lust or fear, she had no way of separating.

Ben and Olivia were sitting together on the couch in the family room when she breezed into the kitchen through the back door. They were watching *The Lion King* for the ten millionth time, or she should say that Olivia was watching while Ben worked on his homework next to her. They really weren't such bad kids. Naomi called him over to the kitchen and they each took a stool on the same side of the island.

"Did you have a good day?" she asked.

"Yeah, went okay."

They both started to speak at the same time and stopped together. Naomi laughed. "How about I go first? I've got an appointment after work tomorrow and was wondering what you thought about watching Olivia after school? Your dad will be at the track meet. I would pay you for the hour of kidsitting." She noticed the flash of delight that crossed Ben's face before he dropped his eyes and nodded.

"No problem."

"The thing is …" She waited for him to look at her. "Your dad doesn't think you're old enough for this responsibility and on that point, we disagree. I think you're plenty old enough."

Ben's forehead wrinkled in worry. "He doesn't have to know, does he? Olivia won't say anything if I tell her not to."

She pretended to think it over. "Weeellll, I guess we could keep this between us. As long as you promise that you and your sister won't get into any trouble for the hour that I'm at the appointment."

"I promise. You can count on me, Naomi."

"I know I can." She patted his knee before standing. "That's settled then." She stopped and turned back. "What was it you wanted to tell me?"

He looked as if he was searching for an answer. He shrugged. "I forget. It was nothing."

"Well, if you remember, I'm right here. Now go back and get your homework done while I whip up your favourite macaroni and cheese for supper."

"Thanks, Naomi."

"You're more than welcome."

"There's his car." Stonechild pointed to a slate grey Jaguar. "I bet you money."

"One of the sweet perks of owning your own business." Gundersund wheeled his Mustang into the empty spot next to it and they both got out. "How do you want to play this?" he asked, looking at her over the roof of his car.

"You ask the questions. I get the feeling Mitchell will respond better to another male."

Gundersund held up two crossed fingers. "Like this."

Stonechild rolled her eyes. "Happily, I don't see you and Mitchell Eton as blood brothers."

Gundersund didn't know whether to be relieved or disappointed that she'd chosen to ignore his news about Fiona and the dissolution of his marriage. She hadn't seemed convinced. He wondered if she'd got a wager going in the office pool and was waiting for him to cave. Maybe she was hoping to win the pot, which he heard was up around a thousand bucks. He was well aware that his weakness for Fiona was legendary around the water cooler.

An attractive young woman directed them to Mitchell Eton's corner office at the end of a short hallway. Black and white lithographs of machines through the ages lined the pale green walls. They found Mitchell working on his laptop in a sunny corner of his large office. He frowned when he saw them standing in the doorway but recovered quickly, leading them into a small meeting room with two large windows and a view of the woods. "Have you arrested her?" he asked as he sat down.

"We're still following up on leads," said Gundersund. "I'm sure you understand that we need enough evidence for a conviction before we take the case to the prosecutor."

"And I'm sure you can appreciate how frustrated my wife and I are by the pace. However, I agree that you need to ensure the Thompson woman spends the rest of her life in prison. She must never be allowed to corrupt another boy like she corrupted Devon." He ran a hand across his eyes. "What brings you here today then?"

"Some new information about Devon. We've learned that he visited the Limestone Spa Hotel after school on the day he died. According to Ivan Bruster, he met with Devon to discuss a summer job in his company. Did you know about this?"

Mitchell's eyes darted back and forth between them, seeming to look for validation that what Gundersund said was true. His voice came out frosty, the words forced through tight lips. "No. I would have told you if I'd known. Have you spoken with Ivan?"

"Yes. Devon was keeping the job interview a surprise for you, apparently. Ivan let Devon know that he had the job before he left the interview."

Conflicting emotions battled across Mitchell's face. "This brings it all back, you know? My son had such a bright future ahead of him and this makes it real. I'm glad that he at least died knowing he'd gotten the job."

Bruster had said much the same. "Ivan told us that Devon left before six but didn't say where he was going."

"So you've accounted for what, an hour more of his day? That doesn't seem to be nailing down the killer."

"It's one more piece of the puzzle."

Stonechild asked, "How are your wife and Sophie doing?"

Mitchell's eyes shifted over to her. "Not great but better, thanks for asking. I'm leaving after you finish to pick up Sophie from school. It's her first day back."

"We understand you're having a celebration of Devon's life on Friday."

"We've decided against it for now. We'll keep the burial a private service with only our family. Sophie and my wife are not up to anything public at the moment. I intend to start a football scholarship in Devon's name. Perhaps we'll have a celebration of his life at a later date, once we've had some time to grieve privately. Once this business with Jane Thompson is completed."

Kala ate a late supper of scrambled eggs and toast standing at the kitchen counter looking at the black line of trees at the edge of the lake. Taiku had greeted her arrival and immediately gone to lie down on the couch in the living room. She'd had to coax him to go for a walk. He hadn't eaten any of his supper. She was considering whether or not to take him to the vet in the morning when her cellphone rang on the table where she'd left it after calling Rouleau.

"So sorry to take all this time to get back to you." Caroline Russell's voice was loud but friendly in her ear. "I wanted to find out how it really went with Dawn, and don't worry, I'm not expecting it went smoothly. The trust with you will take some time to renew."

"She didn't say much." Kala was hesitant to put her own trust on the line with Caroline Russell. She was too used to having her words used against her.

Caroline spoke with care after a brief silence. "I'm worried about Dawn. She's been skipping school again and won't say where she's spending her time."

"Can't the foster parents ensure she makes it to class?"

"They haven't developed a relationship with her. This is part of the problem."

Kala remained silent. What could she say except I told you so?

Caroline didn't let the dead air last as long this time. "Look, to be candid, I'm not in agreement with Tamara Jones about removing Dawn from your care. However, I'm only babysitting the file until she comes back off leave."

"Could you transfer Dawn back to live with me?"

"I can recommend this, but it's not my decision. I feel, however, that if you develop a relationship with her again, this could go a long way toward a positive outcome."

"So no promises."

A sigh. "I wish I could tell you differently."

Kala thought it over. "When can I see Dawn again?"

"I could arrange something for the weekend."

"I'm not sure of my schedule but set it up and I'll try to make it."

After the call ended, Kala put on her jacket and called for Taiku. She took him across the lawn and down to the rocky strip of beach. The air was cold, but the wind was down and the waves were gentle swells rolling into the bay. The moon had grown to almost a quarter, and stars dotted the black dome of a sky. She found a flat rock and sat with Taiku taking up the space near her feet. She absent-mindedly rubbed his ears while thinking over the situation with Dawn and what she should do next. It wasn't too late to back out completely before she gave Dawn another chance to reject her — but that was a coward's way out. She had to stand firm and allow Dawn to work this through. She owed her that. Gundersund would agree, she knew.

She didn't know quite what to make of Gundersund's announcement that his marriage was over. She knew he believed what he said at this moment, but he'd been down the same road before and Fiona was still his wife. Kala couldn't see her going away easily. Kala wouldn't let herself think about him being single until the deed was done.

On the way back to the house with Taiku loping alongside, she replayed the last part of her workday. She'd spent a few hours watching Jane's apartment after she told Gundersund she'd be heading home. Jane had been inside and appeared restless, walking back and forth in front of the bedroom window. Kala had found herself wondering what Jane was planning, and not for the first time. Once, Jane had stopped and stared out the window, her eyes probing into the darkness of the backyard, and Kala had thought for sure that she'd be seen, but Jane had given no sign. She'd reminded Kala of a tiger pacing in its cage, waiting for the right moment to pounce on the gatekeeper to make its escape.

CHAPTER TWENTY-FOUR

"Will you hurry up and get down here? You're going to be late for school … again!" Roslyn Hanson walked past the mirror hanging in the hallway and grimaced at her tired-looking face and bedraggled hair. If only she had the money for a trip to the salon. She licked her fingers and rubbed a bit of egg yolk from the side of her mouth before going into the kitchen to get her purse. She waved her arms in the air as she passed Charlie sitting at the table slouched over a bowl of puffed cereal. He looked at her from under the brim of his ball cap.

"What did I tell you about wearing your hat to the table?" she asked, not expecting an answer. "Your sister is going to be the death of me. Can you please make sure she gets out the door? I have to get to work."

"Sure."

"You're a pet." She blew him a kiss as she opened the door and stepped outside. "Not raining for once," she said before slamming the door behind her.

Charlie shoved his bowl of cereal across the table. He picked up his cellphone and checked for messages as he got up and headed into the hallway and up the stairs. He stopped at Tiffany's door and banged on it with his fist. "Hey, you decent?" he yelled.

The door jerked open and Tiffany batted her eyes. "More like indecent." She turned her back on him and returned to stand in front of the full-length mirror, picking up her eyeliner pencil and continuing to draw it around her eyes.

Charlie crossed the floor and sprawled on her bed. He pulled her sweater out from under him and held it up before tossing it toward the foot of the bed. "Do you own anything besides black clothes? Mom says to make sure you get to school on time today."

"Yeah, like that's news." She finished with the eyeliner and picked up a lipstick. She applied it thickly and stepped back to admire the slash of red on her lips that contrasted like a bloodstain with her blackened eyes and pale powdered skin. She walked over to the bed and picked up her sweater. "I like black clothes," she said, putting her arm into the sleeve. She looked at him. "How are things going?"

"Fine."

"You can tell me, Charlie."

"I just feel bad."

"I know, but it's better this way. Devon deserved what he got."

"It's weird not having him around, though."

"I know, but you'll get used to it."

Charlie swung his legs over the side of the bed. "Some of the kids in my class think I killed him."

Tiffany was afraid this was going to happen. She was going to have to be tough enough for both of them. She made her voice sound unconcerned. "They can think whatever they like. They have no proof."

"Have you talked to Sophie yet?"

"Nah. She's been impossible to get near. I heard she's back in school, so I'm going to try to get to her today."

"Well, she could blow it for all of us."

Tiffany found herself losing patience. Fighting her brother's battles was one thing. Having to listen to him whine was something else. "I'll look after it." She stared at Charlie again. He was wearing a shirt that said "Just Give 'Er" and his bony arms were sticking out like toothpicks. She thought about what a sad little wanker he'd been his entire life.

"Let's get moving, then." She reached down and poked him affectionately in the ribs. "Make Mom's day and get to school on time."

"She'll know we're up to something if you start behaving." He grinned at her before his face returned to its regular sullen default.

"Yeah, well, if we get to school early, I can have a smoke before I have to sit through another boring math class. If I'm lucky, the teacher won't check homework or there'll be another note home."

Rouleau met with Gundersund in his office at going on ten o'clock Thursday morning. Gundersund looked tired and preoccupied. "Everything okay?" Rouleau asked.

"Yeah, just trouble sleeping. What have you got?"

"I've gone through all the reports and think it's time to bring in Charlie Hanson and see if we can shake something out of him. I'm going to send Woodhouse over to pick him up from school. He knew Devon better than anyone and he's clammed up. We need to break through the wall and find out what he knew."

Gundersund nodded. "You think he has information?"

"I'm sure of it. Best friends since grade five and the last one to see Devon at school. I'd bet money he knows what happened to him. I believe this is worth a try."

"Anyone else we should be putting in the hot seat?"

"Besides Jane Thompson?" Rouleau took a drink of coffee. "Her husband had reason to hate Devon."

"Yeah, Adam Thompson strikes me as a difficult man — unforgiving with a low tolerance for failure."

"A man concerned with projecting a good image?"

"I'd say so. From what he said about Jane, her affair with Devon still rankles. He might have wanted to kill the problem. Take some revenge and restore his pride. Replacing his wife with a twenty-something-year-old might not be enough."

"He also wants to keep Jane away from the kids, so killing Devon and putting suspicion on her could solve another problem."

"Do you want us to bring him in for questioning?"

"Let's wait until after Woodhouse interviews Charlie."

"You really think it's a good idea to let Woodhouse take the lead on that?" Gundersund looked far from convinced.

"I'd like Woodhouse to have a role." He'd decided to give Woodhouse more responsibility in the hopes that he'd start playing on the team. Woodhouse was also rude enough to take on a teenager who might respect that kind of approach. Sometimes, a gentler hand didn't get respect from kids turned off to authority. "I wouldn't mind if you watched the interview from behind the two-way mirror." He might be willing to risk Woodhouse running an interview, but he wanted another set of eyes.

"Will do."

"Stonechild late this morning?"

"She said she had an errand to run but will be in shortly."

"Good. Heath pulled the tail off Jane Thompson during working hours too. Let Stonechild know."

"Any reason?"

"The manpower is needed elsewhere and Jane hasn't done anything out of the ordinary. In fact, the reports on her comings and goings are as exciting as dirt. I couldn't come up with a good enough reason to keep the tail."

"She would be on her best behaviour knowing she was being watched."

"I can't justify tying up somebody when we don't have any proof linking her to the murder. If you get me some evidence, now that's a different story."

Gundersund left to wait for Woodhouse, and Rouleau stared at the pile of paperwork on his desk.

He'd started going through the first file when Vera knocked at the door. He hadn't seen her since the night of the charity musical.

"Come in, Vera. I wanted to apologize for missing the play the other night. How'd it go?"

"Good. I was sorry you didn't make it." She wasn't smiling and cut off his second apology. "Hilary Eton is in the waiting area by the front desk and asking to speak to you."

Rouleau checked his watch. Still twenty minutes before his meeting with Heath. "I can see her now."

"I'll go get her. I could use the exercise."

He watched Vera walk away; he wanted to call her back, but didn't. He wasn't sure she'd accept that he'd skipped the night out for no reason other than he hated sitting through a play, especially when singing was involved. Frances had known this and gone alone or with a girlfriend if there was something she wanted to see.

Hilary Eton was suddenly standing in the doorway to his office, looking much like a bird that wasn't sure if it should land or take off. Rouleau got up and ushered her inside, sitting her in the chair normally occupied by Gundersund. She crossed and uncrossed her legs while unbuttoning her coat. She was wearing kid leather gloves, russet red and expensive looking. Her coat was mohair and her black leather boots came above her knees over black leggings.

Rouleau took the second visitor chair next to her, repositioning it so that he was facing her. "How can I help you?" he asked.

"I've come to beg you to arrest the Thompson woman so we can get on with our lives. I implore you to do the right thing." Her fingers picked at the fabric of her sweater.

"As the investigating officers told your husband yesterday, we need to have more evidence before we can arrest her. I assure you that we're working thoroughly and methodically to make a case against Devon's killer. We're as eager as you are to bring someone to justice for his murder." He spoke gently. "We have to be certain she killed him, but we haven't reached that point in the investigation yet."

Hilary let out a sound of anguish. She half rose from the chair. "That woman was responsible for everything … everything. If but for her, Devon would have turned out differently. He wouldn't … he would …" Her hands waved in the air. "How can you people not see what she's done?"

Rouleau said quietly, "Can you tell me about Devon? I'd like to hear more about him."

Hilary focused on him then and the frantic energy left her like air escaping a balloon. She settled back into the chair. "What do you want to know? That Jane Thompson broke and destroyed my loving boy? He was never the same, you know. She should never have been let out of prison."

"What was he like before the business with Mrs. Thompson?"

Hilary's face relaxed and she closed her eyes for just a moment. She looked at Rouleau. "He was active and advanced for his age right from the start, and such a good-looking boy. We had a special bond, the two of us. Mitchell was jealous, I think, because he wasn't part of it and he tried to toughen Devon up. I think he understands now the bond I felt with our son because he has much the same for Sophie. It's odd isn't it, Sergeant, how one of our children can stir that feeling in us? And I don't mean anything perverted, just simply an affinity with them that can't be explained. Of course, all that disappeared with Devon after he was corrupted. Oh, Devon still had the charm and worked to please me, but he wasn't the same."

Rouleau remembered Stonechild saying that she couldn't get a real read on Devon even after all the interviews. Hilary's ramblings held a truth that he couldn't see yet. He waited, letting her know that he was listening, not daring to interrupt. The look in her eyes was as close to raw pain as Rouleau had ever seen, and he wondered if he'd looked the same when he heard that Frances had died.

"I shouldn't have come. Mitchell won't be happy if he finds out." She started to do up her coat, her long fingers fumbling with the buttons, having difficulty putting them through the holes.

"I'm glad that you did. You've been under a great deal of stress and understandably want answers."

"Please forgive me." She stood quickly. "I need to go."

"I'll walk you out."

"No, you've done more than enough already." She extended a gloved hand and he reached for it. Her eyes held his. "Please let me know as soon as you arrest her. I think I could sleep then."

Rouleau watched her walk down the hall toward the exit and thought about what she'd told him, uneasy at what she'd revealed about her son. He'd relay the conversation to Gundersund and Stonechild and hopefully they'd cross-reference the information with conversations from other witnesses and make sense of it. He wished he was in a position to take a greater part in the investigation, finding directing from the sidelines a frustration. Necessary to have someone overseeing all the bits and pieces, but not the same as speaking with all the people in the victim's life. He missed being on the front lines. That was the greatest loss that came with moving up the ladder and accepting a pay increase. That, and the time that he spent on paperwork that he'd never get back.

He returned to his desk and opened the file he'd been going through before Hilary Eton had entered his office. He'd be the unit's representative at a conference in Toronto on use of force in a week and had a lot of reading ahead of him. He had ten minutes to make some headway before his trip to Heath's office to explain again why they hadn't arrested Jane Thompson.

It might have been the fact that Rouleau had given Woodhouse a job to do that didn't involve door-to-door searches that made him enter Frontenac Secondary School by the front door and wait patiently in the office instead of barging into Charlie Hanson's classroom and dragging the kid out. He'd conceded to Bennett's suggestion that it didn't take two of them to drive Charlie to the station and left him following up on some phone calls.

Charlie shuffled into the office behind the secretary who'd gone to fetch him. Woodhouse was leaning on the counter and turned his head. Kid could have been him at that age. Same awkward looking slouch, hair wild and curly enough to mean he'd never be cool. The black glasses on the kid's face would add to the "kick me, I'm a goof" look. Woodhouse straightened.

"You'll be coming with me, son," he said. He motioned the kid to walk in front of him and they passed by a few giggling girls on their way down the hall to the main doors. Charlie kept his head down.

A group of older kids was standing at the edge of the property smoking, and Woodhouse could almost feel the pain radiating from Charlie as he walked past them.

"May as well sit up front with me. Not like you're under arrest."

Woodhouse's attempt at humour fell as flat as a pancake, but Charlie got into the front seat and did up his belt without comment. He'd brought his school bag and held it in his lap. He'd been in the middle of class and said he'd go home from the station.

Woodhouse eased the car away from the curb, ignoring the rude gestures from the kids that he saw in his rear-view mirror as he pulled away.

CHAPTER TWENTY-FIVE

Jane's Thursday started with a pleasant surprise. The cop car that had become a fixture outside her apartment was gone. She had no idea why but took this as a sign that today was going to be a very good day.

She dressed in her usual jeans and a new second-hand shirt that she'd bought for three dollars at the Sally Ann. She'd found it in one of the bags and recognized the quality of silk and cut from her old life, when she'd buy her own clothes at higher end boutiques. A royal blue shade, the shirt draped mid-thigh and she'd found a used silver belt to tuck it in at the waist. She could almost believe she was that same woman who'd once liked to dress up for a night out with Adam.

She kept to her routine, drinking a cup of instant coffee while waiting for two pieces of bread to brown in the toaster. She threw the last of the loaf into the garbage, and after her sparse meal, checked that all the perishable food was emptied from the fridge and cupboards. She'd only bought what she'd needed and the garbage bag was less than half full. After brushing her teeth and washing her face, she tucked her toothbrush and the toothpaste tube into her purse and left the soap on the side of the sink. She hated to leave the shampoo and conditioner, but she felt it would be wiser not to have anything with her that looked like she was going to be gone longer than a day.

She'd be back to freshen up before leaving this place for the last time. The ringing of the phone in the bedroom startled her as she was putting on her jacket. "What now?" She could leave, but if it was her parole officer making a spot check, she had to be available. Everything had to look like business as usual. She crossed the short distance and picked up on the third ring. The voice she loved and often despaired of breathed into her ear: "I don't know why I felt this urge to call you this morning, but something felt off last night."

Jane kept a groan from escaping. She stared out the window and said, "I'm fine, Sandra. Just on my way out the door to work."

"You aren't going to do anything stupid, are you?"

"Of course not." Jane pulled the receiver away and cursed under her breath. All the good karma from the cop car being gone was disappearing with this call from her sister.

"I thought I could pick you up after work and we could pay Mom a visit at the home. I know this isn't what you want to do, but I've been thinking about it, and I believe seeing her again would be cathartic. You've given her more power in your imagination than is good for you. When you see her, you'll know what a diminished, helpless person she really is. What time are you off?"

"I'm seeing my parole officer after work. Can I think about it? I'm not saying no, but just not today."

"I thought you saw your parole officer on Fridays. Today isn't Friday."

"He had to change the day this week because he's going out of town for a conference." *Stop talking, Jane,* she ordered herself. *The less you say, the less your story sounds like a lie.* "Listen, Sandra, I really have to get moving. Call you later?"

That pause again, and then, "Yeah, I'll call you tonight at seven. I love you, Sis. I don't think I've said that often enough."

Now where did that come from? "Love you, too."

A crackle on the line. "Jane? Jane, are you still there?"

"Yeah, I'm still here."

Sandra's breath was a whoosh in her ear. "I woke up with this bad feeling today and had to call you. You remember how I got those premonitions as a kid? I always knew when you were in trouble. Like that time those kids beat you up and I found you hiding in the park because you were scared to go home and face the wrath of mother for ripping your jacket and getting it covered in mud? Well, I woke with the same kind of feeling today."

"Could this bad feeling be tied to the fact the police think I killed Devon Eton?" Jane tried to make her voice light even as a flutter of anxiety started in her chest. "Then I'm starting to get premonitions too, if that's the case."

"Don't make fun. I'm serious about this. You have to take care today, Jane — and think about a visit with Mom sometime soon."

"Okay, okay, I will." Jane hung up the phone and added the word "not" into the empty bedroom. She didn't plan to visit their mother again in this lifetime. It would take more time to get over never seeing her sister again, but that was a sacrifice she'd have to make to get what she really wanted.

And what she really wanted was almost within her grasp.

She left the apartment, walking quickly toward the bus stop on the other side of Princess while trying to ignore the worry Sandra's call had started in her head. Damn her sister for picking today of all days to play at being a clairvoyant. The weather was co-operating, at least. Overcast and chilly but no rain forecast until after dark. She did up her jacket and scanned the road for signs of a bus. She could see one in the far distance letting people off at a stop. The first leg of her journey was right on schedule. If her luck held, soon she'd be miles away and her life in Kingston would become but a distant memory.

Word didn't take long to make its way to Tiffany that Charlie had been picked up by the cops. Soon after, she'd left history class on the pretext of going to the washroom and slipped out the side door. She chewed on what Charlie's trip in the cop car could mean all the way to Winston Churchill Public School, hoping to get to Sophie as she'd promised Charlie, but not convinced this was the best course of action now that the cops were homing in on him. She knew that she had to do something, though. Charlie wasn't the type of kid the courts would look favourably on.

The school buses were idling out front of the school when she rounded the corner. She quickened her pace to a run, jumping off the sidewalk onto the road to get around a group of girls. She thought she saw Sophie's distinctive white-blond hair but as she got closer realized it wasn't her. Sophie always walked home so Tiffany figured she'd hang out near the entrance and wait. Kids came out in waves and then she recognized a couple of girls from Sophie's class.

"Hey, Madeleine!"

The redhead turned and Tiffany waved. She'd remembered the girl's name at the last second and luckily been right. The two girls walked toward her.

"Hey." Tiffany smiled. "I'm looking for Sophie Eton. Is she still inside?"

Madeleine shook her head. "Her mother came and got her last class for an appointment. I think she's seeing a shrink. Do you want me to pass along a message?"

"No, that's okay. I'll catch her later."

Tiffany walked back to the sidewalk and pulled out a cigarette from the crumpled pack in her bag. She waited until she was out of sight of the school before putting it into her mouth.

Now what?

She could cross the street and go home to wait for Charlie to show up, but something told her that he was going to be a while.

What if he starts talking?

She started across Macdonnell Street toward her house and felt in her jacket pocket for her lighter. Her fingers brushed a hard piece of something. She pulled it out and looked at Officer Stonechild's name and phone number on a business card. The card she'd shoved in her pocket with no intention of using. She walked past her house and kept going as she flicked the card with her fingers, forgetting about the unlit cigarette in her mouth.

When she reached Johnson, she shoved the card back into her jacket and pulled out the lighter. *Chill*, she told herself. *It isn't time yet to do something desperate. Let this Charlie-cop thing play out before you throw yourselves on the mercy of a stranger who might or might not help get you out of this mess. Charlie knows better than to open his mouth.*

She lit her cigarette and continued on, hoping her mom had bought something good for a snack. She hadn't eaten all day and her stomach was rumbling. She picked up her pace. Charlie might already be home waiting for her to show up, and she'd have worried for nothing.

The hours had trudged by like a caterpillar crossing a football field, which Naomi found fitting since Adam was off watching kids run around one. She surveyed her classroom and saw twenty-eight heads bent over the math test she'd given them twenty minutes earlier. Fifteen minutes to go and they'd be handing in their papers. Ten minutes after that and they'd be leaving for the day. Quarter to four couldn't come soon enough.

The anticipation waiting for her rendezvous with Liam had her excited and apprehensive at the same time. She imagined the trouble she'd be in if Adam found out — but he wouldn't find out. He was miles away at the track meet and not due home until six. She'd be back with Ben and Olivia at five and he'd be none the wiser. One hour with Liam might be rushed, but that would make the sex exciting. Hopefully, it would be the first of many encounters. She let herself daydream. She'd leave Adam for Liam once the school year ended — they could both transfer to another school or town where Adam wouldn't cross their paths and get an apartment together. Adam was becoming more and more like a father and a tyrant in her mind as she rationalized what she was about to do. Some part of her knew she was making him into the bad guy to ease her own guilt, but really, she was too young to settle down with a man who had two kids half her age.

A man stalking his ex-con ex-wife with a camera.

Since they only had an hour, Liam had suggested they skip the Holiday Inn and she come to his apartment, which was near Queen's University. He'd kept his place after graduating the year before while starting off as a supply teacher. She hadn't dared put his address into her phone in case Adam checked, but Liam had passed it to her on a piece of paper with directions. She would destroy the paper once she got there.

She checked the clock. "Five minutes left before you hand in your papers," she announced to the class.

And half an hour until I'm lying in bed naked with Liam Brody.

CHAPTER TWENTY-SIX

"Feel like stopping in at the Merchant for a late lunch?" Gundersund asked after checking his watch.

Kala nodded. "I could eat."

They'd spent the morning watching Woodhouse interview Charlie Hanson with a finesse that had surprised them both. She hadn't had anything to eat since an early breakfast of granola and a glass of orange juice before she left the house at seven thirty.

Twenty minutes later, they were at their regular table in the room to the right of the entrance. Kala liked the feel of the bar, a limestone building built in the 1800s near the waterfront that had been a working warehouse with horses on the premises. It retained the warehouse feel with rough-hewn plank floors, fireplaces, red brick and limestone walls, and dark beamed ceilings. Even the tables and chairs were dark wood and utilitarian. A long bar extended across the back wall with a stage set up to its left where bands played on the weekends. The team had come one Friday and found wall-to-wall people standing and listening to a rock band from

Toronto. Kala was pleased to find the place nearly empty now since the lunchtime crowd had already been and departed.

They placed their food order — two whisky burgers with onion rings — and Gundersund asked for a pint of the local Beau's beer while Kala went with coffee.

"Who knew Charlie and Woodhouse had so much in common," Gundersund said after taking a sip of beer. "Both into extreme fighting on television and video games that involve a lot of guns and killing."

Kala smiled. "The two of them almost seem as if they were separated at birth."

Gundersund looked thoughtful. "I sometimes underestimate Woodhouse. It's easy to forget that he's a half-decent cop because he acts like such a chauvinistic asshole most of the time."

"You won't get any argument from me."

"Still, he didn't get anything useful out of the kid."

"Not for lack of trying, although I got the impression that Charlie is scared. Something is going on, don't you think?"

"Yeah, I got the same read, but whatever it is has him as tight-lipped as a clam."

"Didn't know clams had lips. You *are* a walking biology lesson." She smiled at him and stirred cream into her coffee. She'd give anything to see inside Charlie's brain. "Do you think he might be in danger? If he knows who killed Devon or why …"

"So maybe locking him up for the afternoon isn't as hare-brained as I thought."

"I doubt that's why Woodhouse decided to put Charlie into a cell for a few hours. I think he's trying to shake him up so that he'll talk."

Gundersund took another swallow of beer. "Good luck with that. Mrs. Hanson was on her way to the station, and she said Charlie wouldn't be saying another word without a lawyer. By the way, Rouleau told me this morning that the tail on Jane Thompson was pulled altogether."

"You're kidding." She paused. *Nobody is watching Jane.* "Why?"

"Resources mainly. Rouleau wants her brought in again tomorrow for another round of questions."

"He's hoping someone is going to crack."

"You sound doubtful."

"Because I am."

Their food arrived along with a couple that took the table next to them, ending their discussion about the case. When they'd finished eating, Gundersund checked his phone. "Rouleau wants one of us to watch the next round between Woodhouse and Charlie. Should we flip for it?"

"If you'd be okay doing it, I'd owe you one."

"Do you have something on?"

"I have some research I'd like to follow up." She returned his stare. "Nothing dangerous, I promise."

"Okay." He sighed loudly. "I'll take this one for the Gipper, but you'll have to pay up at a time of my choosing, Stonechild."

"Why do I feel like I'm promising you my first-born?" She signalled their waitress to bring their bills. "Although I am awfully grateful to skip another couple of hours of watching Charlie Hanson slumped in a chair avoiding saying anything intelligible."

"He's not the wordiest of kids. He might be bright, but it's hard to tell."

Kala thought about that. Everyone said how brilliant Devon was but none had said the same of Charlie. A few teachers had observed that Charlie was smart enough but not in the same league as Devon. Nobody had had much to say about Charlie except that he was creepy. She wondered about their mismatched relationship and whether something had happened between the two of them that had made Charlie turn on his childhood friend and bash his brains in.

Gundersund drove them back to the station and she got her truck from the lot. Knowing that Jane was free to roam without someone keeping tabs made Kala uneasy. From her hiding place in the backyard the evening before, she'd watched Jane at the window and had known in her bones that this woman was up to something.

It was after three when Kala parked in the Salvation Army's parking lot. She sat in the truck for a few minutes checking out the store and deciding whether or not she should go in. Jane wouldn't be getting off shift until four according to the schedule the parole officer had sent to them the week before. The clouds were thickening off to the east but the rain was on hold for now. She got out of the truck and stretched.

An East Indian woman came out of the store and walked a few paces away from the entrance. She turned her back to the wind and lit a cigarette. Kala crossed the parking lot until she was a few feet away from her. "Do you work in the store?"

"I'm the manager. Can I help you?"

"I'm looking for Jane Thompson. Is she off at four?"

"Jane left early for an appointment about an hour ago."

Kala pulled out her badge. "I understood she was working until four today. Weren't you supposed to call in to her parole officer if she changed her schedule?"

The woman put her hands on her hips. Her tone was defensive. "I would have but she told me that she'd made the call herself. She volunteered the information so I thought … well, maybe she told her parole officer and they didn't tell you?"

"Not that I know of, but I'll check into it."

As Kala walked back to her truck, she called the parole officer. He was away for the afternoon but his assistant said that Jane had not called that week. Kala considered the facts as she opened her truck door. Jane had left work early the first day she wasn't being watched. She'd lied to her manager about telling her parole officer. Nothing terrible in and of itself, but Kala remembered the look on Jane's face the evening before as she stood in the window, her feeling that Jane was waiting for something to happen.

Kala decided to swing by Jane's apartment before placing a call to Rouleau to have Jane tracked down and brought in.

Jane made one final check of the apartment, not sorry to leave this dismal place behind. She'd taken the bus back from the store with enough time to freshen up before lifting the floorboard and retrieving the passports and car keys from their hiding place. She'd been overly cautious but hadn't wanted to carry them on her person in case the police had done a spot check. If they had stopped her, they wouldn't have had any reason to be suspicious and she would have simply changed the timing of her plan.

Still on cautious mode, she exited the apartment building by the back entrance and entered the alleyway through the hole in the fence. The car would be waiting for her two streets over. She looked up at the sky, or what she could see of it through the trees and over the housetops. The air was cooling and the clouds were leaden and grey. She hoped the rain would hold off until after supper.

Walking quickly, she cut diagonally across College Street to Park and followed it to Helen, where she turned north toward Franklin Place. The silver Mazda 3 was in the empty warehouse parking lot right where Hieu told her it would be in the note he'd left with the keys in her mailbox two days earlier. She was grateful that he'd fulfilled his promise and chosen a car that lots of people owned and that wouldn't attract notice. She gave silent thanks to her new guardian angel and checked all around her before unlocking the door and getting inside. Hieu had left a package of butterscotch mints and bottles of water on the passenger seat along with a roadmap, which she tucked into the console. He'd warned her not to use a GPS or any other location device because she could be tracked.

Fifteen minutes later and she stopped at the curb, one block down the street from Calvin Park School. The anticipation and excitement in her chest were almost too much to bear. She didn't exhale until she saw Ben and Olivia standing on the sidewalk, Ben searching up and down the street with anxious eyes. They'd both grown so tall but she'd have known them anywhere. When Ben saw her, he poked Olivia and they both turned their faces toward her car and relief replaced the worry. Olivia raised her hands and clapped. They raced over, and Ben opened the back door and Olivia climbed in while Ben got into the front.

"Mom! You made it." Ben was smiling at her with such delight it made Jane's heart hurt.

"Mom!" Olivia called as she slid across the back seat until she was behind Jane and could wrap her arm around Jane's neck. Jane held on to her arm and leaned her head into Olivia's.

"I'm so happy to see you both, but we have to get moving. We can give big hugs once we're safely away, so sit back Olivia and put on your seat belt." Already, Jane had eased the car away from the curb and turned toward the shortest route out of Kingston.

"We did what you said and left all our clothes and stuff. I don't care about any of it anyway." Ben grinned at her. "We just want to be with you."

Olivia called from the back seat, "We missed you so much, Mommy."

"And I so, *so* missed you both." Jane smiled at Olivia in the rear-view mirror. "Are you ready for an adventure, my sweet Olive?"

"I am! I am!"

Ben opened the map tucked between his seat and the console. "Where are we going to cross?"

"I'm going to drive to the Thousand Island Bridge, and rush hour should still be on so hopefully we won't be looked at too closely. I have passports. Your name is Peter, and Olivia, your new name is Carey."

"Carey. I love that name," Olivia said.

"Good," said Jane, "because you're going to be called Carey from now on."

"And what's your new name, Mommy?" asked Olivia.

"I'm going to be Maureen. Our new last name is Bedard because it's a really common surname."

"Where are we going to be living?" asked Ben.

She glanced at him. "We're going to a place outside of Pittsburgh for tonight. There's already an apartment lined up for us but we won't stay there for long. We'll decide where we want to live in a week or two."

"Good." Ben sat back and looked out the side window. "Goodbye, Kingston," he said. "Been good to know ya."

"What did you say to Naomi about coming home late from school?"

"She has an appointment and won't be home until five. Dad is on that field trip I told you about. I left a message on Naomi's voice mail when I knew she was in class saying that I'd be taking Olivia to the library for an after-school activity that my teacher told me about." Ben smiled at Jane. "It's lame but should buy us some time. Naomi isn't as strict as Dad."

Olivia piped up from the back seat. "Naomi leaves us alone. She wishes we weren't there."

"Well her wish is coming true," Ben said. "I typed notes from Dad to say we had to get out of class early and I forged his name. I practised writing his name a lot."

Jane looked at him and grimaced. "That's the last time you do anything like that. I don't want you turning into a thief or anything."

"I know, Mom."

"Did you leave your cellphone in your locker?"

"I did better than that. I turned it off and hid it at my friend's house in their shed in the garden tools. They'll never find it because they're done with their garden for the season."

"Good. I threw away the one I was using to contact you."

"We're all set, then." Ben settled back in his seat.

Jane took a hand from the wheel and reached over to hold his. "Thanks for not giving up on me. You and Olivia are all that has been keeping me going."

"We know you didn't do what they said."

Jane didn't dare look over at her son, her little boy now almost a teenager. His belief in her had never wavered, not even when everyone around him — and even she — had given up. She wasn't the same person as before all this began, and the proof wasn't hard to find. Here she was stealing her two kids away from their father and home, not sure if this was best for them or just for her.

She may have ruined their childhoods, but God help her, she couldn't give them up.

CHAPTER TWENTY-SEVEN

Gundersund dropped by Rouleau's office after three more hours spent watching Woodhouse interview Charlie. He filled two mugs with coffee that looked to have been made first thing in the morning and added generous amounts of cream. He stirred two heaping spoonfuls of sugar into the second cup.

Rouleau was standing motionless in front of the window and it took him a while to notice Gundersund in the doorway. "Is now a good time?" Gundersund asked.

Rouleau turned, and his eyes focused in on Gundersund. He nodded and walked toward his desk. "Sure. Anything come out of the interview?" He accepted the mug and sat down.

Gundersund plunked himself into the visitor chair and stretched out his legs. He held the coffee cup in both hands and took a sip before lowering it to rest on his chest. "Not really. Charlie wasn't saying anything before his mother and the lawyer showed up, and he said even less after."

"Woodhouse wants to arrest him and hold him overnight for obstruction. What do you think?"

"To rattle him?"

"And shake something out of him."

Gundersund smiled at the image of Woodhouse holding Charlie upside down trying to shake an answer out of his tightly clenched lips. "Your call," he said.

"I told Woodhouse no. We really haven't a good reason to arrest him now. It's his right not to talk and we've been treading on shaky ground even holding him here this long. Luckily, he didn't think to ask for a lawyer until after round one this morning."

"Although nothing came of it. Stonechild and I both think he seems scared."

"No idea why?"

"Not yet."

Rouleau drank from his cup and looked toward the outer office. "God, this coffee is awful. Where is Kala by the way?"

"Doing some research on the case, but I'm about to check in with her."

"How is she?"

"She seems to be coping. She met with Dawn and her child care worker a few days ago but won't talk about it."

"I wanted to call Children's Aid to get Dawn back when it first happened, but Kala wouldn't hear of it."

"She's used to working things out on her own."

"Her strength and her weakness." Rouleau took another sip of coffee, grimaced, and set the cup on the desk. "She's gotten quiet again, have you noticed? It's like she's rudderless."

Gundersund thought that Rouleau had gotten it right. If it wasn't for Stonechild's focus on the Devon Eton case, she'd be lost. "I'm keeping an eye on her," he said.

Rouleau nodded. "Good. I feel like I'm letting her down these days, but I'm swamped in paperwork and meetings. Keep on top of what she's up to and I'll sleep easier."

Not to mention working through the death of the woman he loved most in the world. Gundersund knew the toll Frances's death had taken even though Rouleau kept silent about his grief. "Sharing isn't her default, but she's coming around."

He wished he had more confidence in his words than he did. He had the uneasy feeling that Stonechild was working this case without him. Despite her assurances, she'd gotten secretive and was as withdrawn as when he'd first met her. He picked up his mug and stood. "I think I'll go make that phone call now. Time to get an update on Stonechild's latest research project … and to find out exactly what it is she's been working on."

Kala parked her truck on Regent a block down from Jane Thompson's building. She punched in the number for the apartment directly under Jane's and waited impatiently for one of the students to buzz her in. A skinny long-haired boy with no shirt on opened the door and she walked past him into the foyer. A blast of Foo Fighters filled the hallway. "The Pretender." She'd played the song over and over in her tape deck while driving in the backwoods of northwestern Ontario the summer of 2010. It brought back fond memories of ink black sky and endless pine trees. She held up her police badge and the kid raised both hands as if surrendering before shutting his door.

She took the steps two at a time and rapped hard on Jane's door. When she was certain that nobody was inside, she pulled out a metal pick that she kept in the inside pocket of her leather jacket and worked the lock. The satisfying click took only a few seconds.

She stepped inside and made a silent walk through the small space. She was relieved to see Jane's few possessions still in place, her towel and face cloth hanging on the towel rack in the bathroom, shampoo and soap on the side of the tub, a couple of shirts hanging in the closet, underwear in the ancient chest of drawers. The single bed looked lumpy, and the faded blue blanket covering it had a hole dead centre that revealed a greyish sheet underneath. Kala was reminded of a prison cell, the furnishings so minimal and utilitarian. *How did you survive the fall from grace to land in this depressing existence?* Passing by the bedroom window, Kala looked out at the empty yard below. If Jane had come here after work, she'd have left by her secret exit. She might still be on foot, maybe waiting at a nearby bus stop.

Kala closed the apartment door and sprinted down the stairs to her truck. She'd cruise the neighbourhood before calling this in. Maybe she was overreacting, but her gut told her probably not. She tried to put herself in Jane's place, a woman who'd been a respected teacher with a successful husband and two kids, living in a decent home. What would losing all that do to a person? How far would someone go to try to get some of that life back? Especially a woman like Jane: intelligent, beautiful, and increasingly desperate … with absolutely nothing left to lose. Even her kids had been taken from her.

Jane wasn't anywhere to be seen as Kala drove slowly up one street and down the next. She decided to head onto Princess and check in the window of the nearby coffee shop. She was at the intersection, preparing to turn right, when she checked her passenger side mirror and saw a short-haired blond head ducking into the front seat of a silver car angle parked. Kala hesitated but a car pulled up behind her and she had to make the turn. She weighed the odds and immediately disregarded the blonde when she remembered that Jane didn't own a car nor could she afford one.

Kala checked the sidewalk on both sides of the street as she drove, ignoring the driver riding her tail who was trying to make her speed up. She pulled left into the Tim Hortons and the driver leaned on his horn as he sped away. She ignored him and drove slowly past the plate glass window, taking a long look inside, but there was no sign of Jane.

Back on Princess, Kala had to make a decision. She drummed her fingers on the steering wheel. What was she missing? What would she do in Jane's shoes? Then it struck her. Jane was likely doing the same thing that she'd been doing after Dawn had been taken from her. Going to stand outside her kids' school. Trying for a glimpse of them, seeking some assurance that they were doing okay. In Jane's place, she'd be heading to Calvin Park School if she was finally free of a tail and wouldn't be hauled in for violating parole. Kala knew that one of the conditions of Jane's release was that she leave her family alone. She couldn't initiate contact with her children, and Adam had to agree to any visitation. As far as Kala knew, he hadn't. This must be driving Jane crazy, because if nothing else, everyone who'd known Jane had given her good grades as a mother. Every last one of the witnesses at her trial, including her husband, Adam, had voiced surprise at the double life she'd been leading precisely because she'd appeared such a loving and good mother. A child psychologist had interviewed Ben and Olivia, aged eight and four at the time of her arrest, and found them to be well adjusted and happy. No abuse detected.

She drove slowly, checking side streets as she went, taking Roden Street north until it merged into Norman Rogers Drive. Stopped at the Van Order Drive intersection, she checked her watch. She could see the school set back from the road, but classes were still in. There was little activity on the street except for an elderly man in a green army jacket walking two dachshunds on leads and a couple of kids standing a block away on the same side of the street as the school. She looked back in time to catch the tail end of a silver Mazda driving past her heading toward the school. It looked familiar, but then all silver Mazdas look alike. She turned right in the same direction and pulled over to the curb directly across from the school to answer her cellphone.

"Hey Gundersund. How'd the interview go?" She watched the silver car slow and pull over to the side of the road where the children were standing. "Yeah, I figured he wouldn't say anything. No, I've still got one more thing to do and then I'll be in." The car doors swung open and the kids got into the car, the girl scrambling into the back and the boy sliding into the front. Something about the boy looked familiar. "Gundersund? I've got to go. Can I call you back? Sure. Thanks." She tossed the phone onto the seat and put the truck into gear. The Mazda was turning left onto a side street. She hurried to catch up but kept some distance, still not certain that she'd seen Ben and Olivia Thompson getting into the car and unclear who was driving.

The side street was MacPherson, a short, straight road heading east that ended at Sir John A. Macdonald Boulevard. The Mazda turned south onto Macdonald. Kala had no trouble following at a distance since this was a major roadway. She sped up once to get close enough to read the licence plate before falling back. The rear window was lightly tinted, preventing her from being able to identify the driver or passengers. She was content to keep pace for a while since this route was roughly heading toward the station.

Jane Thompson had left work early and wasn't in her apartment. Could she have gotten her hands on a car? Kala considered this and realized that it wasn't outside the realm of possibility. Jane's sister might have lent her a vehicle. If Jane was at the wheel and had stopped by the school to pick up her kids mid-afternoon, she was going around the court order to see them. They obviously had gotten out of class early and were waiting for whoever was driving the car. Maybe Naomi had left class early and picked them up. They weren't heading in the direction of the Thompson house, though. Perhaps they were meeting Mitchell or going to an after-school activity. Kala kept following, not too closely but always with the silver Mazda in her sightline. The car passed Richardson Stadium on Queen's campus, crossed Union Street West before turning left onto King. The car was picking up speed.

Kala stayed back but decided to follow until they parked and she could see who got out. Lake Ontario was restless and choppy with the thick cloud cover making the water a dull slate grey. The oak and willow trees swayed in the wind blowing in off the lake. The wind and rain had removed most of the autumn leaves from the trees and they lay a thick crimson and yellow blanket covering the lawns while the odd cluster of leaves became caught in the breeze and swirled above the ground. Kala had her window down but didn't smell rain yet. It would be a few hours before the storm hit.

She passed Murney Tower and Macdonald Park where Devon Eton's body had been found, and the Kingston Yacht Club with boats moored and bobbing in the water like so many corks on strings. At West Street, the Mazda swung south onto Ontario

Street and Kala sped up slightly to keep pace, her heart pounding faster because she knew that Ontario Street turned into Highway 2. When the car passed by Princess and kept going straight past the Wolfe Island ferry dock, her unease went from simmering to full-blown worry. The driver took the bridge across the St. Lawrence River and past the Military College and Kala knew with certainty that the driver was taking the kids out of town.

She had a decision to make. Give up the chase, which was based on intuition as much as logic, or follow for a bit longer and see if they were stopping somewhere along the highway. She checked her watch again. She was going to be late for work, but what if her instincts were right and those were the Thompson kids in the car? She'd keep going and deal with the rest later.

After they passed the small communities of Ravensview and Poplar Grove with no sign of stopping, Kala began to wonder where the Mazda was heading in such a hurry. They were driving about ten kilometres over the speed limit — not enough to attract police attention but not wasting any time. This road followed the St. Lawrence and passed by Gananoque on its way to Brockville and Cornwall. There was enough traffic that she could stay back and keep a few cars between her truck and the Mazda.

The Mazda turned onto the 401 highway at Gananoque and Kala continued following. She decided it was time to pass the car and see who was driving. Pulling into the outside lane, she drove alongside and glanced over. Once, twice. Olivia Thompson was in the back and Ben was in the front passenger seat. Jane Thompson was at the wheel, but luckily she turned her head at that moment to say something to Ben and had her eyes turned away from Kala. Kala hit the steering wheel with the palm of her hand.

Damn it, Jane. You've just bought yourself a whole whack of trouble and a prison sentence.

Kala dropped back and changed lanes so that she was directly behind them. When the Mazda took the Ivy Lea exit, her heart sank. There could only be one explanation. Jane was taking her kids across the border into New York State at the Thousand Island border crossing. She grabbed her cellphone from the seat next to her to call it in. As she fumbled with one hand to turn the phone on, she had a sudden vision of Jane standing in her bedroom window, the lamplight glowing behind her. She was leaning on the window sill, stretching her neck to see the stars above the trees and houses, the expression on her face expectant and hopeful. Kala had found this startling under the circumstances. No doubt, Jane had been planning this escape and she just might have gotten away if Kala hadn't set out to track her down.

Screw it.

She tossed the phone back onto the seat and waited for a car to pass from the other direction before pulling into the oncoming lane. She drew alongside the Mazda and stayed there until Jane looked over. Kala could see by the dawning recognition and the near panic in her eyes that Jane knew she'd been caught. Before she could accelerate and make a run for it, Kala motioned her to pull over, speeding up and cutting in front of her and pumping the brakes. Jane made the only decision she could and eased the Mazda off the highway onto the shoulder. Kala pulled over several yards in front of her and hopped out of her truck. She ran back and Jane rolled down her window. Kala checked for weapons and didn't see any. She let her hand fall from her sidearm hidden under her jacket. Since her close call and Bennett's shooting a few months before, she'd taken to wearing it when away from the station during her working hours.

"This isn't going to work, Jane. You have to take them back to Adam."

Ben was glaring at Kala and Olivia was wailing in the back seat. Jane had her hands on the steering wheel and looked straight ahead as if she was thinking of how she was going to get them away from Kala and onto the bridge to the States and freedom. When she finally looked at Kala, her brilliant blue eyes were hard and defiant. "I suppose," she said, but Kala could tell she was still weighing options.

"We don't want to go back to my father," Ben said. "We want to be with my mother."

"Mommy! Mommy!" Olivia was screaming from the back seat.

"Hush, Olive. Officer Stonechild is right, Ben." She turned toward him. "This isn't going to work." She looked back at Kala and spoke quietly so that Ben couldn't hear. "Am I under arrest?"

Kala looked at the terror on the kids' faces. They'd believed they were going to be living with their mother in some new town with a new start.

She could understand a child's simple need to be with their birth mother, no matter what she'd done. What would it do to them when she went back to prison? She looked back at Jane. "Not yet. Not if we get them home now. You're wanted at the station for questioning tomorrow but not because of this. Disappearing with two children is not as easy as you might think. Do you really want them to lead a life on the run, always looking over their shoulders? Do you want that for Ben and Olivia?"

Jane slowly shook her head. A sigh heaved upward from her stomach and Kala knew she'd accepted that her run to the border was over. "No. No, I suppose I don't."

"I'll follow you back. I'll need to go in with the kids to make sure their absence hasn't been called in." Kala took two steps toward her truck.

"Why? Why are you doing this for me?" Jane asked, her voice rising in a cry above the noise of a passing car.

Kala stopped and turned to look at her. Jane's eyes were skeptical, puzzled, challenging Kala for an answer.

"I'm not entirely sure," Kala said, but she did know. She only had to look at the shattered faces of Ben and Olivia. The images would stay with her for a long time. If Jane had killed Devon, she would pay soon enough. She said, "Maybe, I don't want your kids to go through any more trauma until they have to."

Jane bowed her head in guilt or agreement, Kala wasn't sure which.

CHAPTER TWENTY-EIGHT

Naomi left Liam's apartment twenty minutes later than she'd intended. She was surprised at how reluctant she felt to return to her life with Adam. Liam was uncomplicated and easy to make laugh. She didn't have to pretend to be older or more mature than she was. She'd forgotten how good it was to be herself and not be playing a role.

She pulled into the driveway and was alarmed to see the house in darkness. Then, she remembered that Ben had sent a message that he was taking Olivia to the library for some after-school program. She hoped they made it home before Adam. He'd have a fit if he knew they were out and about by themselves.

After turning on a lamp in the living room and the outdoor porch light, she put some OneRepublic on the stereo and set about preparing a simple meal of omelettes and hash browns, dancing around the kitchen to "Love Runs Out" before rummaging through the fridge and pulling out fresh basil, cherry tomatoes, onions and mushrooms, a carton of eggs, and milk. It didn't take her long to cut up the vegetables as she chopped to the beat. She returned to the fridge for the block of cheddar and got the cheese grater out of the cupboard.

By the time she'd shredded the cheese and browned the onions for the hash browns, it was going on seven o'clock. She tried Ben's cell for the second time, but it again went straight to voice mail. She stood at the kitchen window and tapped her fingers on the counter. Where were those kids? Should she get in her car and search for them? She dreaded Adam's anger if he got home before they did and she couldn't account for their whereabouts.

She was trying Ben's cellphone again when she heard the click of the front door. She checked out the side window and didn't see Adam's car in the driveway. "Thank God," she said under her breath. Ben and Olivia were halfway up the stairs by the time she reached the front entrance. "How was the library?" she called up to them.

Ben turned at the landing. "Fine."

He was in darkness and Naomi reached over and clicked on the light. She looked up the stairs to where he was standing. He was blinking, his eyes bloodshot and bruised-looking but his face was pale. "What's wrong with you, Ben?" She started toward him, taking the steps two at a time.

"Nothing's wrong with me." He turned to go, but she caught him by the arm. "Have you been crying?"

"Let me go."

"Where were you two?" She knew he'd been up to something. A disturbing thought crossed her mind. "Were you with your mother?"

His bottom lip trembled.

"Oh my God, you were!"

"You can't tell Dad."

"What have you done? Your father is going to kill us all."

They both looked down the stairs toward the front door at the same time. It had opened with a bang and Adam was stepping in carrying his gym bag. "I'm home!" He looked up and caught sight of the two of them standing suspended on the landing. He stopped. "What's going on?"

Naomi gave Ben a little shove and moved to block Adam's view. "Nothing. Ben is just washing up for supper." She pasted a smile on her face and bounded down the stairs into his arms. "How was the track meet? Did we win the trophy?"

"Hey, take it easy." But he was laughing and dropped the gym bag and grabbed her around the waist. "We placed third overall but got a few firsts in the hundred-yard dash and long jump. A good showing for my first time as a coach."

"Bravo!"

His hand slipped lower over her rear end and she jumped. The last thing she wanted to do at this moment was replace the memory of Liam's hands on her body with Adam's. She slipped out from under his arm and ran her fingertips across his cheek as she stepped back. "I have supper to prepare. The kids are hungry."

"Haven't they eaten yet?" He followed her down the hall into the kitchen.

"They wanted to wait for you." She picked up a

spatula. "You're awfully late by the way. What time was the track meet over?"

He picked up some grated cheese and popped it into his mouth. He avoided her eyes. "Close to five, but I went to the gym on my way home." He started walking toward the family room. "If we're having omelettes, I'll have a four-egger. I missed lunch."

"Coming right up," she said, relieved that he wasn't suspicious of her or the kids. He likely had his own sins to hide.

She opened the freezer and took out the hash browns, her thoughts escaping this drudgery and back with Liam in his bachelor apartment, lying naked in the crook of his arm on his double bed while they checked their cellphones. She was already counting the hours until morning when she'd see him at school again.

Jane stumbled up the stairs to her apartment, light-headed with fatigue and overcome by an overwhelming sense of loss. She knew that she was lucky Officer Stonechild hadn't arrested her or reported her to anyone … yet. She'd taken the passports and car keys and told Jane that she'd be checking on her first thing in the morning and she'd better be available. Jane knew she wouldn't be offered any more lifelines. Officer Stonechild could lose her job for letting her off with a warning, although she hadn't seemed terribly concerned about any repercussions. She was like no other cop Jane had ever met.

At the top of the stairs, Jane stopped, unable to take in what she was seeing. An enormous dread filled her. Spray-painted in red block letters across the door to her apartment was a single word: WHORE. The shock made her stagger back and lose her footing. She caught herself by grabbing on to the banister and clinging suspended over the stairs until she could pull herself back onto the step. Straightening, she leaned heavily on the railing and pulled herself to the landing. She approached the door slowly, as if walking toward living, breathing evil. She reached out trembling fingers to touch the paint. The lock to her apartment had been jimmied and the door swung open under her touch. Her fingers came away smeared in red. Whoever had done this had been here recently.

She stood still, senses on alert and ready to flee. When she didn't hear any noises from inside, she entered and surveyed what she could see from the doorway. She walked through the rooms, exhaustion replacing horror by the time she reached her bedroom. The intruder had been inventive, choosing from a list of nasty words that they'd spray-painted across the walls and mirrors in the bedroom and bathroom. Above her bed was spray-painted in capital block letters: REPENT BITCH OR DIE.

Jane lowered herself slowly onto the bed and curled up into a ball, clutching her knees and rolling onto her side. She pushed her face into the bedspread and tried to imagine herself in the car cutting across upstate New York with Ben and Olivia on their way to a new life. She tried to relive the feeling of them in her arms when she'd hugged and kissed them goodbye a block away from their home. But already the sensation was fading. The warmth of their arms around her neck wasn't strong enough to erase the hatred in this room.

She was too tired to even think about cleaning up the mess tonight. She wasn't even sure what would take the words off the walls. They'd have to be repainted and she didn't want to use her precious money on paint and rollers. She got up and shut the door to her apartment, turned off all the lights, and crawled back onto the bed. Her whole body was shaking as if she had a fever, but she was cold. So cold, she felt as if she'd never be warm again. She wrapped the blanket around herself and closed her eyes.

When the rain started less than an hour later, she was still awake. She listened to large drops pattering on the roof and blowing against the bedroom window and wondered when the universe would reveal what terrible thing she'd done in her life to deserve all this heartache. Whether whatever god was calling the shots would ever stop punishing her and let her have some peace.

CHAPTER TWENTY-NINE

Kala felt guiltier about leaving Taiku alone as long as she had than she did about not arresting Jane Thompson. She arrived home at eight and expected to find him at the back door needing to get outside; instead, he was sleeping soundly on the couch when she stepped inside and took his time getting onto the floor and ambling over to greet her. She reached down and felt his nose but it was cool and wet. She crouched next to him and rested her head on his. "What is going on with you, boy?" Her guilt at having left him alone all day increased. She never had gotten him to the vet.

She took Taiku outside and he disappeared into the darkness while she sat on the steps and waited. She pulled her phone out of her jacket pocket and saw the red light flashing. She accessed the voice message system and listened. Tiffany Hanson had called two hours earlier and wanted to talk … tonight. *Tonight or never.*

Kala checked the incoming number and punched it in. Tiffany answered almost immediately, slightly out of breath. She said that she could meet Kala even though it was late, and Kala let her pick the location, which Tiffany insisted would not be her house. Ten minutes later, Kala and Taiku were on their way to meet her at a coffee shop on Princess Street.

Luckily, a car pulled out of a parking spot close to the café and Kala pulled in before someone else snapped it up. She left Taiku lying on the passenger seat with the window open a crack. It was a cool, windy night and rain had started falling, but Taiku would be fine for half an hour. He seemed unusually sleepy tonight and his eyes were closed when she looked into the truck from the sidewalk.

She'd arrived ahead of Tiffany and took the opportunity to order a chicken salad sandwich and carton of milk. She selected a table away from the windows and began eating. Tiffany walked in a few minutes later, shaking the rain out of her hair, a vision in black: leggings, army boots, pleated skirt, and jacket. The only colour breaking up the bleakness was her bright red lipstick. She ordered a tea from the counter and took the seat next to Kala, who was taking the last bite of her sandwich.

"Your Mom okay with you being out this late on a school night?" Kala asked, wiping her mouth with a napkin.

"She's at bingo. Said she needed a distraction after today."

Kala thought back. The morning seemed like a lifetime ago. "That's right. Charlie was interviewed."

"*And* held in a cell." Tiffany spoke with righteous indignation. "They can't think he killed Devon. Never mind they were best friends."

Kala looked at Tiffany's outraged face and thought about how to play this. "Charlie's a suspect, but not the only suspect," she said in a voice meant to convey hidden knowledge. She relaxed against the back of the chair and waited.

"What about that teacher? Jane Thompson? It had to be her. Everyone says so."

"Not everyone. We have evidence ..." She let her voice trail off.

"Then, it's wrong! Charlie never killed Devon." Tiffany's eyes narrowed as she studied Kala. She looked to be weighing what Kala said and assessing her next move. "What if I told you the truth about Devon? Would you lay off Charlie?"

"Depends on what you tell me."

Tiffany was quiet but her face was going through contortions as a battle raged within. Kala knew exactly what was going on inside Tiffany's head because she'd thought the same way back in the day. Cops were the enemy, not to be trusted, but the trouble Tiffany's brother was in meant giving over to the lesser threat. Kala sat silently and her patience was rewarded.

"You have to promise me you'll look out for Charlie."

"I'll do what I can."

"Devon Eton was nothing like what he showed on the surface."

"No? In what way?"

Tiffany squirmed in her chair. She bit off a hang-nail. "Charlie was scared of him ... hell, I was scared of him. He had no conscience, you know? Like he did things, sneaky, evil things, and he had a way of making everyone look guilty for things he'd done. Charlie told me that Devon would figure out what meant the most to somebody and then he'd hurt them."

"You're going to have to give me some examples."

"You have to understand, Charlie was just a kid when he met Devon, and he didn't have any idea how he was being manipulated. At first, he was so happy to have this upper-class, good-looking boy even want to be his friend that he was like a little puppy, all tail-wagging and doing whatever Devon wanted. It was innocent boy stuff at first. Shoplift a candy bar from Mac's Milk. Upend a garbage can in somebody's driveway. Things like that. Then, it started getting uglier."

"Were you aware this was going on?"

Tiffany shook her head. "Not really. I'm three years younger than Charlie, remember? Charlie is quiet, anyhow, like really introverted. I began to know everything wasn't as it seemed around that teacher's trial. Charlie was thirteen and I was ten, but he started acting weird. Guilty of something and really withdrawn."

A coldness spread through Kala as if a blast of ice water was suddenly pumped through her veins. They were heading into territory she'd considered but discarded. Maybe, a part of her had always suspected. She asked in a flat voice, "Did Devon make up the story about Mrs. Thompson and force Charlie to go along with it?"

Tiffany's eyes were pleading for Kala to understand. "Charlie didn't want to do it, but he had no choice. He only told me this year because of other stuff. That teacher was getting out anyhow so … well, it didn't seem worth saying anything now. You can't do anything to him, you know, for lying, can you? I mean, he should have stood up to Devon, but at the time, he didn't think he had a choice. He was scared."

Let Charlie off scot-free after lying and putting an innocent woman away for four years? For ruining her life? Kala closed her eyes and breathed deeply to calm her anger. Jane Thompson's release from prison didn't end her punishment even if Tiffany wanted to believe it did to ease her conscience. She opened her eyes and stared at Tiffany, who was staring back with a look of defiance. Kala calmly asked, "What other stuff?"

"Charlie wouldn't tell me. He said Devon was capable of anything and wanted to get away from him. They weren't friends like I told you before. It was an act."

Kala detected a subtle change in Tiffany's eyes and her body language and could tell that she was lying. The question was, lying about which part of her story? She asked, "Where's Charlie now?"

"Home getting stoned and listening to head-banger music." She gave a lopsided half-grin. "I guess I shouldn't be telling you that."

"Probably the least of his worries. Did he give any reason for Devon setting up Mrs. Thompson?"

"She gave him a bad mark."

"That was it?"

"That was it."

"Wow." Kala thought she was beyond being surprised by the depravity of human behaviour but obviously not. If true, Devon Eton had been seriously twisted at a young age.

Tiffany bit off another nail. She looked at Kala with her raccoon eyes. "Devon had this thing about being superior to everyone and he'd go ballistic about the stupidest shit. The first time I saw that side of him was last summer when Charlie, Devon, and I were hanging out one Friday night. He said this girl in one of his classes had been rude to him so we went over to her house and Devon slashed all the tires on her car and her parents' car. I was freaked out but Charlie said to let it go. He said she'd gotten off light."

"I don't understand why Charlie kept up the facade that they were friends. Do you have any insight?"

"I already told you. He was scared. To bits. So now you know why that teacher killed Devon. She was getting even."

"That's definitely one possibility. This information turns the investigation on its head, Tiffany. We'll have to reassess." Kala didn't want to point out that it gave Charlie a compelling reason to kill Devon, as well. "Will you repeat what you told me to the other investigators?"

"I guess, yeah."

"I'm also going to need to speak with Charlie again. Does he know you're here?"

"He doesn't know. I can try to convince him to talk to you." She paused. "He won't be in good shape tonight, though."

"As you said. Let him know that my partner and I will be by in the morning. Hopefully, you'll be able to impress upon your brother the need to be truthful by the time we get there." She paused and tried to put her finger on what was bothering her about Tiffany's confession. She asked, "Why now?"

"You mean, why tell you this now?"

"Yeah, why now?"

"Because Charlie's going to be nailed with this murder and I don't want to see that happen. It'll destroy Mom. Charlie isn't innocent of a lot of things, but he's not a killer." She flattened her empty cup with the palm of her hand. "Although if you ask me, whoever rid the world of Devon Eton deserves a gold medal."

Kala called Gundersund and Rouleau as soon as she dropped Tiffany off at home. Tiffany's revelation weighed heavily and needed to be shared before morning. Both agreed to meet her at the Merchant without asking for details. She guessed they'd heard something in her voice.

The rain was coming down in torrents as she backtracked to Princess Street and the pub near the waterfront. Hardly anybody was on the road and the streetlights were ghostly pale in the mist and rain. She could see the light reflecting off the slick black roads, the puddles looking like pooled oil. Sodden leaves filled the gutters and sidewalks. Taiku nuzzled up next to her, his big head resting warmly against her thigh. She was glad for his presence on this dark autumn night that had her feeling alone and on edge.

She parked as close to the Merchant as she could to get a view of the front door and slumped in the front seat, waiting for either Rouleau or Gundersund to arrive. She spoke soothing words to Taiku, telling him what a good boy he was as she rubbed his head. When she spotted Rouleau in his black trench coat, she ran her hand through Taiku's fur one last time and told him she'd be back soon. Rouleau had already disappeared inside by the time she climbed out of the truck into the driving rain.

She entered the Merchant and stood shaking the rainwater out of her hair as she walked down the short hallway. Rouleau had chosen their usual table in the bar to the right of the entrance. The bar was nearly empty but she would have been surprised to see many patrons. This weather was bad for business. Kala joined Rouleau, and Gundersund arrived a few minutes later. He'd been on his way home from downtown when Kala called and the trip to the Merchant was quicker than it would have been otherwise.

"Well, what have you got?" Rouleau asked once the waitress brought their drinks.

Kala outlined what Tiffany had told her and could see the impact of her confession in their faces. They took a moment to think over the implications while Rouleau and Gundersund each took a long drink of beer.

Rouleau said, "Jane Thompson was sentenced to three years in prison for something she didn't do. Why did she confess?"

"She kept saying she was innocent and only confessed after she was in prison. Adam divorced her after her confession but she got out a year earlier than she would have," said Gundersund. He rubbed the scar on his cheek as he thought out loud.

"She must have given up hope of being believed and confessed to lessen her sentence. The judge gave her such a harsh punishment because he said she didn't own what she did and showed no remorse," Kala added. "Should we be going over to tell her tonight that we know Charlie and Devon were lying? I hate thinking that she has to believe we think she's guilty for one minute more than necessary." She chose to keep Jane's run to the border with her kids to herself. Nothing could be gained from sharing the story, or that's what she told herself.

Rouleau tore the label from his beer bottle. "If Devon was the monster Tiffany now tells us he was, he appears to have been good at hiding it from his classmates, teachers, and family. Do you both buy that?"

"You're asking if Tiffany and Charlie concocted this story for some reason?" Kala asked. When Rouleau nodded, she said, "But why? Tiffany was willing to tell me that Charlie had lied about Devon and his teacher even though it could get Charlie into a lot of trouble."

Rouleau continued playing devil's advocate. "We had Charlie in a cell to shake him up but maybe it shook Tiffany more. She thought Charlie was going to be charged with Devon's murder. Maybe, she's using this as a diversion. She must have thought her confession would help Charlie in some way."

"Tiffany told me that this proved Jane was taking revenge out on Devon for ruining her life," Kala conceded. She tried to picture Tiffany's face when she'd said it. Kala had had the feeling Tiffany was holding something back, trading this bit of a confession for ... what? Perhaps Rouleau was right in his questions. Tiffany was trying to get them heading down a track away from something she didn't want them to know.

"I'll send someone to pick up Charlie and Tiffany first thing tomorrow and want you both to interview them. You'll need to also speak with Devon's parents again to find out if there could be any truth to this. Hold off on speaking to Jane until we have some formal confessions from the two of them. No point giving Jane false hope if they decide not to co-operate tomorrow."

Gundersund met Kala's eyes. He said, "Jane might still have killed Devon. This would give her a good reason."

Kala couldn't argue with him, but she said, "You have to admit that if what Tiffany said is true, the suspect pool widens."

"And that's a good thing?" He smiled at her.

"This could mean re-interviewing everyone who knew Devon," Rouleau said. "We need to get this right. Woodhouse is not going to thank you, Stonechild."

She gave a half-smile to them both. "And I'm already his favourite person."

"If you keep this up, next thing you know, he'll be sending you jokes and videos," Gundersund said. "Although, hard to say if he sends them to people he likes or ones he wants to annoy."

She picked up her glass and tilted it in his direction before drinking. "God invented the delete button for a reason." Exhaustion was settling in and she thought about Taiku waiting in her truck. "I'll be pushing off. Looks like we're going to have another full day tomorrow."

"We'll be leaving right behind you," said Rouleau. "I'll pick up the tab on this one. Good work, Kala."

Hilary Eton had taken up smoking again. She'd bought a family-size bag of chips and had the girl toss in a pack of Camels when she'd gone inside the store to pay for her gas. So far, she'd managed to hide her lapse from Mitchell by sitting in the backyard behind the pool shed when he was at work or sleeping. She knew she was going to have to stop after the one pack. Her heart doctor would have a fit if she knew.

Mitchell had come home late as he always did, showered, and gone straight to bed. He'd had supper brought in to a meeting and refused her offer of heating up a plate of roast chicken and potatoes, left over from her dinner with Sophie. Work had been the reason he'd missed so many suppers with her and the kids over the years. He'd been travelling more before Devon's death, but after her heart attack had started coming home earlier in the day when he was in Kingston, and had averaged three dinners a week. Now, he was back to working late and avoiding mealtime. She'd stopped minding because his absence gave her a chance to forget.

The grandfather clock near the front door chimed eleven and Hilary roused herself to get up from the kitchen chair where she'd been sitting in the dark. Should she go outside for that cigarette or head back upstairs and slip in next to Mitchell? She only had a handful of cigarettes left and had herself rationing them out like mini-rewards for making it through another morning, afternoon, evening. She had to stick to her promise to herself and not buy any more. She needed to pull herself together, if only for Sophie.

She left the kitchen and walked down the hallway toward the stairs, leaving the lights off but having no difficulty finding her way in the inky blue light coming through the windows. The rainstorm had passed by an hour earlier, leaving a dampness in the house that chilled her even though she wore a heavy cable-knit sweater. Foot on the third stair, she heard a noise overhead and craned her neck to look up, thinking at first that Devon was home before she remembered that he would never be coming home again.

Nobody was on the landing and she kept climbing. At the head of the stairs, she hesitated. Sophie's room was at the other end of the hall. She'd already checked in on her before going downstairs half an hour earlier and found her sleeping. She took a step toward her own room when a nagging worry made her stop and turn around. What would it hurt to look in on Sophie one more time?

The carpet muffled her footsteps and she avoided stepping where she knew the floorboards would creak under her weight. Sophie's door was shut as she had left it, and she hesitated again before turning the knob and pushing the door open. Her eye was first drawn to the row of stuffed animals on the window seat, Sophie's bear Puddles staring back at her with his beady black eyes and thin thread smile. The covers were tossed back from the bed and she could see the whiteness of the sheets as she stepped into the room. Sophie was not in bed. Hilary looked toward the bathroom and saw the light coming from under the door. The jolt of fear at finding the bed empty fluttered back into its box to be replaced by concern that Sophie might be ill. She thought back to suppertime and remembered the paleness of her skin and their stilted conversation.

"Sophie?" she called softly as she crossed the bedroom floor to stand in front of the bathroom door. She rapped lightly as she said, "Sophie, are you okay? I was passing by and noticed your light on." Hopefully, Sophie wouldn't realize that she couldn't see the bathroom light from the hallway. She put her ear against the door and heard running water. She knocked harder on the door. "Sophie? Everything all right?"

The handle turned under her hand and she pushed the door open. The faucet was wide open and water was running into the claw-footed tub, about to overflow the sides. Sophie was lying with her head resting on the back of the tub, neck elongated and angled just enough so that her face wasn't submerged in the slowly rising water. Her long blond hair spread around her in the water like undulating seaweed, rippled by the flow of water that streamed onto Sophie's feet and ankles before mixing into the pinkish pool. A steady supply of crimson blood was drip, drip, dripping onto the floor and staining the white bath mat where Sophie's left arm dangled. The air smelled sickly sweet with fresh blood. Steam coated the mirror and filled the air in ghostly tendrils.

The scene was horrifying. Obscene. Impossible to take in. The shock froze Hilary like an animal in the path of an oncoming car.

Oh my God. Oh my God. Oh my God.

She tried to unscramble her brain, to make sense of the nightmare in front of her. "Sophie! No!" she pleaded out loud. "No!"

Hilary's body was leaden, her limbs heavy weights that wouldn't hold her upright. The pain in her chest was nothing compared to the fear coursing through her. She clutched at her heart and dropped to her knees on the tile floor, crawling through the blood and water on hands and knees to reach her daughter. Only when she'd pulled herself up the side of the tub and cradled Sophie's head in her hands did she begin screaming for Mitchell at the top of her lungs.

CHAPTER THIRTY

Naomi woke before Adam, the room still dark and a damp breeze rattling the blinds and gusting across her face. Adam couldn't understand her need for fresh air when she slept but he'd gotten used to the open window. She'd reluctantly close it once winter temperatures dipped below freezing, but not before.

She remembered that today was a PD day and they were to use their workday preparing lesson plans with an optional workshop at the school in the afternoon that she planned to miss. She rolled over onto her side, her head resting in the crook of her arm. Adam looked so childlike in sleep, not at all the rugged alpha male that still made her quiver with longing. His vulnerable side was as much a turn-on, but in a softer way. She reached out her fingers and brushed a strand of hair from his forehead. His eyes opened and for a moment they lay side by side staring into each other's eyes.

Adam's hand snaked under her nightgown and between her legs. She tensed and his hand stopped its upward climb. She forced herself to relax and rubbed his chest with her free hand, closing her eyes. Adam's hand spread her thighs and he rolled onto her, his erection at full attention, pushing into her without caring that she wasn't ready. The pain made her cry out, but he rammed harder as his pace increased to jackhammer speed. She wriggled her hips under him and soon began rising and falling with the rhythm of his thrusts. His passion, for that was how she chose to see it, climaxed quickly with a shudder deep inside her. He rolled off, panting slightly, staring straight up at the ceiling without touching her.

"Naomi," he said, turning his head sideways to look at her, "this isn't going to work."

"Sorry?" She closed her legs and moved an arm up to cover her breasts.

"I want you to move out. I'm hoping you can find your own place by next weekend."

She wondered if he'd found out about Liam but knew this wasn't possible. They'd been too careful. This must have something to do with Jane. "I don't understand," she said.

His jaw tightened. "I don't love you and I can't see this continuing. The sex is great but not enough. You must see that. I haven't been fair to you or the kids and it's time you and I moved on with our lives."

He pushed himself out of the bed. "I'm going to wash up and then go to the gym before I go into school, that is, if you don't have plans this morning?" He waited for her to answer, his posture braced as if to take her tearful entreaties and a round of begging.

Her first thought was *how many times can one man work out*, and her next was *I'll grovel over my dead body.* She said, "I'll be here packing and can watch the kids if that's what you're asking. I'll leave when you get back."

"Thanks." He stared at her with a puzzled expression flashing across his features but quickly turned and continued his strut across the carpet.

She watched his tight bum and muscular back as he walked toward the ensuite. She was in shock, angry with how easily he'd discarded her, but the more his words sunk in, the more relieved she began to feel. Even so, pride made her want to fling her betrayal with Liam in Adam's face, to shake his arrogant, conceited ego to the core, but self-preservation vetoed the idea. Adam was capable of cold retribution, and she knew he could crush her and her career. Better to leave with as much grace as possible and forget this unpleasant chapter in her life.

She sat up and reached for her cellphone on the bedside table. She texted Liam as she strode across the room to get her housecoat and let him know that she'd broken it off with Adam. Their after-school sex had left her dissatisfied living with him and she had to get out.

Liam's reply was instant and ended with tiny emojis of a heart and thumbs up. "I knew you'd see the light. Come crash with me."

Naomi turned off her phone and smiled.

At eight thirty Tiffany Hanson was in the Kingston police station giving her statement to Woodhouse and Bennett with her mother at her side, while Kala and Gundersund were in a separate interview room down the hall with her brother, Charlie. Charlie had said that he didn't want or need a lawyer. Kala was sitting directly across the table from him while Gundersund sat silently on her right, his chair slightly back from the table. Charlie had to turn his head to look at Gundersund but so far had only given him a cursory glance. She thought Charlie was worn out and disengaged, his foot tapping under the table to some heavy metal riff likely playing inside his head.

"Sorry to drag you back in here again, Charlie. Did you get a good night's sleep?"

"Sort of." His foot resumed tapping while his head began bobbing up and down and his index fingers played a beat on the table.

Kala reached her hands across the table and covered his fingers. "You need to focus. We're trying to help you here, Charlie, but you have to come clean with what you know. Understand?" She was deliberately repeating his name, trying to make a connection.

His body went still. He looked at her, his eyes owlish and unblinking through the thick lenses of his glasses. He nodded. "K."

Kala released his fingers and pulled back. "Tiffany told me about Devon and the fact you both cooked up the affair with Jane Thompson. Can you tell us more about that?"

"I didn't want to say I saw them together but Devon told me I'd be sorry if I didn't."

"Are you telling me that you both lied about him having a physical relationship with Mrs. Thompson? Remember that the tape is recording what you say and it can be used in court."

"Devon made up the story. He forced me to back him up."

"Does anybody else know?"

"Tiffany. I told her."

She leaned forward, resting her elbows on the table. "See Charlie, the problem I'm having with your story is that Devon isn't here to defend himself. I'll need more than just your word that this new version of events is the truth."

"Mrs. Thompson talked about going out of town one weekend with her family. Devon decided we should go to her house and have a look around. We went Saturday night and he got me to climb in through an open window on the second floor. They'd left a ladder by the back shed so it wasn't hard. I let him in and he worked on her computer for a while, I guess adding some porn photos, and he took some of her panties out of the laundry hamper on our way out."

"Why did you go along with him?"

Charlie squirmed uncomfortably in his chair. "He'd done other stuff. I was scared he'd hurt my mom or sisters."

"What other stuff?"

"I don't want to say."

Kala let silence fill the room. He looked up at her with head bowed and then lowered his eyes to stare at the table. He crossed his arms across his skinny chest and slumped back in the chair. Today, his black T-shirt sported a blow-up of Bart Simpson's face saying, "Don't have a cow, man."

"We need more to go on," she said, "if we are going to be able to help you."

Charlie's foot began tapping again. Kala thought she'd lost him but after a minute of silence, he started talking in a voice that grew increasingly bitter as the dam burst.

"Devon was smarter than anyone I knew. He liked to make fun of people because it made him feel like a big man. I thought that's all it was at first. You know, all talk, but then he started doing horrible things and I didn't say anything. I guess I liked having a friend for a while. Then, I was scared of what he'd do to me if he knew I'd turned on him, so I went along with it. I never told anybody."

"What kind of horrible things did he do?"

"He'd lie all the time. Make up things about people and make sure everybody knew without letting on that he was behind the smear. He loved doing that, especially watching somebody get humiliated or shut out of the group. He told me that the best thrill in the world was to find out what somebody really cared about and then ruin it for them."

Kala asked softly, "And what did he find out you really cared about?"

When Charlie raised his head, she was surprised to see his eyes were red and brimming with tears. He swiped at his eyes with the back of his hand. "I can't tell you."

"Maybe telling will help. Whatever he did must be hard for you to carry around."

Charlie sniffled and wiped at his eyes again. Gundersund left the room and returned with a box of tissues that he pushed across the table as he sat down. Charlie grabbed a handful and blew his nose.

"It didn't start out bad. We were at his house watching television. His mom was out and his dad was at work. I don't know where Sophie was. We were kind of bored so Devon said, 'Let's go into my mother's medicine cabinet and find something to get high.'"

"When was this, Charlie?"

"Not long after his mom was home from her heart attack."

"Okay."

"So we went into her bathroom and went through her pills. She had a lot of shit, including some Percodan left over from her operation, so Devon put some of them in his pocket. He said she wouldn't miss them. We went to my house to take them and listen to music in my room because my mom was working late. Dad was home but he was drinking in the backyard. We took some of the pills, and then Devon said that we should sit with my dad for a while. I was surprised and then worried because Devon thought my dad was low class and not worth his time. Dad had been drinking for a while but he wasn't loaded, just happy and telling stories. I could see Devon was laughing at him and not with him, if you know what I mean, so after a while I said let's go. Devon just kept sitting there with this big shit-ass smile on his face, not budging. Dad offered us a beer and I said no but Devon took one. When Dad left to have a whiz, Devon took out a pill and put it into his beer. He said it would be a big laugh." Charlie's voice broke and he struggled to control his breathing, which was coming in sobs. "Before I knew what was happening, Dad was back and drank that beer in a few gulps. I watched him afterward and he seemed okay, so I thought, maybe nothing is going to happen. The Percodan wasn't doing that much for me except this kind of nice feeling. Devon said he'd get Dad another beer and went over to where he was keeping the two-four on the picnic table. Devon opened one and came back and handed it to Dad. He sat down again and watched Dad drink it and then said he had to go home. Devon told me that he'd changed his mind about the music and was leaving. I went in my room and crashed. Mom found Dad dead in the lawn chair when she came home from her shift."

"You believe the drugs that Devon put into the beer killed your father?"

"I know they did. It wasn't painkillers he put in the beer; it was his mother's heart medication. It didn't compute at the time that the pill wasn't Percodan but I saw the one that he dropped into the open beer bottle and checked his mother's medicine cabinet next time I was over. I think he put more pills in the beer he opened for Dad. Devon had his back to us and he had time."

"Was an autopsy done on your father?"

"No, but it's too late if that's where you're heading. Dad was cremated."

"You never told anybody this."

"I confronted Devon after Dad's funeral. He told me that I'd agreed to the joke and I was as guilty as he was that it turned out the way it did. He said that keeping quiet would be better for me and for everyone else in my family, if I got his drift."

"His mother must have noticed the missing pills."

"She kept quiet if she did."

Kala thought about this for a few seconds. "How did Devon get along with his family?"

Charlie met her eyes and looked back at the table. "You'll have to ask them."

"Surely, you have some idea of how they interacted."

"Let's just say there's a reason they don't have any pets."

"Do you believe their stories?" Rouleau asked. They were gathered in the meeting area going over the interviews.

"The question is why they would lie when they're both implicating themselves by keeping quiet for so long," said Bennett.

Woodhouse gave him a disparaging look before saying, "It sounds to me like they got together to blame somebody who can't defend himself. Saying Devon killed their father shows creativity. Oh, yeah, and can't be proven."

"I agree with Bennett," said Gundersund, ignoring Woodhouse's glare. "Why would they make this up now? To what end? I believe they're telling the truth. What do you think, Stonechild?"

They all stared at her and waited.

"I believe them, but I don't think they've told us everything even now." She turned to face Gundersund. "Do you remember Devon's coach and what he told us? He said that Devon was manipulative and not as he presented. We should interview him again, too."

"You're right. I remember we discussed that the things he said about Devon didn't fit with what everyone else was saying."

"We never got a clear picture from anyone though. Nobody really seemed to know Devon and Charlie except superficially." She smiled at Gundersund before looking back at Rouleau.

"What about Jane Thompson?" Woodhouse asked. "We were supposed to bring her in today for questioning after the Hanson kids."

They waited silently for Rouleau to coordinate their next steps. He was only too aware that they hadn't figured out who'd killed Devon, but he felt like they were getting closer. Heath was expecting him to sit in on another media briefing but that would have to wait. He said, "I'd like Woodhouse, Bedouin, and Morrison to go back to Devon's school and re-interview the coach and his teachers based on this new insight into his character. Dangle some of the new intel you got about the kid's character and see if they reveal anything new. Stonechild and Gundersund, pick up Jane Thompson and bring her back here and let her know what the Hansons told us. Film her reaction. I'll take Bennett over to the Etons' and we'll find out what they've been covering up about their son. Somebody is going to break if we apply the right pressure." He looked over their heads. The desk sergeant Fred Taylor was standing in the entrance between the two dividers, holding a sheet of paper.

"Just got a call that Sophie Eton is in Kingston being monitored. She tried to kill herself last night. Thought you might want to know."

CHAPTER THIRTY-ONE

When she opened her eyes, Jane couldn't believe that sunshine was streaming through the window and the night's storm had passed. She'd been physically exhausted when she lay down but her mind had been going a mile a minute and she'd lain awake in the darkness for what felt like hours. She had no idea when she'd finally fallen asleep but figured it was in the dawning hours of the morning. She stretched under the scratchy blanket and extended her aching legs. Her body felt as if it had been pummelled relentlessly by a less-than-gentle masseuse. Her eyes swept the room and landed on the threatening red words on the wall next to the closet that looked stark and ominous in daylight. She jolted out of half-sleep and sat up. She thought, *This is outrageous, even for you, Adam.*

The idea of giving up was seductive. Get her hands on some pills or take a hot bath and slit her wrists ... or both. No more struggle. An end to the pain and constant disappointment. She thought about the cop Stonechild and her unexpected kindness the day before. She'd said the truth would come out. To have faith. Ben and Olivia might not be gone forever.

Jane wanted to believe.

She got up and gathered some clothes to put on after her shower. Not much to choose from, but nobody was around who cared what she looked like. She showered quickly, washing her hair and leaving it to dry naturally. The beauty of short hair was that this wouldn't take long. Ruffle her hand through the mess while wet and good to go. Dressed in old jeans and a black T-shirt but leaving her feet bare, she put the kettle on to boil a cup of instant coffee. She'd thrown out the milk and would have to drink the brew black. She still had the money she had been planning to take across the border — luckily kept separate from the passports, which Stonechild had confiscated — and she'd splurge after this inferior cup with a Tim Hortons coffee and muffin. She'd allow herself this one indulgence before getting back to saving for when she had the kids again. She would get them back. She'd promised each of them in turn before hugging them goodbye.

She took her coffee into the bedroom and stood in the window, looking out across the fenced-in yard to the red brick building on the street behind. The smell of garbage and pot wafted up through the vent from the apartment below. While she stood trying to figure out the rest of her life, the steady boom of music began thumping from beneath her feet. God, she hated this place, almost as much as she hated what her life had become. She turned her head believing she heard footsteps on the landing but decided the noise was just the music from below. She turned back to look out the window and thought about calling Sandra. She knew that her sister had phoned at seven the night before as she had every evening since Jane got out of prison. She'd be worried when Jane didn't answer, convinced that her ESP had correctly predicted a new disaster. If she only knew how close to accurate her dire prediction had been.

She sensed a movement in the doorway to her bedroom and spun around, dropping the half-full coffee mug onto the carpet. The brown liquid spread in a dirty circle and splashed onto her foot.

"What are you doing here?" she asked, hating the fear in her voice.

Mitchell Eton took a step into the room, effectively blocking her way out. "It's time to pay for all the pain you've caused. You sit here free and waiting to ruin other lives, and I can't let that happen to some other family. Not while we're still paying for what you did to Devon."

His voice cracked and for a moment, she thought he might cry. A strange calmness came over her as she faced this man who believed he had every right to hate her. He was wrong, but she knew that arguing wasn't going to convince the cold anger in his unrelenting blue eyes. The handgun was aimed at the floor but it was threat enough to keep her rooted in place. "Are you going to shoot me?"

"Not here. We have someone else who needs to pay, and you and I will be going on a drive. Turn around and clasp your hands behind your back."

"And if I say no?"

"Then I *will* shoot you right here."

"The boys downstairs will hear. They'll call the police."

"Unlikely over the music. What is that? Kings of Leon?"

"I have no idea." The question was ludicrous under the circumstances.

She turned and did as he asked, and then he was behind her tying a rope around her wrists. He tied it tightly so that it cut into her skin. He whispered into her ear, "You are so beautiful and so evil. My son didn't stand a chance of turning out normal after you decided to fuck him." His breath was hot, his voice breaking. He rubbed the nose of the gun across her cheek and down the side of her neck and seemed to be fighting the urge to pull the trigger. "Let's get moving, shall we? And don't even think about making a scene or I will kill those upstanding young men in the apartment below. Believe me when I say, I won't hesitate to kill everyone in this damn building." His eyes lifted to the red words spray-painted on the wall. "Looks like someone else has you figured out, too."

She tilted her head away from him and let him swing her around to face the door. She started walking, and he was right behind her with one hand holding on to her tied wrists. She stopped in front of her open apartment door. "Do you honestly think you'll get away with this?"

"Honestly? Yeah. Yeah, I do. But here's the thing. I don't care one way or the other. All I want is to see is justice done and to end this torment for my family. Knowing you're back on the street and knowing what your selfish perversion has cost us, I am prepared to take whatever comes. Do you get that, Mrs. Thompson? Mrs. Teacher of the Year? This is all on you, and I am desperate for you to see exactly what evil your affair with an innocent child has caused. I want you to go to your grave knowing why you do not deserve my mercy."

They found Hilary Eton sitting next to Sophie's bed in a private room at the hospital. She was holding her daughter's hand and Rouleau had to repeat Hilary's name three times before she looked at him. He put a hand on her shoulder. "I'm so sorry," he said.

Her shoulder shook under his touch as she stifled sobs. He looked down at Sophie in the centre of the hospital bed under a neatly folded white sheet, her freckled arms straight and resting outside the sheet. White bandages were wrapped around both wrists. An oxygen mask covered her mouth and an IV bag was dripping clear liquid into her arm. Her blond hair had dried in long tendrils that had been pulled to the side so that her hair lay across one shoulder. Her eyes were closed, but every so often her eyelids fluttered without opening. She looked younger than thirteen to Rouleau and heartbreakingly innocent. He asked, "Is Mitchell nearby?"

"He had to leave."

Rouleau hid his surprise. "Did he say where he was going?"

"He had something urgent to attend to but didn't say what. He was so upset ... I thought he needed to do something to take his mind off this ... at least, for an hour. We've been here all night."

"Would you come with me to the cafeteria and we can talk over a coffee? I won't keep you long. Officer Bennett can stay with Sophie and he'll phone me if there's any change."

"I don't know. Can't this wait?"

"A coffee and something to eat will help you to keep your strength up. I could also use your help to move our investigation into Devon's death forward."

"I don't know how I can be of any more help." She looked up at him. "I could use a break. The doctor gave her a sedative and said she'll be asleep until lunchtime."

"Then we should take this opportunity."

She chose a seat in the corner of the cafeteria while he bought coffees and a wrapped ham and cheese sandwich, loading them onto a tray. If she couldn't eat now, he'd have her take the sandwich with her. When he slid in across from her, she was sitting motionless, staring at nothing, her hands folded in her lap.

"Did something upset Sophie besides Devon's death?"

She shook her head. "No. She's been in a bad way but this ... this was unexpected."

"I need to talk to you about something unpleasant, and I apologize in advance for adding to your pain. We've had two people who knew Devon well come forward with additional information about his personal interactions."

"Oh?"

"Would you say that your son had a vindictive nature, Mrs. Eton?"

She looked down at her hands. "Who have you been speaking with?"

"Charlie and Tiffany Hanson. Also, Devon's football coach."

"I see. My son isn't here to defend himself and these people are using the opportunity to destroy his reputation."

"We'd like to hear what you have to say. Help me to understand."

He didn't flinch from her gaze and the defiance in her eyes flickered and crystallized into pain. "My son was strong-willed right from the start, but we … I loved him. Mitchell wanted Devon to live up to his potential and pushed him, possibly more than he should have, although Mitchell always accused me of being too soft. We fought many times over our parenting styles, I'm afraid. Devon might have played on our conflicting approaches."

"Would you say your son was manipulative?"

She tilted her head to one side and pursed her lips as if considering the idea for the first time. "Yes, I would say that he was. He was brilliant but couldn't handle being wrong. I think Mitchell's insistence on perfection influenced Devon and by the time I realized its negative impact, Devon had incorporated the trait into his personality. What makes my husband a great businessman didn't necessarily translate well into parenting." Her jaw lifted. "I believe Devon would have found his way if it hadn't been for Jane Thompson. He spiralled after that."

Rouleau found it revealing that Hilary was sharing no part of the blame for her son's behaviour. "What do you mean by spiralling?"

"Oh, he became moody and difficult to deal with. Quick to anger with me and Mitchell. Obstinate." She laughed, more bitter than amused. "I saw this as typical teen behaviour, but Mitchell wanted him to see a psychiatrist because he thought that Devon's moods were extreme. I felt that Devon behaved properly outside our family and was just exhibiting normal teenage rebellion. I took the brunt of Devon's acting out, anyhow, because Mitchell was away so much. We did take Devon to see someone after the trial, but he convinced the psychiatrist that he was fine."

"Did you think that he was?"

"At the time, but maybe because I wanted to be convinced. After the trial, Devon learned to hide his true feelings under a layer of charm, even with us. Later, I knew he wasn't fine."

"Did Devon ever steal your medication?"

She looked down. "I suspected he had."

"When did you suspect?"

"After my heart attack. Some of my pain killers and heart medication were missing but I thought that I might have taken more than I was supposed to by accident. I asked Devon about it, and he got angry and accused me of not trusting him. I let it drop. I started keeping my medication locked up after that."

"Charlie Hanson said that Devon put your heart medication into his father's beer the night that he died of the heart attack."

She sat very still, eyes darkening as she grasped the significance of what he was telling her. "No." The single word was a filled with pain more than denial.

He pressed on. "Charlie also told us that Devon made up the story about his affair with Jane Thompson and he supported it because Devon threatened him."

She shook her head. "That can't be. We always believed ... we believe that she was the reason he became the way he did. How could the jury at her trial be wrong? She confessed...."

"We think she confessed only because she felt that she had no other option if she wanted to get released from prison early to see her kids."

"My God, I can't take this in." She raised a hand to cover her heart. "Why would Charlie tell you this now? How could he have left it so late and let us believe all this time...?"

Rouleau spoke gently. "It's never too late to tell what's been eating away at you and to set things right for Jane Thompson so she can start putting her life back together, knowing that the truth has come out."

Hilary stood, a look of panic on her face. "Mitchell. I need to reach him."

"Where is he, Mrs. Eton?"

"He was going to fix things. That's what he said."

"Fix things how?"

"I don't know!" Her voice rose in a wail. "He blames Jane Thompson for everything. He wants our family's pain to stop. Sophie put him over the top." She dropped back into the chair, still holding her chest. "My God, Devon. What have you done to us?"

Rouleau's phone rang in his pocket. He grabbed it and checked the number before answering. "What have you got, Stonechild?"

"Jane Thompson was seen leaving her apartment with a man about twenty minutes before we got here." She sounded short of breath, as if she was walking fast.

"Did they get a description?"

"Yeah, and it fits Mitchell Eton. I'm worried."

"I'm here with Hilary. She said that Mitchell left to take care of something."

"This is bad. Does she have any idea where he might have taken Jane?"

Rouleau looked at Hilary slumped in the chair. Her breathing was laboured, all the colour drained from her face. "No, but I have to go." Stonechild started to say something, but he shoved the cellphone into his pocket while yelling for someone to get a doctor. He pushed his chair aside and grabbed on to Hilary as she tumbled to the floor.

CHAPTER THIRTY-TWO

"Well, that was odd." Kala lowered her phone and caught up to Gundersund.

"What's odd?"

"Rouleau hung up on me. I guess he had something urgent going on. I didn't get to tell him about the graffiti all over Jane's apartment walls and door and the spilled coffee in her bedroom."

"Both disturbing as hell. If it was Eton that the kids saw leaving with her, he could have taken her to his house. Nobody else is there."

"We don't have many other choices."

They got into Gundersund's car and he drove down Regent, cutting across the city and making good time on the side streets. Kala's phone rang as they pulled onto Beverly. "Woodhouse," she mouthed to Gundersund as she clicked on receive. "Yeah, Woodhouse. Find something interesting?"

She listened without interrupting and sat for a moment gathering her thoughts after she disconnected. Gundersund glanced over at her. "What's going on?"

"He tried calling Rouleau but no answer so we were the next best thing. He's over at the Limestone

Spa Hotel. The manager called him in to look at video footage from the day Devon went missing. They have a camera on the back locked door, and he had a member of his staff go through the footage for the entire day on a hunch. They found a few frames that show Devon letting Charlie and a blond girl into the hotel. Woodhouse is quite sure it's Sophie Eton. Time on the tape is four forty that afternoon."

"As I recall, Sophie said that she never met up with Devon that day. She waited in the park but he didn't show."

"She obviously lied." Kala thought back to the day she interviewed Sophie and pictured the mother and daughter sitting side by side on the couch across from her. "Her mother was in on the lie. I remember having this sense at the time that she'd coached Sophie about what to say."

"What do you think it means?"

"Devon and Charlie were up to something and Charlie is still keeping it a secret." She thought about Sophie trying to kill herself over her brother's death and didn't like how the pieces were fitting. "We need to speak with Charlie again."

"I agree. After we check out the Etons', we can swing past Charlie's place." Gundersund pulled into the Eton driveway, turned off the engine, and leaned on the steering wheel. He looked at her and said, "Mitchell's car isn't here but it could be in the garage. We'd better be ready for anything."

She gave a half-grin. "My gun is loaded and my trigger finger is sharpened."

He smiled back. "Good. Hopefully, this will go

smoothly and you won't need to shoot anybody."

They tried ringing the doorbell, stepping back with their handguns at their sides. Gundersund banged on the door but there was no movement or noise from within. They went in different directions and circled the house, checking windows and looking for signs of life, meeting up again on the front lawn.

"He didn't bring her here," said Gundersund.

Kala pulled out her phone. "I'll try Rouleau again." She moved into a circle of sunshine while she waited for him to answer, briefly enjoying the fall warmth and the absence of rain clouds. Her call went to Rouleau's voice mail and she left a message for him to call her back. She joined Gundersund in the driveway. He was standing with his back to the road, watching the Eton house. She said, "Rouleau's not answering. What now?"

"We could head over to Mitchell's work. A long shot, but worth a try. Then, we can pay Charlie that visit."

She agreed because she couldn't come up with a better idea. "I'm not liking this, Gundersund. All of this uncertainty about what Eton is doing with Jane is giving me a bad feeling."

"I've got the same feeling." He rubbed the scar on his cheek as he walked toward his car. "Try Rouleau again in a few minutes and let's hope he answers. We might need to get everybody involved looking for Mitchell and Jane if this goes on much longer."

"What would you like for lunch?" Katie Bruster asked, rubbing her belly as she stood in the doorway to Ivan's home office. She felt like a blow-up doll that had been filled to capacity and would soon burst. One more week before delivering this big baby from its cocoon inside her and the day couldn't come soon enough. Fatigue was her constant companion and she was having more and more trouble hiding her grumpiness from Ivan and Kyle, although she had to admit that neither her husband nor son appeared fazed by her sharp words.

"Just a ham sandwich is fine, babe." Ivan was working on his computer and barely glanced at her. She stood waiting until he looked up from the screen and smiled at her. "Sorry, I was working on a file. Everything okay?"

"Yeah, everything is great. I'll be back in a few minutes with your sandwich, unless you'd like to join me in the kitchen to eat?"

He ran a hand through his mess of brown hair, the hair that she'd run her own hands through the night before in bed. "I'd love to but need to get this work done before the next little Bruster appears on the scene. I'll be taking a few weeks off and don't want to have to worry about loose ends."

"I understand." She walked back to the kitchen, catching sight of herself in the full-length mirror as she passed by it in the hall. Was she heavier than the day before or was it her imagination? Her ankles were swollen and her legs ached but she wasn't complaining. She'd had a healthy pregnancy and would soon have a lovely baby. Hopefully, a daughter to complete their millionaire family. She really wanted a little girl.

She got the ham, lettuce, and mustard out of the fridge and made two sandwiches. She poured herself a glass of milk and opened a beer for Ivan. He allowed himself one at lunchtime and nothing more until he finished work for the day, usually after seven when she called him for supper.

She returned to his office and set the sandwich and beer on his desk next to his computer.

"Thanks, babe," he said, catching her hand for a moment in his. "Kyle taking a nap?"

"He is, and I'm going to stretch out on the bed for a snooze after I eat."

"I wish I could join you." He smiled and she bent and kissed his mouth.

She'd eaten half her sandwich when the doorbell rang. She heaved herself out of the kitchen chair and walked toward the front door, making out the shapes of two adult figures on the other side of the beveled glass. *Please not those Jehovah's Witnesses again trying to convert me*, she thought. She opened the door a crack and looked out, taking a few seconds to recognize Mitchell Eton. She didn't know the woman with him. She pulled the door open wider.

"Mitchell, was Ivan expecting you today? He never said."

"No, this is a surprise visit."

"Well, come in." She held out her hand to the woman. "I'm Katie, Ivan's wife."

The woman looked from her to Mitchell and he nodded. The woman held out her hand. "I'm Jane."

She gripped Katie's hand with such force that she was momentarily taken aback. Katie thought she saw a warning in eyes so clear and beautiful that she had trouble looking away. A sense of inadequacy filled her as it did every time she met someone this striking, but she stifled the feeling. She had grown a lot since marrying Ivan and becoming a mother. She knew looks weren't important when it came to happiness … well, not as important as she'd believed in high school and college. Mitchell cleared his throat and prodded the woman to walk ahead of him into the house. He shut the door and shot the deadbolt into place behind him. "Why don't you lead us into Ivan's office, Katie," he said.

She didn't like the tone he was using but didn't say anything. She looked from him to the door. Why had he locked it? "I was just eating my lunch at the table. Maybe I could make some coffee while you go speak to Ivan." She took a step in the direction of the kitchen.

"I'd rather you take us to Ivan," Mitchell said.

Katie half-turned and looked into Jane's eyes. She knew she wasn't misreading the situation. Something was wrong. "Okay," she said.

She and Jane led the way down the hall. Before they reached Ivan's office, he called out, "Who was at the door, babe?"

"I was," Mitchell said. "Take the two seats, ladies." He raised the handgun he'd been holding behind Jane's back and pointed it at Ivan, who was sitting pressed back against his chair.

"I only see one chair," said Katie.

"You take it," said Jane. "I can stand."

"No, Ivan will stand. You take his chair," said Mitchell.

Ivan got up, his hands raised waist level, palms out. "What's all this about then, Mitchell? What are you doing here?"

Katie looked from her husband to Mitchell and something passed between the two men that made her hold both hands over her stomach. A spasm of pain made her gasp. She'd never met Mitchell's wife but she was beginning to think that Jane might be her. Was she about to find out that Ivan had been unfaithful with Mitchell's wife? The crazy idea made her want to giggle, and she knew this was the typical way she dealt with stress. She tried to breathe deeply like she'd been taught for her upcoming labour. The woman stared at her from across the desk with concerned eyes.

"You know why I'm here, don't you Ivan?" Mitchell asked.

"Can't we let the women go into the kitchen while we talk?"

"I don't think so. Your wife will want to know what you've been up to."

Ivan's eyes reddened and he looked as rattled as Katie had ever seen him. He was usually so self-assured and domineering that she knew her world was about to be rocked. Jane, in contrast, looked resigned and calm, as if she'd seen her fate and was okay with it. "Tell me, Ivan," Katie said. "Have you done something the kids and I should know about?"

Ivan seemed to get a second wind. He glared at Mitchell. "My company has done a lot of business with yours. If you want our good relationship to continue, tell my wife that you've made a mistake coming here. We can work out our differences in private once everyone has settled down."

Mitchell looked at the gun he was holding and back up at Ivan. "My daughter tried to take her own life last night because of what you did to her. My son was murdered because of that woman sitting there in your desk chair. You think I really care about our damn business relationship?"

Ivan's eyes found Katie's. They appeared to be begging for understanding and she felt her insides go cold. "Tell me, Ivan," she said.

"Tell her what you did if you don't want me to shoot your wife right now," said Mitchell.

"This is insane. You can't just waltz in here and threaten my family." Ivan took a step toward Mitchell but raised his hands and backed up when Mitchell pointed the gun at him.

"Tell her," said Mitchell. His voice rose to a shout. "Tell her now!"

"Okay, okay, okay." Ivan looked at Katie with a pleading look on his face. "I paid to have sex with his daughter. Her brother, Devon, set it up. I'm so sorry, baby. It just … it just happened. If I could take it back, I would. It was wrong and I was crazy out of my mind to do it and you have every right to hate me. It was only the one time and I've regretted it ever since. I love you more than anything. You've got to believe me. Please, baby."

Another stab of pain filled Katie's belly. She could see Ivan's mouth moving but stopped hearing him after he said he'd had sex with Mitchell's daughter.

Her mind turned sluggishly as she struggled to remember a conversation she'd had with Mitchell the summer before. He had one daughter named Sophie — yes, she was sure he said only one daughter — and she was starting grade eight. *Ivan had paid for sex with a child*. The pain in her stomach had moved up to her chest. Surely, this was what it felt like to die, to feel as if the entire world had stopped spinning and she was about to free-fall into outer space. She cried out and black, fuzzy spots filled her eyes. Jane called to her and Katie turned her face toward the sound of her voice. Like a magnet pulling her back, she looked into Jane's mesmerizing blue eyes.

"Don't think about it now," Jane said. "Slow, deep breaths. You can get through this, Katie."

"Shut up," said Mitchell. "Just shut up." The gun in his hand was shaking and tears were running down his cheeks. He doubled over, but kept the gun wavering in the air. "How could you have done this to my child? My beautiful girl. I thought we were friends."

"I'm sorry," said Ivan. "I'm sorry."

Mitchell straightened. "Sorry isn't good enough." He levelled the gun and shot Ivan Bruster two times in the chest.

CHAPTER THIRTY-THREE

After they found Mitchell's office building locked and empty, Kala called in to the station that Jane Thompson was missing, and conveyed their fear that she was with Mitchell Eton and he could be distraught over his daughter's suicide attempt. Gundersund drove them to the Hanson house while Kala spoke to Fred Taylor on her phone.

She dropped her cellphone into her lap and said, "Taylor's spreading the word and will have patrol on the lookout for Mitchell's car."

"Good. We should be at the Hansons' in ten minutes."

Charlie answered the door after five minutes of ringing the doorbell and banging. His hair was spread out like a rooster's comb and his eyes were red. "I'd just fallen asleep," he said, taking off his glasses and rubbing his eyes. "What do you want now?"

"Is anyone else home?" Gundersund asked.

"Mom's at work and I don't know where Tiffany is."

"We have a few more questions. Can we come inside or would you prefer a trip to the station?"

Charlie's voice was as sullen as he could make it. "I guess you can come in, since I don't have a choice."

Gundersund filled the small entrance and Kala stepped around him "We can talk here in the hall," he said.

They angled Charlie against the wall and stood on either side of him. They'd agreed on the way over that Gundersund would be the set-up man and Kala would ask the questions.

"Charlie, we have you on camera at the Limestone Spa Hotel, entering by the back door with Sophie Eton on the day that Devon went missing. Devon let you in, in fact, at around four thirty. You've been lying to us and it's time you told the truth."

Charlie shook his head.

"What were you doing with Sophie at the Limestone that day?"

"We weren't there."

"We have proof that you were."

"I don't have to say anything."

"Charlie, you need to tell us what you know so we can sort out the damage. Do you understand?"

Charlie stood with his head lowered, hair flopped over his eyes, mouth tightly shut. Kala stared at him, trying to figure out what to say to get him talking.

A voice from upstairs made his head snap up. Kala and Gundersund raised their eyes. Tiffany was making her way toward them. Today she was wearing black leggings under a black tunic, but her eyes looked naked without the usual black smudging. She seemed younger, more vulnerable. "He was there with Sophie," she said as she came down the stairs. "Devon made Charlie do it."

"Why were they at the hotel?" Kala asked.

"Devon wanted to hurt his father. He told Sophie that they were meeting Mitchell in Ivan Bruster's room, but he drugged her with some Quaaludes in a drink when she arrived and left Sophie alone with Ivan. Devon made a thousand dollars, which he shared with Charlie to keep him quiet."

"Is this true, Charlie?"

Charlie looked at his sister before nodding and bowing his head again.

Kala swallowed hard. "Did Mitchell find out what Devon did to Sophie?"

Charlie and Tiffany looked at each other. Tiffany answered for them both. "We don't know. Charlie never saw Devon again after he took off. Devon was going to wait around for Sophie and take her home around seven. He said he'd done the same once before with some girl from school and gotten away with it."

Kala looked at Gundersund. "This must be why Sophie tried to kill herself last night. Are you thinking what I'm thinking?"

"I'll call Ajax police and get someone to check this out."

"Wait, Sophie tried to kill herself? Is she okay?" asked Tiffany.

"What do you think?" Kala said more sharply than she'd intended. "Sophie is suffering. Keeping quiet about what Devon did to her was entirely the wrong thing to do."

Charlie finally spoke. "Devon said she wouldn't remember and if she did, nobody would back her up. He said part of him wanted his parents to know so he could see their faces when they found out, but he'd have to be satisfied with knowing what happened to her. A laugh behind their backs, he said. I have the money he gave me. You can have it back. I don't want it. I never wanted it."

Kala was at a loss for words, the evil in Devon Eton was so profound and terrible. The part these two played was unforgivable. She reined herself back in before she said something she would later regret. She reminded herself that they were kids and victims, too. "We'll talk about this more later. Lock the doors after we leave and let your mom know what's been going on. If Mr. Eton shows up, call 911 and don't let him in."

She followed Gundersund out of the house and down the stairs toward his car where he stood talking on his cell. She stood stock still while he explained the situation and asked someone, perhaps his cop friend in Ajax, to get over to the Bruster house. Gundersund lowered his phone and looked at Kala standing next to him. He put an arm around her shoulders and gave her a hug. "You okay with this?"

She nodded. "Although it's making me sick to hear what they did to Sophie … and to Jane Thompson." His arm was comforting and she let herself enjoy his closeness for a moment. "You know, it's only a few hours to Ajax."

"One and a half, if I floor it."

She pulled back. "Then what are we waiting for? Let's get going."

CHAPTER THIRTY-FOUR

Katie watched her husband fall to the floor, a look of shock on his face. The noise deafened her for a moment and she was surprised to taste salty tears on her lips. She thought there should have been more blood. The room started to become brighter, every part of the scene sharp and pointy, like a movie in slow motion. She watched Jane get to her feet and Mitchell turn the gun on her.

"Don't move," he said. He looked over at Katie. "I hear your son crying upstairs."

His words made her pull out of the foggy realm and back to earth. She looked at him and tried to see some sign of the man she'd eaten dinner with on his trips to Ajax to meet with Ivan. She remembered his boy, Devon, and how excited he'd been to be going to a Jays game with his dad. "Please," she said, "he's just a little boy. He never hurt anyone."

Mitchell shook his head. "I'm not going to hurt you or your son. I never wanted to hurt anybody. Go to your son and don't come back."

She stood on unsteady feet and grabbed on to the desk as the room swayed. She took a deep breath and looked at Ivan on the floor. He was lying on his stomach with his face turned toward the wall. A bright red stain circled out across his back, ruining the blue shirt that she'd bought him the week before at the Bay. She couldn't tell if he was breathing.

Mitchell said, "You might not know it now, Katie, but I've done you a favour shooting your husband. He was a child molester."

Katie raised her head and looked from him to Jane, who was still standing motionless with hands at her sides on the other side of the desk. Katie still had no idea who she was. "What are you going to do?" she asked Mitchell, frightened for this woman who didn't appear prepared to fight for herself.

"Finish. I'm going to finish this."

Katie tried to get him to look her in the eyes. "Let her come with me, Mitchell. I don't want to leave her here."

The phone in the kitchen began ringing. It rang three times and went to voice mail. A few seconds later, it began ringing again.

Mitchell had turned his head to listen. He looked back at Katie. His eyes were resigned. "Go now," he said, finality in his voice. "Before I change my mind."

She walked through the kitchen and down the hallway, her son's cries increasing in volume. She was glad now that they'd put off getting him a bed because the crib was keeping him from coming downstairs. The front door was so close, but dare she open it? She wouldn't do anything to risk Kyle. As she passed by, she saw dark forms moving outside the door and she looked back toward Ivan's office. Mitchell hadn't followed her.

She put her foot on the bottom stair and hesitated. A sharp rap on the door startled her but she knew help was on the other side. She made a final check down the hall and scooted across the space, throwing back the deadbolt and pulling open the door. Three police cars were in the driveway and cops were everywhere. The one directly in front of her motioned for her to stay quiet and asked, "Where are they?" He had a large handgun aimed at the ground.

She pointed down the hall. "He has a gun," she said. "He shot my husband but he has a woman with him."

"Go outside."

"My son is upstairs."

"We'll get him."

Before she stepped outside or the police made it down the hall, the sound of two gunshots in quick succession came from Ivan's office. Katie held on to her belly as her knees buckled. Hands held her up and someone lifted her and carried her down the steps and into the yard.

Jane opened her eyes and wondered if she was dead. She blinked and suddenly Officer Stonechild's face was hovering over her. Officer Stonechild smiled and told her that she was going to be fine. She was safe in the hospital and the surgery had gone without a hitch.

Jane closed her eyes and when she opened them again, some time had passed but Officer Stonechild was still there, sitting in a chair with her head back and snoring softly. The detective was instantly awake and on her feet when Jane tried to sit up.

"You're still here," she said. The words came out hoarse, and Officer Stonechild offered her ice chips from a cup on the tray and helped to prop her up comfortably on the pillows.

"The surgeon took the bullet out of your stomach and said not to expect any lasting damage. You were very fortunate."

"Mitchell. Is he...?"

"Dead? Yes, he shot himself in the head before the police got to him. Ivan Bruster also passed away, likely instantly. One bullet hit his heart."

"Mitchell told me that he killed Devon. He lost it that night when he found out from Sophie what had happened. Devon drugged her, but she knew what was going on. She was a wreck when she got home. Devon tried to bluster it out." Jane searched Officer Stonechild's face to see if she believed her. For some reason, this police officer's good opinion mattered to her.

Officer Stonechild's eyes were kind. "Charlie and his sister Tiffany have given statements that Devon lied about having sex with you in grade seven. Charlie confessed to helping bring Sophie to the hotel where Ivan Bruster molested her. We will do everything we can to make sure the public knows you were wrongfully convicted."

Jane shut her eyes and tears squeezed out the sides.

"I'll let you sleep now, but wanted you to know before my partner and I head back to Kingston."

"Thank you, Officer Stonechild … for everything."

"I wish I could have done more sooner."

Adam and the kids were in her room the next time she was fully awake. Ben and Olivia looked scared but smiled when she opened her eyes. They hugged her carefully and talked a mile a minute, asking her if she was okay and telling her they could see her again. Their dad had promised.

Adam waited until they stopped for air before getting close to the bed. "Here's some money. You two go buy your mom a present from the gift shop while we chat for a second."

He pulled up a chair and sat where Jane could see him easily. He had a five o'clock shadow and his eyes were filled with contrition. "I've been wrong," he said, "about a lot of things. The police told me that the kids made up the story about you and Devon. I'm angry as hell at them for what they did and I'm sorry for doubting you. I wish we could go back in time to before any of this happened."

"I want to renegotiate our custody agreement."

"Of course. I was hoping that we could see about spending more time together after you get back to Kingston. Maybe, you could come live in the house again. We can take it slow."

She studied him and wondered what kind of man would spray-paint the words he did on her walls. Mitchell had had no reason to lie when he said he hadn't done it. That left Adam, whose anger and obsession wanted her to keep paying. He'd promised to disappear with the kids forever if she didn't confess and take the counselling courses. Underneath, he was more like her mother than she'd ever imagined. Rigidly fixated on fire and brimstone and retribution. "I'm going to stay with my sister when I leave here. It's all arranged." It wasn't, yet, but Sandra had gotten a message to her through the nurse that she was on her way.

He covered her hand resting on her chest with his. His eyes drilled into hers. "I've never stopped loving you, Jane. Even through all the bad times."

She studied his square jaw and handsome face. Odd to think how once she'd reveled in his need to have her in his life. From the start of their relationship, he'd put her on a pedestal, idolizing her physical beauty. She'd loved him then, mistaking his obsession for passion and love. The answer was simple, really. She slid her hand out from under his and said gently, "But I don't love you, Adam."

His eyes searched hers. She'd waffled about leaving him before Devon accused her, but he'd always been able to win her back. He appeared to see something in her gaze that rattled him. The certainty left his voice. "I guess I deserve that. Believe me when I say that if we could go back in time, I would do a lot of things differently."

"That makes two of us, Adam. Too much has gone on that we can't take back. I hope we can be friends for the children."

"We can try. I warn you, though, I'm going to try to win you back."

His words felt like a threat, but she knew she was strong enough to leave him now. Odd that it took three years in prison to make her feel liberated. She'd get a teaching job and make a life for herself with the children. The future was wide open; she'd grab on to it and never look back.

She would begin living again.

CHAPTER THIRTY-FIVE

Gundersund dropped Kala off at her house shortly before eight o'clock, following a quick stop at Gibson's restaurant in Napanee for a bite to eat. After checking in with Rouleau, Kala had taken a break from her cellphone but began scrolling through messages as she walked up the driveway. The sun was completely down, but the sky was clear and cloudless and a dome of stars made her tilt her head back and breathe in the night. The cool breeze from the lake stirred up the autumn smell of composting leaves and end-of-season gardens. Someone had lit a bonfire and she caught the scent of woodsmoke as she entered the backyard. She hadn't thought about it before, but she had lots of room for a firepit. It would be pleasant to sit next to a fire on the cooler nights and even cook her supper in the open air. She had to let Marjorie know soon if she wanted to buy the house. Evenings like this one, the idea was tempting — a place to call her own; Gundersund down the road; Rouleau and his father close by in town. Maybe, it was time to put down roots. She could always sell or go on long trips to quench her wanderlust.

She had a couple of voice messages and was accessing the message centre when she unlocked the back door. Taiku was standing in the hallway, tail wagging. He ran over to greet her, and she petted his head while listening to the voice mail. Caroline Russell was phoning to find out if she'd been in touch with Dawn. No cause to worry but Dawn hadn't gone to school or returned home after leaving in the morning. Kala took Taiku outside and sat on the deck to return Caroline's call while he snuffled around in the grass.

"Sorry to keep bothering you," Caroline started, "but has Dawn been in contact with you today?"

"I haven't had any word from Dawn since you brought her to see me last week."

"Damn." Caroline took a deep sigh before saying, "We're going to have to come up with another place for Dawn to live. The foster family where she's placed now isn't working out."

Kala let the empty air stretch between them. Before her meeting with Dawn, she would have immediately offered to take her back, but Dawn didn't want to be with her. She'd made that crystal clear. Kala had betrayed her, and in Dawn's place at the same age, she would not have forgiven either.

"Well, if I hear anything, I'll call you," said Caroline. "Would you please do the same?"

"Of course."

"Dawn has become independent and resourceful. I'm hoping these traits will keep her from getting into trouble."

Kala sat for a long time after the call, sitting on the deck and watching the twinkling night sky. Taiku eventually tired of roaming around the property and came back to sit beside her. When they went inside, he ate a bit of his supper but left most of it in his bowl and came to lie at her feet while she drank a cup of tea and read the news on her iPad. When she stood to empty the last of her tea into the sink, he leaped to his feet and started down the hall to the stairs, stopping and looking back to make sure she was following.

"I'm coming, boy," she said. "I have to lock up and I'll be right behind you."

He'd disappeared up the stairs and out of sight by the time she set foot on the bottom step. She was surprised not to find him in her bedroom and backtracked to the guest room where she found him on the foot of the bed, his bright eyes looking at her from the darkness of the room. Kala stepped closer, and from the light in the hallway, she made out a form lying under the covers and saw black hair spread out on the pillow. She sat down on the edge of the bed and put her hand on the girl's back. She rolled from her side onto her back and looked up at Kala.

The house's secrets revealed. Kala smiled. "Dawn. I'm so happy to see you."

Dawn stared at her. "Are you angry?"

"No. No, I'm not angry. I'm glad that you're safe."

She sat up. "Can I stay, Aunt Kala? I don't belong with that family. We don't have to tell them. They won't miss me."

"How have you been getting here from downtown?"

"The bus. I kept my key. I've been looking after Taiku while you worked the case. I belong with you and Taiku."

Kala rubbed her eyes with the back of her hand. This child had never let go of her even though she had every reason to turn her back. Kala had never had anyone love and need her like this before. She reached out and pulled Dawn to her. "We're both home," she said. "We're both here where we belong."

"It's getting late," Vera said, standing in the doorway to Rouleau's office. "Heath will be pleased that you skirted around the reporter's questions about why he jumped to conclusions before the facts were in." She smiled her Mona Lisa smile.

"Thanks, Vera. This case had some peculiar turns that nobody could predict. I'll be finishing up here in a few minutes. You should run along though and get some supper. Thanks for all your help getting the media briefing together on such short notice."

"My pleasure."

"Will Heath be back in the office tomorrow?"

"He texted me while you were answering media questions that he's taking his wife to Turks and Caicos for a couple of weeks." She shook her head. "Making amends for his trespasses." She paused as if she wanted to say something more but seemed to think better of it. "Don't work too late," she said and beamed a smile at him before turning to leave. He watched her walk down the hall and out of sight.

Rouleau finished typing the report he'd been working on and turned off the desk lamp, sitting in the darkness while his eyes adjusted. His father would be in bed by now and the idea of being alone with his thoughts was not a good idea. He picked up his coat and left the building, getting into his car and heading into town toward the waterfront. He debated stopping at the Merchant for a nightcap, and an empty parking spot near the pub seemed like an omen that he couldn't pass up.

The team's usual table was occupied and he got a beer from the bar and stood at one of the high tables nearby. The band was on a break and the room was filled with lively chatter. He settled in to people-watch and sip his beer.

"Mind if I join you?"

He looked over his shoulder and Marci Stokes skirted around to stand next to him. She'd been at the media briefing and was on her phone calling in the story when he last saw her. He'd manage to leave Sophie's name out of the story, but knew the press would see the holes in the sequence of events eventually. Interest in the story would end sometime, and he'd protect Sophie from the worst of it until then. Ruining her reputation would serve no purpose. Jane Thompson and Bruster's wife knew, of course, but neither would be giving details to the press. "I'd enjoy the company," he said and waved over the waitress. "What will you have?"

"Gin and tonic, thanks." She undid her coat and draped it over a stool. "Well, that was quite a turn in the case. Did you have Mitchell Eton in your sights all along?"

"He wasn't one of our main contenders."

"So Devon concocted the entire story about Jane Thompson and their affair. I see a lawsuit somewhere."

"She might have a right to some compensation, but the court will have to decide."

"Hmm." Her eyes found his. "One wonders what sent Mitchell off to Ajax to kill a business associate, but we may never know. Is that how you see it, Sergeant?"

"People do unpredictable things when they become unhinged."

"Indeed. Perhaps, the trigger was something long simmering. I can understand Mitchell striking out at his son when he found out that he'd concocted the story that put Jane Thompson away for a couple of years." Her drink arrived and she raised her glass. "A toast to closing chapters and new beginnings."

And media not finding out what really happened in the Eton family. He clinked her glass and drank from his. "Are you returning to New York? You make it sound as if the blacklisting has lifted." He grinned and thought that he might miss her if she left this time for good.

"On the contrary. I've been offered an assistant editor job on the *Whig* that I accepted" — she made a show of checking her watch — "not even an hour ago. You're going to be stuck with me for the foreseeable future."

The idea was not unappealing. He raised his glass again. "Congratulations. I trust this is what you want."

She tilted her head and smiled at him. "This town is growing on me, Sergeant. Enough criminals to keep my interest but not too many that I fear for my own safety." She took a drink. "And how about you? Will you be sticking around for a while?"

"Until my father doesn't need me anymore."

She looked thoughtful. "Not to harp on this Eton case, but deliberately setting up a teacher the way Devon did might be viewed as an act without conscience, especially not coming forward with the truth once she was incarcerated."

"Nature versus nurture, you mean? I'm not sure but I haven't seen many truly evil people in my career. Usually, something in their past led them to commit a crime. Often drugs or alcohol are involved."

"But you admit a person can be born without conscience?"

"I do, just not as often as media would portray."

"Touché." She pushed her hair back from her face and took another drink of gin. They watched the band leap back onto the stage and take their places. "Well, it's been a long day so I'm going to push off," she said. "I guess I'll be seeing you around."

"I look forward to it."

EPILOGUE

Hilary Eton parked across the street from Winston Churchill Public School, rolled down the windows, and turned off the car engine. She'd brought a crossword puzzle and spent a few minutes folding the newspaper and finding a pen in her purse. She rested the puzzle on the steering wheel and immediately forgot it was there, instead staring out the front window and going over all of the preparations she'd made for their trip to Bermuda. The suitcases were in the trunk. She'd notified everyone she needed to that they'd be away for two weeks, and she'd exchanged enough Canadian money for American to last them several days. It had been over a month since they buried Mitchell, and she and Sophie needed time away to heal and to reconnect. Sophie's therapist had suggested the trip and her own heart doctor had supported the idea.

Kids started to stream out of the school and raced toward waiting buses or parents standing in groups on the sidewalk talking. Some of the older children were walking home in groups or pairs, their voices loud and animated. Hilary was about to get out of the car, thinking Sophie had forgotten their meeting place, when she spotted her daughter walking in her direction alone. Hilary reached a hand out her open window and waved. Sophie gave a half-hearted wave in return but kept trudging along as slowly as ever. Hilary thought that she was looking stronger than she had even a week before with more colour in her cheeks and some life back in her eyes. She didn't think this was only her wishful thinking.

Sophie opened the front passenger door and climbed in, bringing a blast of cold air with her. Snow was predicted for the weekend, but by then they'd be lying on a beach in the hot tropical sun. She dropped her schoolbag onto the floor and buckled her seat belt without saying anything.

"How was your day?" Hilary asked as she started the car.

"Okay." Sophie was looking out her side window when she asked, "Are we going home or right to the airport?"

"Airport. Did your teachers send along some homework?"

"Mr. Casey wants me to keep a journal of the trip and Mrs. Samuels sent some math sheets. They told me to relax and have fun."

"I bought some books for you to read."

"Great." Her voice was without enthusiasm.

Sophie was asleep by the time they merged onto the 401 on the way to Toronto. The flight left in the evening but Hilary wanted to make sure they arrived good and early. Toronto rush hour traffic would add time to the trip through the city even though they'd stay on the major highway. Sophie had been sleeping a lot since she returned home from the hospital, spending the weekends in her pajamas and needing to be roused for meals, meals that neither of them had wanted. Hilary hoped this trip would break through her depression.

On the outskirts of Toronto, Sophie opened her eyes and stretched. She promptly plugged in her earphones and listened to music the rest of the way, effectively shutting off conversation. Hilary didn't press. She'd do what Sophie's therapist advised and take things slowly. Traffic was steady but moving at a good clip and they arrived at Pearson Airport ahead of schedule. She found a spot in long-term parking and Sophie helped with the luggage. They made it through security without any delays.

"Let's go into the restaurant and have supper," Hilary said once they started down the corridor toward their gate. "We have two hours to relax before our flight."

Their drinks arrived and Hilary was taking a sip of wine when she noticed a man staring at her from two tables over. She held the glass in front of her mouth and said to Sophie, "Don't look now but someone from Daddy's office is about to come over. Let me do the talking."

She stood and let Preston Weaver envelop her in a hug. "I'm so devastated by all that happened," he said, holding her at arm's length. "We still can't believe that Mitchell is gone."

"Thank you. This has been a horrible time for us but we're doing better."

Sophie's abuse at the hands of Ivan Bruster and Devon's role in making it happen had been kept from the media. They'd reported on Jane Thompson's wrongful conviction, but as so often happened in the world of public opinion, many felt sympathy for Devon and believed something had gone on to make him behave as he had. People couldn't believe a boy with so much going for him would lie without a reason. Hilary supposed that evil was not easy to get one's head around, for she knew now that her son had been just that.

Preston dropped his hands but seemed in no hurry to leave. "That's good to hear. Mitchell was a stand-up guy and such a loss." He looked at Sophie and gave her a brave smile. "Where are you headed?"

Hilary answered for them both. "Bermuda."

He turned his face back to look at her. "You'll need a break after all that happened. I'm off to Florida." He paused and Hilary knew he was waiting for her to ask him about his trip. When she kept silent, he said, "Well, I won't take up any more of your time but wanted to say how sorry I am and to let you know that nobody blamed Mitchell for what happened. Anyone can lose it given the right pressures."

"Thanks for saying that."

Hilary sat and willed the fluttering in her chest to calm down. *Would it always be this way when someone from Mitchell's past approached?*

Sophie was watching her. "When are you going to tell the police?" she asked.

Hilary had been waiting for Sophie to ask this question since the night Sergeant Rouleau had come by the house to tell them Mitchell had shot himself in the head. She reached across the table and took Sophie's hand. "Daddy wanted the police to believe that he killed Devon. He made sure the police were told that."

"But he didn't kill Devon." Sophie pulled her hand away and dropped it into her lap. "You did."

Hilary kept her voice calm with effort. "Do you want me to confess, Sophie? I will if that's what you want."

The waitress arrived to take their order and they didn't speak again until she'd gone. Hilary tried to meet Sophie's eyes, but she was looking into her drink glass and punching the straw up and down against the ice. "What is it you want me to do?" Hilary asked again. "Tell me and I'll do it."

"I don't want you to confess to the police." Sophie looked up at last. "I want to forget … everything that happened that night."

"Then we'll make a pact to never speak about this again. Agreed, Sophie?"

Sophie nodded, tears sparkling in her eyes. Hilary took her hand again and clasped it between both of hers. A boy at the next table laughed, and Hilary jolted back in horror as if she'd been struck. The boy's laughter could have been Devon's that night he'd told them what he'd done to Sophie. She took deep breaths and turned slowly in her seat to assure herself that it was not her son.

She wasn't sure how many times she'd hit Devon with the poker she'd grabbed from the fireplace. She couldn't even remember picking up the weapon or raising it over her head. Mitchell had grabbed her arm and pulled her off and she'd collapsed on the floor, her rage spent and nothing left to keep her upright. Sophie's screaming had echoed off the walls and ceiling for a long time afterward. Mitchell had been left to comfort her and clean up the mess. Even now when Hilary closed her eyes, she could see in detail the pulpy mess she'd made of Devon's head and hear the gurgle of his last breath. The image returned to haunt her days and kept her from sleeping night after night after night.

Hilary brushed the hair back from Sophie's face and ran her fingers down the side of her cheek. She said to convince herself as much as Sophie, "Devon isn't going to win this time. Not this time." They locked eyes and Hilary would not let Sophie look away.

The waitress arrived and Hilary pushed back her chair to give her room to set down their plates of food. She and Sophie picked up their forks and Sophie dug into the french fries, filling her mouth so that her cheeks puffed out like a chipmunk. She smiled at Hilary as she chewed and Hilary thought she'd never have imagined that the sight of her daughter eating again would fill her with such joy. She watched Sophie pick up her hamburger with both hands before scooping pasta onto her fork. For the first time in a long time, her own hunger had returned and it seemed that she couldn't get the food into her mouth fast enough: fettucine, salad, garlic bread, a second glass of red wine — she and Sophie scraped their plates clean and ordered more buns and a second round of wine and 7UP. They swallowed every last bite and emptied their glasses before deciding they still had room left over for dessert.

And sometime between the chocolate sundaes and the plane landing in Bermuda, Hilary knew that she and Sophie were going to be all right.

ACKNOWLEDGEMENTS

I would like to acknowledge the great Dundurn team working behind the scenes to bring this book and other Canadian fiction and non-fiction to the shelves. I was fortunate to have editors Shannon Whibbs, Kathryn Lane, Cheryl Hawley, and Shari Rutherford finessing my words and making *Shallow End* come together. Thanks also to my publicist Michelle Melski and to Margaret Bryant. The cover design comes from the creative and talented designer Laura Boyle. As always, I owe a debt of gratitude to Dundurn president Kirk Howard and vice-president Beth Bruder, for continuing to bring Canadian stories to a broad and growing readership.

I would also like to thank the readers who have emailed me directly about the series, posted reviews, and recommended the books to their friends. I'm fortunate to have a loyal group of friends who've been with me every step of the way from my first young adult mystery, and I owe each of you my gratitude. I would like to make mention of a few stalwarts: Janice and Peter Murdoch, Bill and

Kathy Adair, Jan and Frank Bowick, Dawn Rayner, Helen Brown, Ann and Ken Cooke, Kathleen and Paul Schiemann, Denis Fabris and Carol Gage, Kathryn and Claus Anthonisen, Wendy Pell and Keith Carlson, Nancy Pell, Maureen Johnston and Jim McIntyre, Mona and Bruce Simpson, Margaret Cody, Darlene Cole, Katherine Hobbs, Fred Taylor, Glenda Stewart, Judith Kalil, Michael Murphy, Susan Rothery, Janet Claridge, Joanne Lynn…. I could go on … (and will next time!)

A special thank you to Jim Sherman, owner of Perfect Books, for your friendship and support.

And last, but not least, thank you to all of my family who offer support from afar and to Lisa, Robin, Julia, and Ted, who continue to make the journey fun. With a special thank you to my mom, Ollie Chapman, for your belief in the possibilities.

COLD MOURNING

Nominated for the 2015 Arthur Ellis Award for Best Novel

It's a week before Christmas when wealthy businessman Tom Underwood disappears into thin air — with more than enough people wanting him dead.

New police recruit Kala Stonechild, who has left her northern Ontario detachment to join a specialized Ottawa crime unit, is tasked with returning Underwood home in time for the holidays. Stonechild, who is from a First Nations reserve, is a lone wolf who is used to surviving on her wits. Her new boss, Detective Jacques Rouleau, has his hands full controlling her, his team, and an investigation that keeps threatening to go off track.

Old betrayals and complicated family relationships brutally collide when love turns to hate and murder stalks a family.

BUTTERFLY KILLS

Jacques Rouleau has moved to Kingston to look after his father and take up the position of head of the town's Criminal Investigations Division. One hot week in late September, university student Leah Sampson is murdered in her apartment. In another corner of the city, Della Munroe is raped by her husband. At first the crimes appear unrelated, but as Sergeant Rouleau and his new team of officers dig into the women's pasts, they discover unsettling coincidences. When Kala Stonechild, one of Rouleau's former officers from Ottawa, suddenly appears in Kingston, Rouleau enlists her to help.

Stonechild isn't sure if she wants to stay in Kingston, but agrees to help Rouleau in the short term. While she struggles with trying to decide if she can make a life in this new town, a ghost from her past starts to haunt her.

As the detectives delve deeper into the cases, it seems more questions pop up than answers. Who murdered Leah Sampson? And why does Della Monroe's name keep showing up in the murder investigation? Both women were hiding secrets that have unleashed a string of violence. Stonechild and Rouleau race to discover the truth before the violence rips more families apart.

TUMBLED GRAVES

When Adele Delaney and her daughter, Violet, go missing, Jacques Rouleau is called upon to investigate. However, struggling with the impending death of his ill ex-wife, he sends Kala Stonechild and Paul Gundersund instead. Stonechild has been trying to adapt to life as her young cousin Dawn's guardian, and even though Gundersund has offered support, Stonechild is at risk of losing custody.

On the second day of the investigation, Adele's body turns up, dumped on the shoulder of the highway with no sign of her daughter. Her husband, Ivo, denies any involvement with either his wife's death or their child's disappearance, but not everyone is convinced. As the investigation unfolds, Stonechild learns that Adele was once entangled with a Montreal biker gang and heads to Quebec to investigate further.

As Stonechild and Gundersund juggle personal troubles and a complicated, dangerous case, they find themselves piecing together a chain of disasters leading back to a single betrayal.